WHEN TITO LOVED CLARA

When
Tito
Loved
Clara

A NOVEL

JON MICHAUD

ALGONQUIN BOOKS OF CHAPEL HILL 2011

Published by
ALGONQUIN BOOKS OF CHAPEL HILL
Post Office Box 2225
Chapel Hill, North Carolina 27515-2225

a division of
Workman Publishing
225 Varick Street
New York, New York 10014

"Marked Playing Cards" (first appeared in *The New Yorker*) from
Walking the Black Cat, copyright © 1996 by Charles Simic, reprinted by
permission of Houghton Mifflin Harcourt Publishing Company.

"Ave Maria" copyright © 1964 by Frank O'Hara.
Reprinted by permission of City Lights Books.

This is a work of fiction. While, as in all fiction, the literary perceptions and
insights are based on experience, all names, characters, places, and incidents
either are products of the author's imagination or are used fictitiously.

Library of Congress Cataloging-in-Publication Data
Michaud, Jon, [date]
When Tito loved Clara : a novel / by Jon Michaud — 1st ed.
p. cm.
ISBN 978-1-56512-949-8
1. Dominican Americans — Fiction.   2. Immigrants — United States —
Fiction.   3. Domestic fiction.   4. Psychological fiction.   I. Title.
PS3613.I3448W47 2011

813'.6 — dc22   2010037075

10 9 8 7 6 5 4 3 2 1
First Edition

To
Zoraida
and
Atar

Author's Note

In this novel certain liberties have been taken
with the geography of Essex County, New Jersey, and northern
Manhattan, especially with the layout of Inwood Hill Park.

If you love, you grieve and there are no exceptions—
only those who do it well and those who don't.

THOMAS LYNCH, *The Undertaking*

I marked playing cards to cheat against myself.
All my life I kept raising the stakes, knowing
That each new loss assured me of her complete love.

CHARLES SIMIC, "Marked Playing Cards"

WHEN TITO LOVED CLARA

Part One

Clara

Clara drove across the George Washington Bridge. She was going back to Inwood to pick up her sister, Yunis, and her niece, Deysei. Inwood, where she had learned to be an American; Inwood, where she had first fallen in love and broken someone's heart; Inwood, the neighborhood of parks and bodegas, of rivers and bridges, the forgotten part of Manhattan she could not forget. Clara's husband, Thomas, who'd grown up in the suburbs of Maryland, had once expressed a passing, semiserious desire to live there, to be among the mulattoes, the remains of the Irish and Jewish communities of the last century, to be one of the newly arrived middle-class couples who'd been priced out of Brooklyn and Astoria. But Clara wouldn't hear of it. "Why did I go to college?" she'd asked. "Just so I could live down the street from all the dumbass immigrants I grew up with? I don't think so."

It was nine-thirty, still a little early for her late-sleeping sister and niece, but they'd have to lump it. The traffic on Broadway budged forward indifferently, the rush hour coming to an end. Clara turned left on 204 and found a spot near the corner of Cooper Street. She locked the Odyssey and walked around the corner, trying to be as inconspicuous as possible. She never knew who she'd run into when she came back to the neighborhood and she always feared the worst. The first doorway on Cooper was the entrance to the apartment building where Yunis and Deysei lived with Yunis's ex-con boyfriend, Raúl. Raúl was about to become Yunis's ex-ex-con boyfriend, Clara thought. Yunis was moving to the Dominican Republic to live with their mother, who had retired to a rum-softened dotage in a suburb of Santo Domingo. Deysei, who was to be a junior in high school that year, was going to live with Clara and Thomas in New Jersey and finish her secondary education at Millwood High—a prelude, everyone hoped, to college. Clara had no idea what Raúl planned to do now that he was going to be without a girlfriend and a place of residence, and she hadn't lost much sleep over it. Things had been bad between Yunis and Raúl for so long that she was no longer able to recall a time when things were good between them.

In the building's vestibule, she rang the bell and waited for the buzzer. The proportions of the small cement alcove that led from the street to the vestibule corresponded to some sort of golden mean for the capture of stray breezes and the corralling of litter. Sheets of newsprint, candy wrappers, and plastic grocery bags circled the center of the alcove as if riding an invisible carousel. No matter the season or the time of day, the lethargic cyclone spun before the door. In the corner, a Snapple bottle rolled back and forth in the turbulence, as if trying to build up the momentum to join the other garbage in its swirling dance.

Long ago, Clara had dubbed her sister's apartment (and, by extension, her sister's life) the Yuniverse. The Yuniverse was a queendom rife with drama, anxiety, and endless scamming. Its entrance was a brown door on the building's third floor decorated with a bumper sticker that read, VIRGINIA IS FOR LOVERS. A former boyfriend, an ex-navy man turned gunrunner from Newport News, had put it there. (Clara liked to joke that Yunis wouldn't give you the time of day unless you'd seen the inside of a penal institution. The only boyfriend she'd had who wasn't a convict was Deysei's father, and he was an illegal immigrant now living under a false name in Florida.) It had not always been this way. Her sister had once been a sweet, goofy teenager. It had been her good looks, poor grades, and inept use of contraception that led her to the place where she was now.

Raúl answered the door. "Yo," he said, swinging his arms with primate restlessness. Raúl never seemed to know how to act around her—whether to kiss or fist-bump her. There was something of the beaten animal about him this morning and Clara gave him a quick peck on his cheek, which made him smile. Raúl, tall, muscular, strange, moody. He and Yunis were combustible, Clara thought. One a lit match, the other a can of kerosene.

The apartment, like many in New York, was too hot in the winter and too cold in the summer, but today, for once, the place was at a comfortable temperature and, beyond the faint sour whiff of dust, odor free. A hygienic breeze drifted over Clara as she entered. Raúl led her past the kitchen, where a half-eaten *pernil* or lasagna usually sat in a dented tinfoil baking sheet on the table. But the kitchen was clean—spotless. Everything had been put away. The metal basin of the sink had been emptied and recently scoured with a Brillo pad. Most bizarre of all was the rubber drainboard without dishes. Not even a teaspoon in the utensil cup. How odd. Clara wanted to stop and admire it, but she sensed that there were more sights to see up ahead. She wasn't disappointed. In the middle of the living room floor, which had formerly been the home of a Formica coffee table heaped with refuse, suitcases were stacked up. The windows were open. For the first time in the years that she had been coming here, Clara could imagine living in these rooms. She pictured a rental agent saying the word *potential*. Yunis had been trying to sublet the place before clearing out. She aimed to live in the Dominican Republic without working, to exist on a small inheritance she had come into as well as the rental income from illegally subletting the apartment. Keeping the lease in her name, Clara knew, was also a hedge in case things didn't work out as well as she hoped. If nothing else, Yunis had learned from experience to prepare for reversals.

"Wow," said Clara.

"You should have seen the shit we threw out of here," said Raúl, gesturing with his hands as if tossing a medicine ball. "We found newspapers from like four years ago. Busted cell phones, chopsticks, candy with hair stuck to it. Videocassettes. All this *stuff*, just sitting in here waiting to be thrown away."

"It piles up," said Clara and, for an instant, she had the image of her son, Guillermo, in forty or fifty years, going through her possessions after she and Thomas had died, wondering where it had all come from and why his parents ever kept such things.

"Yeah, man. It does," said Raúl, nodding, as if they'd unveiled some profound truth. The two of them had never found enough common ground for even the simplest conversations. Raúl, despite his time behind bars, his muscled frame, and his homeboy manner, had always struck Clara as oddly touchy and vulnerable. He was likely to overreact to the smallest thing.

Nearby, Yunis's bags were stacked like a vinyl Stonehenge: three collapsible columns of varying size along with a shapeless hold-all made of a multicolored substance that looked like nylon wicker. Next to them were Deysei's two smaller rolling suitcases and a hard plastic case that looked like something you'd use for carrying bait or tools. In the corner rested a green duffel and two black garbage bags that were, doubtless, the vessels for Raúl's possessions. Nowhere to be seen was the array of gray-market contraband that Raúl brought home through his mysterious sources: bootleg DVDs of movies that hadn't even been released, handheld gaming systems, watches, clothes, and jewelry. Raúl worked as a mover and Clara suspected that at least some of it came from the homes of the people he'd helped relocate. A couple of years before, he had even brought home a karaoke machine for Deysei. Clara wondered again what Raúl was going to do with himself now that Yunis was taking her love of convicted men to another country. No doubt there were other women in Washington Heights who would not let a little jail time stand between them and Raúl's affections.

"Why you wearing that? You're going to be too hot. It's summer, remember? *Sum*-mer! Summer is hot. You don't have to cover yourself up like a fucking nun."

This was Yunis's voice and her comments were addressed to her daughter. Clara could not see either of them, though the door into the apartment's lone bedroom was open.

Raúl gave her an *oh, shit* look. "Been like this all morning," he said. "Something's going down. I don't know what, but she's been on Deysei's ass since she woke up."

"Change is hard," said Clara.

"I hear that," said Raúl.

They were interrupted by Yunis's arrival in the room. "Hey, Sis! What's cracking?" she said. Yunis was at her ghetto-fabulous finest this morning in black jeans, pointy-toed shoes, and a pink Baby Phat T-shirt stretched across her breasts, the rounded tops of which were revealed by the scoop neck. Her hair, in ringlets, was a glistening autumnal mélange—russet with strands of yellow and gold and a layer of her natural black underneath. She wore huge rock-star sunglasses, the ones that made her head look like a bug's. Her ability to concoct a powerful sexual magnetism from her genetic gifts and these accessories was a large portion of her livelihood. Yunis had never had a full-time job. Her income was an eternally fluctuating balancing act among state and city subsidies, pocket money from the current beau, whatever loose change she could cajole out of her family members (Clara and Thomas included), and wages from the occasional receptionist or babysitting gig, which never lasted more than a few weeks before Yunis got into a spat with her employer and quit in a state of indignation.

"Everything ready?" Clara asked.

"Everything except my *daughter*," said Yunis, almost yelling the last word. "You *coming*?" she bellowed at the bedroom door.

"Give her a minute," said Raúl.

"She's had all fucking morning," said Yunis.

Deysei emerged from the bedroom wearing baggy denim over-alls with frayed cuffs and a black hooded sweatshirt—the usual self-conscious teenage getup, like the vestments of an order. What was different was her hair. Normally worn in braids, it had been styled in cornrows that left the upper portion of her head looking like a crop circle. Somehow, the 'do had changed her face. It made her seem older.

"Your hair looks great," said Clara.

"Thanks, Tía," said Deysei.

"We were up late doing that," said Yunis. "It's my farewell gift to her. I know you won't be making her any cornrows." This sounded defensive, and Clara let it go. There was an edge to her sister this morning and she didn't want to provoke her. Likewise, Deysei seemed even more resigned and subdued than normal. Yunis could do that to you. Eventually, everyone she associated with had the same hangdog air of defeatism about them. She'd worn down ev-eryone in Inwood and now she was off to the Dominican Republic to wear down the unsuspecting inhabitants of Santo Domingo and its suburbs. Clara wondered if she might meet her match there.

"Did you get someone to rent the place?" she asked.

"Yeah. Idelcy's cousin, Carmen. I didn't want to rent it to no man. They'd just fuck the place up." This appeared to be aimed at Raúl, who had gone into the bedroom but was still well within earshot. *Departures are fraught with anxiety,* Clara thought. *Best to get this one over with.* "Shall we?" she said.

CLARA, YUNIS, AND Deysei had loaded the suitcases into the back of the Odyssey and were just about to get in when Raúl appeared, carrying the karaoke machine on his shoulder. "Yo!" he called. "You forgot this!"

"We didn't *forget* nothing," said Yunis.

"This belongs to Deysei," said Raúl. "I gave it to her."

"She hasn't played with it in a year," said Yunis.

"Thing cost me two hundred bucks," said Raúl.

Clara opened the side door of the van. "Here, lay it across the backseat. We can put it in the basement."

"You want it?" Raúl said to Deysei. She had her hood over her head now, the white wires of her iPod running from the marsupial pouch. Without taking her hands out of the pocket, she shrugged.

"If she wanted it she would have packed it, wouldn't she?" said Yunis.

"What the fuck am I going to do with it?"

"You could sell it," said Yunis. "And put some money in those empty pockets of yours."

And then Raúl looked at Yunis with a yearning that, for Clara, was easy to read and painful to see. The message on his face said: *Please take this. Don't tell me I didn't mean anything to you or your daughter.* This is precisely what Clara had wanted to avoid, a scene between Yunis and Raúl. She often wondered how Deysei put up with it, living in a one-bedroom apartment with her mother and her mother's lover, sleeping on the fold-out in the living room while Raúl and Yunis shared the bed next door, listening to them fight, listening to them fuck, inhaling their secondhand smoke, answering the door to their idiotic friends all night, kicking their empty forties across the floor on her way to the bathroom. But, then, Clara reminded herself, hadn't she survived even worse? This empathy for her niece, coupled with her desire for a second child, was the reason she had agreed to take Deysei in.

Staring at Yunis, Raúl set the karaoke machine down on the sidewalk. Clara picked it up and stowed it in the back of the van.

"Come on, baby, say goodbye to Raúl," Yunis prompted her daughter, not breaking the staring contest.

"You be good. Don't let those thugs in Jersey touch you," said Raúl, looking away from Yunis.

"Bye Raúl," said Deysei, and gave him an awkward hug.

"Awright," said Raúl. He swung his arms and watched Deysei climb into the van's side door. Clara kissed him again on the cheek. "Good luck," she said.

"I make my own luck," said Raúl. "Look after her, OK?"

"I will," said Clara. She slid the door closed and walked around to the driver's side to let Raúl and Yunis have some privacy. She started the engine and, unable to help herself, looked in the passenger-side rearview mirror. Reflected there was Yunis's triumph. Clara wasn't sure, but it looked like Raúl was crying. His head was bent, his hand was covering his eyes, and he was saying something. She suspected that Raúl was weeping more for his own plight than any heartbreak he felt over Yunis departing his life, but the sight of him—muscles, tattoo, pinpoint beard, and all—was moving none-theless. She took a quick glance over her shoulder at Deysei, who had her hood on, her face darkened, like a penitent, her headphones securely in place.

The passenger door opened and Yunis got in beside her. "Let's go, Sis," she said, and slapped the dashboard.

Clara pulled out of the parking spot and advanced only a hun-dred feet or so before stopping at the light on Broadway. The silence in the van was explosive. She turned on the radio: NPR headlines, just winding down. Quickly, she hit the button for the FM dial. Yunis and Clara's cousin Manny borrowed the van from time to time and always changed the presets on the FM dial to hip-hop and R&B stations. It irked Clara, even though she rarely listened to the FM dial. She lived on AM in the car—NPR and 1010 WINS.

"That's my jam!" said Yunis, as one of the hip-hop stations tuned in. "Sis, I didn't know you liked this shit."

The song that was pouring from the Odyssey's system was a current hit. The rapper was promising all the ladies listening that there was more than enough of him to go around. Yunis appeared willing to wait. She did a chair dance, wiggling her shoulders and shaking her head. Better by far than the silence of a moment ago, Clara thought, as she headed for the parkway and the bridge.

THE TRIP BACK to New Jersey was an uneventful one. Deysei sat with her arms across her chest, looking out the window and listening to her iPod. Yunis, meanwhile, had spent most of the drive talking on her cell to her cohorts in a mixture of Spanish and English, planning some kind of party when she got to Santo Domingo that evening.

Thomas was waiting for them, sitting on the front steps of the house, sipping from a can of Coke. He had been laid off six months before and Clara wasn't sure exactly how he spent his days aside from putting Guillermo on the bus in the morning, meeting him off the bus in the afternoon, watching baseball games on TV, and cooking dinner. He still had a substantial amount of his severance money socked away but money wasn't yet the issue. He had loved his job and had been gutted when they let him go. The company he'd worked for, BiblioFile, had hired him right out of library school—where he and Clara had met—and she remembered how the job had transformed him from a self-effacing and introverted cataloging specialist into a collegial, confident, professional *man*. They had been dating about a year and a half at that point. Clara always associated Thomas's job with the marriage proposal that came a few months later when he was awarded a small bonus for his contributions to the first project he worked on—a bonus he used to buy her engagement ring.

Thomas had served on a team that digitized paper resources, turning card catalogs, vertical files, and corporate archives into databases searchable through Web interfaces. His team worked for insurance brokerages, law firms, and newspapers on large-scale projects, involving the scanning of hundreds of thousands of pages and the assembly of complex relational databases. Clara, who managed the library at a medium-sized law firm in Newark, occasionally peeked at the work Thomas brought home with the same bemusement she felt when happening upon a piece of twelve-tone music on the radio or a chemical formula on the Internet. She sometimes felt that her rather traditional library career was lacking by comparison, a Victorian scrivener next to Thomas's twenty-first-century cyberman—at least, she did until her husband was laid off.

Losing his job, he seemed to lose his confidence. She feared that he had been too much defined by his career and not enough by his family, that one day, when he took off his shirt, she would discover that he was made of binary code. It was her hope that having Deysei in the house would somehow galvanize him. He'd been withdrawn of late, but he was, for the most part, a good father to Guillermo, and having a second child to parent might coax further engagement from him.

Clara waved at him as she pulled into the driveway. Thomas waved back. Yunis looked over at her and, in a voice not loud enough to be heard by Deysei, said, "Sis, we got to talk."

"Right now?" said Clara.

"Right now," said Yunis.

Thomas had come around the side of the house. He opened the back of the van. "How'd it go?" he asked.

"Fine," said Clara. "Deysei, why don't you help your *tío* take your things into the house?"

Thomas appeared to get the subtext. "Yeah, I'll show you your new room," he said with stagy enthusiasm.

"OK, Tío," Deysei said, pulling the white buds from her ears and getting out of the van. She looked warily back at her mother.

Clara and Yunis watched them go into the house through the back door. Clara had wanted to be the one to show Deysei her new room, the room that had, until a month ago, been set up as a nursery for the baby she and Thomas had lost the previous year. It was now an impersonal space, with no trace of its former intended use—a queen-sized bed, a chest of drawers in which they'd stored linens, and a closet where Thomas had kept his suits back when he had a job. It was the only room in the house without something on the walls. Deysei would have a clean slate.

"What is it?" Clara asked her sister once Thomas and Deysei were inside.

"You ain't gonna believe this," said Yunis. "But my daughter is pregnant."

Clara drew a breath and nodded her head. The news did not completely surprise her. It wasn't that she'd somehow anticipated her sixteen-year-old niece entering her household knocked up; it wasn't that she thought of her as promiscuous or careless; it wasn't that she believed Deysei was doomed to repeat her mother's mistakes (Yunis had given birth to Deysei when she was seventeen). It was merely that, lately, she had come to expect such news—the unpleasant, the inexplicable, the complicating. Every day, she readied herself for the latest in what seemed to be a widening circle of troubling developments—job loss, miscarriage, now teenage pregnancy.

She realized that Yunis was trying to read her reaction, waiting for her to say something. "Let's go get some lunch," Clara finally said.

"Lunch?" said Yunis.

"Yes. Wasn't that the plan?" she asked, deadpanning. "Lunch and then the airport."

Yunis shook her head. "You bugging, Sis. This is serious."

"I know it's serious," said Clara, "but she's not having the baby *today* is she? And anyway, shouldn't we include her in this discussion? Isn't she the one who's pregnant?"

Yunis looked at her with complete bafflement. "All right. You want to have lunch? Let's go have lunch."

Clara was buying a little time, time to think about what this meant. They would go to Church's, a soul food restaurant on a bleak stretch of Springfield Avenue near the on ramp to I-78, with quick access to the airport. It was her favorite place in Millwood to go when she needed comforting. Church's was where they'd gone after Thomas lost his job and Church's is what Clara had wanted after the latest miscarriage. It was the only food in town that made her feel like her mother's cooking did, a menu featuring fatty hunks of pork, crisp fried chicken, heavy starches, and vegetables boiled to mush. She called Thomas and Deysei downstairs and told them what the plan was. On their way out the door, she took her husband into the mud room and gave him the news.

"Is she going to keep it?" he asked.

"I don't know," she said. "I guess we're going to talk about it at lunch."

"My God," he said. "Well, it's ironic, isn't it?"

"What?"

"All the trouble we've been having . . ."

"Yeah, watch me die laughing," she said, and they went out to the Odyssey, where Deysei and Yunis were waiting.

It was a short, tense trip to the restaurant. Thomas drove. Clara was in the passenger seat, looking out the window, woolgathering; Yunis in the first row behind them, sullen; and Deysei all the way in the back, the most animated of the three women. She had her hood down, but the iPod buds were in her ears, her chin jutting ever so slightly to the beat. Thomas left the radio off and cheerily asked Yunis a series of questions to which Clara was sure he already knew the answers: What time is the flight? (4:05.) Who's meeting you in the D.R.? (Tío Modesto.) Do you need to get anything before you leave? (Of course.) This effectively passed the time until they got to the restaurant.

Inside, Church's looked as unprepossessing as the street scene outside. Most of the business was takeout; the interior was dominated by a long red counter. There were four plastic patio tables with red-and-white checkered tablecloths and beach umbrellas—garden furniture brought indoors. To add to the effect, strings of fake ivy climbed the walls near the tables. On either side of the counter were cork boards with photographs of Mr. and Mrs. Church and their daughter, Rose Mary, along with newspaper reviews of the restaurant, including one with the headline BEST RIBS IN ESSEX COUNTY. It was barely noon, and though they were the first customers, the place smelled like food—like grease and barbecue sauce and boiling cobs of corn. Behind the counter was Mrs. Church herself, a slow-moving, good-humored woman who was given, Clara had noticed, to narrating her own actions.

"Got some customers," she said as they entered. She handed each of them a folded paper take-out menu. "Have a look," she said. "Tell me what Edwin and I can make for you today."

They perused the offerings but there was no doubt what their order would be: chicken and ribs, rice and beans, corn and collard greens.

"I'm not hungry," Deysei said, pulling out her earphones and winding the cord around her pink iPod. She put her menu back on the counter.

"The food is great here," said Thomas.

"You've got to eat," said Yunis.

"I'm not hungry, Mami," said Deysei again and went to sit at the nearest table.

"*Dios mío*," said Yunis. "You're not in Washington Heights now, baby. You can't just walk to the corner and get a slice whenever you feel like it."

"I know, Mami. *I'm. Not. Hungry.*"

"*Ayuda me*," hissed Yunis, looking at Clara.

They gave their orders to Mrs. Church, who shouted each item to her husband before going back to help him in the kitchen. Then they joined Deysei at the table. As soon as they were seated, Clara spoke up. "Your mom told us, Deysei. Is it true? When was your last period?"

Deysei looked first at Clara and then at Thomas. She was not used to having a man present during such discussions—Clara had almost asked Thomas not to come. But if he was going to be a kind of stepfather to Deysei, he needed to be a part of this discussion.

"Six weeks," she said.

"Have you taken a pregnancy test?" Thomas asked. That was her husband, thought Clara, always seeking the empirical.

"Yes, Tío," she said, and glanced at her mother.

"I made her," said Yunis. "Last night. She didn't want to. But I knew something was going on. It had been too long since she took one of my pads."

"So, you haven't been to a doctor yet?" said Clara.

Deysei shook her head.

"OK," said Clara. "We're going to get you to a doctor this week. I have a good OB."

Deysei nodded, not saying anything. She looked like a framed corporal facing a military tribunal—frightened but hopeful of exoneration.

"Does the father know?" said Clara.

Yunis interjected. "She won't tell me who the damn father is. It's probably that fool Eduardo. That moron has been following her around for months. 'Hey, baby. Hey, baby.' I told you to stay away from him."

Hidden beneath her overalls and her hoodie, Deysei had the kind of rounded, big-boned, heavy-bottomed body most Dominican men loved. Clara, who was skinny by comparison, could tell it was a burden for her niece and, surely, a big reason for her choice of attire. "Does the father know?" she asked again, ignoring her sister's outburst.

Deysei's face contorted as she tried to keep the tears back. She shook her head.

"It's all right," said Clara, and put her hand on her niece's cheek. "It's OK."

"God damn it. It's not all right," said Yunis. "How can I leave now? How can I go to D.R. now, like this? I can't leave her with you." And Clara saw that this relatively minor inconvenience—missing her flight, delaying her escape—not the larger issue of her daughter's pregnancy, was irking Yunis.

"Let's all try to stay calm," said Thomas, to which Yunis rolled her eyes.

"Do you want to tell us who the father is?" Clara asked. She put her hand on Deysei's and squeezed.

Deysei shook her head.

"Sis, you're being way too nice. You can't ask her. She's got to *tell* us. You've got to *demand*."

"Now isn't the time," said Clara. She looked over at Thomas. He in turn was looking at Deysei intently—as if *he* were the father and about to be blamed for all of this.

Clara continued: "Deysei, sweetheart. You don't have to tell us the father's name, but there are two questions you're going to have to answer before too much longer. The first is, are you going to tell him? The second is, do you want to keep the baby?"

Deysei appeared overcome by the magnitude of these questions. She covered her face and began to weep.

"Why you crying?" said Yunis. "This ain't nobody's fault but yours. If you hadn't been screwing around there wouldn't be anything to cry about." Clara now regretted suggesting they go out to lunch. Her hope had been that a public venue would keep the tone of the discussion civil. She hadn't expected the place to be so empty. It was August. Everyone was somewhere else.

"Yunis!" said Clara. "Don't be so hard on her. It's too late for that now. You did the same thing when you were her age."

"Yeah, like I was the *only* teenage mother in New York," said Yunis.

"All right, all right," said Clara, holding up her hands, wanting to get off *that* subject. "Look, there's no reason you can't go to Mami's today, as long as Deysei is OK with that. There's still a couple of weeks before school starts. We don't have to decide anything right now, except whether you're going to get on the plane this afternoon. And if you don't get on the plane, Mami's going to wonder what's going on."

"I've got to tell her."

"That's up to you," said Clara.

"Please don't tell Abuela," said Deysei, wiping her nose on a paper napkin. "Please don't tell her, Mami."

"Wow. She's going to be a great-grandmother," said Thomas. "And she's not even sixty yet, is she?"

"No," said Clara. She hated the fact, hated every stereotype it conformed to, but it was true.

"My mother was almost sixty when Guillermo was born," said Thomas.

"*OK*," said Clara.

"Shit," said Yunis. "Mami's going to flip. All right. I ain't gonna tell her until we decide what we're going to do."

"You mean until Deysei decides," said Clara.

Yunis looked at her daughter. "Yeah, I guess so."

Mrs. Church emerged from the kitchen door with a basket of biscuits and a pitcher of iced tea. "You look hungry," she said. "I got food for you. A lot of good food. Edwin has outdone himself today. I'm bringing it now. Here I come."

"Let's eat," said Clara. "We have a plane to catch."

CLARA HATED AIRPORTS. It was her conviction that the airport experience was a fair analogy of what awaited her immediately after death—that her credentials for the afterlife were more likely to be inspected by someone who dressed like an airline attendant than a pre-Raphaelite archangel and that the Pearly Gates would probably resemble customs and immigration more than the entrance to an upscale retirement community. As she pulled into the short-term parking lot for Newark Liberty Airport's terminal A, she recalled a flight to the Dominican Republic she'd taken the summer between college and library school. She was going there to be feted by her mother, to be shown off like a prizewinning show dog, the first in the family to get a degree. Half an hour into the flight, the pilot had announced that they were turning the plane around and going back to New York. There was something wrong with one of the engines—or at least the possibility of something being wrong with one of the engines, the announcement wasn't clear. The pilot said that it was nothing to be concerned about, that the other engines could take the weight of the plane in the event one failed. They were just being careful. Clara's reaction to this announcement was emphatic disappointment. "No!" she said aloud, drawing stares from her fellow passengers. Her disappointment was not because of the lengthy delay that was sure to follow, but rather because she thought of air travel, like death, as irrevocable. From the moment the ticket was purchased, the die was cast. It was partly for this reason that she refused to entertain the idea of Yunis not going to D.R. It was fate, fate that Deysei would become her responsibility, fate that Clara would learn that her niece was pregnant the same week that a doctor had told Clara that she might not be able to have another child.

There had been little talk in the Odyssey since they'd stopped at the CVS on Springfield Avenue. Thomas had parted company with them at Church's, walking home to meet Guillermo off his summer-camp bus. The iPod buds were back in Deysei's ears, isolating her as firmly as a language barrier. Meanwhile, Yunis had spent the drive to the airport making last-minute phone calls to her friends and associates in New York and Santo Domingo. While she talked, she distributed her purchases into various pockets of her purse and her carry-on bag as if trying to hide something. Clara had left the radio off and driven in silence, eavesdropping on her sister. There were buried motives for everything Yunis did. There was always an angle, always a scam, and Clara hoped to overhear something that would help her understand more fully what her sister was up to in running away to their mother's house and abandoning her daughter. From the beginning, the decision had seemed impulsive to Clara, but that was how it went with her sister. Plans were anathema. Yunis's cell phone conversations left Clara unilluminated. They were mostly business—making sure that the woman she'd sublet her apartment to was still planning to move in the next day and reminding Tío Modesto that he was supposed to pick her up at the airport. "I hope you got those Presidentes on ice, 'cause I'm thirsty already and I ain't even on the plane yet!" she said, switching off her phone.

They parked and found a cart to transfer Yunis's luggage into the airport. Entering the terminal, Clara felt it—the hollow chill of the place. Because they were late, there wasn't much of a line at the check-in. A family of panicked, abrasive Dominicans ahead of them were squabbling with the agent about the weight of their gargantuan bags. Meanwhile Yunis was delving again through the contents of her purse.

"I hate this e-ticket shit," she said. "You remember when you used to get your ticket in a nice plastic wallet? Like a diploma or something? Now it's these fucking printouts."

Every event in her sister's life was like a scene out of a *telenovela: Days of Our Yuniverse.* Maybe it really was best for everyone if she just went away.

"Here you are, you son of a bitch." From her bag, Yunis pulled a crumpled piece of paper with the Yahoo! logo on top.

"You got your passport, Mami?" asked Deysei.

"Yeah. I got both. Dominican and American. Nobody's going to give me no trouble today. Where are they?" She rooted once more in her purse, as if to pull a loose thread from the lining. Her bag fell from her hands and spilled half its contents across the hard, shiny floor.

"Fuck!"

"Last call. Santo Domingo. Last call," said one of the attendants behind the counter.

"Wait! That's me!" shouted Yunis. Clara and Deysei squatted down to help her gather her belongings. Clara picked up a lipstick, an envelope, and a photograph of a man she'd never seen before, a young Dominican in a muscle shirt and a black Yankees cap, palm trees in the background. Perhaps *he* was the real reason behind Yunis's departure. She handed the items to her sister, who was yelling, "Santo Domingo! Right here!"

Her luggage was checked and her boarding pass issued with alacrity. The attendants told her to hurry. They went down the escalator to the security gate, where the metal detectors and X-ray machines waited. There was no time for a prolonged goodbye, but en route from the check-in counters, Yunis had started crying.

"Oh, baby, are you going to be OK?" She clutched Deysei to her breast.

"*Yes,* Mami," said Deysei.

"I'm not deserting you, baby. You know that, right? I'll come back the minute you need me. You look after my girl," said Yunis to Clara, a pearl-sized tear bubbling out of the corner of her eye.

"I will. Now go. Your flight is about to take off."

"I'll call you from Mami's. Tonight. Bye *mi amorcita.*" She kissed her daughter and her sister and hustled toward the TSA workers, her big booty shaking, her curls bouncing. They watched her remove her shoes and pass through the metal detectors. On the far side, reunited with her bags, she waved at them and raced away.

"Tía?" said Deysei, a moment later.

"What?" said Clara, with more abruptness than she intended. The day's events had left her feeling testy.

"I hope you won't be mad at me."

"What is it? Just tell me."

She hesitated. "I'm hungry."

"Oh, is that all?" said Clara, softening her voice. "How could I be mad at you? You've got to feed that baby. There's the food court over there. What do you feel like?"

Deysei looked abashed.

"What is it, honey? You can tell me."

"A Big Mac, Tía."

"You want a Big Mac?"

"Yes, Tía."

Clara smiled, genuinely tickled. "That's funny."

"What?"

"Big Macs were all I wanted to eat when I was pregnant with Guillermo. I just couldn't get enough of that special sauce. I must have eaten a hundred of them during those nine months. Poor Thomas. They got to know him pretty well at the twenty-four-hour drive-thru on Northfield."

"I'm just hungry, Tía," said Deysei, clearly reluctant to dwell on the procreative bond with her aunt. "It's not like it's a craving or nothing."

"That's what you're saying now. Just wait. Pretty soon, you won't be able to think of anything but Big Macs. You'll be dreaming about them." The memory elevated her mood. No matter what the damn doctors said about her uterus, she had given birth to a healthy boy who was alive and well and busy in the world—probably getting off his school bus right about now.

Clara left her niece at a table by the window in the food court and went to the McDonald's counter. She still felt overfed from their lunch at Church's. Watching the petulant, poorly paid staff assemble her niece's meal, she thought that fast food never looked less appetizing. She couldn't remember the last time she'd eaten a Big Mac. Years. During the second pregnancy—the lost baby—her foods of choice had been gazpacho and spring rolls. Maybe McDonald's made stronger babies, she thought, and felt the absence, as she did from time to time, of the other living organism within her, a kind of physical déjà vu. Deysei's child was going to need every advantage it could get and she was going to do whatever she could to help.

On her way back to the table, Clara noticed that Deysei was hastily putting away her cell phone. Who was she talking to? Maybe the baby's father? What an enabler of subterfuge those devices were. She set the tray on the table with a *voila!* gesture. Deysei was unwrapping the burger before Clara even sat down. She squeezed two tubes of ketchup into the top side of the carton and dipped the massive pillbox of meat and bread into it before taking her first bite. Clara found it hard to watch her niece eat the huge hamburger, the ketchup and the pinkish special sauce smearing on the sides of her face, the soiled napkins piling up on the table between them. She didn't properly wipe her hands on them; instead, she squeezed them tight and set them down like crumpled moths. Deysei was grinning with delight as she chewed. Clara gazed beyond her niece, scanning the other travelers in the seating area: a cute young woman in college sweats talking on a cell phone; an in-love couple who looked like they were going away on their first vacation together; a salesman in slacks and a polo shirt poring over a spreadsheet (the very image she'd always had of her husband when he was on his business trips); a handsome dark-skinned man hugging a small blond boy. This last pair caught her attention for a couple of reasons. First, the striking disparity between them: the man brown and burly, the boy tow-headed and slender. Second, the man was Dominican and she recognized him. It took a moment to put a name to the familiar, if estranged, face. Then she knew who it was.

"You OK, Tía?" asked Deysei, then tucked the last of the hamburger into her mouth and took a long draw on her soda.

"Yes," said Clara, standing up. "Let's go. You can eat those fries in the car."

THEY WENT BACK out to the parking lot, Clara hustling her niece.

"What's the hurry, Tía?" Deysei asked.

"Nothing," said Clara.

"Then why we rushing?"

"Come on," said Clara, not explaining.

In the Odyssey, waiting to pay for parking, Clara ran her tongue along the inside of her lower lip. There was the scar tissue where her teeth had nearly been driven through her own flesh—but the scar tissue also covered another, deeper wound that she could not touch. Tito Moreno. Where else but in an airport—a place of transience, a place of such consternation for her—would she see for the first time in years the boy, now a man, for whom she had such complicated feelings? And, to further complicate those feelings, he was there in the airport with a beautiful blond child. Was Tito that child's father? It hardly seemed possible, but then wasn't she often mistaken for the nanny of her own light-skinned son? He looked well, fit and healthy, though she thought she saw (or wanted to see) melancholy in his face as he hugged the boy. It was conceivable that the boy's mother had just departed on a trip. Clara imagined her as a businesswoman, like one of the attorneys she worked with. It was hard to believe that Tito would have ended up married to a lawyer, but anything was possible.

They were on I-78. Soon they would be home and then she would have to figure out what to do about her niece. Then she would have to talk to Thomas about what the fertility doctors had said. And now Tito. What was she supposed to make of that?

"Tía?" said Deysei from the passenger seat, as if reading her mind. Clara glanced over. Deysei was staring at her, the empty red carton of fries cupped in her hand.

"What is it? Are you still hungry?"

"No, Tía. I want to tell you something."

"What?"

"I want to tell you who the father is."

Whoa, she thought. "OK."

"But first you have to promise me you won't tell anyone."

"I promise."

"You mean it, Tía?"

"Yes. It will be a secret. I won't tell anyone."

"Not even Tío Thomas?"

"Yes. Not even him."

Deysei paused. "It's Raúl," she said.

And Clara pulled off to the shoulder, because otherwise, she would have crashed.

Tito

Now and then Tito got a call for an estimate in New Jersey, usually in Bergen County, where Dominicans from the Heights moved when their ships came in. Sometimes the suburbs weren't all they were cracked up to be and people decided they wanted to move back to the city. They missed the very things they were trying to escape: the noise, the crowds, the filth. One woman actually said that to him. "The streets are too fucking clean over here. It makes me feel like I can't walk on them."

The house was in Oradell, a white Cape with a sloping lawn on a quiet cul-de-sac lined with pear and apple trees. Tito parked the car and climbed the steps, pausing to look around. It was a street he had visited many times in his imagination, the street he dreamed of living on. His wife and two children resided here. In the back of the house were the graves of a dog and two goldfish. To his left lived the friendly neighbor, the one who lent him the expensive lawn equipment and power tools he never got around to buying himself. On the right was the loud, uncouth neighbor, the one who fought with his wife and drank too much—just the sort of person you thought didn't live in the suburbs.

Tito rang the bell.

The door was opened by a good-looking high-yellow Dominicana in her fifties. Her hair was straightened and styled short, like Condi Rice's. She was wearing dark blue jeans, an ivory blouse, and a pair of silver reading glasses, which dangled from a chain around her neck. It was those glasses, as bright and sharp as surgical instruments, that caught his eye. He glanced down at his clipboard to check the name but found that he already knew it.

"*Buenas tardes,* Ms. Almonte," he said. There was an awkward pause as he waited to see if she would recognize him—but why would she? "I'm with Cruz Brothers," he continued. "I'm here to give you an estimate for your move."

"Yes, come in," she said, and walked him around the house, pointing out what was staying and what was going. Inside, it was not at all the cozy, domestic space he'd dreamed up for himself and his phantom family; it was spare and clean to the point of being ascetic, with modern art on the walls, books in every room, and no television. There was an austerity to the wooden furniture that reminded him of church pews—you wouldn't be able to get too comfortable, he thought. Only the bathroom matched his imaginings. It had just been redone, she told him, fitted out with his and hers sinks, a whirlpool tub, and one of those showers that blasted water at you from about eight different directions. To Tito, it seemed like something a long-married couple would treat themselves to in lieu of an active sex life. A lot of the stuff was staying, which in his experience meant a divorce. It was not a house where children lived.

When the tour was finished, they sat in the dining room and Tito asked her how soon she wanted to move. He sipped at the glass of ice water she had given him, making sure to place it on the coaster and not on the glossy surface of the table. The glass was slippery and he was worried about dropping it.

"The first of September," she said.

"*Bien.* Where you moving to?"

"English, please," she said. "I'm moving to Sherman Avenue in Manhattan."

"You're moving *to* Inwood?" he said, and stopped himself from asking her why.

"Yes. But some of the items are going to go into storage. I assume you offer that service?"

"We do," Tito said. "For how long?"

"Indefinitely," said Ms. Almonte.

He nodded and got to work on the estimate, giving her a better price than she would get from anyone else, though there wasn't much he could do about the monthly storage rates. He wrote the figure at the bottom of the sheet and passed it to her along with a Cruz Brothers brochure and his business card. She looked it over. He could read nothing in her face. "I'm getting some other estimates," she said. "I'll give you a call when I decide."

"Of course," he said, taking another sip from his beaded glass. The water in New Jersey always tasted like chemicals to him.

She walked him back to the door. The whole time he had been there, he had debated saying something. Now he had to decide. Just before stepping outside, he asked, "Does your Word Club still exist, Ms. Almonte?"

Her eyes flickered at him. "Were you a student of mine? I never forget a student and I don't remember you."

"I was at Kennedy," he said, "but not in your class." And then, after a pause: "I was friends with Clara Lugo."

She appeared to consider him anew. "So, *you* were Clara's boyfriend?" she asked.

Tito did not answer the question. "Let me know if I can help with your move," he said, and walked back down the steps.

DEPENDING WHO YOU asked, Ms. Almonte was either the greatest teacher in the history of the world or a hard-ass, stuck-up *mulata* bitch who thought she was the Queen of England and Miss Manners rolled into one skinny, titless body. She taught A.P. English and was known to fail students for a few misspelled words or for not knowing where to put an apostrophe. But the worst thing a student could do in her presence was throw Spanish words into an English sentence. "This is an *English* class," she would say. "I want to hear English. Your future employers will want to hear English, too."

She had followers, mostly college-bound girls who imitated her in every way they could—some more successfully than others. These devotees belonged to the Word Club, an after-school program that had begun as a prep class for the verbal portion of the SAT, but soon morphed into an extracurricular finishing school for a handful of bright, ambitious, assimilated girls headed for scholarships to the Ivy League and Seven Sisters. Behind their backs—and sometimes to their faces—they were called lesbians and wannabe whiteys, but the fact was that almost every boy in the school was in love with Ms. Almonte or one of her girls in a way that the boys would never fully understand or admit to one another. She and her girls were beyond them; they lived in the territory of the imagination.

Clara Lugo was Tito's Almonte girl. She was neither the prettiest nor the best dressed of them, but she had, by some measures, come the farthest to be there. She was dark skinned and had Chinese eyes. At her temples grew swirls of hair that looked like wispy reinterpretations of her ears. For a Dominican girl, she didn't have much of an ass, but she was tall and her hair was long and thick.

Tito and Clara had played together as children. Clara's father owned a hardware store on Dyckman Street, and Tito's father was the building superintendent for 222 Seaman Avenue—a good customer. On Sunday afternoons, when the store was closed, the two families met for picnics in the park. Tito retained a clear memory of the last afternoon the families spent together. The Lugos were still wearing their good clothes from Mass while Tito and his parents were dressed casually. He and Clara were in the Emerson Playground, twenty yards from the picnic blanket. Clara came too close to the swing he was on and his foot clipped her in the mouth. It felt like nothing to him, but she cried out and brought her hand to her face. When she drew it away, her fingers dripped with blood. She ran to the blanket, where their parents were sitting with Clara's baby brother, Efran, eating *pastelitos* and drinking beer. *"¡Que barbaro!"* he heard his mami say, and then his papi came and yanked him off the swing to make him apologize.

Soon after that, his father and Don Roberto stopped speaking to each other. At first Tito thought it was because of the bloody lip, but, he later learned, the issue was a faulty power drill that Clara's father refused to take back, saying that it had worked fine when he sold it to Tito's father. The dispute escalated and Tito's papi took his business to the Jewish hardware store on Broadway—a declaration of war. Clara's papi started saying things about Tito's father, implying that he had lived too long in that building full of white people, that he had forgotten he was Dominican, that his son watched too much TV. He was going to grow up godless and unable to speak Spanish. Tito had always been afraid of Don Roberto. He was big and loud, with a chipped tooth and pockmarked cheeks. How could a man so ugly have produced a daughter so becoming? He liked to slam his hands on the counter of his store when he was making a point to one of his customers—and, it seemed, he always had a point to make.

Tito was forbidden from playing with Clara and she became, in time, just another neighborhood girl, glimpsed in the subway station or crossing Broadway. Over the following months, his mother subjected him to a propaganda campaign about Clara's family. She said that Doña Dolores was not actually Clara's mother, that everyone in Inwood knew this. Don Roberto, she claimed, had abducted Clara from the Dominican Republic and brought her to the United States. Her father was strict with her, and her stepmother was wicked—straight out of *Cinderella*. At the time, Tito thought this was all just part of the feud between his parents and the Lugos and he forgot about it. Soon enough, he befriended some of the kids in the building his father managed and Clara all but slipped from his mind. That is the way things stayed until high school, when in a process as mysterious and unmeasurable as the growth of fingernails, she re-emerged from the general population of girls to become, first, a girl and, then, *the* girl. By then, she had grown and filled out, matured. Once she joined the Word Club, she began straightening her hair and wearing stylish clothing. She occupied more and more of Tito's mind and took on a significant role in his fantasy life. Between classes he looked for her, and when she did appear from the throngs in the halls, he trailed behind her, floating in the wake of her smell—of gardenias and candy—like a cartoon character following the scent of a freshly baked pie. Sometimes he would trail her all the way to the other side of the school, far from his next class. The bell would ring and he would come to himself alone in the hallway, late again.

LEAVING MS. ALMONTE'S, Tito drove back to Washington Heights, his mind in turmoil. He had not seen Clara for fifteen years, but he continued to think of her often. When he conjured his imaginary family life in the suburbs, the role of his wife was usually played by a grown-up Clara, especially when he was between girlfriends, as he was now. She was the template for his longings.

Tito had just moved out of his parents' apartment and was still unpacking his new studio on Broadway and 190th Street. When he got home, it took him a while to find the box, the one marked MISC. PAPER. Inside the box he dug through an assortment of documents in plastic sleeves—his tax returns, his U.S. passport, his naturalization certificate, his high school diploma, his Dominican passport, his birth certificate—to find the Ziploc bag of envelopes and postcards that represented nearly all the real mail he had received in life. Within the bag he leafed through the sheaf of birthday cards, valentines, and love letters until he found the note from Clara. He knew the words by heart, but still he unfolded the single page from its smudged and wrinkled envelope and read the following:

Dearest Tito,

I'm sorry I did not write sooner. You are probably wondering what happened to me. I want you to know that I am safe and happy. Don't worry about me and please don't try to find me. I'm sorry I did not have a chance to say goodbye.

Clara

He folded the note and returned it to the envelope, put the envelope into the Ziploc bag, and dropped the bag back into the box. Then he went into the kitchen and poured himself a drink.

Ms. ALMONTE CALLED him a few days later and accepted his offer but only if she could move that Saturday, a week sooner than she'd told him. Tito, who had not worked a move since being promoted into the sales force, would have to drive the truck himself. He scrambled to put together a crew. On such short notice, he had to scrounge around to find a couple of warm bodies. One of them, Hector, had been working for Cruz Brothers since Tito was a crew chief on the trucks, and Tito was grateful to have him. Hector was an older guy from El Salvador who was shaped like a fire hydrant, didn't speak any English, and could carry objects twice his size. He was religious and, even in Spanish, kept his thoughts mostly to himself. Tito felt less fortunate with his other grunt, a young Dominican named Raúl who had muscles on his muscles but also a reputation for surliness and inappropriate behavior—including hitting on young female clients during moves. There was no one else available, though, so Tito was obliged to go with the team he had. He signed the truck out of the garage and picked up Hector and Raúl in the yard on Tenth.

"So, where we going? Jersey?" asked Raúl, as they drove down Broadway to the bridge, the cab bouncing in response to the potholes.

"Jersey," said Tito. "Yes."

Raúl looked like he'd sooner go to hell. "Jersey ain't nothing but a big landfill."

"That's Staten Island," said Tito.

"Same damn difference," said Raúl. On the far side of the cab, Hector sat with his arms crossed, napping. Tito remembered this about him: He could sleep anywhere, seemingly at will.

Ms. Almonte was ready for them. She'd gone through the house tagging everything that was to be taken with Post-it notes, sometimes even writing out explicit directions about how an item should be packed. Normally this would have pissed Tito off, but he knew to expect nothing else from her. How could she fail to be a difficult customer? They got to work. He sent Raúl and Hector to do the kitchen, hoping that Hector's example would keep Raúl out of trouble. Once he saw that they were filling boxes with pots and cutlery, he started on the books in the den. Tito wanted to work alone. He had the vague, hopeful idea that he might find something. He kept looking over his shoulder as he worked, waiting for Ms. Almonte to appear to make sure he was packing the right things or to complain about the mess his boys were making in the kitchen, but once she'd let them into the house, she left them alone, and this made Tito even more nervous. After an hour, he poked his head into the kitchen and saw that Raúl was not there. "Where did he go?" he asked Hector.

Hector mimed a man urinating. Then there was the flush of the toilet. Raúl came back into the kitchen, buckling his belt. "What?" he said.

"Nothing," said Tito. "Get back to work."

"Man can't even drain his lizard," said Raúl, shaking his head.

Tito returned to the books. (There were a lot of books.) He heard her footfalls upstairs and wondered where the husband was. From the wedding photo in the living room, he looked to Tito like an uptight businessman—the sort of guy who didn't own a pair of jeans or sneakers. Shouldn't he be here, making sure his wife wasn't absconding with his ancestral china? Maybe it wasn't a divorce, Tito thought. Maybe it was just a separation. Or maybe the husband had run off with his secretary and didn't care about the ancestral china anymore. This is what he loved about his job—the voyeurism, the constant opportunity to speculate about other people's private lives and imagine, if only briefly, that he lived like them. Tito spun out his thoughts as he put the short stacks of books into boxes, filling the crevices and cracks with paper, sealing the boxes tightly with tape. He'd forgotten how this kind of activity with the hands could free the mind. He was so busy daydreaming that he almost failed to notice the edge of the photograph poking out from the book in his hands. The book was a hardcover edition of Julia Alvarez's *How the García Girls Lost Their Accents* and the photograph was of the members of the Word Club all seated in Ms. Almonte's room, only it didn't look like her room because there were pillows on the floor and teacups and a plate with some kind of pastry on it. There were seven girls sitting in a semicircle around Ms. Almonte. He knew all of their names, as if they had been the heroines of his favorite television show: Yesenia, Milly, María José, Victoria, Julia, Eva, and Clara. None of them lived in the neighborhood anymore (he'd checked, as best he could, in the phone book, he'd asked around). Occasionally he heard stories about one or another of them, though never about Clara. Many had married white men; one was living in Paris. Another was a surgeon. Standing in Ms. Almonte's den, doing a job he had been doing since he was in school with them, he took a long, inspecting look at their faces. They were just girls. He got that now. They didn't have super powers or anything. Some of them weren't even so good-looking, he was stunned to realize. They were trying too hard, wearing clothes that were too mature for them, arranging their hair in styles that now looked ridiculous. Even so, seeing Clara again stirred something in him that he could not explain away so easily. This is what he had been looking for. He slipped the photograph into his pocket and kept packing.

They were done by noon. Her possessions half-filled the truck. None of the appliances were going and only a little of the furniture. It was the small stuff—the books, the bric-a-brac, a few carefully packed pieces of art, and a lot of elegant clothing: five full wardrobe boxes. Tito probably didn't need a two-man crew, but he wanted the whole thing to look official. Raúl and Hector were still securing the cargo in the back of the truck when Ms. Almonte got in her sedan and backed down the driveway, honking as she passed them. Tito started the truck's engine and waited for his boys to close up the back. Then they drove down Route 4, the Washington Heights Highway, to the bridge.

"Damn, she's the whitest Dominican I ever saw," said Raúl. "Didn't have even one can of beans in her kitchen. I looked. Probably *allergic* to beans."

"She's just as Dominican as you or me," said Tito. "I bet she grew up in the Heights just like us."

Raúl sucked his teeth. "I didn't grow up in the Heights," he said. "I'm from Bushwick. There ain't no Dominicans like her in Bushwick, I tell you what."

FROM THE OUTSIDE, the building she was moving into looked like a significant step down in life, a sooty, once glorious Art Deco structure five stories high. Tito stood on the pavement peering at the names in the little glass windows beside the buzzers, a habit of his. Still a lot of Spanish there. In addition to ALMONTE, he saw a PÉREZ, a MARTÍNEZ, and a BLANCO. A couple of Irish names appeared, from the faintness of their type, to be the oldest tenants: DEVINE and McINTYRE. Mixed in with these were two Asians, a ZHOU and a YAO; a Jew, GOLDBERG; and a scattering of others who could only be younger white newcomers, NIELSON, BARRE, RUSSO, the sorts of names you never used to see in Inwood buildings. He pressed the black button next to ALMONTE and waited. When the buzzer sounded, he secured the doors with bungee cords and signaled to Raúl and Hector to open the back of the truck.

It was a ground-floor apartment, the door unlocked. He knocked and entered a long, darkened hall. Ms. Almonte was making the journey from the house of Tito's dreams to the kind of dwelling where he had grown up. It was not a step down in life as he had first thought, but a step *back*. Just inside, he was not surprised to see, stood a glass vase for the water of the saints. Above it, a small portrait of the Virgin Altagracia. He nodded at the Virgin like an old friend. The hallway was clean and otherwise bare. At the end of it was the living room, where Ms. Almonte was sitting with an old woman on a white leather couch wrapped in a clear plastic cover. Something about the room looked wrong, as if the furniture had been shifted around by someone who didn't live there. The television was on, showing *El Gordo y la Flaca*.

Ms. Almonte introduced him to the old woman, her mother. She looked up at him with incomprehension and, seeing his clipboard, said, "Census?"

"No," said Tito. "*Mudancero*."

"Ah!" she said, and took a drink from her glass. She looked at her daughter and asked her who was moving in.

Ms. Almonte appeared embarrassed by the exchange—or by Tito witnessing the exchange. She stood and led him to an adjoining room, which was empty save for a twin bed with a gaudy floral coverlet. It was a large five-sided room with one window and a doorway that led to another room, which, it seemed, was the mother's bedroom. Ms. Almonte was wearing a dress today, loose black linen, which gently shifted around her skinny frame. "I want everything in here," she said. "Everything that's not going into storage." It would look strange, Tito thought, all that modern, highbrow stuff in these immigrant surroundings.

They emptied the truck of everything except the storage items in less than an hour. Carrying in the last of the boxes, he stopped to watch Ms. Almonte trying to feed her mother a lunch of soup and bread.

"You have to eat something, Mami. You're wasting away."

"*No tengo hambre,*" said the mother.

"Please, eat."

"*¡No tengo hambre!*" said the mother, again.

At this point, Ms. Almonte turned and caught Tito looking. "Yes?"

He raised his hands in apology. "We're almost finished. I just need you to sign."

"All right," she said. "*Un momentito, Mami.*"

Out of the classroom, and out of her house, she had lost her aura. Tito no longer felt cowed by her and he was saddened by this realization. Many of the things that had impressed him the most when he was younger—the subway, Christmas, television—seemed perfectly humdrum now and he wished it weren't so, wished he could still be awed. Was it simply because he wasn't young anymore, or was it something worse: an aptitude for disappointment?

Ms. Almonte signed with an ornate, illegible signature, tipped them generously, and showed them the door.

TITO DIVIDED THE tip evenly, thanked Hector and Raúl, and drove them back to the yard. He signed in the truck, filed his paperwork, and went home. Sitting on his couch and sipping from a bottle of Corona, he took out the photograph and stared at it again. It wasn't enough. He had thought it would be sufficient to pilfer this memento of the great mystery of his teenage years, of his first broken heart, but the more he looked at Clara's face and the more he dwelled on the memories and questions she provoked, the more he came to see that the photograph was just like a first kiss—all it did was make you greedy for more. What he really wanted was the impossible—to go back and do something that would prevent

Clara from vanishing. She'd gone off to college and, aside from the one cryptic note, he'd never seen or heard from her again. Tito thought he had made his peace with it, but as he grew older and his losses accumulated, this first one loomed ever larger. The events of that summer assumed the form of a puzzle, which, decoded, would somehow explain why things in his life had not turned out as he had once hoped.

ON A WINDY afternoon in the spring of his senior year in high school, Tito was kept late by a teacher who was "concerned" about his "academic performance." There was a line-up of boys waiting outside the teacher's room. One by one they were summoned into the room to receive versions of the same pep talk. Upon hearing what the talk was about, a number of those who were waiting left before their names could be called. By the time Tito got in there, he wished he'd left, too. "You've got some brains in your head, Moreno," the teacher said to him. He was one of those clean-cut young black dudes fresh out of teachers' college who was going to change the world one kid at a time. He'd raised himself up from a slum somewhere and wanted his students to do the same. Tito waited for him to start in about accepting Jesus as his personal savior, but it never came to that. "Your grades aren't that bad. Maybe you could do something with your life if you *applied* yourself," the teacher said, getting close enough to him that Tito could smell the man's Pep-O-Mint breath. Tito had already started applying himself for Cruz Brothers on the weekends, making good money. He didn't see what the teacher's point was and the meeting came to an unsatisfactory end for both of them.

He headed home. As he made his way down 230th Street past the U-Haul lot, he was thrilled to see a familiar figure up ahead, dressed in a long coat. She tottered as she walked, like someone inside a tube. Then the tube crumpled and down she went. Books were cast across the sidewalk. A three-ring binder sprang open, releasing its pages to the wind like a flock of doves. Tito ran after the papers, snatching them out of the air, lunging and thrusting for them as they circled and danced. Out of the corner of his eye, he saw that Clara had gotten up and was doing the same thing, as best she could in that bulky coat. In the end, they captured every page but one, which was carried away from them on an updraft, gliding and flipping over on itself, rising toward the elevated tracks of the 1 and 9.

"I hope that one didn't have all the answers on it," he said.

She was jumping in vain, beckoning to the departing page, close to tears. Her coat was like a giant roll of shearling. Tito looked at the papers in his hands. The top sheet had a geometry problem, his footprint, and a big red A minus on it. So, she was good at math.

"You all right?" he asked.

"Yes," she said. "Yes I am." She was calming herself. "It's these shoes," she said, lifting up her coat to show him a pair of ankle boots with silver buckles and leather soles. "No grip."

"I'll walk you home," he offered as casually as he could manage. "You still live in that house on Payson?"

That made her look at him properly for the first time. "Hey, you're Don Felix's kid. My dad says your father is a lying sack of shit."

"Yeah, well, my pops says your old man is a tightwad cocksucker." They both laughed.

"I've still got the scar from when you kicked me," she said. She pulled down her lower lip and showed him the pair of short white lines her teeth had made, like a double dash in the bumpy red pulp of her mouth. "I'll never forget how much it hurt to eat," she said. "And brushing my teeth was a nightmare."

"Yeah, well, I had to have my toe amputated, just so you know. I still walk with a limp from it."

"Glad you're not holding it against me," she said.

With her papers gathered and returned to their binder, they headed south along Broadway. "So, were you at the Word Club this afternoon?" he asked.

"Maybe," she said.

"What do you guys do in that club?"

"You mean after we're finished with the sex toys?"

He blushed. "Yeah, when you put the dildos away."

She drew an invisible zipper across her lips. "I took a blood oath. They'll kill me if I tell you. Then they'll kill you, too."

"Thanks for looking out for me," he said. They walked along for a moment without saying anything. He'd daydreamed about talking to her many times, and now here he was—talking to her.

"So, where you going to college?" he asked. There was no question of *if.*

"Cornell," she said.

The name meant nothing to him. "What? Not Yale?" he asked, pronouncing it with a Spanish accent: *Jail.*

"I no smart enough for Jail," she said, copying his accent. "Besides, Jail no giving me no moneys."

"What about the other *muchachas*?" he asked.

"Oh, jes," she said. "They going to some good schools: Preenstone, Wasser, Breen Marr, En Why Joo. ¿Y tu, Señor?"

He shook his head and dropped the accent. "I've got a job lined up."

"A *legal* job?"

"Yup."

"That's good," she said. "Better than most of the fools around here." And he was grateful that she spared him the same lecture he'd just gotten from the teacher. Tito liked to read—comic books, thrillers, pornography—but the thought of studying, of taking tests and answering questions in a classroom for four more years, made him queasy. Clara's proficiency at academics now rendered her all the more remarkable to him. It was the same admiration he felt for acrobats and chess masters, people who excelled at things he had no interest in.

Crossing the Broadway Bridge, they discussed the best way to get to her house. The feud between their fathers was dormant but still acknowledged in the neighborhood, and it would be best for both of them if they were not seen together. Tito was cheered by the underlying assumption that they would walk all the way together, that she wasn't going to ditch him. Any lingering animosity seemed to have been forgotten. He said he didn't want to go down Seaman in case his father was sweeping in front of the building. Clara didn't want to walk on Broadway, in case one of *her* father's cronies was eating in El Malecon. In the end, they went up through Park Terrace and Isham Park, hurrying across Seaman well south of his father's building and walking through the forested part of Inwood Hill Park to a path that led down and out of the trees at Payson Street.

"You better stay here where my mother won't see you," she said when they were walking down the path, the trees thinning as they neared the street. "She's already going to kill me for being late."

"Wait," he said. "Maybe you want to come out with me on Saturday?"

"I can't. I work in my father's store."

"What about Sunday?"

She shook her head.

"Oh," he said, downcast.

She smiled. "But you can walk me home next Friday," she said.

"Friday?"

"Yes. And one more thing. You can't tell anyone about me going to Cornell."

"It's a secret?"

"Yes. Everyone thinks I'm going to Hunter. Even the parents."

"I won't say anything," he promised, enjoying the privilege of her secret.

"Thank you," she said, and turned away to walk down the path and out of the park.

The Lugos owned one of the single-family homes that were

scattered among the crumbling Art Deco apartment buildings of Inwood. It was a three-story brick wreck with boards in the windows of the upper floor and planks on breeze blocks for a stoop. A Dumpster had occupied the short driveway for as long as Tito could remember. If progress was being made on restoring the house, it was all happening on the inside, because the outside was as derelict as it had been when their fathers were friends. In Tito's imagination, the house had, over the years, anthropomorphized into a giant, decapitated head, its chin on the sidewalk, the garage an open mouth, the windows above them like a pair of eyes, and the boarded orifices on the top floor some kind of pagan headdress. As Tito watched Clara walk across the street, it seemed like the house was going to swallow her alive.

WITHOUT HAVING TO be told, Tito understood that the Friday afternoon walks home with Clara would be a secret—not just from their parents, but also from their schoolmates, from his friends. He could tell no one. The romantic lives of the Almonte girls spurred endless speculation among the boys (and, he guessed, the girls) of John F. Kennedy High School. The speculation filled a void. There were rumors of the Word Club girls going on dates with Columbia students and New York Presbyterian doctors, of limousines and downtown nightclubs, of trips to resorts in the Poconos or long skiing weekends in Vermont, but these were merely rumors, never substantiated. The only certainty was that they did not date boys from Kennedy. If Tito had claimed that he was Clara's boyfriend, no one would have believed him; he would have succeed only in attracting ridicule or, perhaps, pity. During the school week he could presume no change in Clara's attitude toward him. In short, he could not expect her to acknowledge his existence beyond sharing her amusement with her friends about the boy who sometimes followed her in the halls. He was fine with this. It was a small price to pay.

The next Friday was Good Friday—something Clara may or may not have realized when she issued her invitation the week before. It was a half day. He waited for her by the U-Haul lot, figuring she wouldn't want to be seen near the school grounds with him. He positioned himself there immediately after the final bell rang and was still there well after the time when he had run into her the week before. Rain threatened and he sensed the disapproval of the people passing by: He must be up to no good. Still she did not appear. Maybe she'd gone to church or something? It was then that he realized there would be no school the following week because of the Easter break and that he would not see her for at least ten more days.

Those ten days passed slowly. He worked a move on the Saturday, a family relocating from a shitty apartment on Nagle Avenue to a slightly less shitty apartment on Fordham Road. Sunday he went to an early season Yankees game with his cousin Hershel. Hershel attended George Washington High, but Tito refrained from telling him about Clara, just in case the rumor leaked back to Kennedy. During the week off he helped his father. He repainted a vacant one-bedroom apartment by himself; he hauled the mounds of trash out to the curb for the weekly collection; he unclogged a drain for Mrs. Canby on the fourth floor. When his father sent him out to buy a new faucet for the Hernández family in 2G, he momentarily thought of going down to Dyckman and buying it from Clara's father, just on the off chance that she was working. But his own father would never forgive him.

On the Monday after the Easter break, Tito saw her in the hallway, walking by herself between classes, and was relieved to learn that she still existed. She appeared to take no notice of him until she was almost past and then, at the last moment, she winked at him. It was so quick that anyone seeing them might have thought she got something caught in her eye. But it was enough.

That Friday—it was mid-April already—he waited for her closer to the school, standing outside a bodega in the weak spring sunshine, pretending to read a newspaper. About an hour after the final bell, she walked by with one of the other Word Club girls, Yesenia Matos, and he followed them, keeping his distance. At Broadway, Yesenia climbed the stairs to the subway while Clara turned and walked south toward the bridge. He followed, catching up with her on the span as a train made its cacophonous passage over them on the elevated track.

"I was beginning to think you didn't like me, Tito," she said.

They walked home together by the same evasive route they'd taken before, talking and joshing each other about the mix-up on Good Friday. Clara's mother, in one of her fits of piety, had made them go to Mass. That afternoon in the park Tito kissed her for the first time. It was on the path in the woods as they descended toward her house. He was motivated by a sense of desperation, a sense that she might contrive ways of avoiding him on Fridays the rest of his life. If nothing else, he would at least have this one kiss. How modest that aspiration seemed to him later, but how immense it seemed to him at the time. He took her by the hand and pulled her close, fully expecting to be struck across the face. She gave no resistance, opening her mouth to his. Tito tasted icing sugar on her lips—a dissolving sweetness—along with traces of lip balm. He felt her warm breath against his cheek. When he finally pulled away, she smiled at him. "See you next week," she said.

FOR THE REMAINDER of the spring, Tito did not have any trouble finding Clara on Friday afternoons. Even after school ended in late June, they maintained their schedule. He worked both weekend days so that his Fridays would be free for her. He moved furniture, hung out with his boys, ate meals with his parents, listened to music, read his comic books, exchanged bullshit with Nelson, did his daily push-ups and sit-ups, watched the Yankees on TV, went to a couple of lame parties, but all of it was just a means of distraction until Friday afternoon came around again. To minimize their chances of being seen together, they took to arriving separately in the forested part of the park. These dates, as Tito liked to think of them, soon turned into extended sessions of kissing and reaching into each other's clothes. The warm weather conspired to make things easier for them—thickening the greenery of the wilder sections of the park, inviting Clara to go bare-legged in skirts and short dresses, the inciting sight of her brown skin on display. They explored each other as much as possible under the cover of the park's flora, but the lack of privacy kept them from going as far as Tito would have liked. There remained always something elusive about Clara. He was increasingly aware of her imminent departure for Cornell. He had tried to talk about it with her, saying that he would visit her at college, promising to do whatever it took to carry their relationship forward, always seeking signs of assurance from her. But Clara inevitably stopped these entreaties by kissing him or taking his hand and placing it over her heart. As much as he loved those gestures, they did not allay his fears—if anything they heightened them. Tito became convinced that the only way to ensure that they would stay together beyond September was to sleep with her. They were both virgins and he believed that sex would somehow create an unbreakable bond between them.

In August, an opportunity finally presented itself. His mother and father were going to celebrate their twentieth wedding anniversary with a week at a resort in Punta Cana. Tito took the time off work to be available for the building's tenants. There was an empty apartment on the third floor. He'd repainted it earlier in the month and helped his father install a new refrigerator. In the refrigerator now was a bottle of wine and some of the food his mother had left for him. The apartment's layout was unconventional, with a bedroom right by the entrance then a long living room opening to an alcove kitchen and leading to the second bedroom. The previous tenants had lived in filth and disorder, with clothes and garbage on the floor, but the place was clean now. All of the rooms had windows that opened into the airshaft—and therefore were visible to people in other apartments—except for the second bedroom, which had a view of the ballfields of Inwood Hill Park. On the hardwood of that second bedroom, Tito had laid out his old sleeping bag, along with a sheet, a blanket, and two pillows. He brought up a vase of flowers. He brought up toilet paper. When the buzzer rang, he was in the bedroom looking out the window at a Little League game.

Clara was wearing nothing special—jeans, sandals, and a lacy short-sleeved blouse—but she looked astounding to him. He tried to kiss her as she entered the apartment, but she danced away, laughing. He could tell that she was in a strange mood. "So, come on, show me around our new place," she said.

He walked her from room to room, describing the apartment as if they lived there together. In the first bedroom, he said, "This is your study. Notice the bookcases over there, and the desk with the nice new computer. See that, I had your diploma from Cornell framed and put up on the wall."

"That's very thoughtful of you."

Every time they went to another room, he tried to take her hand or kiss her cheek, but she moved away. "This is the kitchen," he said, prepared to leave it at that, but she said, "So, who's the cook in the house? You?"

"Of course," he said. "Look what I made earlier today." He opened the fridge and showed her the roasted chicken and the rice and beans his mother had left for him.

"Mmm," she said. "And wine, too? You hoping to get lucky or something?"

"Hoping," he said. She had been willing all summer, but now that they had the opportunity, she had become coy.

He walked her through the living room, pointing out the projection television and the oriental rugs. In the second bedroom, he indicated the sleeping bag and said, "This is our new four-poster bed."

"Let's try it out," she said, and sat down. He got down beside her. He was desperate to feel her skin, even a glancing brush of its warmth, but, continuing to tease him, she rose again and went to the window where he had been when she rang. Tito followed like a dog. She had her back to him and he stood behind her, with his hands on her hips. She did not try to move away. He turned her around and reached up to her face, swept his fingers across her cheek and let his hand glide along her throat. He tugged at her earlobe, teasing the nub of flesh between his fingers like a little piece of dough. She was watching him, her mouth slightly open. His other hand reached behind her and curled up into the back of her blouse. She was naked beneath it and he felt the little canal of her spine between the muscles of her back, the way it flattened out just below her waist. He brought his hand away from her ear and pulled her close. Her mouth felt pulpy. They lowered themselves to the sleeping bag and she was still silent, but busy now, her hands on him, in his hair, clutching at his neck.

Tito was on his knees and she was sitting up in front of him. "Take it off me," she said, pulling at her blouse with a gesture of impatience. Using both hands, he pulled it over her head. He bent forward to kiss her breasts but she stopped him. "These too," she said, squirming as she unzipped her jeans and hooked her finger through a belt loop. "Take them off me." Tito grabbed the cuffs and pulled. They came off slowly at first as her hips resisted his tugs and then they slipped quickly down her legs and she was naked on the sleeping bag before him in the broad afternoon light. Nothing about her was coy anymore and, seeing her this way, Tito was seized by a queasy sense of doubt as he realized how little he really knew her, this beautiful girl he had fantasized about for years. In all, they'd spent a dozen afternoons together. The weight of what they were doing frightened him. Suddenly, he wanted to be done with it, to rush through the act and have it finished, to move on to the next stage of things, but she would not let him. She pushed him onto his back and slowly unbuttoned his shirt, kissing his chest after each button was unfastened.

The buzzer sounded.

"Who's that?" Clara whispered.

"Get under," he said, ridiculously, and lifted the sheet and the blanket for her. Maybe one of the tenants had tracked him down here. Or maybe his parents had come back early. He ran to the intercom. "¿Sí?" he said. He was still dressed and had to adjust himself.

"Yolanda?" said the voice through the speaker.

"No." said Tito.

"Yolanda? Marta?"

"They moved," said Tito. "They don't live here anymore."

The buzzer sounded again, but he was already on his way back to the bedroom.

"Who was that, your other girlfriend?" Clara asked.

Tito said nothing. He took his clothes off and got into the makeshift bed with her. As he lifted the blanket and the sheet, he caught sight of her naked body again, but this time it unnerved him less. Instead, he took pleasure in it, the lovely geometry of her limbs and joints arranging themselves, her breasts swaying, gravity-tugged, and her skin puckering in tiny circles of brown gooseflesh. He felt momentarily that he had created her, willed her into being.

Clara turned and looked at him with a direct and open tenderness that he had not seen from her that afternoon. She kissed him softly, long and drawing with the mouth he had wounded in the playground many years before. Tito felt himself becoming erect again. She continued to kiss him. His tongue went into her mouth and searched for the scars on the inside of her lip. The disruption had settled them and stopped their anxious playing. Tito was not afraid now and he felt calm and watched her and saw that there was none of the nervous, flirty behavior of before. She withdrew under the blankets, kissed him, and turned him so that he lay on his back. Then she straddled him, her body substantial and warm. Tito watched her fingers take hold of him and he felt the firm, bristly pressure as his cock was guided up inside her.

A FEW DAYS after the move, he returned to the apartment on Sherman Avenue. Ms. Almonte opened the door. She did not look surprised to see him.

"I've brought the key for your storage unit," he said. "And, if you don't mind, perhaps you have time to fill out a customer satisfaction survey for me?"

She regarded him for a long moment, a gentle, condescending smile curling one side of her mouth, and then nodded. "Come in," she said. "But you must be quiet. My mother is sleeping." It was six-thirty in the evening. She led him into the kitchen. En route, they passed the mother, who was sitting in a recliner with her eyes closed and her mouth slightly agape, a blanket draped across her.

"Would you like something to eat? My mother made *sancocho*," said Ms. Almonte.

"*Sancocho*? In this heat?" said Tito.

"She's always cold—it doesn't matter what the season. The *sancocho* helps her feel warm. It's just about all she eats these days. Would you like some?"

"Sure," said Tito, sitting at the white, plastic-topped table. Since moving out of his parents' apartment, he'd subsisted on pizza and Chinese takeout. He could smell the *sancocho* as Ms. Almonte ladled it into the bowl. The starchy thickness of it stung his salivary glands to life.

"School opens soon, right?" he asked.

"I'm not teaching this year," she said, bringing the two bowls to the table and sitting down opposite him.

"Did you retire?"

She laughed. "I'm not *that* old. I'm taking a sabbatical. I need to look after my mother," she gestured in the direction of the living room. "It's a full-time job now."

"Why didn't you move her to Oradell? Is it OK for me to ask that?"

She gave the mildest of shrugs, no more than a wince of her bony shoulder. "My husband refused," she said.

Tito nodded. He placed the storage key on the table between them. It was tagged with her name and the unit's location in the Cruz Brothers warehouse. Ms. Almonte did not look at the key, maintaining eye contact with him. "I know why you came back," she said. "So let's not waste time on the survey. My mother will wake up soon and I won't be able to talk to you."

Tito nodded again. "Are you still in touch with Clara?" he asked.

"No," she said. "I was going to ask you the same thing."

"When did you last hear from her?"

"It's been a long time," she said. "Not since her first year of college. And you?"

"Around the same time," he said.

She ate a spoonful of the *sancocho* and seemed to consider what he had said. "It's a shame," she began.

"What?"

"That she didn't go to Cornell."

"Uhh—yes," said Tito. He stirred the *sancocho* with his spoon, steering a piece of carrot around the bowl.

"I'm sorry," she said. "I see that I'm upsetting you. I didn't mean to do that."

"None of the other Word Club girls know where she is?" asked Tito.

She shook her head. "They weren't as close as you might think. I guess Clara's whereabouts remain a mystery." She looked at his left hand and he felt himself being assessed anew. "I take it you're not married now?"

"No," he said.

She raised her eyebrows. "A girlfriend, at least? Surely. You're a handsome fellow, after all."

"No," he said, looking up from his bowl. "Not right now."

She nodded once, a kind of directive. "You should eat your *sancocho*," she said. "Before it gets cold."

AFTERWARD, TITO GOT in his car and drove across the bridge. It was rush hour and traffic was heavy. By the time he reached Oradell, it was dark. He parked on the street and climbed the steps, but instead of going in, he went around the side of the house, past the graves of the deceased pets and the shed where he kept the lawn equipment. He stopped at one of the back windows, hoping to spy his wife and children at play—a golden moment of domestic happiness that would affirm everything. But all he could see was a middle-aged man eating dinner alone in a room where the art had recently been removed from the walls.

Clara

The envelope must have come in the mail while she was at the airport—big as a kitchen bulletin board, with DO NOT BEND stamped in red letters beneath the address. She'd been expecting it, dreading it. Thomas had left it for her on the sideboard in the front hall and it was the first thing she saw as she and Deysei entered the house.

"What's that?" said her niece.

"It's nothing," said Clara. "Just some medical records. Why don't you go upstairs and unpack? Make yourself at home. I'll call you when dinner's ready."

"OK, Tía," said Deysei agreeably, and climbed the steps to the sanctuary of her new room.

Clara was still reeling from her niece's revelation about Raúl, still reeling from seeing Tito Moreno in the airport. She decided she wasn't ready to look at the envelope's contents. She needed a few minutes to compose herself. The television noise coming up through the floorboards told her that Guillermo was safely in his cave; through the dining room window, she could see Thomas at the grill on the patio preparing dinner. She left the envelope and busied herself setting the table, seeking solace in the quotidian on such a nonquotidian day.

Clara took pride in setting an attractive table. One of the first things she'd done after moving out of her mother's apartment was to buy herself a set of new dishes at Fishs Eddy. While Guillermo was still very much in the age of paper and plastic, she and Thomas regularly unfurled linen napkins into their laps, ate off their wedding china, and drank from Tyrone Crystal tumblers. She saw no point in owning these beautiful things if she wasn't going to use them. Would you buy a new car and not drive it? Would you get a new plasma television and not watch it? She'd eaten from chipped plates with bent-tined forks and pitted spoons all of her youth and she associated those indignities with where she had come from, not with where she wanted to be. Putting out her gilt-rimmed dishes every night and setting a soup spoon and dessert fork for a meal that would feature neither soup nor dessert was a daily affirmation for her. Some people leaned on Bible passages, others their bank balances: Clara had the flatware from her wedding registry.

Once the tablecloth had been changed, the napkins folded, and the places set, she crossed her ams and admired the result, quickly noticing that something was still missing—a centerpiece. In the living room, there was a vase of week-old flowers, a thank-you gift from her firm's Westlaw rep for renewing their contract. A small bouquet could probably be salvaged from them, but when she went into the living room, she discovered that the flowers were gone. Had Thomas thrown them out? Such attentive housekeeping would have been unlike him.

She walked through the kitchen to the back door and out onto the patio, where her husband stood at the grill listening to a ball game on an ancient transistor radio and drinking a bottle of beer. The radio, a shiny chrome-and-plastic tablet with its rapierlike antenna, was a relic from Thomas's adolescence, one of several out-of-date contraptions he self-consciously cherished in a kind of sentimental rebuttal to his digital-age profession. Up in his study, there was an Olympia manual typewriter so ancient that the lowercase *l* had to be used for the number 1. From time to time Thomas rolled a sheet of paper into the thing to write a letter, an actual old-fashioned letter placed in an envelope and sent through the mail to his mother in

D.C. or to one of his college friends, all of whom seemed to have made their careers in technology startups in Boston or Silicon Valley. The cackle of the keys on the platen always sounded to her like the chatter of a diabolical monster, but Thomas took inordinate pride in still using the machine. He was similarly attached to the Raleigh ten-speed that hung from hooks in their garage. Like a marine with his rifle, Thomas could disassemble and reassemble the thing blindfolded. Clara had once floated the idea of buying him a new bike—a Trek or Cannondale—but he'd shot her down. "What's wrong with my old one?" he'd asked. Back when they were dating, she had found his attachment to these objects endearing (she'd received more than a few typewritten letters from Thomas during their library-school courtship), but now that they were married, she had to admit, it bugged her. There was intransigence in it—an unwillingness to move forward, a trait, she believed, that was hampering him from finding another job, almost as if he were rhetorically still asking himself, *What was wrong with my old job?*

"Hi," she said, kissing him. He smelled of charcoal smoke and beer, and his eyes were a little swimmy, either from the smoke or the beer or both.

"Hello," he said, and smiled a weird smile at her.

"Everything OK?" she asked.

"Sure," he said.

"What's cooking?"

"Fish," he said. "Salmon. I figured we'd have something light after going to Church's for lunch."

"Sounds good," she nodded. "By any chance did you throw out those flowers I had on the coffee table?"

"No. Guillermo knocked them over," he said. "He was playing with that squeaky ball when he got home and bam! Down they went."

"Oh," she said, wincing. "What about the vase?"

"Broken," said Thomas, "but I think a little Super Glue will put

Humpty Dumpty back together again." He gave her that weird smile once more.

"I wanted it for the table. Oh, well. So, how was Gilly this afternoon?" She felt a sudden bolt of guilt as she realized that she hadn't yet gone downstairs to greet him.

"He was a little out of control, actually," said Thomas.

"What? Really?"

"Yeah. I was trying to get him to help me clean up the basement and he ignored me. Have you noticed? He's obsessed with that robot that Max left here."

"I know," she said. "He wants us to buy him one before he has to give that one back." Max was a classmate of Guillermo's and Clara had arranged the playdate in the hopes of befriending Max's mother, Jessica, but she'd just had a baby and had taken the offer as an opportunity to drop Max off for an hour while she took the infant to a pediatrician's appointment. Max had spent the duration of the playdate asking Clara when his mother was coming back. No treat, television show, or video could distract him from her absence. "I can't thank you enough," Jessica had said, when she came back to pick up her son, who in his delight at seeing his mother again had forgotten about his toy.

"They cost like fifty bucks, don't they?" Clara said to her husband.

"They're $59.99 at Toys 'R' Us," said Thomas. "I priced one on the Web last week."

"So what happened with Gilly? Did he finally calm down?"

"No. Like I said, I was trying to get him to help me clean up and he kept shooting me with those plastic missiles. *'Ka-blam, ka-blam!'* Then he knocked over my beer and I kind of lost it." He looked at her. "I spanked him."

"You *what*?"

"Just once. First the flowers and then the—"

"You *hit* him, Thomas?"

"Just once. Not hard."

"I can't believe you hit him. Oh my God. Promise me you'll never do that again! No matter what he does." Her eyes stung with tears.

Thomas must have seen the tears brimming because he suddenly looked panicked and tried to reassure her. "C., you know me. I'm not that kind of guy. I just lost my temper."

"I'm going to see if he's OK."

"He's fine. It's not like I punched him in the face or anything. I just spanked him once on the ass." But Clara was already headed back to the house, rubbing her nose with her wrist to keep the tears inside. An old fear was squeezing her chest, something she thought she'd never have to face again. She went through the kitchen and down the stairs, her pace quickening. She called out to her son, "Guillermo! Guillermo!"

The basement was their son's lair: Guillermoland, the People's Republic of Preschool, a domain of toys, arts and crafts supplies, stuffed animals, crumbs, and bacteria. Thomas liked to joke that he and Clara needed visas to enter. There was Guillermo, lying on the couch in a sultan's repose, his sandals on the wrong feet, watching Yogi Bear. Max's robot stood sentry on the floor.

"Mommy!" he called, sitting up.

She hugged him. "Are you OK, sweetie?

"Yes, Mommy. I'm OK."

"Did Daddy hit you?"

He looked at her. "Daddy doesn't like me," he finally said.

"That's not true. Your Daddy loves you."

"No," he said. "Daddy doesn't like me."

"He just got mad, Gilly, that's all."

Guillermo crossed his arms and looked past her at the television set.

"I'm sure he's very sorry."

Guillermo did not respond. After a moment, he said. "Mommy,

I'm sharing this with Max, right?" He reached down and picked up the robot.

"Yes, baby, but you know what? We're going to get you your own robot! Would you like that?"

"I don't have to share?"

"No—one for you to keep."

"Oh, yes! Mommy! Yay! I like it." He hugged her again.

"You're OK now?"

"Yes. I'm getting a robot, right, Mommy?"

"Yes, sweetie. Your father's going to buy you a robot."

Gilly let out a whoop of delight.

"Good, I'm glad to see you happy, baby. I'm going to help Daddy get dinner ready. I'll call you up in a minute."

Reassured about her son's well-being, and with the threat of her own tears averted, Clara went upstairs and got Guillermo's food ready. He ate the same meal almost every night: six Tyson chicken nuggets, a cup of white rice sprinkled with grated Parmesan cheese, and half a Gala apple, peeled, cored, and cut into crescents. She didn't know what they would do if Tyson went out of business or if the miracles of modern agriculture failed to generate a Gala crop somewhere in the world throughout the year. Guillermo's palate was *that* discerning. The only other dinner he would eat was Red Baron frozen pizza, and that was reserved for the weekends. Now and then he also consented to eat a piece of grilled steak. Clara took a martyr's pleasure in preparing a separate meal for him every night. It drove Thomas nuts and he refused to participate. "I can't believe we have to make two dinners—one for us and one for him. Remember when he was younger? He used to eat grilled vegetables. He used to eat tofu. What happened?"

"I don't know, but what are we supposed to do, let him starve?"

"Let him go hungry until he eats what we eat. Kids all over the world would love to eat our food."

In her mind some things were not negotiable. She could no more let her son go hungry for an hour than she could abide him being struck by her husband.

As she was peeling the apple for Guillermo's plate, Thomas came in from the patio with a platter of the aromatic salmon. Brown lozenges of caramelized garlic studded the streamlined fillet. Thomas looked at the food she was assembling for Guillermo and shook his head.

"FYI, mister, you're going to be buying your son one of those robots," she said to him as he went into the dining room. "The sooner the better."

Clara summoned Deysei from above and Guillermo from below. In addition to the salmon, Thomas had made a salad and sliced a baguette. She couldn't tell whether the beer he brought to the table was a new bottle or the same one he had been drinking out on the patio. She had passing nightmares about him becoming an alcoholic while he was out of work, though there was little evidence to support such fears. He looked a bit buzzed tonight, but it was not your typical evening on Passaic Street, she was willing to concede. Clara herself wouldn't have minded some wine, but Deysei couldn't have any and it seemed wasteful to open a bottle just so she could have a glass, so she drank iced green tea instead.

Guillermo appeared from the basement stairs and went straight to his chair, biting into his first ketchup-dunked nugget before he was even properly seated. Deysei was the last to arrive and Clara eyed her closely. Dinner at Yunis's apartment, she knew, was usually eaten on the couch in front of the TV, often in the form of Chinese or Dominican takeout. Deysei was dressed for the couch, too. She had changed into a pair of pink-and-white plaid pajama bottoms, pink flip-flops, and a baggy white T-shirt with the word PRINCESS written across the front in silver cursive. Clara still didn't understand the whole nightwear as daywear fad among teenage girls, but that was probably the point—to piss off the older generation. She was still getting used to seeing her niece with cornrows. Yunis was right: Clara never would have styled Deysei's hair that way. She would have ironed it flat.

"What can I get for you?" Thomas asked.

"Umm. Just salad, Tío. Thanks."

"Really? You didn't eat anything at lunch either."

"We stopped at a McDonald's in the airport," said Clara.

"Oh," said Thomas. "Well, I'm glad I didn't go to any trouble with dinner or anything."

Clara ignored this. "I was telling Deysei how I always sent you out for a Big Mac when I was pregnant with Guillermo."

"You too, huh, Deysei? Craving that special sauce?"

Deysei shrugged. "I don't know, Tío. I was just hungry. I won't be asking you to get me no Big Macs in the middle of the night."

"That's what you're saying now," Clara said, laughing.

"And don't forget french fries!" said Guillermo—another item on his restricted menu. Clara found that she often discounted her son as a listener only to discover that he'd taken in every word.

"The fish is delicious, Thomas," Clara said, and it was.

"Thanks. You want to try some, Gilly?" asked Thomas.

"Yuck!" said Guillermo. "Fish eat people who die in the ocean."

"There you go," said Clara, who, with Deysei, was laughing. Guillermo, pleased with himself, beamed at his father—a *fuck you* grin if Clara had ever seen one.

"Right. Whatever," said Thomas, and took a drink of his beer.

AFTER THEY HAD finished eating, Thomas, as the un-employed member of the family, cleared and washed up, while Guillermo savored a last half-hour of cartoons. Clara and Deysei went into the sunroom and called the Dominican Republic to make sure that Yunis had arrived safely. Clara's mother answered. From the music and chatter in the background and her mother's tone of voice, it was obvious to Clara that Yunis had said nothing about Deysei's pregnancy.

"Is it good to have her there, Mami?" Clara asked. Her mother and sister did not always get along (there was, in fact, nobody that Yunis *always* got along with), but that didn't stop her mother from complaining that she never got to see her children or her grand-children anymore.

"It's good right now," said her mother. "But she just got here. There's plenty of time for her to make me mad."

"It'll be fine," said Clara, and realized that it was actually some-thing of a relief to have her sister out of the country—that she wouldn't be calling unexpectedly to ask for money or to borrow the car.

"I hope you told that to Yunis," said her mother.

"Can we talk to her?"

In a moment Yunis was on the line. "Yo, Sis. We're having a little party up in here. Chi Chi, Angel, Plinio, Porfirio, Kenya, they all came. I'm getting real nice on Plinio's Brugal."

"I'm glad you made it safely," said Clara. "Be sure to say hi to everyone for me."

"How's my girl doing? Let me talk to her," said Yunis.

Clara handed the phone to Deysei, whose part of the conversa-tion consisted of three words repeated in varying sequence: "*Sí*, Mami. . . . *Sí*. . . . *Sí*. . . . Bye. . . . *Sí*, Mami. *Sí*. Bye."

"Everything OK?" said Clara when Deysi had turned off the phone.

"Yeah. I think she was drunk."

THE ENVELOPE REMAINED unopened as Clara put Guillermo to bed. She loved their nighttime ritual, loved her role as the arbiter of his slumber. She dreaded the day when her son would no longer need her in this way, when he would be able to brush his teeth properly, put his own pajamas on, read his own bedtime stories, and fall asleep without her in the room. Since their first night in the hospital together, when she had disobeyed her nurse's orders and let him lie on her chest, Clara had found this—sleep—to be the strongest bond between them. (Breastfeeding was too painful and too much work and she'd abandoned it early on for the ease of the bottle.) Sleep had also been a source of acrimony between her and Thomas. Throughout Guillermo's first year, Thomas repeatedly told Clara not to let him fall asleep in her arms, to put him down, to let him cry it out. She disobeyed him, as she had disobeyed the nurse. She didn't care what Dr. Spock or the *What to Expect* women said. She didn't care what nurses or pediatricians or husbands said. To see her son's fretless features snuggled against her breast made her feel that she was doing for him what her parents had never done for her—providing safety and love. *I haven't abandoned you; I'm right here.* As Guillermo grew older and advanced from crib to toddler bed, she started getting under the covers with him, a human teddy bear. At some point, she came to understand that she needed it as much, if not more, than he did, this nightly shepherding into slumber. He was five now and still affectionate, still cuddly, but the day was coming, she knew, when he would not want her help, when his definition of being a big boy would mean getting changed by himself, brushing his own teeth, reading his own books, entering his dreams alone. She was already preparing herself for the event, reminding herself not to feel rejected by him. It was her hope that she would have another baby by then and that she could start the process all over again. But, for tonight, that long-dreaded event remained in the future. Tonight Guillermo wanted to wear his Lightning McQueen pajamas. Tonight he wanted to use his Hot Wheels toothbrush. Helping him change, she was pleased to see how dark he was getting from the summer sun. It was only in July and August that he began to approach her skin tone, to look like her. The rest of the year, he was pale and yellowy, *white*. The rest of the year everyone said how much he looked like his father, thinking they were being nice. But in the summer, his skin was a rich, honeyed brown, and while he would always remain at least two shades lighter than she was, he seemed more her child then.

They got into bed. Tonight he wanted her to read *Where the Sidewalk Ends* and *Goodnight Moon*. When they had finished reading and shut off the light, they went around his room saying "goodnight" to his toys and posters, to his dirty clothes on the chair and his water glass, to the glow-in-the-dark solar system Thomas had hung with fishing line from the ceiling. "Goodnight Mercury. Goodnight Venus. Goodnight Earth. Goodnight Moon. Goodnight Mars. . . ."

Tonight, like most nights, Guillermo wanted to lie in the crook of Clara's arm so that she could not escape once he'd fallen asleep.

"You stay in my bed all night, Mommy?" he asked. "Pleeease?"

"Yes," she said. And they both knew she was lying, but it was enough to get him to close his eyes and surrender to sleep.

CLARA WOKE UP, not knowing whether it was ten p.m. or four in the morning. Guillermo was in deep sleep beside her. There was no light coming in through the windows, no sound from the street outside. For a long moment, she felt like the only person awake in the world, but it did not last. Presently she heard Thomas in the nearby bathroom, brushing his teeth; she heard Deysei in the next room talking to someone on her cell phone, a mumble through the wall, indecipherable. And then she remembered the envelope. No delaying it any longer. She freed her arm from Guillermo's weight, releasing pins and needles from elbow to fingertip, and went downstairs to fetch it from the sideboard, tearing open the flap as she climbed back up the stairs. By that time, Thomas was in bed, reading a William Gibson novel. Clara slipped the X-rays out of the envelope and spread them across the bed: spectral images of her reproductive organs. Thomas put down his book and watched her lay out the blue-black sheets as if she were a fortune teller with a deck of giant tarot cards. He looked a little bleary-eyed, maybe still buzzed, or maybe just tired.

"So here they are," she said. The X-rays had been taken at an imaging center in Newark and she was supposed to deliver them to the doctors at the fertility clinic they were using.

"I know you tried to explain this to me a couple of days ago, but I'm still not quite getting it," he said. "They think you might not be able to have another child because of the shape of your uterus?"

He sometimes pretended to be dense to avoid dealing with difficulties, sometimes hid in his box scores and science fiction novels. Many men did. Perhaps he was still mad about being laughed at during dinner. Clara smiled as though speaking to a foreign dignitary. "Well, they think I could have a T-shaped uterus, which would make it hard for eggs to implant and increase the chances of a miscarriage."

He was looking closely at the X-ray images, the dark spaces inside her where they were hoping to create another life.

"What shaped uterus are you supposed to have in order to bear children?"

"I don't know," she said. "But not that shape. I'm barren."

"Hold on a minute," he said, wincing at the last word, which even she would admit was overdramatic. "There's a five-year-old in the next room that says otherwise. If you've got a T-shaped uterus or whatever, then how do they explain Gilly?"

"A fluke," she said. "We got lucky."

"What? He's some kind of miracle child?"

"Basically."

"They're sure about this?"

She shook her head. "No, they're not sure. They can't tell for certain from these X-rays and MRI scans. They need to do a hysteroscopy."

"Hysteroscopy?" he asked. "What the hell is that?"

"It sounds worse than it is," she said. Thomas's mother had been diagnosed with uterine cancer a couple of years before. It was in remission after a course of chemo and radiation therapy. His mother's illness and Clara's own fertility troubles meant that gynecology was not her husband's favorite topic and she was sometimes wary of discussing the subject with him. "They send a little telescope into my uterus to see its shape from the inside."

"Wow," he said, "a telescope." Glancing at the X-rays, he said, "These kind of do look like galaxies, like images from the Hubble."

"Deep-space vagina," she said, and they both laughed, clearing away the tension. "It's like a fiber-optic cable they use. More like a microscope, I guess. They won't even think of letting us start IVF until I've had this done. We're lucky that this clinic does both evaluation and fertility, but if they're right about the T-shaped thing, we're going to have to think about adopting, because we won't be making any more babies." She gathered up the X-rays. When she had them all, she slipped them back into the giant manila envelope and laid it on the floor on her side of the bed.

"Doesn't it feel like ever since you started going to this clinic, getting pregnant is getting harder and harder, not easier and easier?" Thomas asked.

She didn't answer. She was getting undressed, aware of him watching her.

"I mean, it's just one hoop after another—first they had to get your thyroid levels sorted out, then there was the whole mess with the insurance."

"I know, Thomas. I know. But if we want to have another child, this is what we have to do." She got into bed wearing a tank top and her panties. "I've scheduled the hysteroscopy for next week. I'll need you to give me a ride home."

"Of course," he said, looking away, as if he'd been chastised.

"They have to knock me out."

"I'll be there," he said, and put his hand on her arm. "I'll be there," he said again, soothingly. "And let's not jump to any conclusions. They obviously don't know for sure or they wouldn't be doing this hysteria-oscopy."

She smiled at him, liking his hand on her, the same hand that had struck Guillermo, she reminded herself, but that now seemed like an aberration, a result of this crazy day.

"So, how did everything go at the airport?" he asked. "We haven't had a chance to talk about that yet."

"Oh, you know, the usual," she said, and the image of Tito Moreno in the food court with a beautiful young child came into her mind. Tito Moreno, whose baby she had aborted when she was eighteen. Yes, what a crazy day. "We nearly missed her flight. And then Yunis started crying at the gate."

Thomas nodded, as if that were to be expected. "And Deysei? Do you think she's going to be all right?"

"I don't know. To be honest, I think she's kind of glad to be away from her mother," Clara said. She intended to keep her promise to Deysei and not tell Thomas that Raúl was the father—at least for a little while.

"On some level I bet you're glad this happened, aren't you?" he said. "I mean, if the hysteroscopy comes back and they tell you you've got the wrong-shaped uterus, then you can just have Deysei's baby. Isn't that what you're thinking?"

Whoa. His directness took her breath away. He wasn't hiding in his Gibson novel any longer. "If we can't have another baby, don't you think that's something worth considering?" said Clara.

"No," replied Thomas. "I don't want to raise someone else's child. I want to raise *our* child. And besides, like I said back when we first talked about Deysei coming to live with us, teenage girls are not exactly known for being stable, obedient, and cooperative. Now we've got a *pregnant* teenage girl living under our roof and you want to raise her child for her?"

"I haven't even mentioned it to her. She needs to decide if she's going to keep it," said Clara.

"She should get rid of it," he said.

"Thomas! Come on!"

"Wouldn't that make life simpler for everyone?"

"For everyone except the unborn baby."

"When did you become so pro-life, Clara?"

"Maybe our problems have made me rethink a few things," she said and sighed, thinking of Tito again. "Look, you know Deysei is basically a good kid. And she's never had a true father figure in her life. You can be that for her."

"I'm already a father figure to Guillermo. And right now I'm focused on trying to find another job," he said.

"Oh, really? You could have fooled me. How many interviews have you been on this month?"

"Times are tough," he said, "but I just applied for something that looks promising." A long moment of frustrated silence followed, as Clara decided whether to believe him.

"Thomas, I don't want to fight with you," she said. The next thing that came out of her mouth surprised her as much as it did her husband: "In fact, what I really need you to do is fuck me."

Normally, she would have said something more playful: *Are you feeling lucky tonight?* or *Want to get with some of this, big guy?* But she was glad she'd said it the way she did. That's what she needed and she was not in the mood to be subtle. Church's hadn't done it for her. Nor had putting her son to bed. She needed something more. She and Thomas had been making love with less frequency the last few months and it worried her. Thomas said that the visits to the fertility clinic, with its diagrams, its plastic scale models (plus, now, X-rays), and its clinical language of reproduction had turned him off. She didn't care. Not having sex was not going to help them conceive a child.

Thomas took a moment to compose himself, as if remembering

lines he'd memorized. "Turn off that light," he said, at last. "And maybe we should try to keep it down. Deysei might be listening."

"Nothing we do will be news to her," said Clara, reaching for the lamp.

ASIDE FROM THE obvious sensual pleasure and the reassurance it gave her about her marriage, Clara loved sex with her husband because it returned her to the blissful early days of their relationship when they could not be in the same room without wanting to take each other's clothes off. Why, she wondered, could that passion not be sustained? Why did such irresistible attraction fade? It perplexed her. Was it merely novelty? She wanted always to feel about Thomas the way she'd felt when they had first met in library school; she wanted him always to feel that way about her.

She had been twenty-five then. At the time, she was working as a paraprofessional in the law library of a large Midtown firm, filing supplements, shelving books, doing basic reference queries, acting as a translator for depositions, running down to the courts whenever needed. It was her second library job (during college, she'd worked part-time for an indexing service). Her employer offered tuition reimbursement and, with the encouragement of the head of the firm's library, Clara enrolled in Pratt's part-time program, which met evenings and weekends. Her first class, Introduction to Reference Resources, a kind of Librarianship 101 that was required of all the students in the program, was taught by a woman named Mrs. Molloy, an old-school librarian who, Clara thought, must have been chosen because she so thoroughly fit the received idea of what a librarian should look like—a drill sergeant of the Dewey Decimal System. Tall and slender, with short-cropped gray hair and half-moon glasses, she was dressed in a long beige skirt and a salmon-colored cardigan from which a high lace collar emerged. To go with this appearance, there was her demeanor: severe, proper, and responsible, with a devotion to her profession that verged on the ecclesiastic.

Seeing Mrs. Molloy at the front of the room perusing a copy of *Library Journal* while she waited for her students to arrive, Clara was reminded of previous teachers she'd had in middle school and high school—all of them women—who had helped her overcome the difficulties of her childhood in Inwood. In fact, she viewed her library degree as the culmination of that process. In the two decades since she had been brought to the United States, Clara would have, with the help of these women, transformed herself from a terrified, picked on, barely literate, non-English-speaking immigrant to a self-sufficient, well-spoken, assimilated, professionally employed American. It was a matter of enormous pride for her.

She got to that first class early and sat near the front. Four years removed from college, she was excited to be going back to school and excited to be learning new skills. On top of that, she held out the vague hope that she might meet someone. She'd had plenty of boyfriends in college, but it was clear from early on in each of those relationships that nothing long-lasting would come of them. Clara had been indiscriminate about her boyfriends' backgrounds, eager to experiment. There were broken hearts and hurt feelings, arguments and crying. More recently, she had gone out with one of the lawyers at the firm, a man in his late thirties who was just coming out of a divorce. He was decidedly more mature than the boys she'd been with in college but, maybe, *too* mature, and a little jaded. He had proposed to her after six months, a proposal she'd rejected. They broke up, and not long after that, he left the firm. She hadn't met the right person in college or at work. This is what her romantic aspirations had been reduced to—hoping she'd find a like-minded man in library school.

By the time she got to the classroom, there were two other students already seated, a young black woman and an older guy who looked like he'd come from an off-track betting parlor. Clara inspected the rest of her classmates as they entered the room. They were a pleasingly varied group, some younger than her, but most older. The ratio seemed to be two-to-one in favor of women and two-to-one in favor of people over thirty. Some had clearly come from professional settings; they wore suits and carried briefcases. But more than a few had a just-gotten-out-of-bed-graduate-student look. Toward the end of this stream, there was a preppy guy wearing chinos, a white shirt, and a blue blazer. He had on Buddy Holly/Clark Kent black-framed glasses and had a laptop bag on his shoulder. To Clara, he resembled one of the first-year associates at her firm, but without the cockiness. He surveyed the room and made eye contact with her—a brief moment of connection that caused her to blush—*yeah, you caught me checking you out*—before sitting down near the back. Clara wondered if it was as obvious to everyone else in the class as it was to her that, one way or another, she and this well-dressed young man were going to get together.

The class was scheduled to start at 7:00, and at 7:01 Mrs. Molloy stood up and introduced herself, listing the positions she'd held at public and academic libraries in her long career. The students were then invited to introduce themselves, saying their names, where they worked, and what they hoped to do with their degree. Most in the group were changing careers to accommodate marriage and children; almost everyone cited a love of reading, a comment as obvious and unnecessary, Clara thought, as a beauty contestant's wish for world peace. Around the class the introductions went ("I'm a social studies teacher and I've been feeling burned out," "I just got laid off from a job on Wall Street") until, at last, "Thomas Walker. I just moved here from Boston, where I went to college. I'm temping right now. I'm not really sure yet what field I want to go into. Maybe something with archives." When her turn turn came: "Clara Lugo. I'm from Queens. I work in a law library, but I'm not sure I want to spend my career in law. Archival work might be interesting." The last part was a complete lie, but it seemed to get Thomas Walker's attention.

Mrs. Molloy handed out the syllabus and talked through the

semester's work with them. Each week they would be given a series of reference queries that they were required to answer using the resources discussed in the class: encyclopedias, directories, indexes, databases. "You may work alone, or with a partner, as you wish," she said. She went over the assignment for the following week and dismissed them.

Clara couldn't help but notice that Thomas Walker did not rush to leave the classroom like almost everyone else. He carefully packed his laptop back in its case, glancing her way now and then. She stood and walked slowly, self-consciously, to the exit. She was wearing a short-sleeved dress and low heels and was aware of the air on her shins as she walked along the corridor toward the elevator. The doors were closing on carload of her classmates and she let it go. Then she waited a moment before pushing the down button, just to be sure the doors of the crowded car would not reopen. The arrow lit up and she sensed his presence beside her.

"It's Clara, right?"

"Yes." Turning, she looked right at the lapels of his blazer. He was taller than she'd thought. Then she looked up at his face. He was clean-shaven, had a smile with one tooth slightly darker than the rest. No errant hairs poking from his nostrils.

"Did you say you already work in a library?"

"A law library, yes."

"Well, I wonder if you'd like to be my study partner for this class?" He smiled. "I'm new to this and I think I could use all the help I can get."

"Oh," she laughed. She was surprised and charmed by the self-deprecation. Very unlawyerlike. "Um. Sure. I work up near the SIBL. Do you want to meet there sometime this weekend to do the first assignment?"

THEY BOTH SEEMED to know that it was as much a date as a work session. They dressed better than they needed to, and they were both edgy. Clara was already familiar with many of the reference resources on the syllabus and did most of the research. Thomas assumed the role of scribe, typing both of their names atop the document on his laptop, filling out the description of how they'd looked up the gross domestic product of Mongolia, the patent number for Amazon's one-click purchase feature, the average age at which Californians got married, and the origin of the phrase "in a pickle." When the assignment was completed, they went to a café nearby to talk and eat. And that was how it went for the rest of the semester, the homework for the class becoming, it was increasingly obvious, just a pretense for the date afterward.

There was a lot to like about him. He was courteous. He listened. He was careful and precise. He showed restraint, both in advancing the physical side of things and in his inquiries about her background. Most guys were nosy and blundering. "So, what are you?" they asked. "Are you black?" In her own mind, Clara thought that, save for her modestly sized backside, she looked stereotypically Dominican. But she had learned from years of interacting with people who hadn't grown up around Dominicans that her ethnicity was not so obvious to many. On train platforms, other brown-skinned, dark-haired people came up to her and spoke to her in languages she did not recognize. An Indian attorney had once asked her if she was from Madras. "Another fifty pounds and you'd look Samoan," she'd been told at a party in college. When she finally did reveal to Thomas where she was from, he laughed. "Aha!"

"Why, what did you think?"

"I didn't think. I was waiting for you to tell me."

"Come on, really, you must have had at least a guess."

"When I first saw you, I thought maybe Filipino or Brazilian, but when I heard your last name I didn't know what to think."

He'd gone to Boston College but had somehow ended up sharing a house with a group of engineers from MIT, and from them he had learned a lot about new technologies. Unlike most people she met in the library world, he was excited about what digital innovation might do for the profession.

About halfway through that first semester, a typewritten letter arrived in her mailbox. Up in the left-hand corner of the envelope was his return address:

> T. Walker
> 24-24 24th St.
> Astoria, NY 11218

Standing in the lobby of her Morningside Heights apartment building, with the brass mouth of her mailbox agape before her, she rubbed at the envelope and knew, just *knew* before she opened it, that it was a love letter. If she opened it and read what he had written to her, there would be no turning back: The feelings that had been gathering force in her heart during their weeks of studying together would overwhelm her caution, her fear, her desire not to rush into anything just so quickly. She believed that there was no end in sight for where the relationship might go, no end except for the one she hoped for most.

She tore open the flap.

IT HAD BEEN a love letter, of course, the first of many. Thomas enjoyed writing them (and enjoyed her response to them) so much that Clara feared that when it came time to propose he would do so by mail. But he had not. Instead, he'd fumblingly, charmingly, proposed to her on one knee in Astoria Park at sunset with the engagement ring he'd purchased with his first bonus, just as an Amtrak train went over the viaduct on its way north to Boston, the sky orange and red behind the skyscrapers of the East Side.

Lying in bed with Thomas now, after he'd complied with her request for sex, Clara thought how you never, at the outset of a love affair, looked ahead to the difficulties. You never thought, *I'll marry this guy and three or five or seven years from now, we'll be arguing about our inability to have a child and I'll have to beg him for sex.* You never thought your relationship, the one you'd been waiting all your life for, would be anything but magnificent. Clara did not rue the false-ness of such optimism now; if anything, as she glided in to sleep, she found herself hoping for its improbable return.

Tito

People liked to point out how strange it was that Tito worked for a moving company when he himself had never moved. Until earlier that summer, the only address he had ever had was: Small Bedroom, Basement Apartment, 222 Seaman Avenue, New York, NY 10034. His parents put no pressure on him, their only child, to leave, and he knew that, as his father grew older and the demands of the job became harder for him, his mother was (even beyond the usual coddling Dominican mothers give their sons) increasingly grateful to have him around. There was a local kid, Nelson, a skinny teenager with big round glasses and a shaved head, who helped with the painting and the endless sorting of recyclables, but when it came to dealing with the tenants, Tito's father wanted them handled only by Tito or himself. Nelson, earnest and hardworking, spoke almost no English and the building was full of tenants who spoke nothing but.

Tito had his dream life, of course. That was how he survived the indignities and embarrassments of cohabiting with his parents at an age when everyone he had gone to school with had moved out, gotten married, sired children, or disappeared into the world. The posse of neighborhood friends he'd grown up with had crumbled away, rendering him the lone holdout. *Last Man Standing.* The only people he saw now were those kids' parents. He saw them in the supermarket and the liquor store, buying their *gandules verdes*, their bottles of Brugal, and their lottery tickets. He saw them in the park, walking their dogs. They looked completely lost, as if life had gotten too easy for them now that they'd emigrated, raised their children in America, and made it into late middle age. What was left for them now? He sometimes felt that he was a stand-in for the departed. How quickly it had all vanished, the life he'd had in his teens and early twenties: the ball games at Yankee Stadium, the trips to City Island beaches and New Jersey amusement parks, the pickup basketball and touch-football games, the sledding in cardboard boxes on the hills near the river, the snowball wars fueled with beer and cheap brandy, the pranking and talking smack, the weekends out at the bars and nightclubs uptown and downtown, drinking and bullshitting and trying to meet girls. At the time, it seemed like it would go on forever, but one by one his friends had succumbed to other lives. Alejandro had been the first. He had gotten his crazy Grenadan girlfriend pregnant and moved to Staten Island, where her people owned a bunch of businesses—a bicycle repair shop, a car service, and a chicken joint. Jansel was next. He had finally married that girl Eva, the one he'd been chasing since the eighth grade, the one who'd always played hard to get with him. Eva had a job in a hospital in Englewood Cliffs and Jansel moved out to Paramus, where he was working part-time in the billing department of a Ford dealership. Meanwhile, Tito's distant cousin Hershel, always the least stable of the posse, had let his drug problem get out of control and started stealing from everyone. Watches, cell phones, rings, chains. One minute there, the next gone. Finally, someone got tired of it and called the police. Hershel had been in a halfway house in Long Island City, a place with a cheerful name and a seven o'clock curfew, until he'd fallen off the wagon. He was up top now, in the state pen. Also Edgar, who'd had a football scholarship to some school in the middle of the country before a doctor reset his broken leg out of line. Edgar walked with a limp after that and couldn't play football anymore. He worked nights as a doorman in a rich building downtown. It was a job for life, he'd told Tito, but he was the lowest on the totem pole and wouldn't get a day shift or a regular weekend day off until he was forty. Lastly, there was Ruben, the most successful of them all, a bona fide entrepreneur, who'd made a fortune with some Web site and bought his mother a house in Fair Lawn and drove a Range Rover. Ruben was always flying to Atlanta or California or Chicago for some convention, always making deals on his cell phone, but he'd gotten too big for the neighborhood. Tito still saw them, his boys, sometimes, on birthdays and holidays, for the Super Bowl or the Dominican Day Parade, but they were no longer a part of his normal existence. And with their departure, his life went back to being what it had been when he was a schoolboy: routine, repetitive, and limited.

Sometimes, when he was sitting down to dinner with his parents or dealing with a tenant complaining about the noisy people upstairs or looking for something to do on a Friday night, he felt stagnant and festering, felt that the very simplicity and lack of change were poisoning him. At such times, he always went back to Clara's disappearance as the root of all his problems, as the missed chance to change his life's trajectory. There had been plenty of other girls since then—most recently, the luscious but difficult Jasmina, who'd finally broken up with him for not proposing after they'd been together a year. Jasmina was a teller at the Banco Popular on Dyckman. She had once confessed to him that she'd taken the job in the hopes of meeting a Dominican businessman, but she'd ended up with Tito instead. Tito didn't want to settle for a woman and he didn't want to feel settled for. It didn't work out with Jasmina just as it never seemed to work out with anyone else. The relationships ended and he looked around at the wreckage as if a natural disaster had been the cause. Some guys would have welcomed the serial monogamy, but not Tito. He felt cursed, snakebit, and as he grew older, he became simultaneously resigned to and terrified of the rut he was in. He coped by withdrawing into a vividly imagined alternate reality in which he was married and living in suburbs like

Jansel or Ruben; in which he and his family came into the city on Sundays to dine with his mother and father; in which, after those Sunday lunches, he took his kids to the Emerson Playground.

Now and then, the real collided with the imaginary. For a few weeks, earlier in the summer, Tito had taken a flesh-and-blood child to the playground, a five-year-old boy named Wyatt. Pretending became a lot easier as he sat on the benches with the nannies and stay-at-home moms calling to their kids. Because Wyatt was freckled and blond and Tito was as brown as the mulch in the park's flowerbeds, the women on the benches initially gave him the hairy eyeball. But repeated appearances in the playground along with the boy's obvious affection for him soon vanquished their suspicions. He instructed Wyatt to call him Tío—close enough to his real name—and that seemed to satisfy the curious.

Wyatt and his mother, Tamsin, had moved into the building in June, two months before Tito's sales call with Ms. Almonte. Tito saw the U-Haul as he came up the street from the subway after work one evening, saw Tamsin and another woman—her friend from Philly, it later turned out—carrying a sofa into the building's front entrance. Halfway up the steps, the friend set her end of the couch down and said, "I can't. My arms are killing me."

By the time she said this, Tito was right behind Tamsin, admiring her square shoulders and her lobeless ears. Normally the last thing he wanted to do when he got off work was help someone lift furniture, but the women were good-looking and he sensed that he needed to do something to change his luck. It had been almost a year since his breakup with Jasmina, and the loneliness was getting to him. *When a Stranger Comes to Town,* he thought. He offered to lend a hand.

"Wow, that would be great," said Tamsin, sweeping her fingers through her hair.

With Tito's help, they got the couch into the elevator and took it up to the second-floor apartment, which had previously been the

home of two gay men his father was glad to have out of the building. (The management company handled the showing and leasing
of apartments; Tito and his father often did not know until moving day who would be coming in.) He went back down and helped
them with the last things in the truck: a futon and a dresser—not
much work, really, to have earned the gratitude of the attractive new
tenant. It was only after all that, when they were standing outside
on the sidewalk saying goodbye to the friend, that he noticed the
kid sleeping in the cab of the truck, his face half-hidden by a book
with a train on the cover, the windows cracked open for air. Tito
relished the idea that anybody watching the scene from one of the
apartments across the street might have come to the conclusion that
he and Tamsin were moving into the building together. While he
was having this little daydream, she unlocked the rental truck and
lifted the boy, still sleeping, onto her shoulder. "It's been a tough
move on him," she explained. "Thanks again for your help."

"No problem," said Tito, and held the door open for her.

He expected to have to contrive ways of running into
her in the lobby, or the deli, or the subway. He imagined these
encounters, played them out in moment-by-moment detail in his
mind—*Oh, hi. Sure, I'd love to come in*—and then, with the rapidity
of a plot being advanced in a porno movie, he was taking off her
clothes.

All of that was wiped away the next night, however, when she
knocked on his father's door. Tito, thinking it was a tenant looking
for a package, answered. Tamsin wore a pair of denim cutoffs and
a T-shirt with the word RICE across the front. It would be a week
before he learned that Rice was the name of the college she'd gone
to and not her favorite football player—or food.

"Hey," she said. "Sorry to bother you, but I was just wondering:
Is the park safe?"

He stood in the doorway, next to the pile of signed-for packages, trying to minimize her view of the inside of his parents' apartment while simultaneously scoping her out. She had a heart-shaped face, reddish-brown hair, and sensitive skin that bruised easily—her arms were covered in black and blue marks from the move. On her neck and biceps there were large, jagged freckles, like pencil shavings. She looked slim but athletic, tensile. Tito could see that she was not wearing anything underneath her T-shirt.

"Ah, you know . . ." he started off, hesitant to tell her that a girl had been murdered in the park earlier in the year—a white college student. Not only that, but a white college student who had been a Cruz Brothers client. Rebecca Waverly was her name. Tito hadn't been involved in the move, but he'd monitored the coverage of her murder closely—as had everyone at work. The Cruz brothers sent flowers to the funeral. Attracted by cheap rents and an express subway line, so many people moved to the neighborhood without knowing anything about it. Tamsin was still looking at him, waiting for an answer. "I've never had any problems," he said, finally.

"So you think it would be OK for me to go jogging in there?"

"Yes," he said. "Only I wouldn't go in there at night."

"Right. Sure. And the playground? For Wyatt?"

"I played there as a kid," he said. "He'll be fine. Just not at night."

"That's good to know. And thanks again for helping us yesterday. I'm not sure what we would have done without you."

"It's nothing," he said. If his parents had been away, he would have invited her in, but they were eating in the kitchen and he knew they hated to have their meals disturbed. His mother was crazy about it. And besides, Tito could tell from the way Tamsin kept looking over her shoulder that she was worried about leaving Wyatt alone upstairs.

"Well, see you around," she said.

A FEW DAYS later, a package came for her. It was DHL, not the usual FedEx or UPS. He took it up to her in the evening, knocking on the door.

"Oh, hi!" she said. Today she was wearing capri pants and a halter top, her hair held back from her face by black barrettes. The bruises on her arms were yellowing. *Naughty Neighbor Next Door,* he thought.

"This came for you," he said. "It looks important."

"Oh, it's probably from my husband," she said.

"Husband?" he asked before he could stop himself. He'd taken care to notice that she didn't wear a ring.

"Yeah," she said. "He lives in Peru. We're kind of separated right now. You want to come in?"

The scene was so familiar to him that he hardly registered the chaos of the apartment: Moving cartons everywhere, many opened. Half-assembled IKEA furniture. A pizza box with a pair of crusty crescents amid the crumbs and oil stains. It took him a moment to notice that some of the cartons had been shifted into a fortification in the back of the living room. The boy's head appeared from the space behind the wall of boxes.

"Is that your castle?" Tito asked.

"It's my station," said the kid.

"What kind of station?" Tito asked. "A radio station?"

"No!" said Wyatt. "Train station!"

Tito walked across the room and peered behind the line of boxes. An oval of wooden track was laid out on the floor. Wyatt was pulling a long, multicolored procession of cars around it.

"You like trains?" he asked.

"Yes!" said Wyatt.

"*Like* is an understatement," said Tamsin. "What did we do all day yesterday, kiddo?"

"Rode subway trains!" he said.

"Cool," said Tito looking around at the mess. He turned to Tamsin. "You need a hand with anything?"

"That's OK. You've already helped us a lot."

"What about that AC? Aren't you kind of hot in here?"

"Well . . . yeah. That would be great."

He installed the window unit, propping it on the windowsill outside with a can of soup the gay guys had left in one of the cabinets, screwing the accordion wings into the seams of the window to hold it in place. Then he assembled a bookcase, furtively scoping out her stuff, trying to learn more about her. That was when he noticed the framed diploma from Rice University on the floor. Meanwhile, Tamsin was emptying boxes, putting things away, clearing a space around the couch. After a while she disappeared and returned with two bottles of beer.

Wyatt had come out from behind his fortifications and stood in the flow of cool air from the Fedders. "Wa!" He said. "That's nice."

Tito twisted the top off his bottle. "So, is your husband Peruvian?" he asked as nonchalantly as he could.

"Oh—no," she said. "An all-American boy from South Dakota. He's an epidemiologist."

"A dimelo-what?" said Tito.

A giggle escaped her. "He studies infectious diseases," she said. "Pandemics, plagues, that kind of thing."

"Like that chicken flu everybody keeps talking about?"

"Yes. Like that. We lived in the jungle—in the Amazon basin—for a year. His research took a lot longer than he expected, though maybe he was just lying to me when he said it would only take six months." She rolled her eyes. Tito thought it was a gesture she might have made in the company of a girlfriend.

"Must have been hard," he said.

"It was. Harder than I expected, anyway. I used to think of myself as intrepid, a risk taker. I lived by myself in Houston and backpacked around Europe after college, but having a kid changes everything. Stuff that wouldn't have been a big deal when I was single suddenly seemed impossible. I just couldn't handle it anymore—the weird superstitions, the goddamn insects, the fear of disease, having to boil the water, nobody speaking English."

Tito laughed.

"What's so funny?"

"Sounds like the Dominican Republic," he said.

WEDNESDAY, HIS MIDWEEK day off work, Tito was lying in bed half awake with his hand down his boxers, passively playing with himself, thinking about the word *rice*. His mother knocked and immediately entered the room.

"*La muchacha esta aquí.*"

"What *muchacha*?"

"The new one. She just moved in. The one you've been sniffing around."

"Tamsin?"

"*Sí.* Tom-*seen*."

"She's here?"

"*Sí.* I don't know why you're wasting your time on her when you could have had Jasmina."

"Forget Jasmina, Mami. I know you liked her, but it's over."

"I know it's over. Her mother still calls me sometimes. Jasmina's down in D.R. right now with her new man."

"Good for her," said Tito. "Tell Tamsin I'll be right out."

He waited until his mother left before getting out of bed and putting on a pair of jeans to hide his middling hard-on. He found a clean T-shirt and messed with his hair. Barefoot and euphoric, he went out to meet her.

She was sitting on the sofa in the living room, wearing more clothing than he'd seen on her since she moved in: a knee-length skirt with a matching jacket and a white blouse. She looked like the star of a different movie altogether. *Classroom Confessions*. His mother was waiting silently with her but got up once he entered the room.

"What's the matter?" he asked, because it was clear from her fretful expression that something was.

"I'm supposed to be at work in an hour, but the woman who said she was going to look after Wyatt today just called and said she got another job—a full-time job—and that she wasn't coming."

"That's terrible!" he said.

"I don't know what to do. Today is my first day of summer classes. I'm supposed to be teaching English Comp to a bunch of eighteen-year-olds. I have to be there. I mean, what am I going to do? I can't bring Wyatt."

"I could look after him," said Tito.

"Really? You could? I thought maybe you might know someone who wouldn't mind, but, well—you! That would be so great. I mean, don't you have a job? Sorry, I didn't mean it to sound that way."

"It's my day off. Just give me five minutes. I'll be right up."

"Wow. You don't know how much this means to me," she said.

"It's OK," he said.

Upstairs, she was hurrying around the apartment while Wyatt watched cartoons. Tito got sucked into the vortex of her motion. She showed him where every kid thing was: the juice boxes, the snacks, the aloe-scented wipes, the changes of clothes. "There's just one thing you need to be really careful about. I mean, in addition to crossing the street and letting him pet dogs and all those things I'm sure you already know. The thing is, he's allergic to nuts—especially peanuts. A peanut could kill him."

"*Kill* him?"

"Yes. That's why, if you guys go out, you should take snacks with you. Everything in the kitchen is safe for him. There are no nuts here."

He was going to make a joke, but held back.

"If you buy anything, you've got to read the ingredients. Even if it says it was made in a facility that processes nuts you can't let him have it. OK?"

"Got it. No nuts."

"Here's my cell phone number if you need to reach me. I should be back around four. Really, I can't thank you enough." She squeezed his biceps and then reached for her fancy leather briefcase, which was on a pile of boxes.

Through all of this, Wyatt was sitting on the couch, mesmerized by SpongeBob. His mother kissed him and said. "Tito is going to look after you today. You be good for him. You hear me, big guy?"

"That's a 10-4, Mommy," he said.

Once Tito was sure she was gone and before the cartoons hit their next commercial break, he did a little snooping. The place was a wreck, though Wyatt's room was starting to come together. Everything in Tamsin's room was still in boxes, bubble wrap, or furniture pads, except for the bed, which he had helped her assemble. What he really wanted to see was a photograph of the husband, but he couldn't find any photographs at all, except for a single framed portrait of Wyatt as a baby. Unsatisfied, he next looked for the DHL boxes. He had brought up three of them in the week since she'd moved in. He wanted to know what was being sent with such urgency between two people who were "sort of separated." Divorce papers, he hoped. He found the boxes, but they left him none the wiser—they were collapsed and leaning against the garbage can in the kitchen. A few days later, he would put them out on the curb with the recycling.

He ambled back into the living room. "So, Wyatt," he said, hitting the open palm of one hand against the closed fist of the other. "What do you feel like doing today?"

"Can we ride trains?"

"Sure."

"I love to ride trains. There were no trains in the jungle."

"Then let's go."

He made the kid pee and threw some snacks and a change of clothes into the backpack. At the Dyckman Street station, they caught the A. The rush hour was over and they had the first car almost completely to themselves. Wyatt stood at the train's front window as it barreled down its tube. He hopped with joy as it entered the stations headlong and braked to a stop. "Wa!" he said. "Wa!" and Tito wondered where he'd gotten that expression of joy. Maybe it was something he picked up in Peru, though it sounded more Asian to him than South American.

That was how they spent the afternoon, underground, like motormen, at the front of trains. Wyatt's appetite for it was surpassing and required no contribution from Tito. At one point, he picked up a copy of the *Daily News* and read while the train traveled to the ends of the city, going through stations he'd never heard of—Zerega Avenue, Intervale Avenue, Briarwood—into parts of the outer boroughs he knew only from the eleven o'clock news. Wyatt pretended to be driving an out-of-control train. "Get back! I can't stop this thing. We're all going to *die!*"

Riding back uptown later that afternoon, Tito felt bedraggled, hungover. What time was it? Was it even light outside? At 145th Street, the conductor announced that there was a "sick passenger" on the train, and Tito had the sense that he might be trapped down there for the rest of his life.

"How did someone get sick on the train?" Wyatt asked.

"I don't know," said Tito, but already he'd learned that answer was unsatisfactory to this five-year-old.

"Do they have a sore throat?"

"Maybe," said Tito. "But I think it might be more serious than that."

"Like what?" said Wyatt, genuinely intrigued. "Like malaria?"

"*Malaria?*" said Tito.

"Yeah. I had to take malaria medicine in Peru." He pronounced it *Pru*.

"But you didn't get sick, did you?"

"No. I got lots of mosquito bites but none from No Fleas."

"No Fleas?"

"That's the kind of mosquito that gives you malaria. No Fleas mosquito."

"Your father tell you that?"

"Yeah. I've still got the medicine in my backpack. It's right there, in the pocket." He pointed at one of the zippers on the bag.

Tito opened it and took out an orange pharmacy bottle with a cluster of white pills on the bottom.

"You think the sick person can use my malaria medicine? They can have it. My mom said I can't get malaria in New York."

"That's really nice of you, Wyatt. But I don't think they have malaria."

Tito stood and looked down the train. A police officer and two EMS workers were walking up the platform. The emergency seemed to have passed. Moments later, the doors closed and the train departed the station.

TAMSIN WAS ALREADY home when they got back.

"Oh, there you are," she said, opening the door. "I was starting to get worried. Where were you guys?"

"On the train!" said Wyatt, jumping into his mother's embrace.

"I should have known. Hi, honey," she said, squeezing the kid. Tito wanted to lean in and kiss her, as if they were married, but he held back. That was *la otra vida,* he reminded himself.

"How did it go?" he asked her.

Tamsin shook her head. "It's going to be tough. Most of my students can barely write their names." She put down Wyatt and went into the bedroom, returning with her purse. From its maw, she pulled three twenties. "I was going to pay that woman ten dollars an hour, so here you go. I really can't thank you enough." She extended her hand to him, proffering the cash.

Tito wanted to cry. He'd been thinking that maybe they could all get takeout and eat dinner together. "No, really. You don't need to pay me," he said, holding up his hand.

"I didn't know my lease included a babysitting service. You sure?"

"Anytime I'm not working. Really. He's a great kid. I'll be happy to look after Wyatt next week, if you need me to. Maybe we can ride the Metro-North for a change."

"Yeah!" said Wyatt. "A commuter train."

WEDNESDAYS FOR THE next few weeks, Tito took the kid on every train he could think of. They rode the Metro-North from Spuyten Duyvil into Grand Central. From Penn Station, they took the LIRR double-deckers out to Babylon and back. They went to Hoboken for lunch on the PATH and took the New Jersey Transit out to Montclair, a town he sometimes dreamed of living in. On the return trip, they'd disembarked on a platform opposite a high-speed Acela train, the supreme being in Wyatt's railroad pantheon. Its long sloping nose was shaped like the front of a supersonic jet, but the vents on the side of the engine made it look more like a huge metal shark. Before Tito could stop him, Wyatt dashed into the train's open door. Tito chased him through the empty first-class cabin, finally catching him in the café car, which was also deserted. They sat in a booth and pretended they were on their way to Boston, Wyatt sucking down his juice box and Tito glancing through an out-of-town newspaper someone had left behind. Finally, a conductor came and shooed them off.

Tamsin was cagey with him, hot and cold, though she never again offered him money for spending time with Wyatt. He did not think her so innocent that she didn't suspect his ulterior motives and he hoped she was doing more than just using him for convenient babysitting and handyman help—hoped, but feared the worst. After the first week she'd asked him to watch Wyatt for a little longer when she got home from work while she went out for a run. He didn't mind. He sat on the couch with the kid, one eye on the cartoons and the other on Tamsin's bedroom door as she changed. The door opened and she came out wearing a pair of expensive-looking running shoes, a thin and very short pair of running shorts, and a tank top. *Titillation at the Track.* He and Wyatt went out to the Emerson Playground, where they waited for her return. The dream life never seemed more real than those minutes when he was with the other parents. When Tamsin came back from her runs, she was slick with sweat and the muscles on her legs twitched.

She was driven, lonely, and he soon learned, more than a little neurotic. Watching her open her mail became a favorite spectacle. She opened everything she received, even the junk mail. Not only did she open it, but she read it, scanning through the credit-card solicitations, environmental newsletters, and pleas for money from the Patrolmen's Benevolent Association. When she had read them, she tore the pages into pieces—half, then half again, then again and again until it was too thick to tear. She tore the paper with vitriol and panache. It was a performance. Then she spread the pieces among the three garbage cans in the apartment.

"What?" she asked, as Tito stared.

"I've never seen anyone do that."

"I had my identity stolen," she said.

"Really?"

"Yes. The bitch ruined my credit for years."

"She got your credit card numbers?" said Tito.

"More than that," said Tamsin. "Bank accounts, voting records. Everything. She was a professional con artist. I was one of six or seven identities she used. And you know where she found the information about me?"

"On the Internet?"

"In the garbage."

"Why don't you get a shredder?"

"I *like* tearing things up," she said.

HIS PARENTS' ANNIVERSARY was coming up and, as usual, they were planning a trip to celebrate. This year they were going to Santo Domingo for a week. Tito had taken the time off work to look after the building. On the morning of his parents' departure, suitcases were arrayed in the living room like the skyline of a small city: three slabs of vinyl stuffed with the bounty of New York, destined for his cousins, aunts, uncles, and their miscellaneous mistresses, moochers, and hangers-on. It was nothing fancy—tube socks, blue jeans, clock radios, disposable cameras, and Teflon frying pans—but his parents would be greeted like astronauts returning from a moon shot. And while they were away, he could pretend that the apartment was his own uptown bachelor pad.

His parents were the only people he knew who still got dressed up to fly. His father wore the old-guy summer formals: a linen suit and a Panama hat. Meanwhile, his mother, with her pressed white blouse, her knotted yellow scarf, and her sunglasses, looked like a Latina Jackie O. "You never know who you're going to run into on the plane," she said.

"Yes you do," Tito replied. "On this plane you're going to run into a bunch of Dominican hicks and their noisy-ass kids." But he knew his parents had to dress the part they played when they returned to Santo Domingo: the cosmopolitan couple of means. What everyone back in D.R. didn't know was that most people in America looked like slobs when they traveled. They wore sweatpants and shoes with Velcro closures. Tito had even seen teenagers getting on planes in their pajamas.

His father went over everything with him one more time. Here were the keys, the numbers to call at the management company, the schedule for the garbage pickup, as if Tito had not been putting out the garbage since he was seven. He said, "Yes, Papi," and drove them to the airport.

At the check-in, he waited in line with them to make sure they didn't get any grief for the size of their bags. Then he walked with them to the security gate, where they endured the solemn humiliations of the terrorist age. Before she followed his father through the metal detector, his mother said, "Listen to me, *mijo,* you've got to stop this foolishness with the *blanquita.* You hear me?"

"What *blanquita?*" he asked.

"Tamsin," she said.

"Oh, don't worry about that, Mami, that's nothing," he said and kissed her.

"You stop it, now, hear? You're wasting your time. You're looking for something she can't give you. I don't know why you couldn't work things out with Jasmina last year. *Tu eres un hombre incompleto,*" she said, and went through the metal detector.

Tito drove home thinking about his mother's parting words. *Un hombre incompleto.* An incomplete man. An unfinished man. He had to give it to her. Nobody could slay him with a sentence the way she could. But no matter what his mother said, Jasmina had been wrong for him, spoiled and shallow.

Home from the airport, he went to the closet and took down a box he had not opened in years. He shifted the furniture around in his room and spent the afternoon assembling the box's contents. He had barely finished when the knock came at the door. It was Tamsin and Wyatt.

"Are they gone?" whispered Tamsin, looking into the apartment.

"Yes," said Tito, whispering, too, for no good reason.

Wyatt rushed through the door. "Where is it? Where is it?" he asked.

"He's been asking all day," said Tamsin. "I wanted to be sure your parents had left before we came over."

Wyatt was no longer in view. "Here it is! Here it is!" he called from Tito's room.

"Come on in and see," Tito said, closing the door behind her.

There it was: his old Lionel O Gauge Super Chief with two coaches and the observation car at the back on a figure 8 layout with a station house and a trestle bridge.

"Can you turn it on? *Pleeeease?*"

"Sure," said Tito. "The switch is over here."

An old tenant had given him the train set many years before when her son went to college. Tito set it up in his room and for a week—it was winter, there was nothing else to do—he played with it (if watching a toy train go around and around could really be called *playing*). Looking to expand the layout, he went to a hobby shop in the Bronx to buy some more track, but once he saw the price, he felt like an idiot. It would take him a month to save enough to extend his line by a couple of feet, a year to buy another car for his train. He went home, put the train back in its box, and stowed it in a closet, where it had remained until that morning.

And now he was glad he'd kept it. Wyatt was on his hands and knees prowling around the chugging, smoke-emitting locomotive like a giant cat. "Mommy, Mommy," he said. "You see it? You see it? There's a signal crossing."

"Yes, sweetheart. I see it."

"It's cool, right, Mommy?"

"Very cool," said Tamsin, smiling at Tito.

"Do you have any more passenger cars, Tío?"

"No," said Tito. "Each sold separately."

"You can still collect them all?"

"Yes. But batteries are not included," he said, and they both laughed. "So, you guys hungry?" asked Tito. "My mom left me a ton of food."

"Starving, actually," said Tamsin.

Tito started to set the table and became suddenly indignant that none of his parents' plates or cutlery matched. They had been acquired, over the years, from the odds and ends that people left behind when they moved out of their apartments, and they reflected the subtle changes in generational taste. Some forks had four tines, some had three; some knives were serrated, some weren't; some plates had a floral border, some had gold trim. It was as if their wedding registry had been at a flea market. He turned the gas on to warm up the soup. There was also rice and beans and some *bacalao*. Wyatt didn't want to come to the table, but they showed him that if he left the bedroom door open, he could see the train as it made part of its circuit.

"So, can you still look after him tomorrow?"

"Yes," said Tito. "I've got a surprise for him."

"What?" said Tamsin. Wyatt wasn't listening to them; he was spellbound by the train.

Tito said, "M-O-N-O-R-A-I-L."

"No way. Where?"

"Newark Airport. I saw it today when I was dropping my parents off."

"He's going to freak out."

"It'll be great," said Tito.

"How are you going to get out there?"

"I've got the car. You said you had a booster, right?"

"Yes. I don't think it's unpacked yet, but I'll find it."

They ate for a time in silence. Finally, Wyatt said, "Mommy? You see it? It's picking up passengers at the station. It's the express."

"I see it, sweetie."

"Mommy, can we stay here tonight?" Wyatt had gotten off his chair and was drifting in the direction of the bedroom watching the train. He'd eaten next to nothing. Tito looked at her with an expression indicating that he would not have any objections to them staying.

"No, sweetie, we should go home."

"Please!"

"You're going to spend the day with Tito tomorrow."

"Please!" he said, more plaintively. "Please, Mommy." He was about to cry.

"No, Wyatt. I'm sorry."

"But I want to see the train tonight," he said, his voice cracking. "I want to! The Super Chief is my best friend."

"I thought *I* was your best friend."

"You *and* the Super Chief are my best friend, Mommy. Please?"

"Wyatt and I should get going." She stood and carried some of the dishes into the kitchen.

"No, Mommy, no!" said Wyatt, running into Tito's room and slamming the door.

"Why don't you stay?" said Tito. He'd followed her into the kitchen and had unintentionally trapped her against the counter. "We could watch a movie. My parents have the pay-per-view on the box." He set down the bowl he was carrying and reached toward her, touching her bare elbow.

She flinched—no more than a spasm of the shoulders—and shook her head. "It's late," she said. "And I should really get Wyatt to bed. Thank you for the food."

THE NEXT MORNING, he was eating breakfast when Tamsin knocked on the door. He'd been up late watching pornos on the channel he never got to watch when his parents were around. They were like potato chips, those pornos. *Brazilian Gang-bang,* volume 1? Why not. Volume 2? OK. . . . Volume 3? Sure, just one more. . . . Volume 4? This is the last one. Next thing you knew it was three-thirty in the morning and you were watching volume 8.

"Hi," said Tamsin. "Are you still OK for today? You look beat." She was dressed like a teacher again, but this time Tito felt like her hired help.

"I'm fine," he said.

"I better get going, then," she said. "Here." She set the booster seat down and handed him a knapsack.

"Right," said Tito.

"Wyatt, you be good, do you hear me? Tito has a nice day planned for you."

"Yes, Mommy," said Wyatt, also looking a little sleepy. "Bye."

She kissed her son and left.

Tito let the kid play with the Lionel while he got himself together. Then they went out to the car. An hour later, he parked at the Newark Airport rail station, and they took escalators to the upper level to wait for the monorail. A guard was waiting there, a black guy younger than Tito, wearing a uniform that was too large for him, the tips of his fingers almost lost in the cuffs. Tito sensed the guard looking at him, dwelling on the disparity between his brown skin and nappy hair and the kid's pale face and blond thatch. Wyatt could not stop jumping up and down while holding on to Tito's hand.

"Monorail! Monorail!" Wyatt chanted.

The train slid smoothly into the station as if on ice, and Wyatt stopped jumping. He rubbed his hands together and said, "Heh-heh-heh," like a cartoon villain. It was the first time Tito had heard him do that, but not the first time the kid had surprised him with some expression or gesture. He was constantly coming up with strange turns of phrase and exclamations. One day, on the 2, Wyatt turned to Tito and said, "Are you kidding me?" Another time, Wyatt refused to get off a train. Tito picked him up and the boy said, "Oh, so that's how you're going to play it, eh?" Wyatt had his own fantasy life filled with trains, cars, and superheroes who never lost in their struggles against the bad guys.

They rode the monorail for more than an hour, gliding back and forth among the terminals and long-term parking garages in the driverless, air-conditioned glass pods. Their companions on the little train replaced themselves every two or three stops. There were the pilots, looking like viceroys in their epaulets and gilt-cuffed splendor, the flight attendants, sexy and exotic in their airline colors, talking and laughing in strange languages. There were family groups returning from vacations, people who'd come to meet their beloveds. As every group departed, Tito felt that he and Wyatt had been left behind, that when they got back to the city everyone would be gone.

Finally, Wyatt said he was hungry. They got off at terminal A, amid a dozen members of an Italian sports team, all wearing matching blue tracksuits with white stripes, carrying identical Adidas duffel bags. In that crowd, he managed to lose sight of Wyatt. The athletes piled into the cars and the doors closed and the monorail pulled out of the station.

"Wyatt?" he said, too softly to be heard by anyone but himself.

Another monorail had come in and was disgorging its passengers on the other side of the platform. He felt the tendons behind his elbows and knees twang with panic. A woodpecker was trying to hammer its way out of his throat. Could the kid really have gotten back on the train with the Italians? He remembered how Wyatt had dashed aboard the Acela that afternoon in Penn Station. The second monorail pulled out and everyone dispersed, leaving only Tito and the guard on the platform, facing each other like gunfighters. Tito started walking toward the guard, toward a miserable showdown, alibis cranking through his mind. *I don't know how it happened. He was right there. He's usually a good kid*—ding!

The bell for the elevator rang like an alarm. The doors slid open and Wyatt sauntered out onto the platform with a smile on his face. "Tío!" he said. "I rode the elevator by myself!"

TAMSIN WAS IN the apartment when they got back from the airport. Tito had held Wyatt's hand the rest of the time they were in the terminal and in the parking lot—held his hand, clutched his shirt, given him a piggyback ride, anything to maintain physical contact with him. Those moments of total terror on the platform completely undid him. He didn't scold the kid, didn't yell at him or give him the guilt trip. He just hugged him and took him down to the food court for some lunch, a sense of gratitude and relief welling up within him. What a cataclysm he had averted. He was still holding Wyatt's hand as they entered the apartment.

"Did you see the monorail?" said Tamsin.

"Yes!" said Wyatt. "Heh-heh-heh."

Tamsin looked at Tito and raised her eyebrows as if to ask, *Did you teach him that?* Tito shook his head. "We had a great time," he said. "We rode that thing forever. We saw a lot of airplanes, too, right Wyatt?"

"The planes were coming in for a landing!"

"That's great, you guys," said Tamsin. "Well, guess what? I had a pretty amazing day, too. I talked to your daddy this afternoon, Wyatt."

"Daddy?" said Wyatt.

"Yes. He says he's almost finished with his work. He should be here in two weeks!"

"Daddy's coming?" said Wyatt again.

"Yes, Daddy's coming."

"Yay!" said Wyatt. "I want to see Daddy!"

"Me, too!" said Tamsin.

"I want to see Daddy!"

"Me, too!"

And they both laughed.

"Wow, that's wonderful," said Tito. "You must be really happy."

"You have no idea," said Tamsin. "It is such a relief. And you can have your days off again," she said. "I can't thank you enough. You don't know how bad I've felt about imposing on you like that."

"It was nothing," said Tito. "He's a good kid. He really is."

"Do you want to stay for dinner?" she asked. "I was going to order some pizza."

"That's all right, I've still got all that food my mom left me."

WHEN HIS PARENTS returned a few days later, Tito was able to tell his mother that he'd broken it off with the *blanquita*. She nodded and patted him on the shoulder, as if he had just made his bed for the first time. And then she told him that Jasmina was getting married—to a sugar heir, or something. She raised her eyebrows as if to say, *See? She was ready. And you blew it.* Sugar heir was probably an exaggeration, but it irked him. "She was looking for someone to spoil her," he said.

Having had the real thing—a real child to pamper—the formerly rich fantasy life into which he had retreated after each of his breakups suddenly felt tepid. He sat at the kitchen table eating meals with his mother and father and he could not imagine that a wife was sitting in the empty chair, could not imagine promising dessert to his son if only he ate his vegetables, could not imagine the house in the suburbs where he lived.

Tito had come to know Tamsin's routine so well that he was able to avoid her for a while. There were no more knocks on the door, no more DHL packages to deliver. He didn't ask if she needed him to look after Wyatt the following Wednesday; he picked up an extra shift at work. Everybody thought he was crazy.

Two weeks later, the husband—Josh—showed up. Tito saw them in the playground, the husband pushing Wyatt on a swing. Tito skulked along the perimeter fence, feeling an immense sense of failure and exclusion. A few days later there was the inevitable encounter. *Four's a Crowd.* The reunited family unit emerged from the building's front door as he was on his way up the steps. No way to pretend he hadn't seen them, nowhere to hide.

"Tío!" cried Wyatt, who was being carried piggyback by his father.

"Hey, little man!" he called, and reached up to give Wyatt a high five, which was enthusiastically returned. At least the kid remembered him. Tamsin, looking like someone without an umbrella on a rainy day, held her husband's arm. "Hi there," she said.

"You must be Tito," said the husband, who was large and handsome in a shambling, unkempt way.

"Yes," he said, and they shook hands.

"Wyatt talks about you nonstop. Sounds like he had a great time with you."

"We just rode some trains. It was nothing."

"Well, thanks for taking such good care of my boy—and my wife, I might add."

"No problem," said Tito, looking over at Tamsin, who was looking down at the sidewalk.

"So, you guys heading out?"

"We're getting dinner," said Tamsin.

"Would you like to join us?" asked the husband, apparently sincerely.

"No," said Tito. "No thanks. I bet my Moms has something waiting for me."

Moms. Talking to an educated white dude—a dimelo-ologist—and he says *Moms.* He wanted to kill himself.

"See you round," said Josh.

"Bye!" said Wyatt.

SINCE THE HUSBAND'S arrival, Tamsin had started running every evening. Tito saw her bare legs go past the basement window, a pair of skimpy shorts and a sports bra the only things covering her. He wondered now if he should have told her about the murder of the Barnard girl earlier in the year. She, too, had been a jogger, and it was on one of her runs through the most remote part of the park that she had been killed, her body mutilated and left near the Hudson Bridge toll plaza. No arrests had been made in the case, which meant that the murderer was still at large. For a month or so after the killing, there had been a significantly increased police presence in the park. A mobile command center was stationed on Seaman Avenue near the Emerson Playground. Mounted officers patrolled the trails. Female runners no longer went alone into the forested parts of the park. They went in groups during daylight hours or kept to the paths that were out in the open—in plain view of everyone. But as the months had gone by and a second murder had not occurred, the police found better things to do. The mobile command center vanished. The mounted officers returned south. The groups of runners dissipated back to their single units, running at all hours. Each day that passed without a crime emboldened them further. The fact that there had been no follow-up murder led Tito to believe that the Barnard girl had been killed in a crime of passion. A stalker or a spurned boyfriend had done it, he felt sure.

In the waning weeks of the summer, he, too, returned to the park, taking after-dinner walks with a bag of stale bread. Feeding the ducks by the lagoon, he saw Tamsin go by, heading into the forested part of the park to the west. Half an hour later, she returned, coming back down to the ballfields and waterside paths from the trees, running at a very fast clip, pushing herself. Tito wore sunglasses and a ball cap, kept his back to her, crouching by the ducks on the banks of the inlet.

THE NEXT DAY, he found a good spot, below the trail and screened by a fallen branch, where he would be able to see her coming without being seen himself. He sat there in the humid evening dampness, waiting for her. He had no weapon. He had no plan. He just wanted to see her, perhaps talk to her. Maybe that was all he needed—to be able to talk to her, just the two of them. In his mind's eye, he saw it all unfolding, the dream-life version: Her struggling against him as he pulled her off the path into the deep forest down by the toll plaza. Old growth they called it. He felt the slippery sweat on her neck, her muted attempts to scream through the gag.

He sat behind the fallen branch and watched her come down the trail, alone, and as she drew nearer, he began to weep. It surprised him completely and a sob escaped from his mouth.

She stopped. "Who's there?" she called.

He stifled his sobs and exhaled silently through his mouth.

"Who's there?" she called again.

He did not reply. A tear slid down his cheek.

She called out one last time in a hesitant, frightened voice: "Is anyone there?" And then she turned and ran back the way she had come.

Within a week, Tito moved out of his parents' apartment.

Clara

The day after Yunis's departure for the Dominican Republic, Clara went back to work. She was a solo librarian, which meant that she was the director, middle manager, and lackey for Singer and Watkins's little research center, a glass-walled sanctum of legal volumes, reference texts, Formica carrels, and computer terminals where lawyers occasionally holed up as much to escape their secretaries and their ringing phones as to conduct research. Mostly though, Clara passed her days there in seclusion, fielding requests by e-mail and voicemail, dispensing information through the wires, organizing her collection, as if preparing for a surprise inspection from Mrs. Molloy. Because she worked by herself, there was no one to cover for her when she took a day off and, inevitably, even in August, she returned to find her desk covered with rubber-banded bundles of envelopes, her in-box chockablock with unread e-mail, and the voicemail light pulsing on her phone. Today was no different. She gathered the heap of paper mail into a plastic postal service bin and stashed it under her desk. She would look at it after lunch. Logging in, she went through her e-mail, making notes and prioritizing the requests—partners always first unless one of the associates absolutely needed something yesterday. She also tried to weed out the no-brainers, the queries that were beneath her, where the lawyers were just being lazy. These she forwarded to the appropriate secretary to handle, sometimes with terse instructions about where to find the information. She occupied a curious place in the firm's hierarchy, below the lawyers, but above the secretaries, and off to the side of everyone else. She was simultaneously indispensable and easily forgotten: praised upon the completion of a project, but always the first to have her budget cut when there was a fiscal crunch. Lately, she'd been under pressure to lower the cost of the firm's Lexis and Westlaw bills, and she had, with the help of one of the partners, renegotiated contracts with both, saving the firm nearly fifty thousand dollars a year. Any chance she'd see some of that savings in the form of a bonus? Dream on. Teaching the lawyers how to search more efficiently on their own would have saved the firm even more than the contractual nit-picking she and the partner had engaged in, but the lawyers felt that their time was at a premium: They were too busy to take such a seminar, even if it would save them time down the road.

Before Clara had finished opening all the unread messages in her in-box, Lauren Wakefield, a fifth-year associate and one of Clara's best friends at the firm, appeared in the library. She was a petite blond fireplug who wore suits in solid colors and heels that made the muscles of her calves look as hard and defined as a Tour de France cyclist's.

"How was your day off?" she said. "How'd it go with your sister?"

Clara rolled her eyes. "Crazy," she said. "Lots of family drama. How was it here?"

"It's always a little nuts when you're not around," said Lauren. "Everyone acts as if they suddenly forgot how to use Martindale or Lexis."

"I know. You should see some of the requests I got." Clara laughed.

"So, you want to get some lunch later?" Lauren asked.

"Sure," said Clara. It was good to be back at work, she realized, work, where she knew how to answer the questions that came to her. That was the pleasure of librarianship—finding answers, solving problems, sending people away happy. The problems in her private life seemed harder to solve. There were no databases or reference books to help her figure those things out.

CLARA HAD BEEN born in the town of La Isabela, not far from Santo Domingo. When she was three, her parents left the Dominican Republic to seek their fortunes in New York. Clara stayed behind in the care of her *abuelo* and *abuela*. New York, for her, was a distant and mysterious place, like heaven or the moon. From New York, money sometimes made its way to La Isabela. From New York there was sometimes a letter. Now and then, a relative would visit from New York with word of her parents and, maybe, a gift.

She and her grandparents lived in a three-room wooden farmhouse with a galvanized steel roof and no glass in the windows—only shutters to keep the winds out during hurricane season. This was the house where her mother had grown up; from this house her mother had gone out one night and met her father at a dance. In this house, a little more than a year later, Clara had been born. The farm grew bananas and mangos. There were a few cows and a pen of pigs down the hill behind the house. There were chickens and a manic, jealous rooster that her grandfather had named Fidel.

Her father reappeared at the farm one day when Clara was six. Her grandmother was in town at the *botanica* and her grandfather was in the fields working. Clara was outside the house, killing salamanders. She picked them up by the tail and whipped their heads against the wall. *Whap!* went their little heads. Sometimes she had to do it more than once to kill them. When the salamander was dead, she tossed it into the grass for the dogs. Years later, returning to visit the farm from New York, the sight of a salamander would make her scream.

A man came walking down from the road toward the house.

He wore new clothes and shiny shoes. He was tall and thin. He seemed familiar, but she did not recognize him right away. "Clara, *mi amor*," he said.

She looked up at him. A salamander wiggled in her hand. He had high cheekbones, small eyes, and pockmarked skin. He took off his Panama hat and showed a chicken scratch of tight curls on his head.

"*Es Papi,*" he said. Without saying a word, she dropped the salamander and went into the house and found the framed photograph of her parents on their wedding day. She brought the photograph out and held it up beside his face.

"Papi!" she said.

"*Sí!*" he said, laughing.

"Where's Mami?" she asked, looking back at the photograph. She was happy to see her father, but it was her mother—or the idea of her mother—that she missed the most.

"She's in New York." He glanced at the fields behind the house and then back at the road from which he had come. "Do you want to go to Santo Domingo with me, *mi corazón*? I have a car."

She said yes and, holding hands, they walked out to the road where his car was parked. She would not see the farm again until she was in college.

"Where are we going, Papi?" she asked him.

"Shopping," he said, unlocking the door. "Wouldn't you like some new clothes, *amorcita*?" He spoke softly.

Clara nodded. "Yes, Papi."

They drove into Santo Domingo. She sat in the front passenger seat. Her little body bounced around on the seat as her father maneuvered through the traffic on the unlined, potholed roads. Her eyes barely reached the bottom of the window. She looked up at the passing streets, the grimy facades of buildings, the undersides of trees, the sky—like looking up the city's skirt.

"Can Mami come and meet us in Santo Domingo?" she asked.

"No, *mi amor*," he said. "But maybe you would like to go to New York with me to see her?"

"Yes, Papi!" she said. "Please."

"Good," he said. "We will go to New York. But first you need some clothes."

They parked and walked into a pedestrian shopping area lined with stores and food vendors. In store after store, they were fawned over by female clerks—a father buying clothes for his daughter. He bought her a brown dress with yellow ducks on the bodice; he bought her a pair of long pants made out of a thick, ribbed material she had never seen before; he bought her new underwear; he bought her a pink cotton cardigan; he bought her a pair of white tights, which looked like two squashed, milky snakes to her; he bought her a pair of shoes with hard, smooth leather soles; he bought her a raincoat made of a slick, slippery cloth. The last item of new clothing she had owned was her baptismal dress, a gift from her father's mother. Everything else she had worn in her life had been worn by someone else before her.

"Papi, you have money?" she asked. Money was something her grandparents almost never had but the supply of bills in her father's wallet seemed endless.

"Yes, Clara. I have money."

"New York money?"

He smiled. "Yes, *mija*. New York money."

They had dinner in a restaurant and while they were eating a man came up to the table. The man was fat and not as tall as her father. He had longer hair, a tangled black corona around his head. He was introduced as Tío Miguel.

"I want to go back to see *mi abuelitos*," Clara said.

"I thought you wanted to come to New York."

"No," she said.

"Don't you want to see your mother?"

"Yes, but we need to tell Abuelo and Abuela."

"We are going to New York, Clara."

"No, Papi. I don't want—"

He slapped her. *Whap!* went his hand against her face. Now she knew what the salamanders felt. She vowed never to do that to them again—a vow she would keep. Nobody in the restaurant paid any attention to her father striking her; it was just a man disciplining his child. The blow rang in her ears and silenced her. She was terrified of saying the wrong thing and getting slapped again. She would wait until she saw her mother and everything would be fine then.

From the restaurant, they went back to the car. It was getting dark. Tío Miguel drove now, taking them along a road that ran beside the sea to the airport. The terminal was brightly lit and full of people. Her father led her into the men's room, where the smell of shit made her gag. Men, zipping their flies and turning away from the urinals, were startled to see a girl in the room. They gave an embarrassed smirk and left without washing their hands. In the stall, her father flushed away the stew of paper and feces in the toilet and told her to take off what she was wearing—a pair of shorts and a T-shirt. "*Que flaquita!*" he said, looking at her. She stood there, naked and trembling, as he dug among the bags. The tiles felt cold against her feet. Piece by piece, he made her put on almost everything they'd bought that afternoon. "It is cold in New York," he explained.

She had said nothing since he slapped her and she said nothing now.

"Come, Clara. Don't be that way."

"Mami," she whispered.

"You'll see your mami soon," he said.

When they came out of the men's room, Tío Miguel said goodbye to them, hugging her father and kissing her on the head. She never saw him again and would never know who Tío Miguel actually was.

Her father had only a small suitcase and she had nothing—he

had thrown her old clothes into the trash in the men's room. They waited in line at the ticket counter and Clara started to feel overheated. She took off the raincoat and the cardigan. It was inconceivable to her that New York was cold enough that she would need to wear both. The ticket agent took her father's suitcase and put it on a baggage cart behind the counter. They crossed the terminal to a doorway where a man in a uniform sat behind a raised desk. Her father handed the man a small red book. The man looked through the book, flipping the pages rapidly. Then he stopped. Inside the book, like a patch of mold, was a wad of folded New York money. She saw it for only a second before it vanished into the man's palm. The man stood up and peered over the desk, laying the book flat, as he inspected her. Clara saw that the book was open to a page with her photograph. She had not seen her father in three years. Where did that photograph come from? It made her father seem more powerful and more mysterious than before. No words were exchanged. The man behind the desk nodded and handed the book back to her father.

CLARA FELL ASLEEP during the flight and missed the descent into the city. She did not see the crisscross of lighted streets, the darkened parks burnished with week-old snow. She was woken by her father shaking her shoulder as the plane came in for its landing. Still groggy, she walked up the jetway into Kennedy Airport. They waited in a long line to stand before a judge, who looked at her picture in her father's book and asked him questions in English. This time there was no New York money in the book. For a moment, Clara thought they might be sent back. The judge looked down at her from his podium, nodded, and—*boom*—delivered his stamp into the book.

"Welcome to New York, Clara," her father said.

A man was waiting for them in the terminal—a squat, burly Dominican man who was introduced as Don Felix.

"Where is Mami?" she asked, looking up at her father.

"At home. We are going now."

"*Pobre muchacha,*" said Don Felix, bending down to look at her. "You won't like New York at first. It's a hard place. But one day you will thank your father for bringing you."

Don Felix told them to wait by the revolving door while he went to get the car. Clara looked out into the night, the cabs and buses pulling up and departing, everyone dressed in heavy coats. They had not even left the airport building and she was already feeling cold. The draft came in from the revolving door and reached up the insides of her pants with its icy fingers. She felt like she was standing in a shallow, cold bath. When Don Felix's little car pulled up to the curb, she and her father walked out of the airport through the revolving door and the March wind struck her body. She had never felt cold with such force. It was like having a fever. All strength left her.

"*Ven,* Clara," said her father, and took her by the hand again and pulled her across the pavement into the car's frigid vinyl backseat.

Don Felix and her father talked as they drove. She did not listen to what they said. She was too busy looking out the window. The car was taking her to see her mother! But the drive never seemed to end. Traffic slowed. There was always another road with more cars, more signs. Arrows pointing this way and that. At last, they were on a bridge and Clara could see the row of tall buildings with their lights on—a wall of lighted boxes reflected on the water. They came off the bridge and drove along the river. There was less traffic now and Don Felix was driving fast. The car had finally warmed up inside and she was feeling sleepy again. Then the highway ended and they were driving down a congested street. She looked out the window and saw a Dominican flag above the door of a bodega. There was a Dominican man waiting at the corner while his dog squatted. The signs were in Spanish. She recognized some of the words—*comida, cambio, banco.* They went through a traffic light and stopped.

"Here we are, Clara," said her father. "This is your home."

They had parked in front of a house that looked like it was still being built. There was an enormous metal trash container in the driveway, and the steps were made out of wooden planks on cement blocks. Across the street, dark as a jungle, was a park. On this side of the street, rising up a gentle slope were other houses in better condition than the one they'd stopped in front of.

"How long do you think it's going to take to fix the place up?" asked Don Felix, gesturing out the window.

"A year," said her father. "Maybe two. Come, Clara. Say good-night to Don Felix."

Clara did as she was told.

Don Felix smiled at her. "I live just there, a couple of blocks," he said, pointing up the street. "I have a boy, your age. I hope you will come and meet him."

Her father opened his door and went to the trunk of the car, where he retrieved his small suitcase. Don Felix was still looking at her, as if he wanted to say more. The door beside Clara opened and her father said, "*Vámonos.*" They climbed the planks, and as her father unlocked the door, she turned and looked back at Don Felix, who waved before driving away.

"*Vieja!*" her father called out as he opened the door.

They went into a small, dark entry hall with a flight of stairs going up. To the right was a door. A light was on at the top of the stairs and Clara could hear someone moving—the sandpapery scrape of slippers on a dirty wood floor. Her mother! Clara was ecstatic. The shadow of her mother came slowly into view at the top of the stairs. "Roberto? It's late." She sounded like she had been asleep, and as she came down the steps, one heavy tread at a time, Clara saw that she was wearing a floral nightdress. Her ankles were encased in wooly gray socks.

"Yes," said her father. "It's late, but we made it." He flipped a switch and the lights in the hallway came on and Clara could see the face of the woman descending toward them, one hand steadying herself on the banister, the other hand gathering the front of her nightdress around her engorged belly. The woman was not her mother.

"Where's my mami?" asked Clara, her voice cracking. The woman was coming closer and closer. Only four steps separated them now.

"This is your mami," said her father, who was at her side. He reached up to take the hand of the woman on the stairs, helping her down to the landing. He kissed her once on the mouth and then bent over and kissed her stomach. "How's the baby?" he asked.

"Ay, Roberto. He's kicking me all the time," said the woman who was not her mother. She looked down at Clara. Clara had never seen a Dominican woman with such a straight, narrow nose, with such thin lips. Her hair was in curlers and the proximity of the great mass of her belly frightened her.

"Kiss your mother," said her father.

"That's not my mother!" said Clara, edging away from her.

Whap! The blow came from the woman and it had as much force as her father's slap earlier that evening. Clara staggered back a step and began weeping, her hands covering her face where the blow had struck her.

"Listen to your father!" the woman said. "Don't be an ungrateful child."

"You're not my mother!" Clara yelled.

"Clara, kiss your mother," said her father, gently but insistently. He grasped her by the arm and pulled her toward the woman who was not her mother. "Kiss her now."

"No!" shouted Clara. Her hands were still over her face and she was sobbing.

Encircling her waist with one arm, her father picked her up. He pulled her hands away from her face, which was wet with tears. Clara struggled, but her father was too strong. He lifted her until she was looking into the eyes of the woman who was not her mother. She had brown bloodshot eyes, the whites of which were gray at the edges, as if diseased.

"Kiss her!" said her father.

Clara moved her head closer, as if to comply with her father's request. At the last moment, she opened her mouth and caught a piece of the woman's cheek between her teeth. The woman screamed and Clara's father pulled her away, but not before Clara tasted the woman's blood in her mouth. Her father flung her to the floor and went to console the woman who was not her mother. She was sitting on the stairs with her hand on her face.

"Dolores," he called. "*Estás bien?*"

Dolores looked up. "She's an animal!"

Clara's father produced a handkerchief to blot the wound. "It's not deep," he said as he dabbed the gash. "You'll be fine."

Dolores pushed Clara's father aside so that she could look directly at Clara, who was still on the floor where she had landed.

"Now I see why your mother abandoned you, little animal," Dolores said to her.

"No!" said Clara. "She did not abandon me."

"Yes! Your mother has forgotten you. It is your father who remembered you. You will have to put her out of your mind, because now I am the only mother you will ever have."

CLARA AND LAUREN took their lunch at a café in the concourse that led from Newark Penn Station to their office building in the Gateway Center. Lauren and her partner, Abby, had gone through IVF the year before to conceive their daughter, Kate, and Clara often sought advice and comfort from her friend. Abby had had a miscarriage during her first cycle, but her successful delivery of a full-term baby a year later gave Clara enormous hope. She told Lauren the latest news about the hysteroscopy. Lauren, with the same thoroughness she brought to litigation, had researched every aspect of reproductive medicine before she and Abby had embarked on their course of IVF.

"You know, in the chatrooms we joined, a lot of people were saying that the whole T-shaped uterus thing is like a get-out-of-jail-free card for the doctors when they can't figure out another obvious reason. It's something to say that sounds better than 'we don't know.' It's good they're doing the hysteroscopy. That's how they will know for sure. I bet that's not the problem at all. I bet that you've just been unlucky, or maybe you've got some kind of infection. After all, you already had one healthy delivery."

Clara nodded, grateful for Lauren's strident certainty. Such confidence is what she needed to hear from Thomas the night before. He'd said some of the same things, but there was doubt or distraction in his voice.

"I've been thinking of starting a fertility club," Lauren said. "Kind of like a knitting circle, only we could tell our stories. Isn't that what you need? To hear that someone else has been through this and that everything turned out all right?"

"Yes," said Clara. "That's exactly what I need."

Tito

Tito flipped open his cell phone and listened again to the message: "Mr. Moreno. This is Alicia Almonte. A valued possession of mine seems to have gone missing. Please contact me at your earliest convenience to discuss the matter. . . . Perhaps I will have to fill out one of your surveys after all. Thank you."

It was eight o'clock in the morning, the week after the Almonte move and, with only beer and sour milk in his refrigerator, Tito was on his way up Broadway to get some breakfast before starting work. He couldn't believe that she'd checked on the photograph. First time he steals from a client and he gets caught! He shouldn't have gone back to talk to her about Clara. It had obviously sent her down memory lane to the Julia Alvarez book. He had the photograph in his pocket, ready to return it and throw himself on her mercy. He'd already been into Kinko's the day before to have it scanned. A copy of the image was in his phone and another rested in his e-mail inbox at work. Even so, he didn't want to part with the original. He sensed that she would understand, that she would forgive him—at least he hoped so, hoped that some kind of connection had been forged because of their mutual curiosity about Clara.

Tito closed his phone and went in through the streaked glass doors of El Malecon. He favored El Malecon over other local eateries for the simple reason that his ex-wife worked there. Her name was María Luisa; it was a green card marriage. She was the cousin of his mami's friend Merida. Tito had been paid a thousand dollars on the day of the ceremony at the Bronx courthouse, and another thousand was promised to him once the green card was safely obtained. This was cheaper than the going rate, but Merida was an old friend; she and his mami had known each other as kids in Barahona. The ceremony took place on a bleak winter day, just a week after María Luisa had arrived from Santo Domingo. The bride didn't speak more than a dozen words of English. She was young and fat, uneducated but sweet. She said her vows through chattering teeth, which the justice of the peace probably ascribed to nerves. Tito played his part and gave her a big kiss, tilting her great bulk slightly as he embraced her.

The reception was back at Merida's: *chicharrones* and Presidentes, *bachata* and merengue. Then he didn't see her for a few weeks. That was their honeymoon. Merida was taking care of the legwork. She appeared with an apartment lease, which he had to sign; she opened a joint bank account for them and found María Luisa the job at El Malecon. In the week before the INS interview, Tito returned to Merida's apartment. María Luisa had gained some English and lost some weight. With Merida as their teacher, they went over their story again and again. How they met, where they had gone on vacations together, when the other's birthday fell, what their favorite foods were, what music they listened to and movies they loved, who their in-laws were. Tito, much practiced in fantasy, had no trouble with the notion of a fabricated marriage, a fabricated life. He even offered little twists and enhancements to the story Merida had conceived for them. The week of study paid off. They passed the interview and María Luisa was approved for resident alien status.

In due time, Tito received the rest of his payment, but it wasn't until three years later that María Luisa took care of the final piece of business. She came to him with divorce papers, severing their union because she wanted to get engaged to an MTA track worker named Manuel (a regular customer at the restaurant, Tito later found out). By then, María Luisa's transformation from bewildered immigrant to barrio eye candy was complete. This was before he had met Jasmina, and it occurred to Tito that his mother might have set the whole thing up in the hopes that he and María Luisa would fall in love and stay married, like one of those arranged marriages. There was no chance for such a scheme—if that's what it was—to succeed. Tito could not think of María Luisa as wife material. She was a *campesina,* a hick.

His new apartment was much closer to El Malecon than to his parents' place and, without his mother to cook for him, Tito found himself going there more often. He went in now and sat at the counter. The place was bright and glassy, with chrome furniture and Plexiglas sheets laid over the green tablecloths. Fake flowers adorned every table. María Luisa was taking an order from an older couple at one of the few occupied tables. A female MTA employee Tito recognized from the Dyckman Street token booth sat at another table reading the paper and eating eggs. In the corner table a high school girl, who looked like she was cutting class, whispered into a cell phone. Though it opened at six a.m., the place was much more about the meals consumed later in the day. At nine o'clock that night, most of the tables would be filled and a ball game would be on the TV where the Univision morning news was now being shown. At the counter he could hear loud and clear the chime of dishes being unloaded from a washer in the kitchen.

"*Ay, Tito, mi amor. ¿Cómo estás?*" María Luisa asked, having taken the elderly couple's order. She kissed him on the cheek.

"*Bien. ¿Y tu?*" He checked her out. Looked like she was putting some of the weight back on. She didn't need to be so careful now that she was married.

"*Bien, bien.*" She went around the counter. "*¿Café?*" she asked.

"*Sí,*" said Tito. "*Café y pan, por favor. ¿Y Manuel?*"

"Working hard," she said, placing coffee on the counter before him. She fetched him a roll and some butter. Tito never liked to eat a big breakfast.

"So, you like being married again?"

"Yes," she said. "Second time is better."

"That's because I broke you in," he said. "Manuel ought to thank me."

"I'll have him send you flowers," she said, looking at him mischievously, smirking.

"What's that smile for?" said Tito.

"I'm pregnant," she whispered, leaning across the counter toward him, showing off her generous cleavage.

"Ah! *¡Felicidades!*"

"Shh!" she said. "I haven't told *her*."

Her was Lourdes, the owner of the restaurant.

"When are you due?"

"January," said María Luisa.

As if on cue, Lourdes came out of the kitchen and gave María Luisa a get-back-to-work look.

"I better place this order," María Luisa said, holding up her pad. "Coffee is on the house, you hear?" She disappeared through the swinging doors into the kitchen.

Tito put five dollars on the counter and walked out. María Luisa could get into trouble for giving him food.

He went up Broadway and then turned on Vermilyea, going past the fire house and the post office, taking 204 over to Sherman. He had thought María Luisa might have been pregnant before she and Manuel tied the knot—that would have explained her haste to divorce Tito—but a January due date meant they'd probably conceived on their honeymoon. Some kid was going to be born an American citizen because of what he'd done. It didn't feel like a crime.

At Ms. Almonte's building, he was buzzed in without a greeting. She was waiting at her mother's door, wearing those scalpel-like glasses and another sleeveless dress, her arms as narrow as dowels.

"Ah, Mr. Moreno. Thank you for coming so quickly." She opened the door to let him pass into the apartment. It had been a little more than a week since the move but the change in the place was apparent. It was cleaner, brighter, more orderly, as if a dozen unsightly objects had been removed from each room.

"Of course, I'm sorry to hear—"

"I don't care about your apologies. It's very important to me. My mother gave it to me for my *quinceañera*."

"What?"

"The bangle. A gold bangle. It was in the top drawer of my bureau and now it's not there.

"A bangle?"

"Yes. You know what a bangle is, don't you? A circular piece of jewelry worn on the wrist. It's only gold-plated. Whoever stole it won't get much for it—if he is even able to sell it. But it means a great deal to me. I don't like to make accusations, but it was there the day before the move and I haven't seen it since."

Now that he understood, Tito was elated that he wasn't going to have to give back the photograph. "I'm very sorry," he said. "I will look into it."

"Good. I thought you might try to deny that things could go missing during a move."

"No," he said. "I can't deny that."

"Then you should know that there was also two hundred dollars in cash that vanished on the day of the move, but I blame myself for that. You shouldn't leave money lying around when you have strangers in your house. But I'm not worried about the money. It's the bangle I need."

"I promise, I'll do everything I can," he said. "And where *is* your mother?"

Ms. Almonte put her hand to her hair, just a gentle pat, though, from her expression, you'd have thought her head was about to fall off. "She hasn't been feeling well the last couple of days. I finally had to take her to the hospital."

"The hospital?"

"Yes, we were in the emergency room last night, so please forgive me if I'm not quite myself."

"I'm sorry. How long do they think she'll be in there?"

"The doctors don't know." She looked away from him.

"I'm sorry, I should go. I'll do whatever I can to get your bangle back."

"I'd be shocked if it was the little Mexican. You should start with the tall, muscular one," said Ms. Almonte. "I'm sure he took it."

THIS WAS TITO'S thought, too. He could not remember having seen Raúl since the Almonte move. He walked back to where his car was parked, near the restaurant, and drove up Broadway to the Cruz Brothers yard. In the lot, he pulled into his designated spot: T. MORENO—SALES. The yard was almost empty. Only one truck was parked there and its hood was up. The mechanics, Armand and Juan, dressed in soiled red Cruz Brothers T-shirts, sat on folding chairs near the truck drinking bottles of Arizona ice tea and talking about the pennant race. Tito waved at them as he walked along the line of parked employee cars toward the office entrance. Moving, like auto repair and garbage disposal, was a mostly male profession. When he had been on the trucks, he had grown weary of all the macho talk—"I'll-kick-your-ass" this and "Suck-my-cock" that. Now that he was in the field, he dealt mainly with women and was happier. Closer to the office entrance were the three European luxury cars driven by the three Cruz brothers: Ozzie, Ronnie, and Orlando. You could measure your place in the hierarchy by your parking spot, and though Tito had been with the company longer than anyone with a parking space, he was still separated from the brothers by a number of spots.

The offices were in a small building adjacent to the main warehouse. Tito walked through the entrance and turned down a corridor to the cramped room where he and the other sales reps worked.

Only Fat Carl was in there now. He had his feet up on his desk, his head cocked to pin the phone against his massive shoulder. Carl gave Tito a mock salute and Tito thought about going in to shoot the shit. Though he had no other appointments scheduled that morning, he was certain there were messages on his voicemail and e-mails in his in-box. Orlando had promised the reps they would be getting BlackBerrys soon. Tito dreaded the thought—the total intrusion of work into his nonworking hours. He saluted Carl back and proceeded to the dispatch room.

Orlando Cruz, the youngest of the brothers, was in his accustomed place, seated on a chrome-wheeled office chair that had been patched with duct tape, holding a cup of coffee in one hand and a cigarette in the other. He was an old-fashioned two-pack-a-day addict, with a voice to match. Through half-moon spectacles, he looked down at the schedule on his desk and out through the large picture window, monitoring the comings and goings of the company's fleet of trucks. Ozzie and Ronnie Cruz, the elder brothers, were the dealmakers, the public faces of the operation—they negotiated with the corporate clients and insurance companies, bought and sold the trucks and supplies, handled payroll and benefits—but it was Orlando who made the business run day-to-day. He knew every employee by name and could tell you without looking at the schedule where everyone was working on a given shift. It was Orlando who had implemented a computerized inventory system that bar-coded every box and manifest. Señor Homeland Security they called him. Some of the guys liked to joke that pretty soon he'd be implanting GPS chips into their asses so that he'd know when they were cheating on their girlfriends, too. As Tito entered the room, Orlando was busting the balls of one of the crew chiefs on the radio about a parking ticket.

"Don't tell me you couldn't find no parking on Riverside Drive at two in the afternoon."

"Yo!" said the crew chief (Antoine, thought Tito, though he

couldn't be sure). "There was *no* parking. They were filming some dumb-ass movie. There were trailers and trucks all over the mother-fucking place. I double parked, blocked some dude in. All he had to do was ask me to move the truck but he went over to Broadway and found a traffic cop to give me that goddamn ticket."

"It's coming out of your check, man," said Orlando, smiling at Tito. He'd given Tito this treatment many times back when he worked on the trucks.

"No fucking way! You can't do that to me," said Antoine.

"You know what garnishing means? I'm not talking about the cilantro they put on your steak. I'm talking about taking the money for this ticket out of your check."

"That's bullshit, man. You take that out of my check and I ain't gonna have anything left. Not even for a bottle of beer after work on Friday. Not even for that Old English piss."

"Good, you shouldn't be drinking, anyway." *Click.*

Laughing out loud, Orlando swiveled his diminutive self around in the office chair. "Tito Suave!" he said, when his guffaws had subsided. "What's good?"

"Poor Antoine," said Tito. "How are you?"

"Good. You liking your new place? You haven't called your mami begging her to take you back yet?"

"Not yet," said Tito, refusing to take the bait.

Orlando looked a little disappointed not to get a rise out of him. "So, what you need? You come to check on Phil? He's already load-ing up that job of yours on 183rd. You going to swing by there and see how it's going?"

"Probably not. I'm actually looking for Raúl Herrera. Where's he working at today?"

"Nowhere. Raúl hasn't shown up for work in a week," said Orlando.

"A week?"

"Yeah. And if he shows up again it'll be so I can fire his ass.

Should have done it a long time ago. He hasn't been too *consistent* in making it in lately, if you know what I mean. He gave me some story about how his girlfriend left him and he was homeless. What do you want with him? You putting together a crew?"

"Nah. I think he stole something from a client."

"Shit. This guy. Nothing but trouble."

"Yeah."

"You know he was in Rikers, right?"

"No. I thought he was clean."

"It was small-time shit. Drugs. Whatever. I took him on as a favor to a friend of my wife's." Orlando affected a high-pitched voice: "'He needs a job or he'll just go right back to selling.' Last time I do that. You could tell that there was something wack about that kid."

"You know where I can find him?"

"Like I said, he was homeless last I heard. Evelyn will give you whatever address we've got on file. Probably the girlfriend. Did you ever see her?"

"Raúl's girlfriend? No."

"Mmm. She has an ass on her to make you weep. Anyway, maybe someone in her building will know where Raúl is. You want to file insurance for what he stole?"

"Nah. It's worth nothing. Sentimental value."

"One-of-a-kind type deal?"

"Yeah."

"That's the worst. Money can't fix it."

"But it fixes everything else, I guess," said Tito. "I'll see you later."

The hallway that led to the "executive suite" where Ronnie and Ozzie had their offices and private bathroom was lined with photographs of the various iterations of the Cruz Brothers truck, from the seventies when the company was started with a secondhand pickup to the current models, which had air-conditioned cabs and

Orlando's beloved GPS systems. ("You know how much money we lose because our stupid drivers don't know the difference between east and west?" he asked his brothers when they were arguing over the cost.)

Evelyn, the company secretary, sat at her desk with Ronnie's and Ozzie's doors (both closed) behind her. There was a small waiting area with a water cooler, a couch, and a coffee table bearing a two-year-old copy of *Money* magazine's Best Places to Live issue and a *Latina* with J-Lo on the cover. Evelyn was at her desk, trussed into a peach-colored pantsuit, her dyed, wax-colored hair falling to her shoulders in curls, her lipstick glistening, all of this part of her daily effort to disguise her age, which was unknown, though Tito figured she was at least fifty. He always thought she looked and smelled like a dessert—some kind of sundae that sounded irresistible on the menu but turned out to be too rich to finish. They were the two longest-tenured employees of the company not named Cruz, and there was a familial ease between them.

"Tito, baby. How you doing today?"

"Fine, Evelyn. And you?"

"I'm keeping it together. You unpacked yet?"

"Getting there."

"Your momma been sending over care packages for you—*arroz con guandules*? What? *¿Rabo?*"

"Nah. I been eating Chinese, like everyone else in the world who can't cook."

Evelyn laughed. "Ain't that the truth. So what you need? You filing for vacation?"

"No, I'm looking for whatever address you have for Raúl Herrera."

"Raúl. Hmmm. Haven't seen him around in a while. Let me check what we got." She stood and walked to the filing cabinet, which she unlocked. Tito moseyed over as casually as he could to watch her finger the files. She had manicured nails painted with shooting stars. A manila folder came up and was opened. It held a single sheet of paper. Evelyn turned it over.

"Here it is. We was sending his check to 86 Cooper Street, apartment 3G. Why you looking for him?"

"He stole something from a client."

"Oh no he didn't."

"'Fraid so," said Tito.

"You know he was in Rikers, right?"

"Yeah, I do now."

"And you know he was trying to hook up with that chick—the one that got murdered."

"No," said Tito. "He hit on her?"

"She called Ronnie the day after the move and said she was going to sue for sexual harassment or something."

"Did she?"

"No," said Evelyn. "Ronnie talked her down. This is all confidential. You can't be telling nobody. Ronnie would kill me."

"I won't say a word. Thanks, Evelyn."

FOR REASONS HE did not completely understand, this pursuit of Raúl was becoming increasingly urgent for Tito. It jangled déjà vu deep inside him. He turned it over in his mind as he drove south along Broadway. The brothers had a collection agency at their disposal, but he didn't see how he could ask them to recover a bangle, and a cheap one at that. He swerved around a triple-parked car and came to a stop at a light. Nearby, on Dyckman, was the storefront that had once been Lugo Hardware. It was now a place where you could cash checks and send money overseas— probably a front, Tito thought. Staring at the sign ENVIOS DINERO, he connected the déjà vu sensation with the actual memory.

It was his search for Clara, of course. After recovering from the initial shock of her farewell letter, he tried to be stoic, to accept that she was gone, and to be grateful for the pleasures of the summer.

He tried to see it all through her eyes. She was starting anew, going to college, on a path that would take her away from her miserable life in Inwood. (Never mind that he was part of that miserable life.) She didn't want anything—or anyone—holding her back. He talked to himself like this for most of the autumn, talked to himself until he nearly bought it, talked to himself so much that he started to think that he *was* Clara. The explanations and excuses for what she had done became more convoluted and insane every time he went over them. But finally he reached a point where he had to acknowledge the idea that he could not see things from her point of view, that he could not understand what she had done. All his elaborations were no more than an attempt to overcome the fundamental *wrongness* of Clara's note. It didn't add up. Something was missing. As the weeks had progressed toward winter, he'd felt an increasingly frantic need to see her again, even if it would only be an opportunity for her to say, "Can't you read? What part of 'Do not try to contact me' don't you understand?"

Over the Thanksgiving weekend, he took repeated walks past the Lugo house on Payson Street and spent excessive amounts of time sitting on the park wall across the street in the hope that Clara, home from Cornell, would look out from her bedroom window and see him. It was, of course, no more than a continuation of the vigils he had kept earlier in the spring and summer, always waiting, waiting for her. Sometimes it had actually produced results. Clara would emerge from the house and they would go for a walk, kissing in the trees and finding a spot where they could watch the barges and sailboats on the river. But this time there was no sight of her. Her younger brother came out of the house and looked across at him with a *What's-it-to-you?* scowl as he headed down to Broadway. That kid always seemed confused to Tito. Confused and mad about something. Darkness came and Tito climbed down from the wall and went home.

A month later, in the week before Christmas, he encountered

Clara's mother in a discount clothing store on 207th and Sherman. He had not seen her close up in years. Whereas she had once looked fierce, she now seemed embittered, scowling, as if unable to let go of some grievance.

"Señora Lugo?" he said to her as they stood before a rack of winter coats. "How is Clara? Does she like college?"

"Who are you?" she said to him. He'd worried that she might recognize him, but it had been a long time. "Why are you asking me about Clara? What do you know about her?"

"Nothing," said Tito. "She was in my class at Kennedy, that's all."

"How did you know who I am?" she asked, walking around the rack of coats toward him. "How did you know I was her mother?" She looked demented. "Why are you asking me about Clara?"

"Never mind," said Tito. "*Feliz Navidad.*" He got out of there as fast as he could. He heard her voice receding behind him as he made for the exit: "What business is it of his how Clara is doing, hmm? You tell me."

Señora Lugo's vehement reaction and her use of the past tense made him consider, briefly, the idea that Clara was dead—that she had killed herself, that her letter to him was a suicide note. But he knew that wasn't it. She wasn't suicidal. More likely, she was someone who would run away and hide. The way they had conducted their affair over the summer told him that she knew how to pretend, how to deceive. Soon enough, he would become skilled at those arts, too. That autumn, he'd talked to some of their former classmates, going through lists of friends, asking about what so-and-so was doing. Nobody had any news about Clara. The Almonte girls had all dispersed to their fancy schools and it never occurred to him that he could have asked Ms. Almonte herself.

If Clara was home for the holidays, she would be working. During the week between Christmas and New Year's, he went into Lugo Hardware with the hood of his sweatshirt worn over his baseball cap. Don Roberto, probably thinking he was in there to steal something, had watched him the entire time. Tito browsed the aisles of plumbing parts, mini blinds, and cheap saucepans, hoping Clara would come out of the back room. There was no sign of her. After half an hour, he bought a roll of duct tape and left. Maybe Clara's father recognized him, maybe he didn't—he'd said nothing.

Perhaps she had not come back to New York. Perhaps, having had a taste of life away from the city, she was in no hurry to return. Perhaps she had stayed up at Cornell the whole time. There was only one place to go now, and that was to Ithaca. In January, he took a couple of days off work and drove up to the Finger Lakes. The journey took much longer than he expected—almost six hours—and it was dark when he arrived. The farther north and west he'd gone, the whiter the world had become. Snow covered everything from the Catskills through Binghamton and Ithaca. Once in town, he followed the mortarboard signs to the campus, which in its architectural splendor reminded him of Yeshiva University in the Heights. The registrar's office was closed. His search would have to wait until the morning. He took a room in a motel on Route 13. That night, with nothing else to do, he walked around the downtown. It was unbearably cold and there were piles of snow on the sides of all the roads. Tito felt as though he had traveled to another country. He thought of a movie he'd seen once: *Ice Station Zebra*. He half-expected people to speak to him in a foreign language. There was a bar not far from his motel, a student hangout full of people his own age, people who had recently graduated from high schools all across the country, people whose parents were proud to send their children to this frigid, remote town. It was the era of grunge and everyone was wearing denim and flannel. Tito, in his baggy jeans, his Yankees jersey, and his black skullcap, looked like no one else there. He was the only person of color in the room but nobody seemed to notice. Somehow that was even more unnerving. He went back to the motel and watched a movie.

In the morning, he was at the Cornell registrar's office when it opened. The woman behind the window told him that Clara was not currently enrolled at the university. How readily she had given him that information, he thought as he stood outside 86 Cooper. The middle-aged secretary had looked in her computer and said, "We have no record of a student by that name." Tito asked the woman if Clara had been accepted to the school. "I don't see anything to that effect, sir, but you'd have to check with admissions." How the world had changed. *We live in a time of secrets now,* he thought. Secrecy could mean different things in different situations. The openness of that earlier time had not helped him find Clara. He hoped that he would have better luck tracking down Raúl, especially now that the two quests had become fused in his mind—as if returning the bangle to Ms. Almonte would somehow reunite him with Clara. He pressed the button for apartment 3G.

After a time, a voice came over the intercom. "*Sí?*"

"Is Raúl Herrera there?" Tito asked.

"He don't live here no more."

"You know where I can find him?"

"What are you, the police?"

"No. We used to work together."

"Oh," said the voice, pausing. And then, as if speaking to someone else in the apartment: "I thought he wasn't doing that shit no more."

"Do you know where he is?" Tito asked.

"No."

"Can I leave a message for him?"

"You can leave a message, but he ain't gonna get it, 'cause he don't live here no more."

"Thanks."

He looked at the list of names next to the buzzers: FELIZ, CASTILLO, JACOBS, SCHMIDT, ALLEN, ESPINOZA, DAVIES, FRANKEL, LÓPEZ. Still a lot of Spanish in this building, which was not as nice as his father's—not as well maintained, not as close to the park. The neighborhood was changing all around him. On weekends, yellow cabs appeared early in the morning dropping off passengers after a night out downtown. There was a farmer's market now that closed off Isham Street every Saturday afternoon and, in the summers, a Shakespeare festival. He saw the young white kids fresh from Cornell and God knows where else showing their parents around, walking them through the park, boasting about the Cloisters. He saw the older white couples pushing their strollers and talking in the playgrounds. The names beside the doors of apartment buildings were an index of these changes. At the bottom of the tenant list for 86 Cooper was the button for SUPERINTENDENT. This was Santiago's building, Tito remembered. He walked around to a tunnel-like entrance with a grated metal door on the side of the building. The tunnel led through to the airshaft where the garbage cans and recycling containers were kept. Tito knocked. Waited. Knocked again. "Santiago!" he called.

In time, there was the squeak of a hinge followed by the scrape of shoes on cement and a crash of bottles. Tall and thin, with thick glasses and his trademark blue baseball jacket, Santiago emerged into view. His coarse, bristlelike hair was now completely white, but still it looked like you could turn him upside down and paint a wall or clean a toilet with him.

"*Oye,* Santiago! It's Tito Moreno."

"Ah!" said Santiago, tilting his head so that he could see Tito through his bifocals. "Come, come." He unlocked the metal door.

Tito followed him back through the little tunnel into the court-yard, then down a short flight of steps to another door, which led into the boiler room. The sound of those massive boilers—the symphonic hiss and rush of them at work—always comforted him. That sound said heat and hot water for winter mornings. It was a refuge from the elements in this cold city. He had spent all of his life falling asleep to that steam symphony coming through the wall from his little bedroom, and now that he lived on the third floor of his new building, he missed it. What he heard now were horns and sirens and garbage trucks and drunken arguments over some "ho." Being in the basement of Santiago's building somehow made him more nostalgic for his parents' place than when he visited them on the weekend. This may have been because Santiago, who was close to Tito's father in age, lived alone now. His wife had died five years before and his daughters had married and moved out. Santiago had not said a word since opening the gate for him. Tito followed him past the boiler into the basement apartment, which was full of junk.

"*Café?*" said Santiago, leading him into the kitchen.

Tito looked around at the untidiness, registering the complete lack of embarrassment with which his host had invited him into this mess, and he felt an alarm go off inside himself, the alarm saying ·that this was how he was going to end up if he wasn't careful, if he didn't do something soon.

"No, *gracias.*" His heart went out to Santiago, and for a moment he thought he should play matchmaker. He should introduce him to Ms. Almonte's mother. She was probably ten years older than he was, but they had the same unhurried, un-American peasant manner about them. Then he dismissed the idea. Ms. Almonte's mother would probably be dead soon. No point getting Santiago's hopes up.

He watched his host unscrew a metal espresso maker and spoon Bustelo into the filter before filling the base with water and twisting the contraption back together. Santiago set it on the stovetop. Click, click, click, click, poof! The gas came on.

"*¿Tu Mami? ¿Y tu Papi? ¿Cómo están?*" asked Santiago, sitting down at the table.

"*Están bien,*" said Tito.

"You still living there?"

"No. I moved out."

Santiago nodded and once again looked down at him through the lower lenses of his bifocals.

"How are your daughters?" asked Tito.

"Good, good. Elie, she married a policeman. They live in the Bronx. She comes to visit every week. A good daughter. She brings me food all the time. Like I'm going to starve living by myself." Tito remembered Elie, a chunky girl who had grown breasts before any other girl in the fifth grade. The boys used to chase her around the schoolyard trying to grope them. Tito had been one of those boys but had never succeeded in catching Elie.

"And Laura?"

"In Miami." He shook his head. Laura was one of the neighborhood's beauties, a great dancer who had boyfriends early and often.

"Still with the trumpet player?"

Santiago nodded gravely. "What can I do? She's in love. He's in some group down there." He cleared his throat with a tectonic hawk. "So, is somebody moving out upstairs I don't know about? Is that why you're here?"

The espresso maker began to gurgle and percolate, filling the room with the smell of coffee.

"No. I'm looking for a tenant."

"Yes?"

"Raúl Herrera."

Santiago waved dismissively. "He's gone. Wasn't a tenant, either. He was here illegally. Nothing but bad attitude."

"INS got him?"

"No, no. He was illegally in the building. The apartment was in his girlfriend's name. Yunis. She lived here for years."

"Lived?"

"She moved back to D.R. a couple of weeks ago. Sublet the place."

"And Raúl. Did he move with her?"

"Don't know. But I doubt it. Hold on." Santiago stood up and walked out of the room. The espresso maker percolated with an accelerated, percussive bubbling. It sounded like it was going to explode, so Tito switched off the gas. The stove top was covered in spills and coffee grounds.

Santiago returned, holding a piece of paper.

"I've got an address where I'm supposed to send the mail," he said, looking at the words on the paper as if they were written in Cyrillic. "Someplace in New Jersey."

TITO WAS LATE for his first estimate of the day, a big house in Riverdale. He often wondered why someone this rich would call Cruz Brothers and not Allied or Mayflower. Maybe his estimate was a bargaining chip. Maybe you ended up in a house like this by going to the effort of finding the best price for everything you bought.

After that, he stopped for a late lunch at the Riverdale Diner, bringing his New York and vicinity road atlas to the table to look up the address that Santiago had given him. Millwood. One of those generic town names New Jersey was full of: Springfield, Union, Somerville. It was in Essex County. Millwood's proximity to Newark suggested a lateral move for Raúl, from one ghetto to another. Maybe some of his old pals from Rikers lived out there.

On his way to the George Washington Bridge, he stopped back in at the Cruz Brothers offices to check in with Orlando and pick up a box of flyers. This would be his business justification for the trip. Planting the seeds of new business. Expanding the customer base. All that horseshit the brothers liked to say.

When he got off the Garden State Parkway in Irvington, his suspicions were confirmed: burned-out buildings, twenty-four-hour go-go bars, and not a white face to be seen. He drove through Irvington and headed south and west along local roads, the neighborhoods improving every couple of blocks. He passed a shopping plaza and turned onto a tree-lined street with large, old houses and well-tended lawns. It reminded him of the street in Bergen County where Ms. Almonte had moved from and it gave him pause. What was Raúl or his girlfriend doing having mail sent to this address?

He parked across the street from the house, a gabled white colonial, and decided to sit there for a few minutes. The driveway was empty and the light outside the front door had been left on the night before. He scanned the windows for movement, but saw nothing. It was a warm, beautiful early autumn afternoon. The leaves had not yet started to fall and there was not even a hint of winter in the wind, but he knew it was coming. In a few weeks the gutters would be choked with nature's orange and yellow refuse. Tito reclined his seat to hide himself as much as possible from passersby while keeping his lookout for Raúl. He covered his eyes with the brim of his cap. In five minutes, he'd fallen asleep.

The sound of a door slamming woke him. For a second he had no idea where he was. Then he remembered and anxiously thought that maybe a police officer was coming. His shirt was damp where it had been in contact with the upholstery. He rubbed his eyes and lifted his cap. A minivan was now in the driveway of the house across the street. The engine cut off and a chubby, brown-skinned girl in overalls and short sleeves walked from the car toward the front of the house. On her arm—*son of a bitch*—was what looked from this distance to be a gold bangle. But he didn't have time to dwell on that, because the driver's side door slammed and, around the back of the minivan, here came Clara.

Thomas

Thomas walked Guillermo down to the corner to wait for the school bus. The intersection of Passaic Street and Irvington Avenue, where they waited every day, marked the border between Millwood and the westernmost encroachment of the city of Newark. On their side of the road, there were single-family homes leading, block by tree-lined block, to a town center that boasted a country club, microbrewed beer, and handmade ice cream. On the other side of the avenue, facing Millwood, was a strip mall with a decrepit dollar store, a supermarket that smelled like rotting meat, and a Chinese takeout joint where the cooks worked behind bulletproof glass. The brown brick towers of the Ivy Hill apartments loomed above the stores as if ready to mug them. He and Clara had come to Millwood because they'd heard a lot about the town's ethnic diversity—that it was a place in the suburbs where no one looked twice at a mixed-race family. What they hadn't heard as much about was the high cost of real estate there. It was only the ominous proximity of those Ivy Hill high-rises that brought the asking price of the third house they saw within their range.

The scene on Irvington Avenue no longer alarmed or amazed him as it had when they'd first moved. It had taken a little while to get used to the idea that the poor and middle class lived so close to each other here. In this part of New Jersey, half a mile separated a street you wouldn't walk down from a street you'd never want to leave. That seemed fine for the city, but not for the suburbs—and certainly not for the suburbs where Thomas had grown up. Barely a week went by without a story in the *Star-Ledger* about a fire in one of those nearby neighborhoods in which an elderly person or a young child died because their rental quarters were not equipped with smoke detectors or a fire escape. The previous week an explosion had destroyed half a dozen vacant houses in Hillside when drug addicts scavenging for scrap metal had accidentally cut a gas pipe. People always talked about the inconveniences of New York City—the crowds, the high prices, the noise—but what about all the conveniences of the place? They sometimes only became apparent once you'd left.

The school bus arrived in due time, halting at the curb in front of them, deploying its STOP sign and bringing the traffic on Irvington Avenue to a standstill. The doors accordioned open to reveal the two West African men—the driver, Jin, and his aide, Kimbe. Both wore tropical shirts and straw fedoras. Thomas always imagined them as missionaries delivering kids from a war zone. "Good morning, Germo!" they bellowed, abbreviating his name into something they could pronounce.

Guillermo said, "Hi!" and climbed the three steps, a smile on his face because riding in this big yellow machine never got old for him. Thomas handed Kimbe the backpack and leaned in to kiss his son on the cheek.

"Bye, Daddy!" said Guillermo. All had been forgiven with the purchase of the robot.

"Bye," said Thomas. "Have fun today."

The doors closed, the STOP sign folded back, and the bus pulled away. Traffic resumed behind it. In the tinted glass of the bus's window, Thomas could just see Guillermo waving. He waved back and watched the bus head down the avenue. Saying goodbye to his son every morning never failed to break his heart, but these last few weeks, when everything seemed to be turning to shit, it was especially poignant for him—as if, each time, he were rehearsing a much bigger goodbye.

Walking back to the house, Thomas considered with some amazement just how screwed up things had gotten. Miscarriage, layoff, and now he found himself a pseudo-stepfather to Clara's pregnant niece. What would that make him in relation to her child once it was born? Pseudo-stepgrandfather? Did they have greeting cards for that? Deysei had been living with them for almost two weeks now and so far, it had not yet been as bad as he'd feared, but it was only a matter of time, he knew, until something else happened, some new complication that would make them all wish Deysei had never moved in. There was always this kind of kicker in every dealing with Clara's family. They agreed to meet you at an expensive restaurant and then announced they were broke. They borrowed your car and returned it with no gas in the tank. They asked you to look after their teenage daughter and then revealed that she was pregnant.

Thomas bypassed the front door and proceeded to the driveway, where the Odyssey was parked. He got in and backed the van out. At the corner, he turned left on Irvington Avenue, passing the discount gas station that served as his barometer of the economy—and thus, his employment prospects. If the price of a gallon of regular had gone down, all was well. If the price had gone up, there was reason to be worried. He'd submitted several job applications in the past few weeks and so was disappointed to see that the plastic numerals atop the faded blue filling station sign showed an increase of three cents a gallon.

Putting this omen out of his mind, he motored into the center of Millwood and parked in the municipal lot. Just off the main street was a florist's shop, where he bought a bouquet of flowers—a spray of irises and snapdragons. He got back in the van and drove out to the far side of town, ascending the hill to the lower slopes of South Mountain. Carved into the gently graded base of the hill was Newstead, a neighborhood of multimillion-dollar homes, the beginning of a swathe of wealth that continued south and west through Short Hills and Summit to Morris County.

Thomas parked the Odyssey in front of a mock Tudor mansion complete with exposed beams, cross-hatched windows, and mushroom-shaped chimney pots. He walked along the paved walkway to the front door, looking at the neighboring houses as he did so. The street was deserted. People who lived in these houses either went to work early or enjoyed the privilege of not having to work at all. Thomas had come to see one of the latter, who was a widow to one of the former.

On his way up the path he couldn't help but notice that the FOR SALE sign planted in the lawn now had a CONTRACT PENDING banner attached to it. This house had been a place of respite and escape from his troubled year. He pictured her, Melissa, his mistress, sitting in the kitchen right now, reading the paper, the long, tanned length of her arm revealed by one of those sleeveless tops she liked to wear in the summer. He imagined her looking up as he rang the bell and walking through her house toward him. He understood now that he had come here too often, dropping by unexpectedly whenever he had an hour to spare. And it wasn't always for some quick satisfaction against the kitchen counter or a make-out session in her sumptuous living room. More often than not, he was happy just to be near her, to shadow her as she worked in the garden, to sit with her for a few minutes while she watched something on TV, to enjoy the kind of stress-free pleasure he rarely felt in his own home. It was like dropping in on the life he might have with her, a tantalizing prospect. *Let's go see what I'd be doing right now if I married Melissa.*

That is the way it had been throughout the spring and summer until, in August, Melissa had informed him that her period was late. The irony of it, coming after Clara's latest miscarriage, was not lost on him.

"What are you going to do?" he had asked her.

"I'm keeping it. The question is, what are *you* going to do?"

A few days later, her period arrived and, he thought, the catastrophe was averted. But Melissa saw it differently. "Baby or no baby, I need an answer from you, Thomas. Are you going to be with me? Are you going to leave your wife?"

He cradled the flowers and rang the bell and stood back on the brick porch expectantly. Moments later, Melissa's shape became visible through the translucent pebbled glass of the front door, just as he'd imagined. The door unlatched and there she was, saying, "Somehow I knew it was going to be you." The cold front of air-conditioned interior air flowed onto him, evaporating the sweat on his forehead.

"Hi," he said. He leaned in and kissed her. "You have time for a quick cup of coffee?"

She smiled and shook her head. She was leaning on the open door in such a way that he could not see her left arm and leg. What parts of her he could see—the right arm with its Wonder Woman–like silver bracelet, the right leg encased in a pair of blue linen capri pants, her head, with the short strawberry-blond hair and blue-gray eyes—were as enticing and appealing as ever. He noticed that she was wearing a pair of those rubber gardening shoes that had become so trendy that year. They looked terrible on her and obscured her pretty, pedicured toes.

"Have you thought about what I said last week?"

"Yes," he said. "I've thought of hardly anything else."

"And," she said, swinging the door toward him a fraction of an inch. "Do you have an answer for me?"

He looked past her for a moment, into the house. Right behind her was the living room, which was darkened, but, beyond that darkness, he could see into the kitchen, which had a skylight and was flooded with the summer sun. The kitchen is where he'd hoped to be this morning.

"No," he said. "Not yet."

"OK," she said. "Then I'm afraid I don't have time for coffee this morning, Tom. And I can't accept those flowers, no matter how beautiful they are."

"Come on," he said. "It's not easy."

"I know it's not easy; it's not easy for me, either," she said. "But I need an answer. Come back when you have one, sweetheart." And she closed the door. It was not quite a slam, but abrupt enough to sound like a rebuke.

MELISSA HAD BEEN his last client, the final job for BiblioFile, before he'd been laid off. Thomas continued to view his time there as halcyon, more so with each passing week of unemployment. He still recalled, with anguish, the winter morning he'd been summoned to his supervisor's office. Broadly speaking, there were three kinds of employees at the company: the programmers, or "techs"; the librarians, or "knowledge managers"; and the salesmen, or "money guys." Thomas's supervisor, Anderson, was a former tech who'd risen to the executive ranks. Thomas knew that people (including Clara) thought of him as a geek, but Anderson was a geek of a different magnitude, a geek's geek.

Anderson's office was bland and not large—not corner. You wouldn't know about Anderson's family from his desk; only his wedding band told you he was married. There were no honeymoon pictures, no kids' drawings. On the wall, in a chrome frame, was a certificate of merit from the corporate headquarters in Kansas City, and on the desk—its centerpiece and conversation starter—was the motherboard from Anderson's first computer, a Commodore 64. The strip of circuitry and soldered metal had been ripped out of its casing and mounted on a lucite base, like some ancient Sumerian relic. Thomas had once made the mistake of asking him about it. For twenty minutes, Anderson had recalled the details of the machine's life—its purchase, its central place in his teenage years, and its ultimate obsolescence and replacement. Those circuits had carried his first attempts at machine code and he was sentimental about them the way others were about their Dick and Jane books.

"Come in, Walker," said Anderson. It was January 3, the second work day of the new year.

He went in and sat on one of the cold, metal-framed chairs before Anderson's desk.

"We have a new job for you. It's a little unusual—a solo project. But before I get into the details, there's something I have to discuss with you." Here Anderson paused and adjusted his wire-frame spectacles. "As you know, there have been great improvements recently in machine-generated indexing and taxonomies. Increasingly, the role of the knowledge managers on our staff is to monitor the programatically generated databases rather than to do indexing by hand. The feeling among the folks in Kansas City is that a dedicated librarian is no longer needed on each of our major projects. Henceforth, librarians will be asked to work on multiple projects simultaneously."

"Sure," said Thomas, still not suspecting where this was going. "I used machine indexing on the Rutgers job last year."

"And with good results, I might add," said Anderson. He cleared his throat. "What it also means, Walker, is that we need fewer knowledge managers on our staff. Each office has been asked to eliminate one position. I'm afraid that the position New York is eliminating is yours."

Thomas felt a low-voltage current course through his shoulders and down his arms. With difficulty, he swallowed. "I'm being fired?" he asked.

"Not fired," said Anderson. "Laid off."

"Why me?" asked Thomas. There were four other librarians in the New York office and he knew he was a better worker than at least two of them.

"We figured that the only fair way to do this was by seniority. You have the shortest tenure with us."

"But Chen and I started at almost the same time."

"Chen was hired three months before you. It just took us a little while to sort out his visa. Besides, in addition to his MLS, Chen has considerable programming experience. I'm sorry, Walker, there's no nice way to do this. It's not personal and it's no reflection on your work, which has been more than satisfactory. We'll be giving you six months' severance pay and a package that also includes a fund for retraining. I strongly suggest you use that time and money to improve your programming skills. If you can learn to write code, you can punch your own ticket."

Thomas looked at the motherboard on Anderson's desk. He wanted to throw it out the window behind Anderson, wanted to watch it explode into pieces on the Midtown pavement below. "I'll bear that in mind," he said.

"Good. Go see Mindy Evans in HR tomorrow. She'll give you all the details and there will be some paperwork for you to sign. Now, the job I mentioned is something we think you'll be perfect for. The technical requirements are relatively modest and you'll have the resources of the programming and Web design departments at your disposal. The client is a widow who wants her husband's library cataloged. It's in your town in New Jersey, which is one of the reasons we thought of you. You've been doing a lot of traveling for us lately. We hope it will give you a chance to seek other opportunities and also see some more of your family." What Anderson didn't know was that Clara was, at that time, pregnant again—just six weeks along.

Thomas had heard that BiblioFile took on private libraries, but he had never worked on such a project himself. He was given a primer for estimating job costs and dispatched to the site, told to take the rest of the day off after he made his visit. He was distraught. He had pictured himself working at BiblioFile for decades, maybe one day rising to the executive ranks in the New York office—when Anderson was inevitably promoted to the inner cabal in Kansas City. On the train ride out to Millwood, he called Clara.

"Those shits," she said. "I can't believe those bastards. Are you all right?"

"I don't know," he said. "I feel like I need to rethink everything. Start from scratch again. They kicked me in the nuts."

"Take it easy, Thomas. You'll find another job. No problem. They'll regret it. When's your last day?"

"In about six weeks," he said. "They're throwing me a bone. I'm going to be cataloging a library in Newstead."

"In Millwood?"

"Yes."

"Well, at least you'll be near home," said Clara. "Promise me you won't worry too much? Please?"

"I'll do my best," he said. "But I really don't know . . ."

"Man, what timing. We only just found out that I'm pregnant."

"Well, I'm sure I'll be able to find something before the baby comes."

He got off the train and went to the Odyssey, which was parked in the station lot and drove to Newstead. All joy had been sucked out of his world. Here he was, in the darkest, coldest part of the year, a little tired and wrung out, about to be unemployed, squinting toward spring and rubbing his hands together for warmth. It was the third day since a moderate snowfall and a cold snap had combined to put a crust of ice on everything in the region, which only added to the sense of gelid torpor.

He parked in front of the house, next to the two-foot-high alpine ridge the snowplows had left along the length of the road. Up and down the street, discarded Christmas trees lay half-submerged in the roadside snowdrifts, their branches poking through the snow like fingers. Walking the salted flagstone path, he became self-conscious about how much he resembled a door-to-door salesman:

suit, overcoat, briefcase. He would not have felt so conspicuous in the reception area of a bank or the lobby of a high-rise office building, but here, a mile from his own home, he was the victim of something close to embarrassment. He already felt unemployed, already felt as if he were begging favors. Pausing, he glanced up and down the street at the wintry, socked-in houses and gave a little snort to reassure himself. Who would even be looking?

The door was answered by a young, attractive blond woman wearing white jeans and a white woolen turtleneck, the weave of which was just loose enough to show the white outline of her bra. Thomas assumed she was the widow's daughter. "Hello," he said. "I'm Thomas Walker, from BiblioFile."

"I'm Melissa Logan. Come in," she said, and extended her hand. She had long, warm fingers and the strong grip of a tennis player or golfer. Even now, in the middle of winter, she displayed the solid, season-defying tan of someone who spent time in warmer climes. Thomas imagined her flying in from Sanibel or La Jolla to comfort her desolate mother. Melissa allowed him to pass through the entry hall into a formal living room formidably turned out in neoclassical style. Two years after he and Clara bought their home, they were still furnishing it, and every time he saw a room like this—a finished idea with a coherent style and a tasteful palette—he realized how far they still had to go.

"The library is this way," Melissa said, closing the front door and gesturing at a passageway off the living room. The motion pulled the sleeve of her turtleneck down her forearm, and Thomas saw a chunky silver bracelet emerge from the flared cuff. *These rich girls and their distinctive jewelry,* he thought. At the end of the passageway there was a large room lined with books and furnished with a Stickley desk and two wood-paneled filing cabinets. It was cozy but decidedly masculine in its details. The bust of someone he didn't recognize—not the usual Shakespeare or Beethoven— stood on the desk. Maps and portraits of generals on horseback decorated the walls. *Prussians,* thought Thomas, for no reason. *Hessians.* A vitrine nearby contained weapons and military accessories. At a glance, he saw a Samurai sword, a long-nosed revolver, and a brass field glass. Automatically, he began scanning the shelves. The bookcases were expensive built-ins, with slide-out browsing tables and good lighting. He saw a biography of Bismarck. Or maybe it was a book about the battleship *Bismarck,* because next to it was a book about the *Graf Spee* and another about the *Tirpitz.* Already he was free-associating, thinking about index terms, moving away from the disappointment of the morning. At least there was still pleasure in his work. Phrases drifted into his mind: *pocket battleship, Allied shipping lines, Scapa Flow.* What would the proper sequence be? Naval Vessels—Germany—Twentieth Century? Second World War—Battleships—Germany? Taking the book from the shelf, he checked the copyright page, but it was in German and he couldn't make heads or tails of it. He flipped to the seam of glossy photo pages in the middle. There was the *Bismarck* in dry dock being constructed. There was the *Galahad,* one of its victims. There was the British aircraft carrier *Ark Royal* with its cloth-winged biplanes. A map showed the pursuit of the *Bismarck* across the seven seas to its final standoff in the Rio Plata. The sound of Melissa seating herself behind the desk startled him and he looked up from the pictures. He'd assumed that she had gone to fetch her mother. Maybe the mother was still too distraught to conduct business.

"Ah, sorry," he said, slipping the book back into place. He picked up his briefcase and moved to one of the chairs before the desk.

"Military history," Melissa said. "That was my husband's passion." She paused, as if caught in a fib. "More than a passion," she said, with the same pained and bemused condescension that Thomas had heard from women all his life when discussing their husbands' pursuits and interests: hunting, stamp collecting, rock climbing. Whatever it was, the wife had to endure it, like a preexisting medical condition or a thorny set of in-laws. Thomas's own father was an amateur astronomer. Copies of *Sky and Telescope* and the *Journal of the British Interplanetary Society* had piled up in the basement of his childhood home. Many times in his youth, his father had woken him in the middle of the night to show him some comet tracing its once-a-century trail across the heavens, or a lunar eclipse, which was inevitably obscured by an overcast sky. The scale of time and distance involved in astronomy and the optical leaps required to participate in it were too daunting for Thomas. He needed something more immediate. His own experience with marriage was that these kinds of interests became increasingly developed and intransigent the longer you were together. It was a way of differentiating yourself, of holding on to an identity within the marital unit. A fiancé with passion for old wars might not have seemed such a problem to tennis-playing Melissa when she was engaged, just as his own mother, a needle-pointer and knitter, might have downplayed his father's interest in the heavens.

Thomas nodded and smiled, sympathetically.

Melissa pointed at the shelves. "That's just part of it. He belonged to this gaming club." She paused, as if she was about to reveal something long-guarded about her husband. "Rather than trying to explain, maybe you should just follow me." They went back into the living room and then through the formal dining room into the expansive, light-filled kitchen—the room where he would spend many hours with her in the coming months. A flight of stairs descended into a finished basement. It was a dull, functional space, like a bachelor apartment under the house. The furnishings were Spartan: a minifridge, a TV/DVD set up on an old faux-lacquered cabinet. Maps and charts were tacked to the walls along with the well-known portrait of a black sailor from the Revolutionary War. In the middle of the room was a Ping-Pong-sized table on which a green baize had been spread in an undulating layer. It was a landscape, like one you'd see on a model railroad layout, only there were no tracks. Instead, there were configurations of lead soldiers, cannon, tents, and a church painted as if on fire, cottonballs of smoke rising from the shattered stained-glass windows.

"Shiloh," she said. "I think."

Thomas cocked an eyebrow. "Is this part of the job?"

"No," she said. "But these are."

Shelved in a bookcase near the table were dozens of composition books with flecked black and white covers. Thomas pulled one down and opened to a random page. "The Battle of Austerlitz," was written at the top of the page. There were lines of text in some kind of shorthand describing the moves in the battle.

"Logs," said Melissa. "They need to be scanned."

"Right," said Thomas. "Anything else down here?"

"No," she said. It seemed like she couldn't wait to leave.

He was there for another hour, taking a closer look at things and asking her questions. In addition to cataloging the library and scanning the game logs, Thomas was to cross-index them on a Web site so that a log from a battle would be linked to the appropriate titles in the library. This was to be her husband's parting gift to the members of his gaming club. Once the library had been cataloged, it would be transferred, he was told, to another gamer's house. Thomas gave her the name of a moving company that specialized in libraries. He went over his notes and arrived at a figure. The pricing for private collections was the same as for corporate clients. When he presented her with the estimate for the job, he assumed she would blanche. But Melissa glanced at it for the briefest of moments before saying, "Great. When can you start?"

Two days later, having been to see Mindy Evans in HR, having agreed (what choice did he have?) to the terms of his severance, having received the sympathetic handshakes and backslaps of his colleagues, who were, he could tell, relieved that it wasn't them, he returned to Melissa's house with a scanner, sheets of bar code stickers, and a laptop computer. The house had high-speed Internet access, and so he could download MARC records and wireframes from the Web developers. Despite his initial reaction, he was intrigued by his client. He felt that he had known women like her since high school; or, more precisely, he felt that he had been unable to know women like her since high school—attractive, cultured, and somewhat bored daughters of privilege who had seen so much of the world by the time they were eighteen that it was impossible to talk to them, let alone impress them. They'd had boyfriends ten years their senior, tried every drug and every position in the *Kama Sutra,* knew ahead of time what was going to be in fashion that season, and had already developed tastes in obscure writers and indie rock bands. Bethesda, where he'd grown up, had been full of such young sophisticates; so had Boston, where he'd gone to college. They could be found in New York, too, of course, but, by the time Thomas got there, he had given up on them; he was moving in another direction, a direction that would bring him to Clara.

He set up in the library. The deceased husband, Stephen, had his books organized chronologically, starting with the Babylonians and ending with books about Al Qaeda and the war on terrorism. (He'd like to see the layout for that game!) Many of the books were already in OCLC, so it was a simple matter of copy cataloging. At some point he'd have to access the library of the Imperial War Museum to process the more rarefied stuff. He played Stan Getz on the laptop's meager sound system as an antidote to the bleak weather outside and the bleak news about his career. The house was warm. He took off his jacket and rolled up his sleeves: the image of hard work. Soon he was contentedly lost in it.

At twelve-thirty, Melissa knocked on the door. "Would you like some lunch?" she asked. He had not seen her since his arrival that morning, when she'd given him a key and told him how to deactivate the alarm system. She said she would be in and out of the house all day, and he figured he'd drive into the center of town for lunch. As he worked, he'd heard her elsewhere in the house—footfalls and closing doors. And now she leaned on the entrance to her dead husband's library, her arms folded across her chest. She was more casually dressed—light gray cords, a pale pink Izod shirt, and a pair of matching Pumas, which looked like the shoes worn by tightrope walkers. Maybe she was a little older than he'd thought the day he'd come to give her the estimate. Maybe she was closer to him in age than he'd first figured.

"OK," said Thomas, setting down a book on the Battle of Thermopylae.

"Good!" She gave him a little nod.

In the kitchen, he washed the dust from his hands. The farmhouse-style table had been set with two places. There was soup, a loaf of crusty bread, and a plate of cheese and grapes. A colorful bottle of mineral water stood like a maypole in the middle of it all.

"I didn't know this was part of the deal," said Thomas.

"It's nothing," she said, seating herself and indicating that he should do the same. "So, how's it going?"

"Fine." Thomas tasted the soup—minestrone—and wondered if she had made it herself. The sink and the Viking range were spotless, as if the meal had been brought in by a caterer.

"My husband, Stephen, spoke highly of your work."

Thomas gave her a quizzical look.

"Your team worked for him at Norse McConnell. He was a partner there."

"Stephen Logan?"

"No. Logan's my maiden name. Stephen Epstein."

"Ah," said Thomas. "Right." Norse McConnell was an accounting firm that had hired BiblioFile to digitize its archives. Stephen Epstein was the partner they'd dealt with. Thomas recalled talking to him about Suetonius's *The Twelve Caesars,* which he had been reading after seeing *Gladiator* on DVD with Clara. "If you like that, you should read Caesar's *Civil War.* I have a copy. I'll bring it in for you," Epstein had said to him, but he'd never followed through, and Thomas had never gotten around to reading it.

"It was in his will," said Melissa. "He wanted BiblioFile to do this thing with his library."

"He asked for us by name? In his will?"

"Yes."

"That's flattering," said Thomas. "I guess he liked the work we did for Norse."

"You should be flattered. Stephen was hard to please." She immersed her spoon in the soup. "Do you think your estimate is realistic? Six weeks?"

"Definitely. We're going to have the notebooks OCR'd by a subcontractor in Bangladesh."

"You're sending the notebooks to Bangladesh?" There was a note of distress in her voice.

"No, just the page scans. By FTP."

"Ah," she said, vaguely. "I don't mean to rush you. It's just that I can't sell the house until you finish."

"You're selling the house?" Thomas didn't know when her husband had died or where in the grieving process she might be. He knew well enough how people could become unmoored by losses of this kind and briefly had a picture of Melissa wandering the world's sunny spots in grief, living off the million or more she was bound to get for the place.

"This summer. It's too big for just me. Besides, I've never really loved the suburbs. I'm more of a city person. Stephen grew up in Newark and always wanted a place like this. He'd already bought this house when we met."

"I see," said Thomas. He remembered Epstein as being mid-fifties, smart and assertive, a little portly and graying, but hardly in decline. *What killed him?* Thomas wondered. He would have to look it up. This was going to be the strangest job he had ever worked. Out of the office, with no colleagues around, the trappings of the professional world gone. Somehow, it didn't feel quite legitimate. Anything might happen.

"You shouldn't have any trouble selling this place," he said.

IN HIS MIND, that week was when the affair, which was not consummated until early March, had begun. Not during the lunch itself, but during the nights that followed, when he found himself behaving in peculiar ways. There were many things about this new job that he did not discuss with Clara—things that got overshadowed by the larger discussion of his pending unemployment. For one, he did not tell her that the widow was young and attractive; he simply let his wife assume that he was working for some crone who'd been married for half a century to a Seton Hall professor. He also did not tell Clara that the widow was making him lunch every day. Thomas even went so far as to pack himself a decoy lunch sometimes, saying it was too cold to leave the house to get something in town. These small deceptions and omissions added up, over time, to the big lie. The affair, which began as a guilty dalliance in his imagination, an escape from job loss and other troubles, eventually manifested itself, weeks later, in reality.

As the days passed, he looked more and more forward to going to work. While the long-term forecast was gloomy, there was warmth and light in the short term. He was pleased and surprised at how much time Melissa spent with him. She would bring him coffee, sit in one of the leather chairs in the study, and read one of her husband's books while Thomas worked, sometimes calling out a bit of information. "Did you know that Napoleon put buttons on the sleeves of his soldiers' coats to stop them from wiping their noses on their uniforms?" There were also stretches of time when she was not there. She had a twice-weekly tennis game at an indoor court in Montclair. Through the Tudor windows, he saw her departing in her form-fitting sweats and a puffy down jacket, the Prince bag over her shoulder. When she was out of the house, he fought hard against the temptation to nose around. Once, he gave himself a tour of the upper floor. The house was well kept except for the master suite, which was in disarray. There were bags and clothes piled up on the carpet, towels left on the floor. It looked like she might be going through her husband's things, or maybe she'd already started packing for when she sold the house. He touched nothing but stood in the room with the blunted winter light coming in through the blinds and briefly imagined how his own house would feel if Clara and Guillermo suddenly vanished. Stillness would come to mean sadness. The mundane sights of his existence would suddenly seem melancholy. He could see himself looking for company, becoming chatty with the UPS driver or the plumber, desperately wanting relief from loneliness and emptiness.

When she returned from tennis, she was not alone. At first he thought it might be a man she'd brought home, and he was simultaneously relieved and jealous. But it was a woman she led into the library, the pair of them holding bottles of Vitaminwater. Melissa's tennis partner was a little older, with thick auburn hair, wrinkles in her cleavage, and a big shiny diamond on her ring finger.

"So *you're* Tom! Nice to meet you," said the woman, who was introduced as Lynne. He had the sense of being evaluated by her.

"You, too," he said. "Good game?"

"No game. We just knocked the ball around for a while."

Later, he heard them laughing in the kitchen, but he couldn't make out what they were saying. It was the first time he had heard Melissa give a full laugh. Something was making her happy.

THE JOB TURNED out to be easier than he thought, requiring less time than he'd predicted. (Epstein was, not surprisingly, a very organized man.) Thomas had looked him up on Nexis. He'd died of a brain aneurism in November, aged 49, survived by his wife, Melissa, 31. Thomas hoped that the collection would tell him more and searched the books for underlining, highlighting, marginalia, and ephemera, but the books were pristine. They looked unread, like books in a bookstore, except each volume had a bookmark on the last page, and the bookmark—a three-by-five index card—held a list of page numbers. Next to some of the page numbers were symbols, such as an asterisk, a question mark, or a check. On the card for the first volume of Shelby Foote's *Civil War: A Narrative,* he found the following:

36
37
293*
305
335
580
792
794

That wasn't many numbers for a very long book. As Melissa had said, Epstein was hard to please. Thomas followed the asterisk to page 293 and saw the tiniest of dots in the margin next to a sentence about how Jefferson Davis had once imported camels to try to facilitate populating the southwestern United States. It was an interesting enough historical anecdote, but it told him nothing about Epstein. Many of Thomas's investigations wound up this way, which is to say inconclusively. Nor were there many revelations to be found in the log books from the battles. They were a bore to read, no more than chronicles of troop movements, feints, attacks, counterattacks, casualty tables, wins, and losses, the handwriting so exactly precise that OCR was a breeze. Thomas wanted the human element—evidence of fear, dismay, and, occasionally, triumph—but he suspected, from the evidence of the library and the logs, that Epstein's goal in life had been to squash such things. About the only thing Thomas gleaned from his work on the library was Epstein's admiration for certain generals: Grant, Rommel, and Pershing. And so, maybe the library did tell him something in the end: that Epstein had been all about control.

Thomas slowed his pace of work in February; he began lingering over the lunches with Melissa. He began pausing to read passages from some of the books. He was dreading his looming idleness, but even more he was dreading not having a reason to come to Melissa's house every day. The scans arrived from Bangladesh, where they had been sorted into a fielded database, searchable by date, nationality, commanding officer, and so on. Thomas had never been to BiblioFile's facility in Dhaka, but he had often spoken to the staff there, Bangladeshis with Anglophone (and probably bogus) names like Rupert, Winston, and Matilda. Business hours in New York meant that it was the middle of the night in Dhaka, but he could always hear the hum of the call center in the background, the sound of hundreds of BiblioFile clients across the United States receiving customer support. He could not help thinking that the workforce in Dhaka was also partly to blame for his downsizing.

Melissa seemed to be aware of his dawdling, seemed to welcome it. A kind of heightened conspiratorial intimacy had developed between them. Two of Thomas's college love affairs had begun in the last weeks of the academic year, when nobody seemed to care about consequences and everybody was bent on not letting opportunities slip away. As he neared the completion of his work on the Epstein library, he had the same feeling. During one of their February lunches, he asked her how she had met her husband.

"Ah," and here she hesitated, dipping her spoon into her soup. "I worked for him. After college, I was with a temp agency and they sent me to Norse McConnell to replace his secretary, who was on maternity leave. He dismissed me after a week, called me into his office on Friday afternoon, and I remember thinking how upset he looked. I thought he was going to ream me, to tell me I'd been doing a terrible job, but he explained that he was transferring me to another department because he wanted to ask me out on a date and it wouldn't be appropriate for him to do so while I was working for him. He said he hadn't been able to concentrate all week because of having to talk to me and walk past me every day. 'Look at me,' he said. 'I fire people all the time and never give it a second thought, but here I am talking to *you* and suddenly I'm all flustered.'" She dropped her voice to imitate her deceased husband, fretted her brow and clutched her fists. Thomas loved it.

"Stephen was a gentleman," she went on. "He had these very old-fashioned manners, wore a pocket square, all that. All of that stuff was very important to him. He'd grown up poor—he was a self-made man. He took me once to the street in Newark where he'd spent his early childhood. It was one of the streets that was burned in the riots in the sixties. I don't know if you've ever seen it, but there are still blocks of Newark that haven't been rebuilt from the summer of 1967."

Thomas *had* seen them. Not long after he and Clara moved to Millwood, he'd taken a drive through Newark. The city frightened him.

"So, did you feel like a prize?" he asked her.

"You mean a trophy wife?"

"Sort of, but more than that."

"No one has ever had the guts to ask me that, though I'm sure most people think it. You know what? Yeah, sometimes. And, you know what else? I didn't think it was so terrible to be his prize. To be valued that way. Whatever else happened, I always felt important to him, cherished." She paused. "I'm only starting to figure some of these things out now that he's dead. Do you ever feel that way with your wife?"

"Like a prize? No. It's different—" Thomas got up from the kitchen table and the vegetable soup they had been eating to answer his cell phone, which was ringing in the library. He thought it might be Anderson checking in with him, but the caller ID showed an Essex County area code with a number he did not recognize.

"Hello?"

"Thomas?" It was Clara's voice.

"Yes?"

"I'm at Summit Hospital. I need you to get over here. Dr. Simeon's office."

"What is it?"

"Just come. Now."

"I'll be right there." He knew what this meant. He flipped his phone closed and went back into the kitchen, where Melissa had stopped eating.

"I have to go," he said.

"Is everything OK?"

"That was my wife," he said. "Sorry. Family emergency."

Melissa held up both hands in a gesture of surrender. "Go," she said.

Thomas felt ashamed of himself. He wanted to get the hell out of there. He did not want to have to explain what was going on.

"I'll see you tomorrow," he said.

He drove out to Summit. The hospital was on a large campus with landscaped grounds and lots of new construction. He took the elevator up to the OB/GYN offices and failed, at first, to spot Clara in the waiting room, which was crowded with pregnant women turning the pages of magazines like some kind of bizarre, silent book club. Already he felt an unreasonable dislike of them, the bloated fertility so proudly flaunted, clutching at their bellies as they moved, wearing their babydoll tops to show off their enhanced breasts. Then he spotted his wife.

"Hello Clarita," he said, feeling the need to use the diminutive.

She looked up at him. "I'm being punished," she said.

"What are you talking about?"

"There's no baby in there, Thomas."

"What? The pregnancy test was wrong?"

"I've got what they call a blighted ovum."

"Blighted ovum," he repeated. Sometimes he longed for more euphemism in medicine. And then he wondered what the opposite of euphemism was. What was the name for a word that made something sound worse than it actually was?

"The egg was fertilized, but nothing ever developed inside it. It's an empty shell. Apparently it happens a lot."

"If it happens a lot, how come neither of us has ever heard of it?"

"Because people don't talk about this shit. 'How are you?' 'Actually, not so good, I just learned I have a blighted ovum inside me.'"

Thomas wondered how anyone ever got born. He noticed a woman nearby glance up at them from her copy of *Fit Pregnancy*. "Come on," he said. "Let's go."

They went back out to the car and drove home. She was inconsolable. It seemed worse even than the miscarriage the year before. Not for the first time, he had the sense that there was something he did not fully grasp about his wife, some depth of pain or loss he had not reckoned with, that she had deliberately kept from him, perhaps because she was afraid of scaring him away, perhaps because it was difficult for her to relive the memory.

THEY BOTH TOOK the next day off. He tried to convince her to see a movie, but she lay on the couch watching home decorating shows. That night, she broke from routine and let him put Guillermo to bed. By the time he was done, Clara was already asleep. He lay in bed, full of futility. Unable to make a second child, unable to console his wife, unable to keep his job.

In the morning, Clara got up and went to work as if it were just another day. As she was going out the door, she turned to him and said, "I can't take any more of these. I'm going to call a fertility clinic and set up an appointment so we can find out what's wrong with me."

"There's nothing wrong with you," he said, but she was already closing the door and on her way.

He went back to work, too. At Melissa's, he let himself in and went straight to the library. Most days she was in the kitchen or the living room, reading the *Times,* sometimes checking her e-mail on a laptop, though he always felt that what she was actually doing was waiting for him. Usually, she would stop what she was doing and offer a cup of coffee from a freshly brewed pot. Thomas frequently wondered whether she'd shown Stephen Epstein such hospitality, whether Epstein woke in the morning, like the hero of a midcentury movie, to the aroma of frying bacon and percolating coffee, whether he returned home in the evening to find the proverbial hot meal waiting, the hot wife wearing nothing under her housecoat.

On this morning, however, Melissa was not in the kitchen, not in the living room. The ground floor of the house did not smell of coffee, and the silver laptop lay closed like a clamshell on the sofa. He went into the library, took off his coat, and booted up the computer. Normally, thoughts about work drifted through his mind during nonwork hours, but he hadn't thought of Stephen Epstein's library once since Clara's call two days before. Now his mind felt sluggish, distracted. This was always the hardest part of any job—wrapping everything up, correcting the typos from the data that had been processed in Dhaka, tweaking little inconsistencies in the taxonomy, asking for a few more grace notes from the Web programmers. Thomas hated these niggling touches; he much preferred the deep, focused work that preceded it. He hated it even more in this case because, when it was done, a void loomed.

On his computer, he brought up the staged version of the interface between the catalog and the game journals. Entries could be sorted alphabetically by author, subject, or title and also chronologically by date of conflict or year of publication. The site had features that the club members would probably never use—all of them were detailed in a finding aid/user's guide Thomas had written. He was toggling the alphabetical list of authors, A-Z, Z-A, A-Z, Z-A, trying to think of what he should be doing, when Melissa came into the room.

"Everything OK?" she asked. She was wearing a brown corduroy skirt with wooly gray tights, equestrian-style boots, and a puffy down vest over a form-fitting crewneck shirt.

"Yes," said Thomas. A-Z, Z-A.

"Your wife's all right?" said Melissa with apparent concern.

"She'll be all right," said Thomas. "We both will." A-Z, Z-A, A-Z.

"What are you doing there?"

"Oh, nothing." He took his hand off the mouse

"I was worried about you," she said. And then: "I've got a surprise."

"Yes?"

"I'm giving you the day off."

"That's not necessary. I missed yesterday."

"I called your supervisor, Anderson, after you left. I told him you'd had a family emergency and that I'd pay BiblioFile for the extra day."

"What did he say?"

"He said it was fine."

"Anderson said it was fine?"

"Yes. I talked him into it."

"You didn't have to do that."

"He also told me that you will be leaving BiblioFile when you're done with this job. Is that true?"

"Yes," said Thomas.

"Where are you going? You have another job lined up?"

"No," he said. "I'm being laid off."

"Oh," said Melissa, looking startled by the news. "Well, then you're definitely not working today. Maybe not tomorrow, either. Come on, bring your coat. We're going out."

He logged off from the computer and followed her through the kitchen to the back door, which led to the driveway. It was cold and gusty, a few small flakes of snow whirling in the air around them. Spring still seemed a long way off. They got into her white and gray Lexus, with its heated seats and dual climate controls, and backed down the driveway.

She drove to 280, taking a route through East Orange that people had told him about but that he'd always had a hard time navigating. He tried to remember the street names but soon was lost. They got on the turnpike going north, as if to the city.

"Where are you taking me?"

"It's a surprise," she said, and again smiled at him. The car had a cream-colored leather interior. Melissa wore driving gloves, her knuckles showing through holes in the perforated brown leather. Classical music played, though turned low, something from the romantic period. Brahms, he thought. All things considered, this wasn't so bad.

They crossed the George Washington Bridge and got on the Hudson Parkway going north across Spuyten Duyvil into the Bronx. Through the lattice of the bridge's railings, he saw Inwood Hill Park. Thomas almost mentioned that his wife had grown up in that neighborhood but thought better of it. They exited to the Mosholu Parkway and he remembered that Melissa was from Connecticut and wondered if she was taking him there. But what for?

In the end it was perfectly clear where they were going. She drove them around a corner through the entry gates of the New York Botanical Garden.

"Ever been here before?" she asked him.

"No," he said. He'd only ever ventured into the Bronx with one destination in mind: Yankee Stadium.

"Good," she said, parking the car.

The wind was stronger here, and the snowflakes, which were small and dry, whipped by in clusters, like insects. At the ticket office, Melissa showed a membership card and they were admitted. There was an open expanse of brown winter grass with a path through it, leading to some greenhouses in the distance. "Quick," she said. "Let's get inside." They walked briskly to the nearest structure, which looked like a bleached whale rib cage. Inside, it was warm and humid, like being inside a whale, Thomas thought. They walked along a path that wove through lush green plants, all of them identified with small gray signs. Melissa took off her down vest and draped it over her forearm as she walked. "Whenever I can't take the winter anymore, I come here," she said.

They moved into the next greenhouse, which offered a desert climate. Outside, sleet was falling. Thomas could hear its insistent rattle on the glass above them.

"Isn't it nice?" she asked. "All that going on outside and us safe in here." She took his hand, in a quick, confident gesture, and led him around a large rock formation. Thomas still had not removed his coat, but he felt himself warming up—felt it in tingles at the end of his nose, the tips of his fingers. Melissa led him to a secluded area between the rock and the wall of the greenhouse. There was a brown stone bench there and a thin stream of water falling off the rock into a pool. They sat down. Behind them, beyond the glass, was a gray metal utility shed with scraps of ice clinging to its side. In front of them was a vista that, with some squinting and imagination, could pass for something you might see outside a hotel room in Santa Fe.

"This is one of my favorite places in the city. I used to come here all the time. I'd bring a book or the paper. It always made me feel better, like it reminded my body that things wouldn't always be cold and miserable. I thought maybe it would help you feel better."

He recognized it as a romantic, flirtatious gesture, but he was grateful nonetheless to be the cause of so much concern from her. "Thank you," he said. "It's really nice in here."

"I don't think you can appreciate how much it has meant for me to have you in the house these past few months, Tom." He'd never corrected her initial use of the abbreviated form of his name. Now it was too late. He was Tom to her, Thomas to everyone else. "Before you came, I thought I was going to lose my mind in that place. I did not realize how much I depended on the routine I had with my husband. But just knowing that you were coming every day got me up, got me moving, made me give a damn. It helped me remember that my life is far from over."

"Did you really think that? That your life was over?" he asked.

"It seemed that way at the time. At least, that *a* life was over, the life I'd had for the last nine years with Stephen. I didn't see an end coming so soon and I didn't see where I could go next. Like I said, since graduating from college, I've kind of existed without a plan. There were times I felt like such a parasite, just living off his money, doing my thing—spending my days playing tennis or visiting the Botanical Garden. You'd think I could do all that just as well without him, right? I mean, I still have the money. I can do whatever I want. I can even do this," she said, and kissed him.

Despite the boldness of her words, it was a tentative, closed-mouth kiss that she planted on him, her lips puckered into a small ring of flesh. He felt his body responding reflexively, his hand going to her hip, and then he stopped himself and pulled back.

"No."

"It's OK," she said.

"No. My wife."

"I won't tell her. I promise."

He smiled.

"I'm serious," she said. "No complications. Not from me. Now come on. Take off your coat. Look, it's really snowing out there."

Beyond the glass walls of the conservatory, everything was a swirl of white and gray. "This is what we can be for each other," she said. "A place of warmth and comfort where we can escape from the world."

She put her hand on his cheek and pulled his head toward hers. He thought, briefly, of Clara and Guillermo, but they seemed very far away, as if they belonged to another lifetime, a lifetime in which he still had a job and in which Clara was still pregnant with their second child. That life felt less and less real to him now, his time with Melissa more and more real.

She kissed him again and he did not resist.

Part Two

Clara

Clara took Deysei to her obstetrician at the end of August, hoping that it might prompt her niece to open up a little about what had happened with Raúl. She and Thomas had left her niece mostly alone during her first week in the house. Deysei had been spending her time either online or out in the backyard sunning herself and listening to her iPod while she read magazines. Clara suggested that she could invite one of her friends from Inwood to come stay overnight, but Deysei refused, saying that her friends would never come out to Millwood. "I got friends who never even been to Brooklyn," she said. "Jersey's like going to Africa for them."

Clara counted on the power of the ultrasound to provoke a reaction, but when the doctor inserted the white wand, the embryo revealed was still so early in its development that it showed up on the screen as no more than a sac filled with grayish matter. There was no heartbeat to hear, no recognizably human shape to see. They might as well have been looking at sonar from a naval vessel. The doctor performed a full exam. Her due date was calibrated as April 2. At the end of the visit, the doctor prescribed prenatal vitamins and asked to see Deysei again in a month, indicating, without actually saying it, that she should get in touch sooner if she decided that she did not want to go through with the pregnancy.

Clara got the prescription filled and gave the vitamins to her niece, but she did not monitor whether Deysei took them. She got the feeling that Deysei was leaning toward keeping the baby but also that she was in no hurry to make that decision final. It was quite possible, Clara thought, that her niece intended to avoid making a decision until things had gotten far enough along that the decision would be made for her.

Deysei spent much of the remaining days of August either on the cell phone or logged into a social-networking site. It amazed Clara how much of the girl's life was mediated through electronic devices. She desperately wanted to see Deysei's MySpace page, but resisted, thinking that it would be an invasion of her niece's privacy. She was also amazed by the extent to which Yunis had disappeared from her daughter's life, completely abdicating to Clara the role of shepherding Deysei through the early stages of her pregnancy and the difficult decision ahead. Every time Clara called D.R., Yunis was either out, or sleeping—a pattern their mother had been less than thrilled to report to Clara.

Clara accepted the role. During the interlude between the visit to the OB and the start of school, Clara gently prodded and interrogated her. She wanted to be precisely the sort of older-and-wiser adviser that she herself had never had as a teenager—not accusing, not criticizing, just trying to get her to disclose what had happened, trying to move her toward a decision. Early on, these attempts to get Deysei to tell her more had been unsuccessful. "That's all I'm going to say for now, Tía. I got to think about what I want to do."

"Deysei," said Clara. "You have to tell me one thing, at least."

"What?"

"Did Raúl rape you?"

"No, Tía," said her niece, looking her in the eye, and Clara believed her.

On the final day of the summer vacation, Deysei finally opened up. They were in the Roy Rogers in the Livingston Mall (there was no McDonald's to satisfy what her niece still refused to admit was a craving). Clara had taken her out for some last-minute back-to-school shopping. The place was full of mothers doing the same for their children. It was far from the first time Clara had vicariously treated Deysei as her daughter. Before she'd met Thomas, and before her sister had shacked up with Raúl, Clara had been almost as much a parent to Deysei as Yunis had, spending most weekends with them, taking her to the movies, helping her with schoolwork, and footing the bill for birthday parties and wardrobe upgrades. Thomas often said that his courtship with Clara was in part a process of wooing her away from her niece. Since then, as Deysei had entered her teenage years, Clara had seen less of her and felt that she did not know her nearly as well as she once had. You could not be a parent from a distance and, besides, she had her hands full with Guillermo.

Livingston was a prosperous suburb, but the Roy Rogers seemed to have been lifted, customers and all, out of the Port Authority bus station. In the midst of artisanal olive oil retailers and Abercrombie & Fitch, the restaurant offered a haven for the unkempt, the uncouth, and the homeless. Across from them sat three generations of women from the same family separated in age, Clara guessed, by no more than thirty-five years. Deysei registered it, too, watching the grandmother scold her teenage daughter about letting the infant put the paper straw cover in her mouth.

"Do you want to tell me a little more about what happened with Raúl?" Clara asked. It was her first direct question on the subject in a couple of days. Clara still believed Deysei had not been raped—that the worst possible scenario had been crossed off the list. That left more complicated scenarios, scenarios in which right and wrong were less clear-cut. Had Raúl seduced Deysei in the waning months of his relationship with Yunis? Was it some kind of pre-emptive revenge? Was Raúl, God forbid, in love with Deysei? This seemed ridiculous, but Raúl, for all his bluster, his misdemeanors, and his felonies, was a kind of emotional naïf. And who knew what went on in that one-bedroom apartment with its complete lack of privacy and its steady flow of malt liquor and marijuana? Another scenario that Clara did not want to dwell on was the Lolita theory, the possibility that Deysei, despite her slovenly dress and her sometimes surly teenage manner, had somehow seduced Raúl, that she had bewitched him in a usurpation of her mother.

"How did it happen, Deysei? Can you tell me that?"

"I don't really know how it happened, Tía. It was like it happened all of a sudden. One night Mami was out late. Raúl came home from work and he was all full of himself. I don't know how to describe it. He got like that sometimes, all gangsta. Like he was waiting to surprise everyone with how *bad* he was. Maybe he'd been doing something he shouldn't have been doing, you know, for his probation or whatever, and he was acting that way because he was getting away with something. I didn't smell no alcohol on him, but maybe he was high. I was watching *Gossip Girl*. Raúl sat down and started watching it with me, saying things like 'stupid white bitches' and 'dumb-ass white girls, what do they know?' But there was this sex scene and Raúl got all quiet. He looked over at me. 'You ever do that with a boy?' I said no. And then he said, 'You know you finer than any of the girls on that show.'" Deysei mimcked Raúl's inflection with uncanny accuracy.

"What did you say to him?" asked Clara.

"I didn't say nothing. But he kept asking me more stuff like that. 'Did a boy ever do this to you?' And then he kissed me. 'Did a boy ever do this to you?' And then he touched me."

"You let him?"

Deysei said nothing. She was blushing.

"He was gentle, Tía. It felt good. Not like the other boys I been with. I don't know. I didn't want him to stop."

"You didn't say no?"

"No, Tía. I know you can't believe it, but he was nice. He didn't do nothing to hurt me."

"What about contraception?" Clara asked.

"What?"

"Condoms."

"He said we didn't need that. He said I wouldn't get pregnant this time of the month."

"And you believed him?"

"Yes. Mami been sleeping with him a long time and she never got pregnant."

"Your mother's on the pill, Deysei."

The girl said nothing.

Clara asked, "What happened when you were finished?"

"He said it was going to be our secret, that we weren't going to say nothing to my mami when she got home."

"It must have been weird when she did."

"I pretended I was asleep. Raúl went out."

"You don't think she ever suspected?"

"No. Raúl mostly didn't pay no attention to me after that. But I think he was acting that way so Mami wouldn't know. Sometimes he'd wink at me or pinch me when she wasn't looking. I thought we were going to do it again, but we were never alone in the apartment before Mami left for Santo Domingo."

"Oh, Deysei."

"What, Tía?"

"Are you in love with him?"

"I don't know what that feels like, Tía," said Deysei.

"Have you been talking to him?" Clara asked.

Deysei would not look her in the eye.

"Well?"

"I talk to him sometimes."

"Have you seen him since you moved out here?"

"No. I guess he's been busy." Deysei sounded disappointed.

"And did you tell him about being pregnant?"

"No. Not yet."

CLARA WAS STILL mulling over all of this a few days later when Thomas drove her to the fertility clinic for the hysteroscopy. Deysei's pregnancy and her own fertility issues had become entwined in her mind. Today she would learn if she could have another child, and the weight of that verdict, like a sudden awareness of her own mortality, had put her in a fretful mood. She knew she'd been acting strange for a while and, in the Odyssey, Thomas asked her if she was all right.

"There's something I need to tell you," said Clara, as they waited at a light. A fateful sentence, she thought.

"What is it?"

"A long time ago, when I was just a little older than Deysei is now, I got pregnant. I'm sorry—somehow, I feel like this is something I should have told you before we got married, before we started all this fertility stuff, but I've been putting it off and putting it off."

Thomas looked over at her. "What happened?"

"I got an abortion," she said.

There was a long silence. "That must have been difficult," he said. She wished she'd said something sooner. There was a time for such confessions and the seventh year of marriage was definitely not it.

"Yes," she said. "It was difficult."

"Who was the father?"

"A boy I knew in Inwood. A sort of secret boyfriend." *Here we go,* she thought.

"A *secret* boyfriend?" Thomas asked.

"My father wouldn't let me go out on dates. I told you about all that. In his ideal world, I would never have spoken to a boy until I left his house. If he saw a male customer flirting with me at the store, he'd yell at them. 'You think my daughter's a whore? Do you? Pay up and get out.' So I had to keep the relationship a secret from him."

"What was the secret boyfriend's name?" asked Thomas.

"Tito Moreno," she said.

"Did he know that he'd gotten you pregnant?"

"No. I never told him."

"So, you just took care of it?"

"Yes. On my own."

"What happened to Tito? Are you still in touch with him?"

"No. I haven't seen him since I went to college. I have no idea where he is or what he is doing now."

"Do you think you should have told him?" Thomas asked.

"I don't know. It was a crazy time, right around when my mother found me again. If I told Tito, I'm pretty sure he would have wanted us to get married and to keep it. I would probably never have gone to college. I never would have met you. Guillermo would never have been born. I mean, that's what we're talking about here. A completely different life. And a life without you and Gilly isn't one I want. By the time I realized I was pregnant, I was already living in Queens. There was a place in Manhattan that did the—" She stopped. "But . . ."

"What? What is it?"

"It's all part of why I'm so freaked out about this—about today. Even though I know it was the right thing for me to do, I think about that aborted baby all the time. A lot more than I think about Tito. It was just a little less further along than the one we lost last year. I sometimes think I'm being punished for not having that baby. I should have put it up for adoption. I was just so scared and alone. I couldn't tell anyone."

"If you were really being punished, then what about Gilly?"

"I don't know. Who said curses have to be logical? They aren't. They're random. It's when you least expect it that it comes back and bites you in the ass. Having Guillermo almost made it worse because, for a while, it seemed like I wasn't going to be punished. For a while there, I felt like I was getting away with something."

"I know what you mean," he said. It would be a couple of weeks before Clara understood that her husband's words were not intended to console her, that they were a confession of his own.

THE SHINING STAR Center for Reproductive Medicine was housed in a brown cement building on a secondary thoroughfare connecting Millwood and Springfield. To Clara, it always seemed like a strange stretch of road, neither fully commercial nor fully residential. There was a nowhereness to the streetscape. Modest split-level houses were interspersed with gas stations, medical plazas, and the sort of low-lying office buildings that were usually home to mortgage brokers, fly-by-night investment firms, and insurance agencies. Shining Star seemed, from the remains of the scratched-off lettering on the glazed front doors, to have been home to a financial services company called Alpine Securities. Patients entered through glass doors on the ground level and went up the stairs to a waiting room that had obviously once been a lobby. The first time Clara and Thomas came to the center—their second choice upon discovering that the esteemed fertility clinic at Summit Hospital did not accept their insurance—Clara had almost turned around and left after catching sight of the waiting room with its uncomfortable-looking chairs, its imitation Fauvist still lifes (painted by one of the doctors, she later learned), its massive console TV tuned to a conservative political pundit's talk show, its coffee station with powdered creamer and pastries wrapped in cellophane. It reminded her of a place she did not want to remember—the waiting room of the abortion clinic. But, before she could turn and pull Thomas back down the stairs, she saw something that made her stop. On the far wall of the room, opposite the receptionist's window, there was a large bulletin board bearing dozens of photographs of newborn babies. While Thomas went to get the registration paperwork, she was drawn helplessly toward the board. As she came closer, she saw that many of the pictures were either thank-you notes or birth announcements with handwritten expressions of gratitude. *We are so blessed. . . . Thank you for bringing our little angel into the world. . . . We were about to give up hope. . . .* Clara looked at all those little faces on curling photo paper. Black babies, Asian babies, white babies, Latino babies, mixed-race babies. All of them with the same open, curious, and innocent expression of life as not yet lived. Every one of these babies had been made here, she remembered thinking, fertilized in petri dishes in some room not a hundred feet from where she stood. Right now, in a darkened, silent lab nearby, eggs and sperm were being united, fertilized eggs were dividing, life was being created. Whatever reservations she may have had upon arriving vanished in the presence of those pictures, the best evidence there could be that the place knew its business—even though the old stockbroker's disclaimer applied just as well here: Past performance is no guarantee of future success.

She looked at those babies each time they came to the clinic in the months that followed that first visit—the visit that had concluded with Dr. Davidian, in full game-show-host mode, saying, "Let's get you pregnant!" She looked at them again this morning, searching for new faces, for proof that the clinic's success was ongoing and contagious, that the place had not lost its magic. When she'd finished her inspection, she went and sat next to her husband, who was already engrossed in a copy of *Sports Illustrated*. He immersed himself in baseball the same way he immersed himself in sleep and, formerly, work, she thought—completely. How she wished for that kind of focus, that ability to exclude things from her skittering mind. This time of year, in the run-up to the World Series, he always became a little remote, his brain consumed by pennant races, triple-crown pursuits, and God knows what else. Perhaps it was merely her own anxieties at play, but his withdrawal seemed more severe this year.

There had been one bit of good news, though. He'd had an interview the previous week with the New York office of a company that indexed and disseminated trade publications. A second interview had been scheduled at the company's corporate offices in northern Virginia on Friday. Thomas was going to spend the night with his mother in Bethesda and return on Saturday.

"How are you feeling?" asked Thomas, as if sensing her line of thought.

"I'm OK," she said.

"You worried about the anesthesia?"

"No. Not so much. Actually, I could really use the sleep."

Thomas laughed and touched her arm. The nurse called her name and she went into the consultation room alone so that they could take her weight and blood and ask her privately if her husband beat her. They asked all their patients this every time they came for an appointment—as if spousal abuse might suddenly erupt during the course of treatment. Every time, Clara said, "No," and every time, the nurse apologized and explained that they were obliged to ask. The question always depressed Clara, and this morning it struck her more than usual. What would have happened if she had said yes?

She went back out to the waiting room, clutching a cotton ball to the inside of her elbow. A few minutes later, she and Thomas were told to head downstairs to the surgical suite. Another nurse admitted them to a locker room, where Clara stripped and donned a white paper smock and sterile hospital socks. Thomas sat on the bench and watched her, not saying anything. She felt as self-conscious undressing before him as she ever had—like the first time they'd slept together. She didn't know what it was. Perhaps the distance she felt between them these past weeks, or the weird stirring of her emotions that had been caused by the confession in the car, or just her anxiety about the outcome of the day's procedure. They hadn't had sex since the night of Yunis's departure. Clara had been waiting to see if Thomas would take the initiative for a change, but he hadn't. So much hung on this inspection of her insides. She gave the key to him. "It's going to be fine," he said, and kissed her. "No matter what happens, it's going to be fine." She gave him a half-hearted nod and went through to the nurse. Thomas would wait upstairs.

The nurse led her to a bed behind a curtain. She was told to stay there until the doctor was ready. She got under the sheets and listened to the other nurses talking at the nearby station as they looked through a menu for lunch.

"I'm hungry. I want lasagna."

"Girl, you eat lasagna every day."

"I know. I like lasagna."

"Lasagna likes you, too. You better be careful."

"You calling me fat?"

"I'm just saying."

All of which reminded Clara that she had been fasting since midnight, reminded her how her life had become ruled by the demands of obstetricians and gynecologists. The nurse parted the curtain and smiled at her. "OK," she said. "They're ready." She had a wheelchair and Clara sat down and was pushed past the other curtained beds in the ward, occupied by women who'd just had eggs extracted or transferred into their wombs or by women undergoing the kind of procedure that was about to be performed on her—exploratory, evaluative. Down the hallway, in the operating theater, the doctor, the anesthesiologist, and a nurse were waiting, all in their scrubs. The removal of her clothes and her transport in a wheelchair left her feeling like an invalid. Suddenly, she wished Thomas could be in the room with her. Whatever his faults, he was usually calm and sensible. She stood up from the wheelchair and got onto the table, sliding her legs into the stirrups. She had the feeling of vulnerability that she always had before a gynecological exam, opening the most private part of herself to someone who was, essentially, a stranger.

"Are you ready?" asked the doctor.

Clara nodded.

"You might feel a little tickle in your throat," said the anesthesiologist, "but by the time you do, this'll all be over." He applied the mask to her face.

CLARA RECEDED FROM that suburban New Jersey operating room, receded back through the years to her bedroom in her father's house in Inwood, where she lay in a dreamless sleep. Into this blackness and silence came Dolores's voice:

"Wake up!"

The covers were pulled from her and a stick was brought down on her legs. Clara became fully conscious of everything at once: the shouted words, the sunlight coming through the thin curtains, and the terrible fact that she was no longer on the farm with her *abuelos*—that the farm, for her, had ceased to exist. She thrashed among the bedsheets, looking for a way back into sleep, back into her old life, as the second blow hit her.

"*¿Qué pasa?*" said Clara, freeing herself from the threadbare linens and jumping off the bed. "*¿Qué pasa?*" she cried. The room was small and cold and unfamiliar and there was no place for her to go that was out of range of Dolores's stick, a wooden extension pole for a paint roller that was covered in white and yellow drippings. It had a threaded steel top, which struck her on the knee as she tried to dodge the third blow. Dolores was tall, with an almost masculine build, and long arms. Clara could see the crescent wound her bite the night before had left on Dolores's cheek.

As if reading her thoughts, Dolores said, "You think I'm going to let you bite me again, you filthy child?" She swung and Clara blocked the stick with the meat of her palm. The sting sizzled from her elbow to her shoulder and then into her chest like an electric shock.

"I'm going to tell my papi!" she cried.

"Ha!" exclaimed Dolores, striking her again, this time on the shoulder. "If you tell your father that I beat you, I will only beat you harder!" She swung again, the stick rapping against Clara's forearm.

"*¿Por qué? ¿Por qué?*" asked Clara, weeping and looking for some-place to hide. But there was no such place.

THOSE FIRST WEEKS of her life in New York—before she started school—were spent almost entirely within the walls of the house, seemingly always within range of Dolores's stick, which she used to compensate for the impediment of her swollen midsection, poking Clara with it if she didn't pay attention, rapping the floor with it to emphasize the seriousness of something she was saying. Clara might as well have been in prison. And like a prisoner, she was kept to a strict schedule and subject to random acts of cruelty. Every morning she was berated from sleep, struck with the stick. She put on her clothes and went downstairs.

Downstairs was Dolores's domain. Downstairs was dirt. Down-stairs was the disarray of a house that had never been fully moved into, a house that was only half-habitable, semirenovated. Down-stairs were filthy floors that Clara would sweep and scrub with a handheld brush. Downstairs were dusty windows that she would clean with newspapers she could not read. Downstairs were photo-graphs of Dolores's family with their bony noses and high-yellow complexions. There was no picture of Clara, no picture of any-one in her father's family. Downstairs was an archaeology of dirty dishes in daily layers going back a week. Downstairs was a place far from what she had imagined when she thought of her parents' life in New York. Downstairs was the refrigerator, which bore drops of blood from leaking plastic meat packets, hardened mounds of molding cheese, the sour scrim of milk. Downstairs was Dolores herself, demanding, displeased, uncomfortable, talking constantly on the phone, complaining about her, listing her woes to family members near and far. When Clara asked about where her father was the answer was always the same way: "He's at the store."

Downstairs the stick was never far away.

On the farm, she had come and gone as she pleased, unremarked and unscheduled. Only darkness reigned her in. But here her life was reduced to her bedroom, the ground floor, and the basement. The basement was unfinished, with a dirt floor and no lights, the only illumination coming through the small cellar windows. In a corner stood the washing machine, a cantankerous, jittery white beast that gurgled and snorted its way through the loads, foam bubbling at the seams of the door, a drool of water leaking out from its undercarriage. When it had whined and barked its last, Clara took each item out and hung it on the lines her father had strung from wall to wall. The lines were high—intended for Dolores's reach—and the wet clothes seemed to get heavier and heavier as she worked her way through the load, until she could barely lift her arms, could hardly pinch into place the ancient clothespins, smooth and pallid, with rusty springs and eyes like dragonflies. Clara never made it through hanging a load without dropping something— usually something white: her father's undershirt, her stepmother's brassiere with padded cups the size of pot holders—onto the floor, where it immediately became filthy. When Dolores saw the soiled item hanging on the line, she would bring out the old wooden washboard and make Clara wash the soiled garment in the bathtub, scrubbing the dirt from the cloth and rubbing the skin from her fingers, up and down on the ribbed wood, strumming and strumming to no tune.

She always seemed to be going down when what she wanted was to go up—upstairs to the unfinished third floor of the house, where she could grow wings and escape through the window, up into the sky to fly home to her *abuelitos*. New York, the little she'd seen of it, was not anyplace she wanted to stay, and she could not understand why her parents had ever come here, why people back home spoke of it like heaven. In the rare moments when she was left alone, when Dolores had gone to visit a neighbor or stepped out of the house on an errand, Clara climbed the wooden steps to the gutted top-floor rooms, imagining it was the *ranchito* of her *abuelitos,* the beams of the ceiling visible, the shutters open, and the sounds of the pigs and the chickens drifting in. There were no salamanders up there, only spiders and mice, but she did not mind. She sat by the window, looking down on the people walking along the sidewalk, waiting for Dolores to return. She never thought of running away. As frightening as Dolores was, the unknown city around her was even more terrifying.

CLARA'S FATHER WAS rarely home. Six days a week he worked at his fledgling hardware store. Sometimes she saw him briefly in the mornings, but usually he was gone by the time Dolores woke her with the stick. He stayed away for lunch and came home late, the three of them sitting in the kitchen eating Dolores's gruesome food: flavorless yucca, *bacalao* that was too salty, soggy rice, and underripe avocados, which had the same consistency as slivers of soap. If her father was not drunk by the time he got home, he became so as quickly as he could after his arrival, kissing, in succession, Dolores, Clara, and a bottle of Brugal, the last kiss being the longest. Inebriation was a mission, a calling, pursued with intensity. One night, when Dolores had gone to bed early, Clara complained to her father about the way she was being treated, but even in his rum-fuzzed state, he had no sympathy for her. "That is your mother you are talking about. She has welcomed you into our home. You must show her the proper respect. Then she will treat you better."

"But, Papi, she hits me."

"That's your fault. If you were good she would not hit you."

"When are you taking me home?"

"This is your home, Clarita."

"Why did you bring me here, Papi?"

"Because you are my daughter."

"Where's my mother? Does she know I'm here?"

"Your mother is upstairs, sleeping."

"I wish you never had come for me."

"No more, Clara! No wonder Dolores hits you, talking back like this. If I hear that you are misbehaving, I will spank you myself."

In despair, she went to bed and wept.

Clara changed her tactics for a few days, as her father suggested. She called Dolores "Mami," even though it caught in her throat. She did not protest when she was told to get on her hands and knees to clean the floor with a scrubbing brush, that this was the only way to clean it properly, that Dolores would have done it herself if she wasn't pregnant. She accepted the stick without resistance or evasion, even when she had done nothing wrong and wondered if this was how she was going to spend the rest of her life, cleaning the house and being hit with the stick. But her passivity and obedience made Dolores even angrier. "I know what you are!" she said. "You can't fool me." And then she brought the stick down on Clara again. "Stop pretending. I will never believe you."

Once the wound on Dolores's cheek healed, Clara measured time by the swelling of her stepmother's stomach. As she became bigger, her moods became even less predictable. Everything would be fine, then the phone would ring, there would be shouting, then Dolores would take her anger out on Clara. Dolores would depart, leaving Clara alone for a few minutes; she would return in a rage and chase Clara around the house with the stick. Once, in a paroxysm of anger, she'd hurled a gallon of milk at her stepdaughter, but she'd missed and the plastic had burst on impact with the floor, sending a torrent of white washing across the tiles. The cascade made Clara laugh, which in turn made Dolores even angrier.

"Clean it!" she shouted. "Do you see how you've made me waste our milk? Do you know how much a gallon of milk costs?" Clara did not know how much a gallon of milk cost, but she did know that money wasn't the problem. Dolores and her father had money from something referred to only as "the accident." That money had bought the house and paid for the hardware store. That money meant there was always food in the refrigerator, even if it was poorly cooked. That money had purchased her father's ticket to the Dominican Republic. That money had brought her to New York. Clara thought that maybe the "accident" was what had made Dolores so angry. She got out the mop and cleaned up the milk. The next day there was a half-gallon in the refrigerator, but Clara had to eat her cereal dry, had to drink water with her dinner.

CLARA STARTED SCHOOL in April and from the beginning she saw it as an escape from the prison of her father's house and the unpredictability of Dolores's moods. In her mind, she would always connect the start of school with the end of winter, the end of being trapped in the house. She retained a clear memory of standing in the schoolyard on her first day, having been deposited there by her father, and feeling that she needed to take her coat off because, in the direct sunshine of the April morning, she was too hot, the only time since her abduction that she'd felt so warm. Unfortunately, the moment she took off her coat, one of the older kids standing nearby made a comment about her sweater.

It was the first of many comments she would hear about her accent, about her hair, about her clothes, about her teeth, about her skin, about her breath. As far as she could tell, she was just like the rest of the kids in the school, but she had simply not learned yet to identify the subtle distinctions that announced her as being just off the boat. Clara was picked on by the picked-on. There wasn't a person in her grade who wasn't cooler in some way. "Cool" was, in fact, one of the first words of English she learned, followed quickly by "dumb" and "black." Later she would understand it for what it was: the cruelty of immigrants who were merely passing down the same rite of passage they had received when they had arrived.

None of it mattered much to her, partly because she didn't really understand what a lot of the taunts and jokes meant, but mostly because however bad school was, it was always preferable to being home with Dolores. At school no one swung a paint-stained stick at her. At school, she did not have to hang laundry or clean the floor. At school, the buildings were heated and the food was better than the dried out and overseasoned meals Dolores begrudgingly made. Most of all, though, at school there were teachers whose job it was to help her learn. Clara was immediately drawn to her homeroom teacher, Ms. García, who was Puerto Rican and tall and pretty with clean clothes and straightened hair. Ms. García spoke to her kindly, explained things to her in Spanish, talked down the bullies who liked to ask Clara if she knew how to use a toilet. It was Ms. García who took her aside in the first week and said, "It's hard now, but every day it will get easier. Every day you will understand a little more." No one else had said anything encouraging to her and Clara immediately adopted Ms. García as her unofficial stepmother.

ONE NIGHT, NOT long after she started school, Clara was woken from her fitful, dream-rich sleep. Someone was shaking her. Reflexively, she held up her hand to fend off the blow, but the blow did not come. Even before she was fully awake, she was moving out of the bed to get away from the stick, but instead, she was embraced by a pair of strong arms.

"¡Ja, ja!" It was her father, trying to calm her. "Some nightmare you must be having, *mija*." There was rum on his breath and urgency in his voice. Clara could see him now, his features coming into sight in the light from the hallway. "Come, Clara, get dressed."

In that moment she thought the impossible had happened. He was going to take her back to Santo Domingo.

"Are we going to the airport, Papi?"

"Airport?" he snorted. "We're going to the hospital."

"Hospital?" she asked.

"Yes, hospital. The baby is coming."

"Oh," she said.

It was still dark outside and she felt slowed by the mud in her brain. The daily muscle aches and bruises mewed along her body as she got out of bed. Her father left the room, turning on the light. In that starburst, she found some clothes, dressed, and went downstairs. Dolores was sitting on the living room couch in her flannel housecoat and *chancletas,* holding her belly, and moaning in a way that Clara had heard animals moan on her grandparents' farm. Dolores seemed to take no notice of Clara as she entered the room, a reprieve she welcomed even in her drowsy state. She blinked and blinked again. Dolores was still there, moaning. Her father came in with a small suitcase—the same suitcase from her abduction—and sat on the couch, putting his arm around Dolores, rubbing his face with his other hand. The suitcase kept alive the idea of the airport in Clara's muddled thoughts, even though her father had said they were going to the hospital. They remained like that for several minutes, the only sound the grunts and moans from Dolores. *What is going on?* wondered Clara. Was the baby going to be born in the living room? She had been born in the house of her *abuelitos,* as had her mother. It didn't seem such a preposterous idea. But what about the hospital? Her father said they were going to the hospital. Then Dolores stopped moaning and, in the sudden silence, there was the sound of a car pulling up to the curb outside the house.

"The cab is here," said her father, helping his wife stand. "Clara, bring the bag." She lifted the suitcase, which felt empty, and she wondered if her father had forgotten to pack everything—or if he had picked up the wrong case. But she said nothing about it, fearing a reprimand. They went out the front door and descended the stoop, Dolores pausing after each step to breathe loudly. "Ay!" she said. "Ay!" Clara went behind them like a footman.

The cab took them up Seaman Avenue. Dolores had resumed her moaning with a new urgency. Clara wished the cab driver would hurry because she did not want the baby to be born in the back of the car—she did not want to see the infant come out of that cave between her stepmother's legs. The cab finally stopped in front of a large building on the corner of Indian Road and the park.

"Is this the hospital?" asked Clara.

"No," said her father. "This is Don Felix's building. You are going to spend the night there. In the morning, he will take you to school. Now go. See, he is waiting for you."

On the side of the building there was an open door with a man standing, silhouetted by the indoor light behind him. Clara remembered him from the night of her arrival in New York. That had been only weeks before, but it seemed longer than the entirety of her six years in the Dominican Republic. He waved at her as she stepped out of the car and began walking down the hill toward him. It was a cool but comfortable night and the park seemed especially placid in the soft darkness. When the cab had pulled away, there was almost total silence, interrupted only by her leather-soled shoes on the sidewalk. Don Felix beckoned to her: *"Ven, mi amor. ¡Ven!"*

The doorway opened right from the street into the Morenos' living room, a comfortable, untidy place that reminded her—in its trappings if not its structure—of the place where her cousins lived in Santo Domingo.

"Come with me," said Don Felix, closing and locking the door. He was wearing a bathrobe over green-and-black checkered pajamas. "You will sleep with Tito."

He took her by the hand and led her to a short hallway at the end of which was a half-open door. Through the door there was a small, darkened room with a bed. Don Felix pulled back the blankets and pushed his sleeping son closer to the wall so that there would be room for Clara to get in.

"What's this?" he asked, pointing at a bruise on her forearm "You have an accident?"

"Sí," said Clara, worried that he would press her for details.

"*Pobre muchacha,*" he said. "Come. We still have a few hours before we have to wake up."

She slipped off her shoes and got into the bed in her clothes. She had packed nothing, brought nothing, and she wondered, for a moment, if maybe the suitcase her father had brought down had been for her. Don Felix drew the blanket up to her chin. "Tito talks in his sleep," he said. "You can talk back to him. Say whatever you like. It's OK. He won't remember anything you say in the morning. I like to talk about the *salseros* who tried to steal his mother away from me before I married her. She was a real dancer and popular in all the clubs. You'd never know it now." He gave a little laugh and stroked her head once with his hand, a reassuring gesture. "Things change. We wanted a daughter, too, but the man upstairs had a different idea. I sometimes talk to Tito about that. Those are things it's OK to talk about in the dark. You understand?"

"*Sí,*" said Clara, though she didn't.

Don Felix stood up and exited the room, leaving the door slightly ajar so that some light would filter in. "Good night," he said.

Clara lay in bed, the elements of the room slowly coming into view: a baseball glove on the floor, a poster of spaceships, a small metal robot. She was wide awake. Tito breathed steadily beside her, now and then his breath interrupted by a gurgle of the sinus. From far away, she heard something click, then click again. A door with a faulty latch, a radiator cooling off. Then, through the bedroom wall, the rumble of the boiler coming to life. She waited for Tito to say something. She wanted to have an answer ready for whatever he might ask her. She decided she would tell him about killing the salamanders, how she now wished she had not done it. But he said nothing and she was still waiting for him to speak when she fell asleep.

• • •

"Papi!"

Clara opened her eyes.

"Papi!"

It was the boy, Tito, standing beside the bed and yelling. She recognized him now, from school, one of her tormentors. "Papi!" Don Felix came in the room, tying the belt of his bathrobe about his waist

"What is it? Why are you yelling?"

"Papi! There's a girl in my bed."

"What a bright boy I am raising," said Don Felix. "This is Clara, Don Roberto's daughter."

"Why is she in my bed with her clothes on?"

"You want her to be in your bed with no clothes on?"

"Why, Papi?"

"Because Doña Dolores went to the hospital last night to have the baby. *Ven,* Clara. Let's let the genius get dressed in private."

She slipped her shoes on and followed him through the living room into the kitchen, where Tito's mother was making breakfast. Clara did not dare believe that the delicious smell filling the apartment was what she hoped it was; and if it was, she did not dare to think that she would be given some of it to eat. But, as she came closer to the table, there it was, *mangú,* a heaping bowl of it.

"*Buenos días,* Clarita," said Doña Sylvia, though they had never met.

Clara did not answer. She was still staring at the *mangú.* It looked just like what her *abuelita* made. Smelled like it, too.

Doña Sylvia chuckled. "*¿Tienes hambre?*" she asked.

Clara looked at the older woman to see if she was being mocked. That is what Dolores would have done. But Doña Sylvia was looking at her with a bemused concern.

"*Sí,*" said Clara.

"Sit, then. Please."

As Clara seated herself, Don Felix came to the table, slipping a rubber band off a copy of *Hoy*.

"Where's Tito?" asked Doña Sylvia.

"Probably figuring how to put his pants on," said Don Felix, turning to the back page of the paper and winking at Clara.

Clara looked back at the *mangú*. What was taking so long? When would she be able to eat it?

At that moment, Tito came out of his room.

"*Buenos días, mi amor,*" said his mother.

Tito sat without a word. His chair was directly across the table from Clara's, and she smiled at him. He looked away.

Doña Sylvia brought a bowl of scrambled eggs and peppers to the table. Then she served them, picking up each plate and placing a spoonful of eggs and a spoonful of *mangú* side by side, like two yellow hills. Clara's face convulsed when she took the first bite. She was trying not to cry. Don Felix saw this and said, "Don't you like it?"

"*¡Sí!*" said Clara. "*¡Es delicioso!*" And she put another spoonful of *mangú* in her mouth to prove the point. During the meal, the Morenos continuously interrupted Clara's enjoyment of the food with questions—questions that required her to stop chewing and speak. They asked her if she wanted a sister or a brother. She said sister, though she did not explain that she wanted a sister to help with the chores.

They asked her how she liked school. She shrugged.

"Tito," said Doña Sylvia, "Are you introducing Clara to your friends?"

"How can I?" he said. "I never met her before today."

"Maybe you were never introduced, but you knew she was Don Roberto's daughter, didn't you?"

"Yes, but she's a *girl*."

"That doesn't matter."

"Everyone calls her *jíbara*."

"Tito!" said his mother.

"I'm sorry, Clara," said Don Felix, cuffing Tito on the head. "Pay no attention to this fool."

Clara blushed. She didn't care. All she wanted was more *mangú*.

THE BABY WAS a boy. He and Dolores came home from the hospital the following day and, for a time, Dolores had better things to do than chase Clara with her stick—though she still had plenty to yell and complain about. The baby's arrival also made the house a little less of a prison. Dolores's friends and relatives came to pay their respects. They also came to have a look at Clara. Some of them were courteous and kind to her. Others made comments, noticing how dark she was and wondering if her mother was Haitian. Clara had heard it all at school and the words barely made any impression on her. She had already begun to develop the forbearance of someone with an open mind raised among people with closed minds.

On Sunday afternoons after the baby was born, Don Felix and Doña Sylvia made a point of seeking them out and helping with the newborn. They would spread a blanket in the park near the Emerson Playground and Doña Sylvia would bring a basket of her delicious food and she would hold the baby, talking to it and singing to it while everyone else ate. The four grown-ups would drink beer when the meal was done and the baby was asleep. Tito and Clara would go to the playground.

Tito's hostility to Clara provoked in her the urge to smother him. She was always chasing after him. She couldn't do it in the school, not without being laughed at, but in the park she would not let him get away from her. It was how she bullied him back. She insisted on doing whatever he was doing. There he was on the monkey bars. She joined him. "Get away," he said. There he was going down the slide. She followed. "Leave me alone," he said. There he was on the swings and there was an empty swing next to him. She ran toward the empty swing, but before she got there, something hit her in the chin, knocking her down, filling her mouth with blood. And then there was Tito's voice.

"I said get away from me!"

SHE WENT AWAY from him then, back to New Jersey, to a hospital bed surrounded by white curtains and the nurse—the one who liked lasagna—standing there, saying, "Your husband's here."

They'd made him put on a paper jumpsuit over his clothes and a kind of shower cap on his head. He looked like a too-big kid dressed up for trick-or-treating.

"Hi, sweetie. How are you?"

She tried to say, "OK," but she could tell from Thomas's expression that something incomprehensible had come out of her mouth. He came forward and sat on the bed, reached out to stroke her cheek.

"You want some water?" he asked.

She nodded.

"That's better," she said, after the drink had washed her mouth clean, had made it possible for her to speak again.

"Have they said anything to you?"

"No," she said. "I just woke up."

"Hi Mama," said a different nurse, sticking her head through the part in the curtains. "You hungry? You want some crackers?"

Clara nodded. She didn't mind all the attention. Not one bit.

She heard somewhere down the row of beds separated by their curtain walls the doctor saying, "You're going to have a little bleeding for a couple of days. That's normal. If you're still bleeding after five days, you need to call us. Do you understand?"

She heard the patient say, "Yes." Clara wondered what news the doctor would have for them. She felt the fogginess in her brain dissolving, like an antacid tablet in a glass of water.

The nurse returned with some packets of Saltines. "Here you go, Mama. You want some apple juice, too?"

Clara shook her head.

"Awright," said the nurse, and left them.

After two failed attempts to get her fingers to open the cracker wrapping, she handed the packet to Thomas. He handed her back two Saltines like some magic trick. Obviously she was still not completely out of the anesthesia yet. She chomped the crackers and asked her husband for another packet. As she was about to eat seconds, Dr. Davidian parted the curtain.

"Hello, Mrs. Walker. How are you feeling?"

"Fine," she said, through crumbs.

"Well, the procedure went smoothly and I'm happy to tell you that there is no physical reason that you should not be able to have a baby."

"I'm OK?" she asked. It was not what she'd been expecting.

"Yes, everything looked fine. We're going to let you have a week to recover from the hysteroscopy. Then we'll put you on a course of antibiotics to take care of any lingering infections. Once you're done with that, you can start your first IVF cycle."

Thomas had plucked a tissue from the box beside her bed and was wiping something off her face. Cracker crumbs? No, she realized. Tears. She took his hand and pulled him close for a kiss.

"I'll leave you two alone," said the doctor. "Just rest another half hour. The nurse will take your blood pressure and then you should be able to go."

ON THE WAY home, she thought about how similar this happiness felt to other joyous occasions in her life—being reunited with her mother, her wedding day, the day of Guillermo's birth. Happiness filled you with the expectation of more happiness. Clara wondered if the lingering effects of the anesthesia—still tingling her scalp, still dumbing her brain—weren't also contributing to her sense of elation and her feeling that the decades had been crushed together, that her emotions were strung like pearls in time.

"Are you pinching yourself?" Thomas asked as he drove.

"Kind of," she said.

"So much for being cursed," he said.

"Well, we did lose one, and there was the blighted ovum, and there's no guarantee that the IVF—"

"I know, but let's not go any further with that thought. Let's be positive for a change." He placed his hand on her thigh and squeezed. It stayed there until he had to make the hard right turn onto Passaic Street. *Yes,* she thought. *Let's be optimistic.*

A white car was parked in front of their house. Thomas swung the Odyssey around it and she saw that both the front seats of the car were occupied. As the van came to a stop in the driveway, Clara turned and saw Deysei getting out of the passenger side of the white car, pausing before closing the door to say something to the driver. For a moment, she thought the driver might be Raúl. The car sped away and Deysei walked up the driveway toward them.

"Hi Tía. Tío," she said, as Thomas came around to open Clara's door. She stepped gingerly out of the Odyssey, planting one foot and then the other on the driveway. "How did it go?"

"It went fine, baby. Who was that?" she asked. "In the car?"

Deysei gave Clara a look of wonderment. "His name is Tito Moreno and he thinks he's my father."

"*What?*" asked Clara and Thomas simultaneously.

"He wants to talk to *you,* Tía," Deysei said.

"I'm sure he does," said Clara, who felt like she'd been hit with a delayed dose of the anesthesia. "Why the hell does he think he's your father?"

"Because he thinks you're my mother."

"Oh, Jesus," said Clara.

"Did you explain to him who your real parents are?" said Thomas.

"Of course, Tío, but he doesn't believe me. He's really nice, but he doesn't believe me."

"You've got to talk to him," Thomas said to Clara.

"I think that's probably what he wants and it's the last thing I want to do," said Clara. She still felt buzzed.

"Do you have his phone number, Deysei? I'll talk to him," said Thomas.

"Yes, Tío," said Deysei, producing a business card.

"Wait," said Clara, "OK. I'll handle this." She snatched the business card from her niece and went into the house.

Tito

Tito almost never took vacations. He had no desire to travel, no need to lie on a beach or hike a mountain trail. The only time he ever took off was to cover for his father. He had plenty of days saved up. That wasn't the problem. The busiest season of the year had just passed at Cruz Brothers, and so that wasn't the problem either. The problem was that he wanted to take three weeks off—in a row. Three weeks was a lot of time, even for someone who took as little vacation as he did. Three weeks was a lot of time, especially for someone whose numbers had been down the last few months, months when all the other reps' numbers had been up.

"Why you need three weeks?" Orlando asked him. "You going to Santo Domingo?"

"No." Tito almost said yes, but there was a good chance someone who worked for Cruz Brothers would see him on the streets of Inwood in the next three weeks and that would be trouble.

"So, what you need three weeks for?"

"I've got shit to take care of."

"We all got shit to take care of. Most of us take care of our shit on the weekends. What is this shit you got to take care of? You getting married or something?"

"No. It's personal."

"Personal. What the fuck isn't personal? You tell me." Orlando looked at him and Tito felt that he was being evaluated, that his whole career at Cruz Brothers was somehow in the balance. "All right," he said, finally. "But you better come back with a whole new attitude. You think I didn't notice the discount you gave that client in New Jersey? You think I haven't noticed the way you been slacking off the last couple of months? Seems like you been a little out of it."

It was true. Until he'd knocked on Ms. Almonte's door, there had not been much latitude for anything more dangerous than a little daydreaming on the job. Since then, though, the separators had collapsed. Customers were real. Commissions were real. Pieces of furniture were real. Bangles were real. But Clara walking down the driveway in New Jersey? Surely *that* was a dream. Surely it was no more real than the fleeting belief that he would become Wyatt's stepfather. Still reeling from that fiasco, Tito did not want to get ahead of himself. He wanted to take his time. He wanted to be sure. He felt like his life depended on it.

And that was why he needed three weeks off.

HE WENT BACK to Millwood the next morning, to the same spot where he'd seen Clara and the girl with the bangle getting out of the minivan. He was going to be patient, he reminded himself. He had three weeks. This day would just be for reconnaissance, to get to know the comings and goings of the household, to see what there was to see.

Around eight that morning, the girl came out of the house with a bookbag on her back and walked down the street away from him. Was she Clara's child? Could Clara have a teenage daughter? Or was she maybe a relative—a cousin or a niece? The way Dominican families were, anything was possible. She was dressed once again in a pair of loose-fitting jeans or overalls and a hooded sweatshirt. He noticed that she walked slowly, almost ponderously. Going to school, he thought, and not too thrilled about it. He would have to find out where the high school was. It couldn't be far if she was walking.

A few minutes later, Clara appeared, dressed for work in a pair of brown slacks and a short-sleeved floral blouse, a satchel in her hand. His entire body hummed with desire and longing for her. Seeing her again, he felt almost seasick and believed, for a moment, that his imagination had brought her back from the past. He took a few deep breaths and calmed himself. He wondered what she did. She looked professional without being too formally dressed. A teacher perhaps? That seemed possible; she was smart enough and she'd always loved school. She walked past him on the other side of the street, heading toward the avenue where the shopping plaza and the apartment blocks stood. It was all he could do not to run over there and lie down in front of her. *Look! Here I am. Remember me?* He wanted to see her up close, to match her face now to the image in his memory—the image in the photograph he carried on his phone. Again, he resisted. There would be time. There would be time to talk to Clara, to look into her eyes again, to ask her all the questions that were bubbling up in his head. First, he needed to learn more. He could not afford to screw this one up. It was a second chance and there would not be, he was certain, a third. He watched as she turned along the avenue and disappeared. A little groan escaped him, as if he might never see her again. But he stayed where he was and turned his eyes back to the house.

A half hour passed and nothing happened. He started to regret not following Clara or the girl. Just when he was about to give up, the side door opened again. A white guy came out with a kid who looked to be about Wyatt's age. The kid was high-yellow but had straight hair. You almost wouldn't know he was biracial. *Clara's son,* he thought. The white guy was dressed in khakis and a pressed short-sleeved shirt, tucked in. He looked like someone you'd see in a commercial for one of those retirement funds. *Have you thought about how much money you'll need when you're ready to stop working? What's your magic number? We can help you get there.* He carried a Hot Wheels backpack. At the corner, across the street from the shopping plaza, they stopped and waited. The white guy—he had to be Clara's husband, Tito begrudgingly acknowledged to himself—peered into traffic as if awaiting a ride. Not long after that, a pint-sized school bus stopped at the corner and the kid boarded it, waving. "Bye, Daddy!"

Tito slouched into his seat, his Yankees cap pulled low on his forehead, so that he'd look like he was sleeping. He watched the guy walk past and go back into the house. Who else could be in there? Was Raúl in there? What about Raúl's girlfriend, Yunis? An intuition derived from years of entering the abodes of strangers told him that there was no one else. This was not the kind place where Raúl would live, even temporarily, and Santiago had told him that the girlfriend had gone to D.R. So, what was he going to do now? He had his box of flyers in the passenger seat. Should he go up there and do a cold call on the husband? The minute Clara saw the name on the flyer, she'd know.

Before Tito could decide, he heard the minivan's ignition. It was the husband behind the wheel. He backed out of the driveway and headed for the avenue, hanging a left toward the center of Mill-wood. Tito started his Sentra and did a quick U-turn to follow him. By the time he made the turn, there were a couple of cars between them. Fortunately, the van was easy to spot and he followed it at a safe distance to a small parking lot in the center of town. The man got out of the van and went into a flower shop across the street, emerging a few moments later with an expensive-looking bouquet. He got back in the van. Tito followed him out to the far side of town, up into a neighborhood of mansions. He was now almost as curious about this guy as he was about Clara—and there was the added advantage that he wouldn't be recognized. What kind of man had Clara married? And where was he going with these flowers?

The minivan stopped in front of a large house with a CON-TRACT PENDING sign planted in the front yard. Maybe a chance for some business, he thought. The house was bigger than the place

in Riverdale where he'd gone to give the estimate earlier in the
week. There would be lots of furniture to haul and a good commission. Not to mention that it might put him back in Orlando's
good graces.

The husband got out of the van carrying the flowers and walked
up the path to the front door. He had no bag, no briefcase. Tito
reached into his pocket and pulled out his cell phone and aimed
its minuscule lens at the man waiting outside the house. A woman
answered the door. From this distance, he couldn't make out much
of her. Blond. Thin. Fit. She kissed Clara's husband on the mouth.
It was not the way you kissed a friend. Tito took a picture, and then
another. Clara's husband offered her the flowers, but the woman
crossed her arms over her chest and shook her head. She was refusing the flowers. Clara's husband scratched his temple, said something, and then turned away. Tito dropped his phone out of view
and let his head fall to one side, half-closing his eyes, as if he were
dozing. The husband looked upset, disappointed. He tossed the
bouquet into the van's passenger seat before driving off again.

Tito followed him back to the house. The husband went inside
and did not reappear during the next hour. Feeling hungry, Tito
decided to go into the center of town. His first stop was the village
hall, where he used the public restroom. Posing as someone who
was thinking of moving to this part of New Jersey, he went into
the property tax bureau and asked about the high school. The clerk
handed him a brochure: "Education in Millwood," paid for by the
local chamber of commerce. Tito read through the glossy pages of
multiracial multiculturality at a bagel place down the street from
the village hall, near the commuter station. The town seemed well-
heeled and calm, though depleted, probably because most of the
people who lived there were in Manhattan office buildings. Rush
hour and the weekends were the times when you'd see the place
alive, Tito thought. In this bagelry, there was a cluster of college
kids in sweatshirts, pajama bottoms, and flip-flops laughing about

some foolishness the night before. A crossing guard, a man in his late sixties, probably a retired police officer, blew on the steam from a cup of coffee while he read the high-school sports section of the *Star-Ledger*. A couple of mothers sat with their toddlers, whose faces were smeared with cream cheese. One mother was black and the other was white, but they both had kids with light brown skin. Maybe the white mother was actually a nanny? He couldn't tell. That's the kind of place it was.

There were still a couple of hours before the high school let out, and Clara wouldn't be home until even later, so he decided to go back to the house on the hill for a little sales call. Start at the edge of this thing and work his way in.

He did a slow cruise through the downtown. It was an odd mix of high-end eateries and places that catered to college kids, with a handful of older establishments that clearly were aimed at a black customer base: a beauty supply shop that sold wigs and extensions, a religious bookstore, and a gallery of African statues and artifacts. There was no Spanish presence in the town at all. He wondered, briefly, if he could live there. If he and Clara had stayed together, would they have ended up here?

Up on the hill, on the street of mansions, he parked in the spot where the silver Odyssey had stood an hour before. He took one of the leaflets out of the box in the backseat as well as his clipboard full of estimate forms and walked up the path to the front door. The house had those old leaded-glass windows that were smoky and warped. Made the place look haunted, he thought. He pushed the bell and waited. The inside of the house was dark and he could see nothing moving in the blurry glass.

"Yes?"

She had come around the side of the house and was standing there in shorts and Crocs and gardening gloves, holding a little shovel. He was not prepared for just how good-looking she was. Her shorts were bunched from squatting in the flowerbed, exposing a length of muscled white thigh. Tito sensed immediately that the distance between them was unbridgable. Sometimes you could just tell. There was no common ground, no way for him to engage her. No matter what he did she was going to treat him like he was from another planet.

"Ah. Good afternoon," Tito said. "I couldn't help noticing the sign in front of your house as I was driving by. I work for Cruz Brothers Moving and Storage. We offer the best rates in the tristate area along with twenty years of experience in relocation services." He realized that he was quoting the flyer in his hand. Relocation services was the new catchphrase he was supposed to use in his sales pitches. "I was in town on another call but I'd be happy to give you a free estimate. May I ask when you're moving?"

"Soon."

And where are you moving to?"

"I'm moving into the city, but I already have a mover, thanks."

"I'm sure we could beat their price."

"I'm sure you could, too, but I'm not interested, thank you."

"If you're moving to the city, perhaps you will need to put some things in storage."

"I've already taken care of that."

"Very good," said Tito. "Let me leave this brochure and my business card. You can look us up on the Web, too, cruzmoves.com. Perhaps you could show it to your husband."

"I'm not married," she said, flatly, crossing her arms over her chest.

"Feel free to call me if you change your mind."

"OK, thanks." She accepted the brochure and the card with her gloved hand. They would be in her garbage can within moments, he knew, or even—what was it called, a compost pile? But he was glad he'd come. It wasn't hard to figure out what was going on between this woman and Clara's husband. And what was going on between them might be good news for him.

THE HIGH SCHOOL reminded Tito of the Cloisters, a big stone building that looked like it had been brought from another country and another time. You could withstand a siege in that place, he thought. Battering rams and boiling oil. At two-thirty, when he coasted past, a police cruiser was parked outside the main entrance. Already, the side streets were filled with idling cars—parents waiting for their children to be released, though they could have passed for a massing invasion force. The school was huge—bigger even than Kennedy, where he and Clara had gone. There would be hundreds of kids spewing out of the place. He parked at the end of the line of parental vehicles and walked the three blocks back to stand across the street from the main entrance, posing as just another father there to pick up his kid. The bell rang at two-forty-five. At first there was nothing—like a remote-controlled bomb that had failed to go off. A minute later, however, the double doors swung open and out they came, slouching, self-aware, laughing, and grimacing, punching one another or walking alone, dressed badly, listening to music, looking shiftily around, fearful of being ridiculed. It reminded him of that Good Friday when he'd waited for Clara outside the U-Haul lot in the Bronx, the hordes passing him.

On the street, traffic was backed up as the police officer stopped the cars to let the kids flood the pedestrian crossing. He was glad he'd parked and walked. He would have been trapped in it, unable to move, unable to see anything. For a good five minutes, he stood there looking at the kids as they emerged and walked into the town. There was a back entrance he'd discovered on his pass through the area, but if she was going to walk home after school, this is the door she would most likely take.

When she finally appeared, he almost did not recognize her because her hood was pulled over her head. It was the way she walked that gave her away, the slow, heavy tread. She was coming in his direction, upstream from the crosswalk, where the police officer was drawing horn blasts from impatient motorists. A moment later, he heard the diesel roar of school bus engines, and a line of the yellow behemoths pulled out of the drive on the side of the school, further congesting matters on the street. It was like a fucking *evacuation,* Tito thought. Like they're fleeing a natural disaster.

Walking by herself, the girl reached the sidewalk across the street from him and turned right, heading downhill, toward the center of town, away from Clara's house. He followed at a distance, hoping the police officer, who was arguing, conveniently, with a guy in a white electricians' van, would not notice that he was unaccompanied by a child. The girl turned left on Valley Street, where the traffic jam had begun to ease. There were still dozens of kids on the sidewalk in little groups of three and four so he could follow her easily and unobtrusively. A couple of blocks down Valley, she went into a pizza place that was already jammed with teenagers. Tito stopped in front of the place and gazed in through the window, trying to look casual—trying to look like a hungry Millwood resident surprised to find his local joint overrun by adolescents, trying, in short, not to look like a stalker.

The girl was waiting in line at the counter. Behind the counter, two unshaven young men in sauce-stained aprons were straining to keep pace with the demand. The girl was last in a line of seven. If he went in now, he could stand right next to her. He reminded himself that he was supposed to be taking things slowly, but he entertained this reminder only long enough to dismiss it. In he went, walking circuitously through the rearranged tables and chairs, navigating the groups of teens huddled around their grease-stained plates and paper cups of soda. The rolled-up sleeves of drinking straws were being propelled from one side of the room to another in the form of spitballs; somewhere a girl screamed as a boy wrestled with her. The girl yelled: "All y'all are hurting me. You need to 'pologize! All y'all are hurting me. Stop it."

He stopped right behind the young woman who was wearing Ms. Almonte's bangle and stared at the rough gray material of her sweatshirt. He could just hear the *tss-tss-tssss* of a high hat in her earphones. *Cuidado,* he thought to himself, as they moved closer to the counter.

Cuidado.

When her turn came she asked for a pepperoni with extra cheese. She was reaching into her pouch when Tito spoke up. "I'll take care of that. And a plain slice for me, too."

The guy behind the counter glanced quickly from the girl to Tito and then shrugged, as if to say, *whatever,* and took the bill Tito proffered. Meanwhile, the girl turned to look at him, pulling her hoodie back from her head and removing the white buds from her ears.

Tito returned her gaze, examining her wide face and large eyes, her dark brown skin, and the ragged cornrows that were begging to be redone. She did not look much like Clara, he decided in that brief instant, though the coloring was right and there was something reminiscent of Clara in her eyes. Besides, who knew what Clara looked like up close now?

"I don't need nobody buying me pizza," the girl said, finally, but Tito noticed that she wasn't taking her money out of her pouch.

"Do you know Raúl Herrera?" he asked, receiving his change from the guy behind the counter.

"Are you the police or something?" the girl asked.

"Why, have the police been looking for Raúl?"

"I don't know." Then, very suspiciously: "Who *are* you?"

"I'm not the police," said Tito. "I used to work with Raúl. I'm looking for him."

They picked up their plates and moved away from the counter. Along the wall of the restaurant was a chest-high shelf with shakers of pepper flakes, oregano, and Parmesan cheese. This is where they set their plates.

"Where'd you work with Raúl?" she asked.

"Cruz Brothers. In the city," said Tito. "Look." He took out his wallet and withdrew one of his business cards.

She looked at the card and handed it back to him. "If you're looking for Raúl, why you talking to *me,* then?"

"Because I think Raúl gave you something that wasn't his to give."

Her hand went to her wrist. "No," she said.

"Yes," said Tito. "The bangle. He stole it."

"Fuck," said the girl. "Fucking shit."

"Dude, hit on someone your own age," barked a kid from a nearby table who was getting up to leave. He wasn't protecting the girl—just trying to make his friends laugh, which he did.

"What's your name?" Tito asked her, ignoring the taunt.

"I'm not telling you my name."

"My name's Tito. I know your mother."

"How do you know my mami?"

"We grew up together. In the Heights."

"My mami grew up in Queens."

Tito gathered himself for a moment. "Are you sure your mother didn't grow up on Payson Street in Inwood?"

"That's where she lives now—or lived, I mean. But Mami grew up in Queens."

"Where in Inwood did she she live?"

"I'm not telling you. I don't even know who you are."

"I told you, my name is Tito Moreno. I'm trying to find Raúl Herrera. I used to work with him at Cruz Brothers. Have you seen him recently?"

"No. I ain't seen him. You want this fucking bracelet? Take it." She pulled the bangle off her wrist and set it down on the shelf next to her plate. "I can't believe he stole that shit."

"Have you heard from Raúl recently? Since you moved out here?"

She shook her head. Her eyes were squinting against tears.

"Keep my card," said Tito, setting it between the bangle and her plate. "If you hear from Raúl, I would like to know, OK?"

She'd never tell him, but she would probably show the card to Raúl. Maybe to Clara. Tito picked up the bangle and put it in the pocket of his jeans. "Thank you for returning this. It means a lot to the woman it was taken from."

A tear escaped the girl's eye and dropped onto her cheek. "This is bullshit," she said.

"Yo, Mister. Don't make her cry." This was said by one of the young men at the next table who'd laughed a few moments earlier.

"Let's get out of here," said Tito. He took her gently by the elbow and led her toward the door. He had the two paper plates with their uneaten slices in his other hand. The girl was wiping her eyes.

"Can I give you a ride home?"

"Are you crazy? I'm not getting in a car with you."

"Look, can I talk to you again after school tomorrow? I would really like to talk to you about your mother."

She looked at him as if he'd started speaking in Russian.

"I thought you were looking for Raúl. Why you talking about my mother all of a sudden?" She shook her head and took the plate with the pepperoni slice from his hand. "Listen, mister, I gave you back the bracelet. Just leave me alone."

"I'll see you tomorrow, then," he said.

She walked turgidly away from him, inserting her headphones with one hand and eating her pizza with the other. Tito watched her go. Had he fucked everything up? He wasn't sure. If nothing else, he'd gotten the bangle back.

THE YEARS APPEARED to be catching up with Ms. Almonte. When he'd first seen her at her house in Oradell, she seemed to have changed hardly at all in the decade and a half since he graduated from Kennedy. She was elegant, ageless, her hair still black and her attire always carefully put together. Now, when she answered the door, she looked worn down, new lines in her face and seams of silver in her hair, which she was no longer taking the trouble to straighten.

"Mr. Moreno. I apologize for not returning your call. It has been a busy time for me. My mother died yesterday and I have been making arrangements for the funeral."

"I'm very sorry," said Tito. He wanted to hug her, this fearsome figure from his youth who had been rendered mortal and vulnerable just like everyone else. Separated from her husband and now orphaned. He wanted to hug her but knew she would not welcome the gesture.

"Thank you for your condolences. I knew it was coming; I just didn't think it would come so fast. I thought I would have at least one more year with her."

"Are you going to go back to work, then?" This was the first thing that came to mind.

"I don't know. I haven't thought about that yet."

"It's good that you moved when you did," he said, wondering if she was going to move back out to Oradell now—if she was going to need a mover again. This was probably not the right time to ask.

She nodded but did not speak. She looked dazed.

"Like I said in my message, I have something for you." He pulled the bangle out of the front pocket of his jeans, realizing, too late, that he should have brought it in a bag or a box. The metal was still warm from his body heat. He held it up. "This is yours, isn't it?"

"Yes," she said, her eyes coming into focus and her face coming to life. She accepted it from him, apparently unconcerned about how it had been transported back to her. "I can't believe you found this. It is a special object for me, especially in light of recent events." She held it against her bony chest and smiled wryly at him. "I need a drink," she said. "Would you care to join me? It has been a long day."

"Sure."

"I have Scotch or rum. Which would you prefer?"

It seemed like a loaded question. "Scotch," he said, still hoping to make a good impression.

"Ice?"

"Yes."

"Sit, sit," she said. They were in the living room, and outside, it was already dark—the dark seeming to come fifteen minutes earlier every night, as if they were accelerating into the colder months of the year. He heard her snapping open metal ice trays in the kitchen and thought what an old-fashioned sound it was. Everyone had ice makers these days. When she returned, she carried two glasses and a fancy-looking bottle with a castle on its label and a long name in Gothic script. Glen something. She had slipped the bangle on her wrist. It looked like a bangle should—loose and mobile. On the girl, it had been tight as a handcuff.

Ms. Almonte sat down opposite him and filled each of the glasses with a good slug. The little piles of ice popped and collapsed. "My husband introduced me to this whiskey. He took me to the place where it is distilled. It tastes like the earth—in a good way, peaty. Like the earth distilled into a nectar." She handed him a glass and then chimed the top of hers against the base of his. "Santé," she said.

"Salud," he said, and took a sip. Well, it was strong, anyway.

"So, tell me how you found it. My bangle. I must admit, I had written it off. Consigned it to the abyss. I didn't think you'd be able to track it down. Certainly not so fast, anyway."

"A little bit of detective work," he said, hoping to keep it at that. "But something weird happened. While I was looking for this bangle, I found Clara."

"Clara Lugo?"

"Yes."

"Where?"

"In New Jersey."

"So close. All this time. Where in New Jersey? Don't tell me Oradell."

"No. A town called Millwood."

"Where's that?"

"Near Newark. Essex County."

"Oh, we never went down there much. Have you spoken to her?"

"No, not yet."

"You know for sure it's her?"

"Yes. It's definitely Clara. I hope later this week I can talk to her. I haven't figured it out yet, but there's some kind of connection between Clara and Raúl—the mover who stole the bracelet."

"They're not—"

"No," said Tito. "Nothing like that. She's married to a white guy as far as I can tell."

Ms. Almonte nodded, as if this was to be expected. "Children?"

"Yes."

"How many?"

"I'm not sure yet. I think two—a boy about six and a teenage girl."

"Really?" said Ms. Almonte. "A teenager?"

"Yes. Why?"

Ms. Almonte appeared to think for a minute. "So she must have kept it."

"Uh—yes," Tito said, not knowing what she meant.

"It all makes sense now."

"What makes sense?" said Tito.

"The last time I saw Clara—right before she went off to college—she was pregnant. It was you, wasn't it? All this time I wondered who it was. Mr. Moreno, that girl is your daughter, isn't she?"

Tito said nothing. The witch was fucking with him. Had to be.

"She said she was going to put it up for adoption. That can't have been an easy decision for the two of you. But Clara must have changed her mind. She must have kept it. How old would she be now? Sixteen?" Ms. Almonte was nodding, thinking to herself, not really paying attention to Tito, who was struggling to keep his composure. He swirled the shrinking ice around his glass and took a long sip.

"Yes," he said. "Sixteen."

"I'm sorry," she said, looking at him again. "I see that I'm upsetting you. I didn't mean to do that. It must be difficult to keep a relationship going when a thing like that happens. My husband and I never had children, but I can imagine how trying it must have been for two young people. I hope that you and Clara can reconnect. I'd very much like to know how she is doing now."

Tito nodded. His head was throbbing.

Ms. Almonte continued. "If that girl is your daughter, you should get to know her. You could bring Clara to my mother's wake on Saturday. A number of my former colleagues from Kennedy will be there."

"I don't know" was all Tito could manage to say.

"Tell her I'd love to see her again. And even if she doesn't come, I hope you will. It's going to be held here. Two o'clock."

WHAT WAS GOING on? Tito had the sense that he'd been caught in some kind of dimensional current or temporal field, towed away from the real into some strange netherworld of past and present, desires and failures, dreams and disappointments. These happenings were exceeding the imaginary life in which he had taken refuge all these years. They were inconsistent with his expectations, which had shrunk in inverse proportion to his hopes. That, maybe, was the one way to know that these things were actually happening—the certainty that, even in his trippiest daydreams, he could not have made this shit up. A daughter? Clara pregnant? His child alive in the world? Is that why Clara had disappeared?

Because of the pregnancy? It was all clicking together. Instead of fighting it, he was starting to think that he should just surrender to it, go for broke, accept that these things were happening to him. Yet a certain caution prevailed. He needed a little more information, a little more *Clara-fication,* he thought, chuckling to himself, on the verge of losing his mind.

He went back to the school the next day to wait for the girl—he didn't quite want to call her "my daughter" just yet—but she did not show up. Probably avoiding him, he thought. And who could blame her? Again he had the déjà vu feeling of looking for Clara and not for this girl who might be his daughter. The following day he waited at the back entrance to the school, which gave out onto the ball fields and parking lots. Again, the bell rang at two-forty-five and, after a long moment, the doors opened and the building emptied. Half-hidden behind a tree, he watched her: the same slow pace, same hooded sweatshirt. He could pick her out anywhere now, he thought.

"Hi," he said.

"You again? I'm going to scream." She pulled the hood down and removed the earphones. Her skin looked as if it had been brushed with a thin coat of whitewash.

"Are you OK?" Tito asked.

"No, I feel like shit," said the girl. Her hand went to her abdomen, which even in the loose-fitting sweatshirt appeared engorged.

"I've got something to ask you," Tito said.

"What?"

"How old are you?"

"I'm sixteen," she said.

He nodded. "I think I am your father," he said.

"What?"

"Yes."

"You're crazy. My father lives in Florida."

"Are you sure that's your father?"

"Of course I'm sure."

"Your mother's name is Clara Lugo, isn't it?"

"No. That's my *tía*."

"Your *tía*? Are you Efran Lugo's daughter?"

"Efran Lugo? I never heard of him. No. My mother's name is Yunis Martínez."

They were standing in the middle of a soccer field with the girl's peers going past, nobody giving them much notice. He felt everything crumbling. What a fool he'd been. The sister. Of course. "I'm sorry," he said. "I'm very sorry. I must have made a mistake."

"What kind of crazy shit are you on?"

"It was a mistake. I'm sorry. But I really need to speak to Clara. She can explain everything. Will you ask her if she'll meet me?"

"Tía Clara? Weren't you looking for Raúl the last time? You're really starting to confuse me, mister."

"I know. I guess I'm confused, too. I *was* looking for Raúl. I was. But now I'm looking for Clara."

"Why do you need to talk to my *tía*?" Her tone had changed. Now that she was no longer the subject of his questioning, she seemed more assertive. Assertive and a little amused.

"It's complicated, but—" He stopped and took a breath.

"You should know, I talked to Raúl last night."

"You did?"

"But you're not looking for him anymore, right?"

"Right."

"I ain't telling you where he is, anyway. You know what he told me?"

"No."

"He said you were OK. But you're too nice. He said he knew you wouldn't do shit to him. Or to me. He told me you still live with your parents."

"Not anymore."

"So, come on, Mr. Nice. How do you know my *tía?*"

"She and I went to Kennedy High School together and, for a little while, anyway, she was my girlfriend."

"She's married, you know."

"I know, I know."

The girl clutched at her midsection and winced. "Ow. Shit. You got a car?"

"Yes."

"You give me ride? *Coño,* I'm going to throw up."

"Sure. Are you OK?"

"Please, if you give me a ride, I'll talk to my *tía.*"

"My car's parked over there," he said, indicating a side street at the end of the ball field. "Are you OK to walk?" He didn't want to leave her now.

"Yes."

"What's the matter?"

"Stomach," she said. "I barfed this morning and I feel like I'm going to do it again."

"You eat something bad?" he asked.

"Yeah, maybe," she said.

They made their way slowly across the grass and into the neighboring streets. Tito took her backpack, which felt like it held a couple of encyclopedias, and, with a free hand, cupped her elbow. She didn't seem to mind and made it all the way without vomiting.

At the car, she appeared to reconsider, looking at him and then at the passenger-side door, which he was holding open.

"You ain't gonna try nothing, right?"

He raised an eyebrow to indicate that the question was not worth answering.

She winced. "All right. We better hurry. God, why do I feel so shitty?"

He let her give him the directions back to Clara's house, did his best not to anticipate her next command.

"Stop here," she said, and he brought the car to a halt right in front of the house. Before the girl could open her door, a silver minivan swung around them and pulled into the driveway.

"There they are," she said. "Tía Clara and Tío Thomas. You want to talk to them now?"

"No, you talk to Clara first."

"Oh, I get it, you don't want her husband around." She smiled at him.

"Something like that," he admitted.

"Thanks for the ride. I don't think I could have walked."

"*De nada,*" Tito said. "There's just one more thing."

"Yes?"

"What's your name?"

"Deysei," she said.

"Deysei what?"

"Deysei Reyes," she said, and got out of the car.

Tito watched her walk up the drive toward Clara, who was being helped out of the minivan by her cheating husband. *Thomas.* Before Deysei reached them, Tito released the emergency brake and pulled away, accelerating down the street like the driver of a getaway car deserting his partner inside the bank.

Clara

Clara was out in the backyard. The previous owner of their house had constructed a stone gazebo in the stretch of grass beyond the patio, and Clara, whenever she got the chance, liked to retreat there, especially at the end of the day, with a drink, for a few minutes, and enjoy the fact that she owned a gazebo. It was a sultry Thursday evening in early September and in a few minutes she would have to go into the kitchen and prepare dinner. Guillermo was downstairs watching cartoons; Deysei was upstairs in her room; Thomas had left before she got home, heading to D.C. for his interview the next day. Clara had the cordless with her and a glass of wine. She slipped Tito's business card out of her pocket: Cruz Brothers, with the Z enlarged and made into a lightning bolt. She had been haunted by the logo for years. Whenever she saw one of the Cruz Brothers' trucks, she would feel a constriction in her chest. On the first and last days of the month, especially in the summer, nearly every building in Inwood had a van, pickup, or U-Haul parked out front and a string of put-upon-looking youths standing amid an assortment of boxes and furniture on the sidewalk and discussing the order in which things should be packed. The neighborhood looked like a giant stoop sale, or a mass eviction. Mixed in among the do-it-yourselfers, in their rented Ryders and U-Hauls, there were always a couple of professional units, or semiprofessional—Moishe's, Student Movers, Schleppers, and Cruz Brothers. This was during the period after college, before Clara had met Thomas, the period when she was living in the studio in Morningside Heights but spending many evenings on Cooper Street, helping Yunis raise Deysei, often babysitting for Deysei so that Yunis could go out on dates. Friday nights after work, she would buy Chinese on Broadway and pick up a bottle of white zinfandel at PJ's Liquor Warehouse and then make her way over to the apartment, threading a path through all the furniture and boxes. Another week gone. If she saw a Cruz Brothers truck, she would cross the street just in case Tito was still working for them, just in case he might be coming down one of those stainless steel ramps carrying a television set. By then, she was more worried about running into him than she was about running into her father.

A few years later, when she moved to Queens with Thomas, she sometimes saw the trucks in traffic on the Triboro Bridge or Astoria Boulevard. The brothers had expanded their business out of upper Manhattan and the Bronx. Now they served all five boroughs, Yonkers, and northern New Jersey. They'd started advertising in the subway and on the sides of buses. *Put your move on Cruz control.* By then, almost a decade had passed since the summer of Tito. He must have moved on, too, no pun intended. She imagined him taking over his father's building or working for the MTA, married, children of his own. She'd seen the trucks less often since the move to Millwood, but every now and then, one would cross her path on the turnpike or the George Washington Bridge, an emissary from her past. The trucks and their lightning-bolt logo no longer elicited the jolt of anxiety that they once had, for she was convinced that by now, there was no way Tito would still be working for them. How blissful had been her ignorance! All this time, Tito could have been in any one of those trucks, sitting in the driver's seat, looking down on her in her little Honda, honking, driving her off the road.

Maybe this was the new direction her curse had taken. No longer was she going to be prevented from having a baby. Now she was going to have to face the father of the baby she didn't want, the baby she couldn't forget. In her most remorseful moments, she still heard the breathy little pop! of the zygote being sucked from her uterus. Tito's DNA fused to hers and turned into medical waste. It was that guilt that made up her mind to talk to him, but it was not an easy thing.

What was she going to say? Her stomach had been churning all day, but there was no avoiding it now. He knew where she lived. He would call. He would pester Deysei. He would knock on the door. She needed to do something now to prevent this thing from getting out of hand. Already, in the days since the hysteroscopy, Deysei had started teasing her about her "boyfriend" when they were alone. Thomas, perhaps stressing about his interview, had said little, an omission that Clara found somehow more worrisome than his initial offer to talk to Tito himself. Yes, she needed to take action, but she felt completely overwhelmed, completely at a loss.

She picked up the phone and dialed the cell number on the card.

"Moreno," said the voice on the other end in a way that suggested he was in the middle of something—driving or eating. It was a business voice, assertive and curt. It startled her.

"Hello, Tito," she said. "This is Clara."

The silence on the other end of the line lasted so long that she thought they'd been disconnected.

"Tito? Are you there?"

"*Sí*," he said. "I am here."

"Deysei said that you wanted to talk to me." The whole thing was so bizarre that she wound up saying this as though they were family.

"Yes, Clara." There was another pause, but this time she heard something, as if he were rubbing the phone's mouthpiece with a cloth.

"Tito?"

"Yes. Clara," he said. "Do *you* want to talk to *me*?"

"I do, Tito. I think we should talk."

"Good. OK. That's good." There was another long silence.

"Tito?"

"Yes. I'm sorry. This is not easy for me."

"It's not easy for me, either, Tito." Why did she keep saying his name? Perhaps it was something to hold on to in this weird conversation.

"Could I come and see you tomorrow?" he asked.

Whoa! "Tomorrow?" she said. So soon.

"Or . . . wait. Do you remember Ms. Almonte? From Kennedy?"

"Alicia? Yes, of course I remember her."

"Her mother passed away this week and the funeral is on Saturday, the day after tomorrow. Maybe you want to go with me?"

"To a funeral?"

"Or just to the wake afterward. It would mean a lot to her if you came."

"I'm surprised she even remembers me. And why did she invite you? You were never in one of her classes, were you?"

"No, but I moved her this summer. We were talking about you, actually."

"And what was she saying?"

He hesitated.

"Is it a secret?"

"Maybe we shouldn't do this on the phone. I could pick you up on Saturday, drive you into the city."

"That's OK," she said. "Why don't we just meet at the Piper's Kilt for lunch on Saturday? I'm not sure about the funeral."

"Piper's. Sure. What time?"

"Two."

"Two on Saturday."

"I'll see you then. Bye." She hung up, glad to have *that* over with.

She took a breath and let the air out through her nose. Her

parting from Tito was so directly connected to her finding—or being found by—her mother that she now felt compelled to hit speed-dial number 4 on the phone.

"*Hola, Mami. Soy Clara.*"

"Clara," said her mother. "*¿Qué pasa?*"

"Is Yunis there?"

"No."

"What's the matter?" she asked. She could tell by her mother's voice that something was.

"I am not going to take it anymore. Yunis thinks she's staying in a hotel. She goes out. I don't know where. She comes back late. Doesn't tell me anything. Then she sleeps until lunch. She thinks she's on vacation."

This was a variation of the litany her mother had been giving her since Yunis's move. Clara had been doing her best to placate her, but she knew only too well how infuriating her sister could be.

"It's going to be OK."

"Please God, *mija*. Yes. It's going to be OK because she's leaving. I told her she has to go. She don't lift a finger around here. Just eating and drinking. Never washes a single dish. Doesn't help me pay for a single thing."

"OK, Mami, take it easy." She didn't want her sister to come back. No. That was the last thing she needed now. "Did you really tell her she had to leave?"

"Yes," she said defiantly. "I'm kicking her out. And you know, the new man is already cheating on her."

"Oh, God," said Clara. She couldn't take much more of this. "What about the inheritance?"

"The lawyers, they are all fighting about it. You know, that man, her papi's papi, had eight children with a bunch of different women. It's going to be long time before she gets those moneys."

"Can you tell her to call me when she gets back?"

"Who knows when that will be?" There was a brief silence.

"Think about giving her another chance, Mami."

"I'm not talking about it anymore, *mija*. She's leaving. How's everything there? How's my grandson?"

"He's fine."

"And Thomas?"

"Fine, too."

"You pregnant?"

"No, Mami. We're working on it."

"It's not really work, is it?" she said, laughing.

"OK, Mami, that's enough. I'll talk to you later. Tell Yunis to call me. Bye-bye."

"Bye, *amorcita*."

Clara hung up. Yunis coming back. It hadn't even been a month. The timing, as usual, was terrible. Just when she started to feel that she was getting somewhere with Deysei. On the phone, she'd heard merengue playing in the background and someone laughing. She could picture the scene: Tía Gigi and Tío Plinio sitting at the kitchen table slicing a mango or maybe smashing the shells of walnuts. A cousin or two with a toy on the floor. The adults would have been sharing one of those large Presidentes, drinking it in small glasses to keep the beer from getting warm. The windows would be open, the doors ajar, and a breeze drifting through the room, an early warning that they could expect rain later in the evening. But later, not now. Now it was time to drink and cook and tell stories. Clara wanted to be there. She wanted to be on vacation in Santo Domingo, to be catered to by her family, to be away from all these troubles. Her aunts would take Guillermo and feed him, entertain him. They would do her laundry; they would make her favorite foods and that oatmeal-milk-and-mango drink she could never quite get right herself. Now that she was in the midst of the kind of craziness that was the norm in Yunis's life, she could see just how tempting running away to D.R. must have been to her sister. And, indeed, it was wonderful in short spells—as long as your money held out. Because there were expectations in the other direction, too. An aunt who needed a new TV, another whose car had broken down, the cousin who had lupus and couldn't afford the medication. These were the unwritten rules of her family relations, the tithes you were expected to pay if you visited from New York. Her mother, now that she had retired there permanently, was the worst of them all, the neediest. She had First World tastes on a Third World budget. There was always something to be repaired at the house, new tile for the bathroom, new cabinets for the kitchen, new locks to keep out the handyman who'd stolen the keys to the old locks. Her mother held the position as the matriarch of the clan, the underfunded provider for the underprovided. That slow financial bleed would have been at least part of the problem for Yunis. The cousins and aunts and uncles and their hangers-on would not have understood that she couldn't keep a job, would not have understood that she relied on welfare to help her with the rent, food stamps to feed her daughter; all they knew was that she came from New York, which meant that she had to have money, an assumption Clara had once made about her parents. As if that were not enough, there would also have been the issue of the boyfriend. Thrice married, twice widowed, and once divorced, their mother was currently without male companionship of a certain stripe. She would not have enjoyed seeing Yunis coming and going with her latest *marido*. She would have undermined, complained, done whatever she could to make sure that the relationship failed. Once she realized that Yunis was broke, that she was there to mooch until this "inheritance" came through, she would have done whatever she could, in her passive-aggressive way, to drive her back to New York. No, it was not surprising at all that it was happening—only that it was happening so fast.

The phone rang. She was never going to make dinner at this rate.

"Hello?"

"Clara?"

"Yes? Thomas?"

"Hi, baby. I'm just about in Philly. I thought I'd check in with you."

"How do you feel?" she said.

"Good," he said. "Optimistic. So Deysei met Gilly off the bus this afternoon?"

"Yes. It was fine. They were eating cereal and watching cartoons when I got home."

"Did you talk to that guy yet?"

Clara hesitated. "No, not yet. This weekend, I'll do it. I'll tell you all about it when you get home." She let her voice trail off, as if there were more.

"What is it?"

"Well, it looks like Yunis might be coming back."

"Already? What happened?"

"It's complicated."

"Didn't she sublet her apartment?"

"Yes."

"So, does that mean she's going to stay with us?"

"I don't know. I haven't talked to her about it."

"Jeez, Clara."

"Look, forget about it for now. We'll talk about it when you get back. It's not definite yet," she said, though in her gut she knew otherwise.

"OK."

"Good luck. I know you're going to do great in the interview. Say hi to your mother for me."

"Thanks. I'll see you when I get back."

ONE SUNDAY EVENING, in her senior year of high school, Clara sat at the kitchen table pretending to read the Spanish-language newspaper her father had left there the day before. Instead of reading, she was listening, listening to a click. It was a plastic click,

a snap-*snap*! She heard it one more time and then heard the rush of
air onto her stepmother's curler-laden head, heard Dolores put her
scaly feet up on the tattered ottoman and begin to leaf through a
copy of *Vanidades*. While Dolores sat under the dryer, Clara went
up the stairs to the master bedroom and turned on the TV. The
room was sparely furnished and yet still untidy—shoes on the floor,
clothes hanging out of drawers. Clara had no interest in whatever
secrets might lie in the bedside tables, in the half-open closets. She
was there to watch television. The set was tuned to Telemundo
and she reminded herself to return to that channel when she was
done. Using the controls on top of the cable box (not touching the
remote, which lay on the unmade bed), she cycled down through
the other foreign-language channels—a Chinese news program, an
Indian dance routine, a sexy Italian woman talking about sculp-
ture—to CBS, just in time to see the stopwatch clicking through
the seconds and the grave, deep voice saying, "This is *60 Minutes*,"
as if it were the word of the Lord. Then an antacid commercial. So
she'd missed the introductory part, but none of the actual reports.
All through dinner, she'd been eyeing the kitchen clock, wondering
when Dolores was going under the dryer. Having missed her usual
Friday salon appointment, she'd rolled her hair before serving the
meal and sat at the end of the table, not eating, but looking like a
pop-art medusa in her pink curlers and her floral robe while Clara
and Efran choked down their dry pork chops and *moro*.

Her assignment for that week's meeting of the Word Club was
60 Minutes. Ms. Almonte had told them earlier in the year that there
were certain resources every educated, independent woman could
rely on for the real news about the world. One was *60 Minutes*. Another was the *New Yorker* magazine. A third was National Public
Radio. Each week in Ms. Almonte's room, they talked about these
sacrosanct cultural outposts—or at least Ms. Almonte and most of
her class talked, while Clara listened. Clara had limited access to
the trinity. She was not allowed a radio in her room, not allowed to

watch English-language television, and she had gotten into trouble earlier that year when Dolores, snooping in her schoolbag, had come across a Xerox of a *New Yorker* portfolio by Richard Avedon in which a fashion model made love to a skeleton.

"What sickness is this?" Dolores had said.

"It's for school."

"School! We never studied anything like this when I was in school."

Clara had to bite her tongue. Dolores had been educated in a one-room school near Higüey, the *salchichón* capital of the Dominican Republic. Of course she'd never seen anything like the Avedon pictures.

"You're lucky I'm not going to show this to your father. After everything he's done for you, this is how you thank him? Pornography? Sex with skeletons?" Dolores frowned and shook the rolled-up Xeroxes at her.

It was a far cry from the beatings she had given Clara with the stick—beatings that had all but stopped around the time Clara went through puberty. A combination of events had put an end to them. Dolores had gained weight after the birth of Efran and suffered from early onset arthritis, she claimed, because of all the handwashing of clothes she'd done in her life. The paint pole was harder to grasp even as Clara was more nimble in avoiding it. The beatings went from a less-than-daily event to just an occasional flare-up. Those dying spasms, it seemed to Clara, represented Dolores's refusal to fully acknowledge that her absolute control over her stepdaughter was gone. They had not stopped completely, however, until Efran, at the age of seven, had gone through a sensitive period. He couldn't bear to see a fly swatted, a mouse trapped, a mosquito slapped, let a lone a thirteen-year-old girl struck with a stick. One night, after he'd witnessed a particularly brutal attack by Dolores, he had started crying. "No, Mami, no! Stop it! You're hurting her. You're hurting her." Efran was nothing if not spoiled, and his pleas were granted by

Dolores—not out of mercy for Clara but because her little *príncipe* always got what he wanted. By then, Clara had reached the conclusion that her home life was something that had to be endured until she turned eighteen and could leave. The focus of her existence was school—her ticket out of Inwood and away from Dolores.

Those pleas from Efran were the high-water mark in Clara's relationship with her half-brother. She'd done her share of diapering and babysitting through his childhood, had done her best not to hold it against her sibling that his mother was such a hypocritical, self-centered *pendeja*. For the most part, they lived separate existences. Efran's room was fixed up, painted, filled with toys. Clara's had remained almost unchanged since her arrival from the Dominican Republic. Efran's birthdays were marked with extravagant house parties at which two enormous white cakes were brought out, while Clara's were barely marked at all. Now, in early adolescence himself, Efran came and went from the house as he pleased, his evenings free of chores, his weekends unencumbered by work at the store. Clara still had her rounds of cleaning, the laundry to do, and a day behind the cash register at Lugo Hardware on the weekends. She tried, tried not to hold any of this against Efran, but it was hard, especially because of Dolores.

Though the beatings had come to an end, Dolores found new ways of tormenting her. She was still engaged in her campaign of disparagement, belittlement, and psychological warfare, the focus of which was Clara's mother, who was accused again and again of doing much worse than coupling with skeletons.

In adolescence, Clara had finally come to accept the idea that her mother was not going to show up and rescue her. She soothed her longings with novels. Early on it was Nancy Drew, whose pluck and self-reliance gave Clara courage. After that it was books by Judy Blume, V. C. Andrews, Sue Grafton, and many, many others, a succession of tales with female heroines who gave her succor. Clara's mother, for all intents and purposes, ceased to exist as a person—

she became less believable than the characters in those books. She became an abstraction, a straw figure for Dolores to abuse and Clara to long for. Early on, Clara believed that there must be some truth to what she was being told, but when she got a little older, she began to think that maybe it was this idea of her mother that had all along been the cause of Dolores's ire—such anger earned for having done nothing more than marrying Roberto Lugo first. Clara questioned just how Dolores knew such details about her mother in the first place.

"We hear things," said Dolores. "Friends tell us."

"You know where my mother is, then?"

"No."

"But your friends know. Can I talk to your friends? I want to see her."

"No. It would be too painful for you to see her. She's a whore. You would be ashamed of her."

"It doesn't matter. She's still my mother."

SHE SAT ON the bed with her notebook, waiting for the commercials to finish. Finally, she was going to have something to contribute to the Word Club. Normally she had to sit in Ms. Almonte's room and listen to Yesenia and Victoria saying clever things about Dr. Kevorkian or Frank Sinatra or the *Exxon Valdez* oil spill. At the end of one of the first sessions, Ms. Almonte—or Alicia, as they were allowed to call her outside school hours—asked her why she'd been so quiet. Clara explained that her father did not allow English-language television in the house.

"Nothing? Not even a news program?"

"No, he says English-language TV will poison me and make me forget that I am Dominican. The only show we ever watch in English is the Miss America Pageant."

Alicia gave a laugh that was also a kind of snort. "Perhaps I should talk to your father."

"No, no, that's OK."

Clara knew that if her father got one look at Alicia, it would all be over. She'd have to stop going to the Word Club, which she'd billed as an SAT prep class, even though she'd already taken her SATs, had, in fact, already been accepted to both Cornell and Hunter with the promise of substantial financial aid. (All of her college application correspondence had gone through Ms. Almonte.) Not only that, but she would have to switch out of Alicia's AP English class just as they were about to start reading *How the García Girls Lost Their Accents.* She would lose everything that she'd spent her entire time in school trying to achieve.

Clara's plan had succeeded. She had taken that name-calling and mimicking of her accent in grade school and used it to push herself to speak better English than all of her attackers—to speak like her teachers. Of course, by the time she had mastered her adopted language—by the time she had removed all traces of her accent, by the time she learned to say bed *sheets,* not bed *shits,* and *thank God,* not *thanks God,* by the time she was reading S. E. Hinton, John Steinbeck, and Madeleine L'Engle—she was being ridiculed for being too smart, for being a little brownnoser, for being a little *Americanita,* for not being street: in short, for being a phony. But she did not mind. She wore those insults as a badge of pride. Clara knew she had achieved her goal when Tito, one of her worst tormentors in her first year in New York, started following her around in high school, giving her the eyeball. He seemed to have forgotten about the names he had called her—the *jíbara* remark on the day of Efran's birth and many other insults. Delighted and surprised, she planned to encourage his interest for a while and then reject him in the most embarrassing manner she could come up with. But the more she got to know this older, less surly Tito, the more she liked him—the more he reminded her of his father, Don Felix, for whom she still felt great warmth. The prospect of thumbing her nose at the ridiculous feud between their fathers by befriending Tito also appealed to her. Her plan to set him up and then spurn him withered with each walk home they took together, with each kiss he gave her. Plus there was the other thing. The sex thing. Tito had grown into a fine-looking young man, his body trim and strong from moving all that furniture. In the Word Club meetings, Alicia had been encouraging them to explore sex before they went to college so that they could be in full control of their liberated selves. She encouraged them to be fearless, not to wait for a boy to ask them out, but to turn the tables on the boys. "You don't need a man to be happy," she said. "But you do need one to have sex. You are going to need men just as you need books, music, and art. And as with those things, you need to be educated, you need to have taste, you need to know what you're doing."

So here she was, getting ready to graduate, on her way to college, the world opening up around her, the possibility of sex with Tito becoming increasingly real, and meanwhile, she could not watch a television news program in her father's house. The ads finished and Lesley Stahl appeared, introducing a segment about Édith Cresson, the first woman to become prime minister of France. Alicia would be all over this, Clara thought as she began to take notes.

As the show went into its next commercial break, she heard something in the hallway—Efran's voice. She turned off the TV (there was no time to reset the channel to Telemundo). She stepped across the room to her father's dresser and picked up a pair of nail clippers that were always there—her ostensible reason for coming into the room, even though her nails were bitten to the quick.

"See, Mami. There she is," said Efran.

Dolores followed him into the room looking exasperated, the curlers still in her hair and her face red from the heat of the dryer. "Clara, why are you in here?" she asked.

"Just cutting my nails with Papi's clippers."

"Efran says he heard the TV."

"No. I'm just about to start on my homework." Clara held up her notebook.

"Let's see," said Dolores, and reached not for Clara's notebook but for the remote. Ed Bradley appeared, talking about the possible detrimental health effects of dental fillings.

"*Coño*, Clara! What did your father tell you?"

"It's homework!" protested Clara.

"Homework? Like that pornography I found in your bag?"

"No, they were talking about the French prime minister."

"Get out of my room. You must think I'm stupid."

On her way out, Clara looked at Efran, who was smiling.

The brief alliance that had been forged between them during his "sensitive" period was long gone. He was eleven now, devious, obnoxious. He was becoming such a Dominican homeboy that it angered her to be even partially related to him. He didn't lift the toilet seat, didn't make his bed, didn't wash a dish. She was amazed that the English-language TV ban applied to him, too, but her father, who was sometimes arbitrary in his rules, seemed to have less of a double standard than Dolores—and the TV rule was his.

As she walked down the hall to her room, Clara heard Dolores say to Efran, "You keep an eye on her. That's a good boy."

LATER THAT NIGHT, Clara was writing an essay when her father came into her room. She almost never saw him sober anymore; this drunk man was her father now. More than anything, she was embarrassed by him, by his inebriation, by his small mind and his dumb Dominican habits—his stubborn refusal to wear socks, even in the winter, by his preference for using his knife like a fork, by the ridiculous *campesino* tin cup he liked to drink out of. Everything he did made her ashamed.

"Clara." He paused and looked around the shabby room, steadied himself with a hand on the wall. "Dolores tells me you were watching American television."

"It was homework, Papi."

"Television is not homework. You expect me to believe that? Ay, how I wish they sold a television that got only Spanish stations."

"Papi, this is an English-speaking country."

"Not all of it. Walk down Dyckman Street and tell me how much English you hear. You are Dominican and this is a Dominican house. When you live in this house you speak Spanish. You eat Spanish food. You dream Spanish dreams."

"Yes, Papi," she said.

He steadied himself and looked at her again. "Gustavo says he saw you in the park with a boy."

"When?" asked Clara, defiantly. Gustavo, who had been a couple of years ahead of her in school, now worked for her father. On Saturdays, when she did her shift at the register, he made his interests known to her. "*Ay, dimelo, mamita!*" he said whenever she arrived.

"Last Friday," her father said.

"Wasn't he working? How did he see me if he was at the store?" This was the wrong approach, but she couldn't help herself.

"He was delivering something. Says he saw you and a boy going into the park at 207th Street after school."

"I came straight home."

"Your mother says you were late. She says you've been coming home late every Friday. She needs your help, Clara. Her arthritis. Her hip. You have to help her."

"I help her."

"Who is this boy?"

Clara said nothing.

"You know what he wants, don't you? You tell him he can't see you anymore. You tell him Roberto Lugo didn't raise any whore for a daughter."

"Papi, what are you going to do when I go to college? You can't watch me every minute. Gustavo won't see what I'm doing—as much as I'm sure he'd like to."

"You'll still be living here. You go to class and come home. Help your mother."

"What if I had wanted to go to college somewhere else? What if I had not gotten into Hunter?"

He looked at her as if he'd never considered the possibility, as if this were the most outlandish idea he'd ever heard. Her father had always wanted her to do well at school and, yes, go to college, so long as she stayed within his gaze, never out of his reach. "Where?"

"I don't know. California. Massachusetts. Lots of kids go away to college."

"Not my daughter. You wouldn't get a penny from me if you went away. You wouldn't be welcome in this house. Do you understand? I'd disown you."

"So, what am I supposed to do, live in this room until I'm fifty?"

"No. Until you get married. Then you can move out."

Clara laughed. "How am I ever going to get married if you never allow me to go out and meet someone."

"You meet lots of boys. What about Gustavo?"

"Gustavo is a *pordiosero*."

Her father shook his head. "You are never going to marry anyone with a mouth like that." He reflected for a moment in drunken solemnity. "There's a party up in the Bronx on Saturday night. Dolores's friend Marti. You come with us."

Her other option, she knew, was to stay home with Efran, who would spend the evening playing practical jokes on her. Efran hated these grown-up fiestas, and so it might be worth accepting just to spite him.

"Come," said her father. "A little food. A little dancing. Some laughing. It's good for you, I think. And I can keep an eye on who you're talking to."

MARTI HAD BEEN in the accident with Dolores the year before Clara had come to New York. The livery cab they were in was rear-ended by a bus. Later it turned out that the cab driver had been drunk. So everyone was to blame except the passengers. Dolores and Marti ended up in the hospital together. The accident and the settlement made them like sorority sisters or something. It also made them—by their standards—rich.

Marti had suffered more serious injuries than Dolores—she'd lost the hearing in one ear (Clara could never remember which one, since it seemed that Marti was just plain deaf) and had a scar that ran from her knee to her ankle. Marti liked to tell everyone how the doctors had almost amputated. *"Marti la pirata,"* she liked to say. She had an eye patch that she liked to bring out when she'd had a few drinks. There were rumors of other scars in places only Marti's husband ever saw, and her lack of children and occasionally weird behavior seemed to lend credence to these rumors. With the money, she'd bought a house in the Dominican Republic to which she would retire when she reached sixty-two. She also must have kept some kind of party slush fund, because two or three times a year, she threw a massive fiesta. People came from New Jersey and Pennsylvania. Once, a relative had flown in from Santo Domingo and flown back the next day.

Marti's building was in the 230s, west of Broadway. There was a low-ceilinged, wood-paneled function room in the basement, which she rented for these affairs. A row of folding tables would be set up along one wall, and on them would be a series of entries in the Best Dominican Food contest: *pernil, moro, pastelitos, tostones, arroz con pollo.* On either end of the row of tables, like sentries, stood garbage barrels lined with black GLAD bags and filled with ice. The long necks of Coronas and Presidentes protruded like bottles stuffed with messages floating on a frozen sea. Another table nearby served as a landing spot for guests to drop off their contributions to the event: Hennessy, Johnnie Walker, and Absolut, along with mixers and cordials. In the back, an aspiring DJ from down the block set up his turntable and two steamer-trunk-sized speakers. The music was loud enough that even Marti could identify the songs. Around the room were odds and ends of furniture, busted up couches, dented metal chairs, and paint-stained stools. There was never enough furniture for the number of people who came, barely enough space in the room to contain everyone. If you stayed long enough, you could rub yourself up against everyone there. Aware of this, a couple of postadolescent boys (too old to be friendly with Efran and too young to know Clara), were pressing the flesh, pressing the cotton, the rayon, the silk, and the polyester. One of them, squeezing past Clara, brought his hand up toward her breasts. "Touch me and die, *chulo*," she barked with such vehemence that the kid said, "*Coño*," and backed away from her, spilling several drinks in his retreat.

Out of the tectonic shifts of bodies came Gustavo. He was dark—darker even than she was. His nappy hair was like a ski cap with springs glued to it. He had eyes set very far apart—a salamander's eyes, she thought—and a weirdly thin nose, maybe the genetic remnant of some Nordic sailor who'd passed through the Caribbean generations ago.

"*Negra*," he called to her. This was a term of endearment he used whenever her father was not in earshot. *Mi Negra. Mi Negrita.* She steadfastly called him Gustavo, now and then referring to him as Señor Benítez, which he hated.

"How are you, *mi corazón*?" he asked, handing her a red plastic cup.

"What's this?" she asked.

"Cognac, baby. Only the best for you. Cognac and ginger ale. On the rocks."

She accepted it against her better judgment—it was hot—and took a sip, looking around to make sure her father couldn't see her, wondering if there was any chance Tito might show up.

"Marti always throws a good party, don't she?" said Gustavo.

"I don't know. I haven't been to one in a while."

"I know. You don't get out too much, do you?"

"No."

"What you say we got to Club Mirage next Saturday—me and you. I already asked your pops."

"My father said I could go to Club Mirage with you?"

"*Sí, Negra.* But *only* if you go with me."

"I don't think so."

"Come on, Clarita. I show you a good time. I treat you like a queen."

"Since I'm not a queen, I think I'll pass."

Gustavo took a sip of his drink. "That's too bad, because . . . I found out who your little homeboy is. The one you been going to the park with on Friday afternoons."

"What are you talking about?"

"Yeah, I bet your pops wouldn't be too happy to hear you been hanging with Tito Moreno."

"Who?"

"Ha! You know who I'm talking about. Your father still hates Tito's dad, you know. Still calls him a traitor to the Dominican race. Look. Here's your papi now. Let's tell him."

Clara turned and saw her father forcing himself through the crowd, pushing people aside and drawing cries of "*¡Tranquilo!*" and "*¡Calma te!*" as he moved through the room.

Gustavo started to say something but her father cut him off. "Come, Clara. We're leaving."

"What? We just got here." But her father had taken her by the biceps and was pulling her away from Gustavo—not a bad thing, altogether. Then she noticed that Dolores and Efran were already waiting by the door.

What was going on? She looked around. Off to the side, deep in the crowd at the back of the room, not far from where the DJ had set up, Clara saw another disturbance, another parting of bodies, and in between the limbs and the hair and the bottles of beer, she saw—could it *be*?

Her father was pulling her even more stridently behind him, like a lifeguard saving her from drowning.

"Wait, wait," she protested.

"No," said her father. "We are leaving *now*."

"Wait!" she shouted, but to no avail.

He dragged her out of that basement and all but carried her down to Broadway, with Dolores and Efran following. Clara struggled against him, but he had her in both arms, pinned against his chest, exhaling his rummy breath into her face. Efran was asking Dolores what was happening, why they were leaving so soon. Dolores didn't respond, preoccupied as she was by waving her arms at the passing traffic. A cab came, separating from the flow under the elevated tracks and stopping in front of them. The four of them got in—Clara's father pushing her into the backseat so that she was trapped between him and Dolores, Efran riding in the front. As the driver guided them into the stream of traffic, Clara looked out the window past her father and saw two women coming down the street—one older and one younger, the younger one either obese or pregnant, she couldn't tell which. In the darkness and the shadows of the elevated, Clara couldn't make out their faces. The signal changed and the cab was sucked south in the rush of cars and buses, across the Broadway Bridge, back into Manhattan.

"What was that witch doing at Marti's?" asked Dolores.

"I don't know," said her father. "But I'm glad I saw her when I did."

"We shouldn't have brought her," said Dolores, glancing at Clara.

"I can't believe it," said her father. "All these years I've never seen her once. Not once. And there she was. Like a ghost."

Clara was silent. She felt an exultation run though her body, the giddiness of her childhood wish finally being fulfilled. Her mother was real, not an abstraction. Her mother had found her, just as Clara had always hoped. It was happening. One way or another, her days in her father's house were numbered.

IT TOOK LONGER than she expected. Having been seen by her mother, Clara expected contact right away, but the days went by with no word—no phone call, no knock on the door. School came to an end and the summer began and she wondered if the night at Marti's party had been nothing more than her overactive imagination combined with a longing for her absent parent. She asked her father about it. "That was my mother you saw at Marti's, wasn't it?"

"I don't know what you're talking about."

"That's why you hauled me out of there like that."

"It was getting late, that's all," her father said.

That last summer in Inwood, Clara saw a lot more of her father than she had in some time, and the more she saw of him, the happier she was that she would soon be away from him. She worked every day at Lugo Hardware. This was partly so that he could keep an eye on her and partly because he wanted her cheap labor. At the end of the week, he would hand her a twenty-dollar bill with a wink and a sly "*Gracias.*" Before Marti's party, Clara's only free time came late on Friday afternoons, when business was slow and her father hosted his weekly card game with some of his best customers: local contractors and handymen. It was an important part of the business and also an end-of-the-week stress release, the lapse in vigilance necessary to blow off steam. Her father and Gustavo set up a table in the back of the store, brought in a case of beer and some *arroz con pollo* from El Malecon, turned up the music, and laughed loud enough to be heard by people across four lanes of Dyckman Street traffic. Gustavo minded the store with one eye while also acting as dealer and cashier. Clara was released, forgotten about. They didn't want a woman on the premises. Friday afternoons were also when Dolores went to the salon to get her hair done—an ordeal that took six or seven hours, the female equivalent of her father's card game. Gossip exchanged, alcohol consumed, the week laid to rest. This was how Clara managed to continue to see Tito once the school year came to an end. Those Friday afternoons were also when she had her occasional meetings with Alicia Almonte, who was the conduit for her correspondence from Cornell. Clara and Ms. Almonte would get together in the Riverdale Diner to go over the university's paperwork and discuss possible courses for the fall. Alicia had helped Clara fill out the numerous forms Cornell required and had written a letter to the university alerting them to the fact that Clara would be unsupported by her family and asking Cornell to consider her for supplementary financial aid, which was granted.

"Are you willing to risk everything for this?" Ms. Almonte had asked earlier in the school year when she offered to handle all of Clara's college correspondence. "Are you prepared for your father's anger when he discovers that your Hunter application was just a ruse? Are you prepared for him never to speak to you again? I have not met him, but from everything you have told me, he won't be happy in the least when he discovers your deception."

"Yes," said Clara. "I'm ready. I know what this is. I am running away from home. I know I'm not going back."

"If you are prepared for that, then I will do anything I can to help you. But be warned, Clara, it's going to be hard on you. Where will you go at Thanksgiving? At Christmas? You can call me if you ever need a place to stay. I think you are very brave to do this."

"I'm not brave," she said. "Just desperate."

That was her plan. Even if her mother did not reappear, she was going to abduct herself.

• • •

MARTI'S PARTY HAD made everything harder. Clara was forced to stay in the store even on Friday afternoons, leafing through copies of *Hoy* and the *Post* until the card game was over and her father locked up and they walked home together, her father's mood dependent entirely on how he had done in the game. If he had come out ahead, they would stop at the Carvel on Broadway for an ice cream cone. If he had lost, he would curse the other players and console himself with the thought that the money would eventually come back to him in exchange for spackle, pipe, and drywall. As far as Clara could tell, Gustavo had not told her father about Tito—perhaps in the belief that he still had a chance to convince her to go to Club Mirage with him, a belief she kept from flatlining by occasionally speaking to him.

A month after Marti's party, on a quiet afternoon in late July, with the fans blowing in the front, and the guffaws booming from the back, a pregnant girl came into the store. She was young and pretty, with good hair—long and thick and curly—and something about her seemed familiar to Clara, as if she'd seen her face in an ad for BMCC or ITT Tech. Gustavo, who was leaning on the storeroom doorway, keeping tabs on the game, saw her, too. Clara watched him watching the girl. Normally Gustavo would have leapt to assist such an attractive female customer, but Clara saw the fact of the girl's pregnancy register, saw Gustavo's attention turn away from the girl and back to the card players in the storerom. With a flick of his hand, he indicated that Clara should attend to her customer.

Clara walked out from behind the counter and approached the girl. "*¿Necesitas ayuda?*"

"*Sí,*" said the young girl, smiling at her. She reached into her purse and pulled out a scrap of stained brown paper, which looked like it had been torn off someone's lunch sack. "My mami is redoing her kitchen. Do you have this?" She handed the paper to Clara.

Clara looked at the scrap. On it were two lines of scrawl in Spanish:

Write your address and we will come for you. Tell us when.
Tu Mama.

Clara looked at the girl. "*¿Es verdad?*"

"*Sí*," whispered the girl. "I'm Yunis. I am your sister."

So, here it was, the message from her mother that she had been waiting for. It had come in human form, in the form of a sister she did not know she had.

"That one's on order," said Clara, stagily. "Maybe next week. Let me give you the phone number here and you can call." Taking a pen out of her pocket, she wrote the address of her father's house, the date for the following Sunday, and eight a.m. She gave the paper back to the girl—to her sister.

"*Gracias*," said Yunis, loudly. Then, under her breath. "Pack a bag. Be ready. You hear me?" And with that, she walked out of the store.

CLARA WAS ELATED and terrified. But what was there to be terrified of? Shouldn't she be just elated? She was eighteen years old—legally an adult—and she had been planning to leave her father's house anyway. Why was she scared? All this meant was that now she had help in abducting herself. But she could not deny it. She was afraid. That night, as she lay in bed unable to sleep, she regretted telling Yunis to come back in a week. The week seemed like a year. Anything could happen. Her mother could lose interest. Change her mind. Clara should have asked her to come back the next day. Or—the idea came to her with an *Oh my God, I'm so stupid!* thwack to the forehead—she should have simply walked out of the store with Yunis earlier that afternoon. Why hadn't she thought of that? No bag. No goodbyes. Just the clothes on her back—the same way her father had taken her from the Dominican Republic. Wouldn't that have been right? Wouldn't that have been poetic? Her father emerging from his card game, drunk, asking Gustavo where the hell his daughter was. Gustavo not having an answer for him, stammering and embarrassed. But in that moment in the store, with the scrap of paper in her hand, Clara was still hemmed in by her old life. She wasn't thinking like a fugitive anymore. She was thinking like someone about to assume possession of herself. Besides, there were things she needed to take care of before she left. The most important of these was Tito.

He had told her that there was an empty apartment in his father's building and that they could use it while his parents were away. The apartment would be empty until the end of the month—Tito was supposed to clean and paint it before his mother and father returned from their second honeymoon. It suddenly seemed urgent to have this final meeting with him, to do the thing they had been building toward all spring and summer. In her heart, she had always known that their relationship would not survive her departure for Cornell. She planned to sever all ties to the neighborhood, and Tito, she knew, would always be tied to the neighborhood.

Clara told her father that there was an all-day orientation at Hunter the following Thursday. Then, during her lunch break, she walked to the phone booth on the corner and called Tito to tell him that Thursday she could come to see him. Now there was something other than the escape to occupy her mind.

The early part of the week went by. During the day, she worked in the store; in the evening, she did her chores at home; late at night, she quietly went through her meager possessions, selecting the few items that she would pack in her school satchel and a plastic shopping bag. Having never gone on vacation, having not flown on a plane since coming to New York, Clara did not own a suitcase.

Thursday came and, at breakfast, she tried to act like it was nothing special. She hadn't dressed for the occasion, choosing jeans and a white blouse. She had a three-ring binder and a couple of pens to make it look official.

"What time will you be coming back?" asked her father.

"I don't know. Like I told you, it's an all-day thing. I'll be back for supper."

"You be careful on the subway. Don't let anyone squeeze into a seat beside you. If they do that, you stand up."

"Yes, Papi."

"Maybe you should cover yourself up. Put on a sweater or something."

"It's August," she said.

"I know, I know. The classrooms might be air-conditioned at the school, You never know." He extended his forefingers like two erect nipples.

"Don't worry, Papi. I know how to look after myself."

She walked to the Dyckman Street station and, instead of taking the train downtown, rode uptown to the last stop, 207th Street. From there, she made her way to Tito's building.

He answered the door looking nervous, which only made her nervous. Immediately, he tried to kiss her, but she moved away.

"So, come on, show me the place," she said, hoping to buy herself a little time, to calm herself down. She didn't feel excited at all. She just felt worried, afraid.

Tito smiled and bowed. "Right this way, ma'am." He showed her a bedroom near the entrance to apartment, telling her it was her study, pointing out the bookcases. "I had your diploma from Cornell framed and put up on the wall."

"That's very thoughtful of you," she said. He seemed to understand what was going on, that he needed to make her feel comfortable, that he needed to seduce her all over again. He made a few attempts to take her hand or kiss her cheek, but they were playful. Many men, she thought, would have grabbed her, forced themselves on her. But Tito was his father's son, a gentleman.

There was food in the kitchen and a bottle of wine chilling in the fridge. "You hoping to get lucky, or something?" she asked, which made him laugh.

"Hoping." He said it in such a way that she knew if nothing happened between them this afternoon, he would wait. He would not force her. The futility of his patience chastened her. She would need to give him something.

They made their way through the rest of his tour, which ended at a second bedroom, where a sleeping bag had been laid on the floor and made up with clean linens like a proper bed.

"Let's try it out," she said, and lowered herself onto the sleeping bag, slipping off her sandals. Tito sat down next to her, but she got up again and went to the window, still anxious. A moment later, he was there behind her, his hands on her hips, his chest pressing gently against her back. She could smell him, a faint whiff of cologne mixed with fresh sweat. Slowly, he turned her around and reached up and squeezed the flesh of her earlobe. It was something he liked to do, like a cat swatting a ball of yarn. Her earlobe must have been some kind of pressure point, because his squeezing of it always relaxed her, always turned her on. With his other hand, he swept his fingers across her throat in a gesture as soft as a breeze. Whatever he was doing was working. She felt desire, like the tickle of someone's breath between her legs.

The hand that had been at her neck reached behind her, up under her blouse, the fingers pressing against the small of her back. Almost of its own accord, her mouth opened to kiss him.

WHEN IT WAS over, she cried, small spasmlike sobs, not much louder than hiccups. She and Tito were mostly naked, mostly uncovered on the sleeping bag, cooling off after the heat of sex.

"What?" Tito asked. "Did I hurt you?"

"No, no," she said. "I'm sorry." It had been uncomfortable, at times awkward, but also pleasurable, the first taste of something she wanted more of.

"What is it? Are you OK?"

"I'm fine," she said.

"Are you hungry? We've got all that food."

"Yes," she said. "I am hungry." She wiped her nose on her wrist.

He got up and went into the kitchen, and while he was in there, heating the food in the microwave, popping the cork on the wine, she decided: She wasn't going to tell him. She wasn't going to ruin this by saying goodbye.

EARLY IN THE morning on Sunday, when everyone else in the house was asleep, Clara got out of bed and made her final rounds, her farewell tour. She was still a little sore from the sex three days earlier. It was not an unpleasant feeling, a tenderness, a reminder of Tito she could carry with her into her new life (unaware as she was of the much more enduring reminder that was already growing and dividing within her).

The dawn came later and later every day. Now, at a quarter to seven, the house was filled with the murky light of hazy late summer. When she had first been brought to New York, Sunday was a church day. Dolores insisted that they all attend Mass, a ritual Clara's father endured for a time because his wife was still undergoing a temporary kindling of religious faith from surviving the accident. It had stopped not long after Efran was born, when sleep became more important than church. Sleep had consumed Sunday mornings ever since.

Clara went down to the basement, to the room where she used to hang the laundry in the years before her father bought the dryer. It was now a kind of storage area and workshop for renovations to the house, renovations that had taken on the status of an elderly relative who would not die. Down there, she found what she had been looking for—her last piece of business before she left, a farewell gesture for Dolores, which, after a few minutes of labor, she left on the kitchen table.

As she went back upstairs, she heard explosions and gunfire coming from the living room. Efran was awake, watching cartoons, sneaking them in before their father woke up. She left him alone, went up to her room. Her satchel and a plastic Mandee bag were behind her bed. She looked around at the unadorned space where she had spent the last twelve years. It had been not much better than a cell. She nodded, as if to affirm this thought and then, as softly as she could, she climbed the stairs to the third floor, where she would have a good view of the street in front of the house. She wondered how this was going to work. Were they coming in a car? In a taxi? Would they knock?

The third floor showed a few improvements from the days when she used it as a refuge from Dolores. The holes in the plaster had been repaired. New windows had been installed to cut down drafts and reduce heating costs. But it still needed paint, still needed wiring, still needed the long-promised second bathroom to be installed. Here she was at last. She was not going to fly out of there as she had so often dreamed as a child. She would walk out the door, into daylight.

A black cab came to a stop, double-parked in front of the house, its windows rolled down. Clara could hear the voices of the people in the car discussing something. Then Yunis stepped out of the back, looking up at the house. She waved. Was it really going to be this easy?

Clara went down to her room, rushing now, not caring about waking anyone up. She retrieved her bags and descended to the ground floor. On her way to the front door, she walked into the den. Efran, in pajamas, was lying on the couch watching *Mighty Morphin' Power Rangers*.

"I'm leaving," she said.

"Where are you going?"

"Away from here," she said.

He sat up, suddenly aware that something out of the ordinary was taking place. "What?"

"Goodbye."

She did not lock the front door behind her. There, on the street, was Yunis, beckoning her into the cab. Clara ran between the two parked cars and got in. Sitting behind the driver, in the back of the cab, was a middle-aged woman.

"*Hola,* Clarita," she said.

"*Hola,* Mami."

They hugged desperately in that backseat, her mother kissing her on the head, as Clara started to weep. Yunis got in the cab and slammed the door.

"*¡Vámonos!*" she said to the driver, and they pulled away.

Still hugging her mother, Clara looked back through the rear window as the cab descended Payson Street and her father's house shrank farther and father away. In the house, Efran would be upstairs by now, waking her father and Dolores from their Sunday slumbers. They would shake their hangover-heavy heads. They would not understand at first what he was talking about. Her father might even tell Efran to *shut the fuck up.* But Efran would persist and finally they would understand what he was saying and they would come downstairs, her father in his baggy pajamas and his wifebeater, Dolores in a ragged housecoat, like the one she had been wearing the night Clara had first arrived in New York. They would come downstairs and look outside and see nothing and lock the front door. Then they would go into the kitchen, shaking their heads in disbelief, and in the kitchen they would see what Clara had left them as her parting gift: the pieces of Dolores's paint pole sawed into harmless foot-long sections and laid end to end. And on those pieces, they would read the message she had written in permanent marker, one word to each sawed-off piece: *You can't hurt me anymore.*

Tito

I n the Piper's Kilt, the four flat screens were showing two college football games and two baseball games—Rutgers, UConn, the Yankees, and the Mets, a tristate sporting flush. It was the month of transition, when both of Tito's favorite pastimes shared the city and its airwaves: summer to fall, hardball to pigskin; warm to cold, vacation to work. He was still on vacation, still had two weeks before he had to go back to Cruz Brothers. He hoped that in those two weeks he would manage a period of transition for himself, too, that he would somehow be different when he went back to work. This meeting with Clara would have a lot to do with that.

He'd arrived at one o'clock, early enough to watch two innings of the Yankees game while drinking rum and Coke to mellow himself out. The Bombers' late-summer resurgence had faded in the past week and they were behind three runs early in the game against the pesky Devil Rays. Unbelievably, it looked like they would not catch the Red Sox this year. And that, in itself, was another transition. For a decade they had always finished first.

The bar held about two dozen other customers, mostly young men in baseball caps and T-shirts. Had he been there earlier, he would likely have seen the hordes of Columbia alumni who flooded the neighborhood whenever there was a game at Baker Field. Parking was hard to find on these mornings. Tempers were short in the streets near his father's building, which were suddenly lined with a better make of car. The alumni came up from the more desirable precincts of Manhattan, down from Westchester and Connecticut, plump, successful men decked out in baby blue attire, cheering for a historically bad team. He thought of them as an invasion force like the Mongols or the Apache: *the Alumni.*

Outside, it was sunny, another in what seemed to be an endless string of beautiful September days. But inside, it was dim and seasonless—bar time. Every minute or so, Tito's eyes ticked toward the door, looking for Clara. It was ten past two and still she was not there. Was she going to stand him up? He didn't think so. He did not think there was that kind of cruelty in her. She wouldn't have called him just to do that. He took another sip of his drink.

He'd been disappointed when she'd refused his offer to drive her into the city. Having listened to countless confessions and confidences of men he barely knew in the cab of a moving truck, he'd formed the conviction that it was easier to talk about difficult things when you were not looking at the person you were talking to. The car ride would have given them that opportunity. But he understood her reasons for refusing, or thought he did. Clara did not know yet if she could trust him. She might even be a little afraid, he supposed.

Awaiting her arrival, he was reminded of the days in late August after they'd had sex in the empty apartment, the stormy, hazy, oppressive days into which the summers in New York always seemed to dwindle. He had been so self-contented, so inebriated with his love for her that he was, at first, completely unconcerned by his inability to get in touch with her. After all, she'd never been easy to reach. She'd told him that her father was making her work every day in the store and that her stepmother was on her every moment at the house. It was a family life so far removed from his own that it sometimes seemed like a fairy tale, like something Clara had made up. While he waited, Tito let himself get carried away. He imagined going to visit her at Cornell, staying in her dorm room; he pictured the two of them getting together during the Christmas break to go ice skating and see the tree at Rockefeller Center. (His dream life, even early on, tended toward the conventional.) This was it; they were on their way.

The door opened and two couples entered. It was a moment before Tito realized that the fifth person, who came in behind them, was not with the first four. The fifth person was Clara. From the doorway, she made eye contact with him and crossed the bar in the direction of his booth. There was enough of a crowd that she had to work her way through them, saying, "*Permiso,*" and "Excuse me." This gave him a few seconds to take her in as she turned and squeezed through the Yankee jerseys. She was much closer to him now than she had been the days he parked outside her house. She was wearing a pair of jeans and a navy blazer with a white T-shirt under it, low heels on her feet. It was not, he noted, funeral attire. Her hair was up in a *moño*. She looked good, he confirmed to himself. Definitely older, definitely a little heavier (and definitely a little more filled out in the breasts, if he wasn't mistaken), but still good. Still beautiful. Still Clara. He wasn't disappointed and hoped that she would feel the same way about him. He'd put on a pair of charcoal gray pants and a white shirt. He was going to borrow a black blazer and tie from his father before the funeral—an excuse to show Clara off to his parents, to take her to the old apartment. He'd gotten his hair cut the night before, gotten those crazy tufts of his trimmed. He felt ready, excited.

As she neared the booth, he stood. What was it going to be? A kiss? A hug? A handshake? He was feeling unsteady on his feet, dizzied by seeing her again. He let her decide and was disappointed when she extended her hand. He shook it and they sat down.

"Hello, Tito. Sorry I'm a little late."

"No, no," he waved. "No problem. I was watching the game." He hoped she couldn't smell the rum on his breath.

"I have to tell you, this is a little weird for me."

"I know," he smiled. "It's a little weird for me, too. But we're here. Thank you. I mean it. You didn't have to come. It *has* been a long time."

"Yes. A long time," she agreed, and smiled, as if in relief. "But I felt like I had to come. I owed it to you. At least that much."

He nodded and smiled. So far so good, but don't push it. "You want something to drink?"

"Sure, what are you having? Is that Coke?"

"There's a little rum in there, too."

"Oh. Well, maybe a glass of white wine. Whatever they've got."

When he returned with her drink, she was still sitting straight-backed with her elbow on the table. She had not looked over at him even once while he was at the bar. "Thanks," she said, accepting the glass. He wasn't getting much from her, but at least she was *here,* he reminded himself. "So, can you tell me how you found me? Not that I was hiding, but, you know, there are ten million people in greater New York. I've been wondering how it happened. It just seemed so random."

He grinned with inordinate pride. "Yeah, sure."

"I mean, you were looking for Raúl—that's what Deysei told me. Why were you looking for him?"

He held up his hand. "Wait. Let me go back to the beginning. Not to the beginning beginning, but the start of this part. About a month ago, I got a call to do an estimate for a move in New Jersey—Oradell, you know it? No? It's in Bergen County. Guess who answered the door? Ms. Almonte. Even though I never had her as a teacher, I remembered her. I mean, how could I forget? Especially since you used to talk about how great she was."

"Wow. Where was she moving to?" asked Clara.

"She was moving back into the city, back here to Inwood, to look after her mother. Did you know she grew up on Academy Street?"

"Yes, she told me that once. She said she wanted to help other Dominican girls do what she did—get out. That's what the Word Club was all about."

"I guess she succeeded," said Tito, realizing too late how that might sound. There was an awkward silence. "Anyway," he continued, "she told me her husband didn't want the mother-in-law moving in with them."

"Harsh."

"Yeah, can you believe it? Probably some uptight white guy." He winced. The same might be said of Clara's husband. He needed to watch his mouth. "So Raúl was on my crew for that move. You know he used to work for Cruz Brothers?"

"I did," said Clara. "But I never thought *you* were still working there."

"The only job I've ever had," Tito said with more melancholy than he intended. He got back to the point: "A couple of weeks after the move, Ms. Almonte calls me up and tells me that something was stolen from her dresser during the move."

"The bangle."

"Right. Anyway, I knew that there was no way Hector—the other guy on the crew—had taken it. Very religious. Sends half his money home to his family in Guatemala or El Salvador or wherever. He wasn't going to risk losing his paycheck. Besides, I also heard that Raúl had been in Rikers."

"Yeah," said Clara. "It's true. He's definitely a little suspect."

"So I tracked him down. The address we had was on Cooper Street. I guess that was your sister's apartment. I didn't know you had a sister."

"She's my half-sister. Yunis. From my mother's second marriage. I have to tell you, I was kind of relieved when she broke up with him."

"Yeah?"

"I never liked the way he looked at me when he thought I wasn't looking at him. Go on."

"Right." He almost asked about Deysei, but thought better of it. That would come later. The conversation was going well. Finish the story first. "So anyway, Santiago, you know—the super in your sister's building—is an old friend of my papi's. He gave me your address in New Jersey. Of course, I didn't know it was *your* address. I was looking for Raúl, and because of that, I was careful. I kind of hung out on the street for a little while checking out the comings and goings. No offense, but for all I knew it was a crack house— Rikers and all. That was when I saw Deysei with the bangle on her arm. And that was when I saw you."

Clara nodded thoughtfully, as if pondering his story, as if looking for flaws in it. "Did you ever find Raúl?" she asked.

"No. Once I took the bangle back to Ms. Álmonte, she was cool. Besides, her mother had just passed." He said nothing for a long moment. Then: "So that's how I found you, Clara. Now it's my turn. What happened to *you*?"

Clara did not speak at first. To Tito, it seemed like she was trying to get the facts straight in her head, like the moments before an exam in school. "My mother happened," she said, at last. "She was at a party my father took me to that summer after you and I graduated from Kennedy. This was right around the time of—you know, that day in the apartment. I hadn't seen her since before my father brought me to New York when I was six. I had the chance to go live with her in Queens. I knew it had to be an all or nothing deal. My father wasn't going to share me with her. I wasn't going to be able to come back. I couldn't show my face around the neighborhood. My mother and her second husband came and got me and I went to live with her. It happened so fast. I'm sorry, Tito. I'm really sorry. I didn't have a chance to tell you. But I just couldn't keep living with my father and Dolores. I had to get out of there."

"I would have gone to Queens to see you," he said, trying to be reasonable, trying not to get mad. "That would have been no big deal."

"I know, but I was really worried my father was going to find me, that he would come and make trouble for my mother. I felt like I needed to break all ties with the neighborhood. What did you think happened to me?"

"I don't know. I guess I thought you'd just gone to Cornell early. I went up there, to Ithaca, looking for you. So I had no idea. They told me that you weren't at the school, told me that you'd never been there. I thought maybe something terrible had happened to you."

"That's why I wrote to you," she said. "I didn't want you to worry."

"And then I ran into your stepmother in December that year and I asked her about you."

"What did she say?"

"She went all crazy. Started yelling at me. I got the hell out of there."

Clara nodded again.

"I wondered if maybe you'd killed yourself, but I didn't believe it. Man, so all that time, you were living in Queens. And you didn't try to contact me?"

Her features fell. She looked spent. "I'm sorry, Tito. It was not an easy time for me."

He nodded. "It wasn't easy for me either, Clara. I was in love with you. I still am. I'm still in love with you."

She glowered. It was the same look he got when he hit on an unreceptive woman, a look that he was all too familiar with. "How can you say that? We haven't seen each other in so long. You're telling me you don't have a wife? A girlfriend?"

"No, Clara. I don't have a wife. I don't have a girlfriend. And I can say it because that's how I feel." Here they were, already at this point. He'd thought it would take longer to get there. "How do you feel, Clara?"

"About you? Tito, I don't know you." She brought her hand to her face.

"Sure you do. I haven't changed much."

"You *should* have changed. It's been fifteen years. You want to know how I feel? I feel lousy," she said. "I feel lousy that I had to do that to you, but I didn't know what else to do. I was eighteen years old."

"It's OK," he said, trying to settle things down. He lifted his glass and finished his drink. Clara sipped her wine and looked around the bar. "It's OK. It's OK," he repeated, under his breath. Then: "You hungry? You want something to eat?"

"No, that's all right. I'll need to get going soon," she said.

"Already? You don't want to come to the wake?"

"I don't know. It would feel a little weird. I bet there will be a bunch of teachers from the school."

"I think Ms. Almonte really wants to see you again. Come on. You said you felt lousy. Maybe this will help you feel a little better."

"I don't know," she said. "A wake?"

"All right," he said. "I'm not going to force you. But maybe we could just pass by the apartment."

"What apartment?"

"My parents' place on Seaman."

She looked unsure about this.

"Come on, they'd love to see you. Especially my father."

He could tell that the idea intrigued her. "Did they know that . . . you and me?" she asked.

"No. I never told them," he said, and this seemed to make the difference.

"OK," she said. "But really, I can't stay long. I've got to get back to New Jersey."

They stood and left the bar. Outside, he had to blink about

fifty times before his eyes got used to the light. He led her across Broadway and they walked up to Isham and turned left toward the park.

"What the hell is this?" asked Clara.

The intersection was blocked off by police barricades and each side of the street was lined with tables piled with produce and baked goods. One of the first stalls promised THE BEST PICKLE IN NEW YORK. Another featured tubs of fresh mozzarella. Farther along there were loose pyramids of Indian corn, apples, and tomatoes. People—Dominican and white, young and old—moved among the stalls pushing strollers, carrying canvas totes that said NOT A PLASTIC BAG, chatting while sipping warm cider and eating fresh-baked scones.

"The farmers' market," said Tito.

"Inwood has a farmers' market? Since when?"

"A couple years now," said Tito. "It runs from Labor Day through Thanksgiving."

"Wow," said Clara. She took it in as if the circus had come to town.

"It's not the neighborhood where we grew up, Clarita. Things are changing."

"I knew things were changing, but not this fast."

"I'm going to get some flowers for the wake," he said. "Do you think that's a good idea?"

"Sure," she said, and they headed for a stall that sold potted plants and fresh-cut flowers. Tito selected a bouquet of autumnal blooms in a plastic vase.

The market had not been part of his plan. Nonetheless, it seemed to have relaxed Clara a little bit. Had she become such a suburbanite that her old inner city neighborhood freaked her out? It could be that she simply felt dislocated as you do when a bodega you are used to seeing every day is suddenly replaced by a bank. Or was it him? *Probably me,* Tito thought. Still, he was enjoying walking beside her, enjoying the possibility that the people milling among the stalls might assume that he and Clara were together, that they were married. As he collected his change, he saw something else that had not been part of his plan, something that was almost too good to be true. Coming toward them was the basic family unit: Tamsin, her husband, and Wyatt. The husband was giving Wyatt a piggyback ride. Tamsin carried a bag with purchases from the market. They looked like they were off to a picnic. Tito waited for, and registered with pleasure, the moment when Tamsin recognized him. As he waited, he put his arm behind Clara's back, not touching her, but holding it there, just behind the small of her back, in a possessive, guiding gesture. Tamsin looked startled, her mouth falling slightly open, but recovered quickly, smiling and pointing, while saying something to her son. Tito lowered his hand before Clara could notice what he was doing.

"Tío!" shouted Wyatt, clambering down from his father's shoulders and running at them. This was too much. Tito could not believe his luck. The kid jumped into his arms.

"Hi Wyatt," he said, setting the boy down and tousling his hair. "Where are you guys going?"

"We're going to Fort Tie-Ron Park," he said, enunciating carefully. By that time, Tamsin and her husband had caught up. Tito saw Tamsin take an appraising look at Clara before saying hello.

"Hi," Tito replied, and introduced Clara to them, deliberately not mentioning what his relationship to her was.

"So, how have you been?" Tamsin asked.

"Fine," he said. "Really good, actually."

"Your mother said you moved out."

"I did," he said. "Not far. I'm just over on Arden."

"We really miss you," she said. "The building just isn't the same."

"Yeah," said the husband. "Wyatt here asks about you all the time."

"I miss you, too," said Tito, looking at the boy.

"Can we ride trains together, sometime, Tío?"

"You got it," he said.

"Can we go back to the airport?" asked Wyatt.

"Sure," said Tito.

"Whoo-hoo!" said Wyatt, pumping his fist.

"There you go, buddy," said the husband. "Give us a call. We'll set it up."

"I will," said Tito. "I'll call you tomorrow. I promise."

"Yay!" said Wyatt, bringing smiles to everyone's lips.

"Well, we should get going," said Tito, not wanting to push his luck.

"Sure. Have a good day," said Tamsin, and then to Clara: "Nice to meet you."

"You too," said Clara, her only contribution to the conversation. She and Tito walked on, turning right on Seaman, going uphill along the boundary of the park where they had spent so many Friday afternoons together.

"Who was that?" Clara asked.

"Just a kid who lives in my papi's building. I looked after him for a while over the summer. The mother—Tamsin—was here by herself and needed some help."

"I see," said Clara. "Where was the husband?"

"Peru. He's some kind of scientist. Studies the chicken flu."

"You know . . . it's the weirdest thing."

"What?"

"I think I saw you and that kid in Newark Airport a couple of weeks ago, maybe a month."

"Yeah. It was us. I took him there to ride the monorail. Wyatt's crazy about trains. So, you saw us? Why didn't you come over? Why didn't you say something?"

"I was with my sister, rushing to catch her flight to D.R. Besides, it looked like the two of you were having a, well, a moment. You were holding him and stroking his head."

"Yeah," said Tito. "That's true. I lost him for a minute in the airport. I thought he was gone for good."

"What do you mean, you lost him?"

"He took off when we got out of the monorail. There was a big crowd."

"That must have been awful."

"Yes. It was pretty bad."

"My God," said Clara. "Did you tell his mother?"

"No," said Tito. "She doesn't need to know that."

"Kids," said Clara, shaking her head. "They can make you lose your mind."

By this time, they had reached the side entrance to his father's building and Tito felt that things were going well, that the farmers' market and the encounter with Tamsin and her family had helped him. He wasn't going to dwell on the airport thing, on Clara not coming over to him. He wanted to stay positive. He drew a set of keys out of his pocket and turned the locks. They went down the three steps into the apartment. Tito's father was sitting at the kitchen table dismantling a faucet with a wrench. The faucet was old and rusty and looked like it had been ripped forcibly from its fixture. He was probably salvaging parts from it, Tito thought. Thrifty as ever.

"Papi, look who I've got with me," said Tito as jovially as he could. He had not warned his parents that he would be coming by, not warned them that he might be bringing someone with him. His father looked up from the faucet and squinted.

"Who?"

"Clara Lugo."

Tito crossed the room and Clara followed him. His father stood up, wiping his hands on a grease-stained rag. He looked bewildered.

"*Hola,* Don Felix," said Clara, kissing his father on the cheek without hesitation. Tito felt the sting of jealousy. It was the greeting he'd wanted.

"*¡Dios mío! Hola,* Clara. What a surprise!" Tito's father put his hand on Clara's arm. "You look more beautiful now than you did as a young girl."

Clara said nothing, but smiled at him. Tito had to admit that his father had a way about him. He could charm anyone.

"I am very sorry about your papi."

"Thank you, Don Felix."

"We may have had our differences, but I knew him a long time— long before he opened that store. I wish we might have been friends again. Nobody deserves a death like that."

Clara nodded, and again said nothing.

"You live in the city?" he asked.

"New Jersey," she said.

"She came for the funeral of one of our old teachers from Kennedy," said Tito, hoping to cut off his father's line of inquiry. "We're heading over there now."

"The mother of one of our teachers," said Clara.

"Right," said Tito. He was no longer sure why he'd wanted to bring Clara here and was surprised by his father's obvious affection for and familiarity with her. It showed him up somehow.

"Where's Mami?" he asked.

"Out. Shopping, I think. Who knows? Are you married, Clara?"

"Yes," she said.

"Any kids?"

"A boy. Guillermo."

"Aha! You have a picture?"

"Yes," she said, and brought out her wallet, unsnapping the clasp to show a photograph of the boy posed on a white stepladder in a photographer's studio. It was cute beyond belief and seeing it ignited a slow-burning rage in Tito's gut.

"He's beautiful," said his father. "God bless you. There's nothing harder than raising a child."

"Thank you, Don Felix."

This was unbearable for Tito. What a fool he had been to bring her here.

"You know any nice girls out there in Jersey for Tito?" asked his father. "My boy wants to die alone and childless."

"Papi, that's not true!" Tito protested.

His father looked at him. "What? You got some master plan you're not telling us about? You got some new girlfriend we haven't met?"

Tito looked at Clara, who smiled and lowered her gaze, not answering the question about girls in New Jersey. She snapped her wallet closed and put it back in her purse. "Didn't you have to get something here?" she asked Tito.

"Yes, hold on," he said, and went into his old bedroom and opened the closet he and his father had always shared, the closet in the master bedroom being given over to his mother's wardrobe. Tito's room had become a storage space for deliveries and supplies. There were two UPS boxes and a big white carton with a diagram of a sink on the outside. In the closet, he found the jacket and an old black tie that he hadn't worn since the last funeral he attended—for one of his mother's cousins. He quickly knotted it and put the jacket on and went back out.

His father and Clara looked up, as if they'd been disturbed during a confidential meeting.

"OK," he said. "Let's go."

"Thank you for coming to visit," Don Felix said to Clara. "It is good to see you."

"You too," she said, and kissed him again. "Tell your wife I said hello."

"I will. Look after that boy of yours."

Tito was drifting toward the exit and Clara at last began to follow him. Outside, as he locked the door, Tito asked her, "What was he saying to you?"

"Nothing," she said.

"It didn't look like nothing."

"He's worried about you, Tito. They both are. Don Felix and your mother."

"He hasn't seen you in fifteen years and all of sudden he's talking to you about stuff like that? He's telling you he's worried about me?" He tried to contain the anger in his voice.

"Yes, that's what he said." She looked at him. "Listen, Tito, I'm not sure I want to go there—to the wake."

"Why not?"

"I'm just not comfortable with it. I made my peace with all of this a long time ago and I don't want to go and reopen the wounds."

"That's great for you, Clara, but some of us haven't made our peace. My wounds are still open. The old ones are still open and new wounds keep opening up, too."

"What do you mean?"

"I mean, I know why you don't want to go to the wake. I know why you don't want to talk to Ms. Almonte."

"Why is that?"

"She told me something else about you."

"What did she tell you?"

"She told me that the last time she heard from you—that summer—you were pregnant."

Clara turned away from him. They had walked up to the waist-high park wall on the corner of Indian Road and Seaman Avenue. By turning away, Tito noticed, she appeared to be looking down into the playground where he had taken Wyatt earlier that summer, the same playground where he had once kicked her in the mouth. He suddenly wanted to change the subject, to ask her about the scar on the inside of her lip—to know if it was still there. He remembered how talk of that scar had loosened her up on the afternoon in the Bronx when he'd helped her gather the swirling papers from her binder, the day all of this had been set in motion. He'd taken the wrong approach with her. It was stupid. He'd rushed into it again. The whole thing with his father had made him so mad. He shouldn't have mentioned the pregnancy. That should have come much later. Instead, he should have talked about the good things they had done together, not the regrettable thing Clara had done on her own, leaving him like that. But it was too late now. He felt everything tipping over, his hopes spilling onto the ground and washing away like a pail of water, impossible to gather up.

"I was," she said. "I was pregnant. I didn't realize it until after I'd moved in with my mother."

"It was mine."

"Yes, Tito. It was yours."

"And what happened to that baby? Is Deysei that baby? Is she my daughter?"

"No." Clara shook her head. "I'm sorry," she said. "Deysei is not that baby."

"Clara, what happened to that baby? Ms. Almonte said you were going to put it up for adoption. Did you put our baby up for adoption?"

"No, Tito." A sob escaped from her and she brought her hand to her face as if to hide behind it.

"What happened to that baby, Clara?" he asked her again.

"It was never born," she said, her hand still at her face.

"Please, Clara. Please. Tell me you didn't."

Slowly she lowered her hand and looked at him, nodding, the tears running in quick succession down her cheek. "Yes," she said. "I did."

"How could you?" His voice sounded strange to himself. It sounded weak. It sounded like a child's voice. "I would have married you. I would have raised that baby with you."

"I know," she said. "But that was not the life I wanted."

Now it was his turn to look away. He took a few steps back from her and placed his hand on the wall. Even on this warm afternoon, the coarse surface of the stone was cold. "How can you say that to me, Clara?"

"I can say it because it is true, Tito. I'm sorry. I don't think it's the life you wanted. To be a father at eighteen."

"How do you know what I wanted? How do you know that wouldn't have been a better life than the one I have now. Any life with you would have been better than what I have now. Any life with that baby alive."

"Don't say that. Don't blame me."

"Why not? You made that decision by yourself. Who should I blame?"

"Tito—"

"Look," he said, reaching into his pocket for the photograph he'd taken of her husband in front of the rich white woman's house. "You think your life is so great now? Look at this." The photograph shook in his hand as he held it out to her.

"What is that?" said Clara.

"That's your husband. And that's the woman he's been fucking behind your back."

"Where did you get this?" she said, taking the photo from his hand and holding it closer to her face.

"I took it."

"*You* took it? You've been spying on me and my family, Tito?"

"I followed him. It was just one day. I wanted to see what kind of man you'd married, Clara. And this is what I found. Not much of a man at all. I thought you ought to know."

"This is insane," she said. "You think this is going to make me come back to you?"

"I would never do that to you, Clara. I would never treat you that way. I would be faithful. I've never loved anyone but you. Please."

"I can't believe this. I haven't seen you in fifteen years and you want me to leave my husband and child for you? You have to be joking."

"I'm not joking, Clara. I'm serious."

She folded the photograph methodically and put it into her jacket pocket. "Goodbye," she said.

"What? Where are you going? We aren't finished talking yet."

"Yes we are. I'm sorry about what happened when we were eighteen. I'm sorry that you had to find out this way. And I'm sorry that you can't get over it. People get over much worse things."

"There's nothing worse than this," he said. "There's nothing worse than losing a child."

"Yes there is," said Clara. "It's worse to give up. It's worse to stop living. That's what you've done, Tito. You stopped living when you were eighteen. You're stuck there and I'm not going back. I moved on. Do you understand? Goodbye, Tito. I am leaving now, and if I see you near my house or my family again, I will call the police. Goodbye."

She turned and went away from him, jogging across Seaman Avenue to avoid an oncoming car and running up the steps into the little strip of greenery called Isham Park, heading for Broadway, for her car, for her home in New Jersey.

"Clara!" he called.

She did not look back.

TITO STOOD ON the corner outside his parents' apartment dressed in his black jacket, holding a bouquet of funeral flowers, watching Clara ascend those steps, watching her go until he could see her no more, until she reached the top and descended the far side, her head dropping out of view. He stood there for a few more minutes, just in case she decided to come back. He was not in any haste to move from that spot, not in any haste to admit that that was it, that he'd had his long-hoped-for reunion with Clara, that the reunion was over, that there would not be another one, and that he'd fucked the whole thing up. He stood there a long time, long enough that he became worried that his father might come out to the side of the building to smoke a cigarette and see him—or that his mother would come walking up Seaman Avenue from shopping and ask him what he was doing standing there like a *pariguayo*. That was the only way this could get any worse—to have to face *her* now—and the fear of it getting even worse motivated him, got him moving along the sidewalk toward the wake. He shouldn't have shown Clara the picture. That was his mistake. Maybe something could have happened, but the picture had killed off any hope of his ever seeing her again. Why had he shown it to her? Because he wanted her to know that the great life she thought she had maybe wasn't so great. Because even before he showed it to her he'd known that nothing was going to happen between them. If she wasn't going to be with him then he wanted her to feel at least a small amount of the pain he'd been carrying all this time.

As he walked along Seaman, he thought about his unborn baby, the child she had aborted. For the last few days, since that afternoon in Ms. Almonte's apartment, he had lived with the possibility that his child might be alive. The child would have been a teenager like Deysei. He had lived with the possibility of already being a father. Now he had to bury those possibilities along with the possibility of ever seeing Clara again. In this stupor, he turned down Academy Street and went across Broadway to the apartment. A couple of other mourners, old teachers from Kennedy, one of them with a cane, were arriving, coming along the pavement behind him. They nodded at him, as they all waited to be buzzed in, but Tito did not nod back. He needed a drink. He needed more than that, but a drink at the very least.

Inside, the apartment's main room had been cleared of all furniture, except for tables. There were probably thirty people in there, with others half-visible in the kitchen and down the hallway in the bedrooms. Every time he came the place looked different, like the stages in a transformation. Set up on the lampstand by the entrance was a large framed wedding picture of Ms. Almonte's mother and father. Along one wall, there was a buffet of the standard offerings: chicken, *plátanos,* rice. The flowers had been distributed throughout the room and Tito set his bouquet down on an empty table. Along the other wall, there was the bar, where an old man in a white shirt polished a glass.

Tito looked around. He was the youngest person there by at least a decade. Certainly, he was the only graduate of Kennedy High School. He recognized a few other former teachers and staff members but no one seemed to recognize him and he was grateful for the anonymity. Most of the attendees were old Dominicans, the first generation who'd come to the United States and blazed the trail for the rest of them—his parents' generation. Is this how they'd pictured their deaths, he wondered. Did anyone ever accurately forecast the circumstances of their own demise? Tito went to the bar and asked for a rum and Coke. He raised his glass in a private salute to his lost child. *I know you're in heaven.* When he finished the drink, he asked for another. He raised his glass to his parents' generation and drained it. Ms. Almonte appeared at his side. She was wearing a simple black dress. She'd had her hair done; it was straightened again.

"Thank you for coming," she said, and kissed him on the cheek as if they were old friends. "I'd like to introduce you to my husband."

Beside her was the portly, bald-headed man he'd spied through the window on his return visit to Oradell, the man eating dinner alone, reading the newspaper. Up close, Tito couldn't help thinking how much he looked like a college football coach—the ruddy jowls and the trimmed no-nonsense mustache.

"Tito Moreno," he said.

"Glen Reid," said Ms. Almonte's husband. It sounded like the name on the bottle of whiskey she had shared with him the day of her mother's death. Hearing the name made him thirsty for a glass of that whiskey.

"Tito is the mover I was telling you about. He moved me to Mami's."

"Oh," said the husband. "Well, my wife will be moving back to New Jersey as soon as her mother's estate is settled. We'll be looking for a mover again. Do you have a business card?"

Tito patted his pockets. It was not his usual jacket. "No," he said. "But your wife knows how to reach me."

"Although, perhaps we should use someone else, given what happened with the bangle." She smiled at him while taking her husband's elbow. "So, where's Clara?"

"She couldn't come," he said.

"No? Did you get to meet with her yet?"

"No," said Tito. "Not yet."

"So you still don't know about the—"

"No," said Tito.

"I hope you do soon," she said. "I think it will be good for you to talk to her."

Tito said nothing. He felt like he was going to vomit.

"Thank you again for coming. And for the bangle." She held up her arm to show it to him. The bangle slid down to her elbow.

"It was nothing," he said.

"Good to meet you," said the husband, shaking his hand in farewell.

They moved on to talk to some of the other arrivals, smiling, hugging, talking. Ms. Almonte did not look like someone who had been touched by death. She looked like someone returning to life.

He stayed at the wake for another half hour, drinking two more rum and Cokes, then began the dreary walk back to his apartment. At the corner an idea came to him and he turned and walked uphill to Broadway, heading north, instead of south toward home. He arrived at PJ's Liquor Warehouse. The place was hopping with the Saturday-night stock-up. Cases of wine and spirits were being rolled out of there, bound for fiestas and celebrations, parties he would not be attending. As usual, there were young girls in skimpy dresses standing in the aisles throughout the store, offering tastes of featured products. Tito sampled everything that was being offered, from a mint liqueur to a new blueberry-flavored gin. Near the back, he came to the shelves of whiskey and found a bottle of the stuff that sounded like Ms. Almonte's husband's name. It was ridiculously expensive, but he didn't care. He waited in line, paid. With the bottle in a brown paper sack, he exited the store and walked west to the park. It was getting dark and he sat on a bench near the lagoon, watching the sun set over New Jersey, the lights coming on in the Bronx, the arching span of the Hudson Bridge illuminated before him like a rusty iron rainbow. He uncapped the bottle, peeling off the lead seal, and took a drink. He did not feel drunk. He felt focused—able to see things clearly.

Tito returned to the line of thought he had been pursuing earlier. Before today there had always existed the possibility that when he found Clara again, his dream life and his real life would merge, that he would no longer need his dream life to escape into because he would no longer want to escape from his real life. That was the ultimate dream life: one that was not a dream at all. He took a drink. Now that possibility was lost. His dream life would always remain just a dream—perfect but elusive—and his real life would always remain real—brutal and unavoidable. Without hope of the two merging, he could not continue. One of those parallel lives would have to come to an end. He took a drink. Tito could see everything plainly now. He knew what his course should be. He knew he should cast off his dream life and finally embrace reality—finally embrace adulthood with its compromised promises and crushed aspirations, accept the fact that he and Clara would not be together, and find a woman he could settle for. The world was full of them.

He'd even dated a few. He knew that this is what he should do, and yet his heart refused to surrender the other life, the life he should have had. He took a drink. He had to choose. He stood up and walked around the perimeter of the lagoon, sipping at his bottle, crossing the open fields and passing the playground, following the path that led into the old-growth trees, the place where murderers hid. He took a drink and went into the forest because that is where his dream life had once been real, Friday afternoons in the summer of his eighteenth year.

Clara

The airport. Again.

Clara waited in the ground floor arrivals hall. As a point of entry to the land of opportunity, it wasn't much, she thought. But then once you got here, it was too late, wasn't it? The only amenities were a newsstand and a coffee shop. Otherwise, the low-ceilinged space was given over to the necessities: rows of chrome and plastic seats, an interactive hotel and car-rental display, and a desk for ground transportation information, where a young woman was typing with her thumbs into a BlackBerry. Outside, buses and taxis pulled up and drove off in sunlight, leaving confused-looking travelers who gawped, unsure if they'd just missed their chance to get into the city. Clara looked back at the gate through which the international arrivals came, the gate through which her sister would be coming any moment. She had been there twenty minutes and had watched the arriving passengers change from mostly pale to mostly brown as flights from London and Frankfurt gave over to the flight from Santo Domingo. She was nervous about how this whole thing was going to go. Once the last blow-up had taken place between Yunis and their mother, her sister had wasted no time booking her ticket, finding an empty seat on a flight the next day. The apartment was still being sublet, and so she was homeless. She'd be moving into the house on Passaic Street. Thomas wasn't happy about it and she couldn't really blame him, but what could she say? It came with the territory. Once Yunis learned who the father of Deysei's baby was, the fun would really begin. She sipped at the carton of orange juice in her hand, trying to get the metallic taste out of her mouth, trying to think of a way to mitigate this disaster, but the acid in the juice only accentuated the taste, turning it into the kind of rusty flavor you sometimes got in tap water. And then there was her meeting with Tito later in the afternoon. She was unable to come up with a solution to the current situation that didn't involve running away. But, with one exception, she wasn't a runner.

Here came Yunis, arriving like a celebrity, wearing a long white sundress with a deep-dropping neckline and a pair of wedges, looking browned and surprisingly happy, the coils of her hennaed hair bouncing as she walked. She had her big sunglasses in place, a rolling suitcase dragging behind her like a subdued captive, and she was talking on her phone—of course. Clara turned and beckoned to Deysei, who had been pushing Guillermo around the arrivals hall on a baggage cart. Deysei, she knew, was looking forward to her mother's arrival even less than she was. Sensing that Yunis's presence could cause Deysei to disappear completely into the world of her iPod, to hide permanently under the hood of her sweatshirt, Clara had spent much of the previous day gently prodding her niece about Raúl. "You're going to have to tell your mami sooner or later, especially if you are thinking of keeping the baby, which it looks to me like you are."

"I can't tell her, Tía. She'll go crazy."

"Waiting will only make it worse. I'll tell her, if you want."

"No, Tía. . . . I guess I'll tell her."

In the airport, Deysei banked a turn and arrived at Clara's side just as Yunis came out of the cordon, snapping her phone shut and smiling.

"Tía!" shouted Guillermo, leaping off the cart, his greeting compensating for the more muted welcomes offered by Deysei and Clara.

"Gilly!" said Yunis, picking up the child and pressing him against her breasts, which, Clara noticed, were unsupported by a bra. *Probably hoping to snag some guy on the plane,* she thought. Guillermo was laughing uncontrollably in her arms. It was a little pornographic. Finally, Yunis put him down and embraced her daughter. "How are you, *mija*?"

"Good, Mami."

"Hi, Sis," said Clara, kissing Yunis on the cheek even though she was still hugging Deysei. "Is that all you brought?" she asked, pointing at the rolling case.

"Yeah, most of the shit I took down with me was for other people. You know how it is. They think you're Santa Claus getting off that plane."

"I guess we don't need the cart then. Is Mami OK?"

"Mami's Mami. Same shit different day. I don't know why I thought I could live with her. She's always into your business. Country full of chickenheads. I must have been out of my mind."

They were walking now, out of the terminal, crossing the drop-off/pick-up lane toward the parking lot.

"You're starting to show a little, Deysei," said Yunis.

"Really? Maybe it's just this shirt." Deysei had left her hoodie in the car; she was wearing a pair of baggy cargo pants and a T-shirt that had once been loose-fitting but was now snug. The shirt said GET STACKED and showed a bookcase. It was a National Library Week freebie Clara had given her the year before.

"Nah, you're showing," said Yunis. "How you feeling? You got any morning sickness?"

"Yes," said Deysei. "I've been throwing up a lot."

"Just like I did with you," said Yunis with relish. "What goes around comes around."

"Yuck!" said Guillermo, and mimed a gag.

"You got that right," said Yunis, laughing.

At least she was in good spirits, thought Clara. That would make it easier. As they drove out of the parking lot, she reached into a compartment where Thomas kept gum and mints. There was a roll of Life Savers there and she prized one out. It did not help.

"You OK?" asked Yunis.

"I'm on these antibiotics—four of them. Like horse pills. My mouth tastes like I'm chewing tinfoil."

"You got a UTI or something?"

"No. It's part of the fertility treatments. They want to kill off any bacteria that might be in there."

"If they don't kill you first, right? So where's Tommy? He didn't want to come see his sister-in-law?"

"He's in D.C."

"D.C.?"

"Yes," said Clara, "he had a job interview."

"For a job down there?"

"No. It's in New York, but the company's executive offices are in Virginia. He'll be back tonight. Listen, I have to ask you a favor this afternoon, Yunis."

"What's that?"

"Can you look after Guillermo? I've got to go into the city."

"So that's why you're all dressed up," said Yunis. "When the cat's away, huh?"

"It's a funeral," said Clara.

"You don't look like you're going to no funeral. You look like you're going on a date."

"Can you take care of Guillermo? I should be back by six."

"No sweat, Sis. Manny and Erlinda said they was coming by to see me. Erlinda made a *pernil* and some *moro*. So you'll have dinner when you get back."

CLARA DROPPED THEM at the house and set off for Inwood for her meeting with Tito. As she drove north on the Garden State Parkway, heading for the George Washington Bridge, she thought back on the morning, more than fifteen years before, of her escape from the house on Payson Street. Clara had ridden in the black cab with Yunis (and Deysei, in utero) and their mother and Yunis's father, Javy. That cab had carried them down Harlem River Drive, under the bridges and past Yankee Stadium, across the Triborough, into Queens, retracing the route Don Felix had followed the night he had picked Clara and her father up from the airport. *Like going upstream to the source of a river,* Clara thought. When they got on the Van Wyck, Clara wondered for a moment if maybe they were actually going to JFK, if maybe they were going to catch a flight back to D.R. and start all over again.

"Where do you live?" she asked her mother.

"Far Rockaway," she said.

"Near the beach," said Yunis. "You're going to love it."

After the initial glee of the escape, after the initial round of hugs and shoulder rubs, after the laughter and the whoops of excitement, after the exchange of the most urgent family news—that her *abuelita* was dead, but her *abuelito* lived on, that her Tío Modesto was married and her Tía Augustina divorced—there had been a period of silence in the car, as if they were all waiting for something to go wrong, for Clara's father to appear behind them in his pickup, for a flat tire to strand them on the side of the road, or for them all to realize that there had been a terrible mistake and that they weren't really related to one another. Clara, sitting in the backseat and still holding her mother's hand, looked at the people around her in the car: the members of her new family. There was Javy, a short, very dark man with bug eyes and a thin, debonair mustache. He was so dark that Clara suspected he was at least part Haitian. He wore a crimson linen shirt and a crisp Panama hat. There was an unlit cigar in his mouth, which he removed now and then to spit a fleck of tobacco out the window. (This was her mother's second husband. He would die six years later in a high-speed accident on the Belt Parkway.) Once they were in Queens, Javy turned up the radio. The mellow country lilt of a *bachata* filled the car.

Up front, next to him, was Yunis, who did not resemble her father in any way. Clara guessed that she was fifteen, maybe sixteen, which meant that her mother and Javy had met very soon after Clara's mother and father had come to New York. Her parents must have broken up quickly after arriving in America. Her mother had been with Javy much, much longer than she had been with Clara's father. Yunis began to dance, moving her shoulders to the music and singing along. Yunis and her father shared a private joke and she punched him on the arm. She was then still just a goofy teenager, not yet the schemer and scammer that single-motherhood and her Virginia boyfriend would make her. Javy turned up the music again.

In the back next to her was her mother. She was recognizably the same woman from the wedding photos Clara had studied in her grandparents' house when she was a child, a beautiful and somewhat daunting woman. In those photographs—there were three of them—her mother had shown the beginnings of the double crease between her brows, a mark of perpetual suspicion and fret. To the attentive observer those lines would have foretold the quick end to her first marriage, which Clara had long suspected was precipitated by her conception. That double crease had now deepened to a double crevice. Only when her mother laughed uproariously (a rare event) did the creases disappear completely. Yes, she was recognizably the woman from those photographs, and yet Clara did not feel at ease with her, did not feel connected to, related to her mother. Not yet.

Her mother wore gold bracelets on her wrists and big hoops on her ears. Clara would learn in the coming months that she spent a great deal of time working on her appearance—her eyebrows were always plucked, her hair was always straight, her clothes were always pressed, and her makeup was always in place. Looking at her now, Clara saw that there was a scar on her lip—a pale incision emerging from her lipstick and running perpendicular to her mouth, as if she had bitten down on a razor blade. Clara would come to believe that her mother's attention to her appearance was a way of spitting in the face of her limited circumstances. Looking good made her feel wealthier than she would ever be.

All of these redolent things—Javy's Panama hat, her sister's pregnancy, the lines on her mother's face—had stories behind them, stories Clara wanted to hear. But for now, not knowing those stories pointed to the scary truth that she had placed herself in the hands of strangers. For all she knew, they were taking her away to be sold into the sex trade. In this scheme, Javy was the pimp, her mother the madam, and Yunis one of the unfortunate girls whose precautions had failed. The idea made her smile. Wasn't that exactly what her father and Dolores had always said? That her mother was a whore? She'd never believed it, but there it was, in her subconscious, feeding her fears. Brainwashed.

THE APARTMENT WAS in a privately developed housing complex near Rockaway Boulevard, a block from the beach. At a first glance, Clara would have written them off as city projects. But they were in better shape—there was no graffiti and no litter around the entrance. The only indication that the ocean was close were the squawking, foraging seagulls standing on the rims of garbage cans. "This is your home," said her mother, as she unlocked the door. It was a tidy, cramped place. "We got two bedrooms here," she said. "One for me and Javy and the small one for Yunis. You're going to have to sleep on the couch."

"Does it fold out?" Clara asked.

"No," said her mother. "But you're not too tall. You'll fit. You can put your clothes in Yunis's closet. Make her throw out some of that garbage she got in there." In Yunis's room, a bassinet occupied the available space between the bed and the closet door. "We're going to set the crib up in the living room when the baby gets a little older," Yunis said. "Maybe then you can sleep in my bed and

I'll sleep out there." Clara nodded. It hit her for the first time how much of a difference Dolores's accident settlement had made to their life in Inwood. Without it, her father would have been pumping gas. Without it, she and Efran would have shared a room.

Clara was given the spare key. She was shown how to turn the shower on and off with the pliers that *must not be removed* from the bathroom. She was told never to touch the radiator valves, no matter how hot or cold it got. She was shown where the iron and the ironing board were kept. The schedule was laid out for her. Javy and her mother worked six days a week. Javy was a gypsy cab driver. Her mother was a chamber maid at the JFK Ramada. Javy worked nights, her mother days. They overlapped for one meal every twenty-four hours: dinner, which was Javy's breakfast. In the mornings and evenings, bathroom times were assigned. Obedience to the schedule was essential to the functioning of the household. Sunday was a day of rest. A day of sleep. When the tour was complete and the schedule explained, her mother said, "*Tengo sueno,*" and retired to the master bedroom, where Javy was already sacked out, his cigar stub in a glass ashtray like a set of false teeth.

While they slept, Yunis took her sister on a walk around the nearby streets, showing her the crucial sites: the supermarket, the drugstore, the Laundromat, and the subway station. It was a much more mixed neighborhood than Inwood. No color or race predominated. Seeing the station, with its blue-circled A, Clara had to smile. All this time her mother had been no more than a train ride away. She would not have even had to change trains to get here! In running away from her father, she had done nothing more than travel from one end of the Eighth Avenue line to the other. And yet, she had changed her life. She was still in New York but felt very far away.

After they had seen the main street, Yunis led her over to the ocean. It was not a beach day—a little too cool—but there were a few clusters of die-hard sunbathers and swimmers arrayed on the brown sand.

"When are you due?" Clara asked.

"November," said Yunis. "I can't wait for it to be over."

"Was Mami upset when you told her?"

"A little. She cried a lot. She said I was too young to be a woman. But she couldn't have been much older when she had you."

"She was eighteen, *abuelita* always said. My age. I'm going to be a *tía*. That's amazing." Clara looked out at the water. "Did she ever talk about me?"

"Yes," said Yunis. "She told me I had a sister, that someday I would meet you. I want you to be the baby's godmother," Yunis exclaimed loudly into the onshore breeze.

"Of course!" said Clara, and hugged her sister. "I would be honored. Do you know what you're having?"

"Yes. But I ain't told no one. Can you keep a secret?"

"Yes."

"It's a girl."

"Who's the father. Do I get to meet him?"

"Luis," said Yunis. "He's down in Florida. Once he finds a place, I'm going down there to be with him."

"He's older?"

"He's twenty-one."

When they got back to the apartment, the door to the master bedroom was still closed. Yunis asked her. "You hungry?"

Clara said she was.

"There's *bacalao* and rice," she said, showing her the covered pots on the stove. "Help yourself. Mami's a good cook."

Clara served herself a modest portion and put it in the microwave. Even before the bell rang, her mouth was watering. She carried the plate back into the living room, where Yunis had turned on the television.

"What shows do you like?" her sister asked.

"I don't know," said Clara. "I never got to watch TV at my father's."

"For real? No wonder you wanted to bust out of there. Oh, good, they're giving *Soul Train*."

Clara put the first bite of *bacalao* and rice in her mouth and closed her eyes with happiness as the memory of eating codfish cooked by her *abuelita* on the farm in La Isabela came back to her. That was the clincher. Only her mother could have made food that tasted like that.

She and Yunis watched *Soul Train,* commenting on the clothes and hairstyles of the dancers. Yunis got up to try a couple of the moves, but was hindered by her enlarged belly. Then the Sunday movie came on. A little later, they heard stirring from behind the door of the master bedroom, stirrings and laughter. The laughter stopped and the stirrings gradually assembled themselves into a steady, accelerating compression and release of bedsprings.

Clara looked at Yunis. "Are they?"

"Bet your ass, Sis. Every Sunday afternoon, Papi gets some action." She aimed the remote at the TV and turned up the volume.

THAT NIGHT, JAVY offered to buy Chinese to celebrate Clara's arrival. The delivery man brought cartons of lo mein and spareribs, which were spread out on the coffee table. Clara's mother brought in the plates, which had the Ramada logo on them. The liter of Pepsi that came with the dinner was poured into glasses. Javy opened a beer.

"So, Clara, do you have a job?" her mother asked.

"Not anymore," said Clara. "I used to work in Papi's store."

"You turned in your resignation today," said Javy, laughing.

"I guess he won't be sending your last check," said Yunis.

"I never got a first check," said Clara, and everyone broke up.

"You're going to need to get a job," her mother said. "You want to buy clothes. You want to go out. You need a job. I don't have money to pay for you."

"It's going to be hard for me to find a job now. I'm going to start school in a couple of weeks."

"School? High school?" asked her mother.

"College."

"Where you going?"

"Cornell."

"Where's that?"

"Upstate. Ithaca."

"*Eee-ta-ka*," her mother repeated. "How far is Eee-ta-ka?"?

"I don't know. Five or six hours by car."

Her mother's face soured and she glanced over at Javy, who raised his eyebrows. Then she said: "You can't do that. I finally get my daughter back and she wants to go away from me?"

"But Mami, it's a good school and they are paying for me. I will be going there almost for free."

"They don't have good schools in New York City? You want to run away from me so soon? You need to be here."

"But Mami."

"If you are going to go to Eee-ta-ka, you are going now." She pointed at the door.

That was the first sign that living with her mother was not going to be the utopia she'd always imagined. The first of many signs. Clara lay on the couch that night thinking about the pictures of the dorms she'd seen in the Cornell brochures that Ms. Almonte brought to their lunches in the Riverdale Diner. Ms. Almonte. What was she going to tell her? Clara lay on the couch and remembered other pictures from the brochure—the view of the snow-covered lake, the stone bridge over the waterfall. She could have those things still. In her bookbag was her life's savings: $512. She could get a bus to Ithaca. She could go right now. The A stopped at

Port Authority. She wouldn't even have to change trains. She could leave both of her parents on the same day. Yes, she *could*. But she wasn't going to. For a start, she'd promised to be the godmother to Yunis's baby. Clara blinked, looking into the gloom of her new home, and considered her options. It was all so sudden that she did not know what to do. Perhaps she could defer her entry to Cornell for a year. Perhaps she could start a semester late. Would they let her do that? It was her first night in her new home—the first night since Efran's birth that she hadn't spent under her father's roof. She didn't want to be rushed into doing anything anymore. She had pined for her mother—for her real family—and now she had her. Clara rolled on her side and looked into the murk of the apartment. *Just sleep,* she thought. *Things will be clearer in the morning. You've come far enough for one day.*

CLARA WAS DOUBLE-PARKED outside the house on Payson Street. She had not been there since escaping with her mother, sister, and Javy. On all her subsequent visits to Inwood, she had avoided Payson, which was easy enough, given that it was a one-way residential street only two blocks long. She had just left Tito standing on Seaman Avenue, had run from him through Isham Park, to the Odyssey, which she'd parked on 211th. Beside her, on the passenger seat, was the folded-up photograph of her husband kissing another woman. Clara had intended to get out of Manhattan, to go straight home. But she was shaken by what had just happened, and as she waited at a light on Broadway, she realized that she might never come back to Inwood again, realized, in fact, that she would make every effort not to come back. She turned right on Academy Street and then cut back to Payson, driving past the forested section of the park and coming to a stop opposite her father's old house. Dolores had sold it not long after her father's death. The new owners—or a succession of new owners—had finally fixed the place up. The stoop had been reconstructed. A shiny red door had been installed. There were modern windows everywhere and curtains visible on the topmost floor, where she had once retreated from Dolores's beatings.

She remembered all that had happened since the morning she had fled in Javy's cab, remembered how she had lived in her mother's apartment for two years, commuting into Manhattan to attend classes, remembered how she'd found a part-time job with a filing service that worked in law libraries all over Midtown, remembered how, when Yunis's baby was born, she took her turn in the rotation of feeding and changing her, sharing these duties with her mother and sister. She remembered taking her $512 and buying a crib and bedding and formula for the baby, remembered how tired she had been all the time in school and at work, remembered realizing one day that months had passed since her last period. She told nobody about it and went by herself to have it done in a place in Manhattan, a place whose address she'd gotten from an ad in the subway.

One day Yunis had stopped talking about Deysei's father, stopped talking about moving to Florida. Not long after that, she met the ex-sailor from Virginia, who had an apartment up in Inwood, where Yunis and Deysei moved. She remembered the long, slow thaw that took place between her and her mother, how it wasn't until she had gotten married and had a child of her own that she felt a real bond develop. She remembered library school and the early days of her courtship with Thomas, a heady time when, she thought, nothing could go wrong for her anymore. But of course it could. Not much later, right around the time she and Thomas had moved in together, she got the phone call telling her that her father had been murdered. He had been killed during a holdup of the store, shot four times in the chest and head. He'd been robbed before and had always just handed over the money. But Clara was willing to bet that he'd gotten sick of it, that he'd put up a fight and paid the price.

That call had come from inside the house she was looking at now. Clara stayed parked there for half an hour, partly in the hope of seeing one of the house's current residents and partly because she was still reeling from all that had happened that afternoon. All these years later, Tito still carried a torch for her. It sickened her to think of it, to admit that the unborn baby had always been more important to her than the loss of Tito—that she pined for it much more than she had ever pined for him. It shamed her to think how little she had accounted for him. But what was she supposed to do now? He was unstable. A reasonable relationship between them was not possible. To see him again would only encourage his outrageous hopes.

And then there was Thomas. Had he really gone to Washington? Or was he somewhere else entirely? At a bed-and-breakfast in Vermont with the blonde from the photograph, sleeping in a four-poster bed decorated with an absurd number of pillows, which they would use to experiment with different sexual positions, sleeping late and waking to classical music and buckwheat pancakes. Or perhaps they were in a hotel suite in Atlantic City, where her husband, who never gambled, would play roulette, the blonde, in a slinky dress, clutching his arm and jumping up and down as the ball landed on his number, bringing him a small fortune, which he would spend on her. Or perhaps they were in a cheap motel on Route 22, the two of them running out to get fast food between fucks, eating it while watching the free HBO.

Clara's imagination could conjure a string of these appalling scenarios with little effort. She'd had her suspicions all along but had always pushed them aside because Thomas was so unflirtatious with other women, so straight, so square, because, until the last six months or so, she had always felt herself to be the main object of his desire. It had been a difficult year, she would admit that. But she was used to difficulty, used to waiting out the bad times. She had counted on Thomas being the same way but, really, what difficulties had he ever faced in his life? Raised in the suburbs. His prosperous parents had divorced, but it had never seemed like a traumatic event for him. He was in college by then and often said that divorce had been the right thing for both of them. It was easy to romanticize hard times when they happened to someone else, even someone you loved. It was much harder when it happened to you. Maybe Thomas was only now finding that out. Yet, she felt that her willingness to trust her husband had somehow made her complicit in his cheating.

It was almost five and no one had come or gone from the house. She took a final look and started the engine. If she didn't get out of there, she was going to have a panic attack. She drove home. The next day, when she tried to reconstruct everything that had happened, she would find that she could not remember anything about the drive home, no landmarks passed, no tolls paid, no fool pulling a dumb move in front of her. It was a quarter to six when she turned onto Passaic Street. Someone on the block must have been having a party because there were a half-dozen cars parked on the street. As Clara pulled into her driveway, she understood that the house where the party was taking place was her own. Through the window, she saw Dominicans: Dominican men holding beer bottles, Dominican women in bright summer dresses. Reggaeton was playing loud enough to vibrate the aluminum siding. She wondered if any of the neighbors had called the police yet. Doubtful—it was still daylight and the party did not seem to be out of control (so far). Last Fourth of July, the Samuels across the street had waited until ten o'clock to call the police on their next-door neighbors, the Carlisles, who were hosting their annual Independence Day bash. A mild scuffle had broken out when LeShon Carlisle had refused, at first, to send his guests home. That was the last thing she needed today.

Clara went in the back door, her mouth still tasting like tin, preparing herself for the worst—for her dining room table to have been broken in half by someone dancing on it, for her kitchen walls to have been charred by someone trying to extinguish a grease fire with a glass of water. The actual state of things was not nearly so bad. It was just a party, the sort of food-drink-and-dancing gathering that accompanied every significant Dominican life event, from a birthday to a graduation to Mother's Day. Clara assumed that this was an impromptu welcome home for her sister. This is certainly what would have been going on at Yunis's apartment this afternoon if she had been able to return there from the airport. Clara's only wish was that her sister had asked her first.

"Clara!" said her cousin Manny, who was standing at the kitchen counter, slicing chunks of meat from a *pernil* in a tinfoil baking dish, his three-hundred-pound body shaking with the effort. Nearby a platter was dressed in a grease-soaked paper towel on which a single *pastelito* was marooned. Glasses everywhere. Bottles everywhere. Plates with bones and crumbs and grains of rice on them. The music thumping away.

"Hi, Manny." She kissed him on his pillowy cheek.

"Yo, you should try some of this. It's slamming. Erlinda outdone herself."

"That's OK, thanks. Where's Guillermo?"

"Downstairs."

"I'm going to go check on him." She nodded and went down to the basement. Guillermo was on the couch, a Hot Wheels car in his hand, Deysei at his side, with her arm around him. The robot that Thomas had bought Guillermo was on the floor close by. They were watching *Tom and Jerry*. It was the one in which Jerry goes to Manhattan, gets scared out of his wits, and comes running back to Tom.

"Mommy!" said Guillermo, getting off the couch and hugging her.

"Hi sweetheart." She hugged him back. No matter what, there was always Guillermo in her life. "How's everything?"

"We're watching cartoons," he said.

"I see that. Deysei's looking after you, huh?"

"Yes, Mommy. It's too loud upstairs."

"I agree. It's too loud. How are you, Deysei?"

"Tired," she said. She had a scowl.

"Have you had a chance to talk to your mother?"

"A little. Manny and Erlinda got here right after you left—like they were waiting around the corner or something. Then everyone started coming."

"Did you tell her?"

"Not yet. I just want to get it over with now, but she ain't interested in me. Too busy having a good time with her friends."

"All right. You guys did the right thing coming down here. Let me go upstairs and find your mother."

Manny was no longer in the kitchen. A woman Clara had met once at Yunis's was reaching into the fridge for a beer.

"You want one?" she asked Clara.

Clara said no and went into the living room. Seven or eight people were in there, drinking and talking. It smelled like at least one of them had been smoking a joint. Someone called out her name, but since her sister was not in the room, she did not bother to respond. She looked into the dining room, where the table was intact and laden with food and her best china. Four or five people were in there getting seconds or thirds for themselves. Again, her sister was not among them. "This is off the hook!" someone exclaimed.

She finally found Yunis in the sun room, on the love seat, holding a bottle of Corona and a cigarette. A guy Clara didn't recognize was sitting next to her, trying to get cozy. Yunis was talking on the phone while laughing and fending off the guy's advances. A third person, a younger guy, maybe in his late teens, was sitting at her computer playing some kind of online video game. The guy who was trying to get friendly with her sister looked up and said, "Oye."

This got Yunis's attention. She said something into her phone and snapped it shut. "Hey, Sis," she said, nonchalantly.

"What the hell?" said Clara. "Huh, Yunis? What the hell? I leave you here to look after my child and you have a party!"

"I told you Manny and Erlinda were coming."

"Yes, you did. Who are the rest of these people?"

"I'm Carlos," said the guy on the couch next to Yunis.

Clara ignored him, kept her gaze on her sister.

"Word got around," said Yunis. "I guess I got a lot of friends."

"Jesus, Yunis. This is *my* house. If you're going to stay here you can't be doing this shit. No wonder Mami kicked you out. This isn't Washington Heights."

"C'mon, Sis. Chill out. Have a drink. And whatever you do, don't bring Mami into this. How was your date?"

"It wasn't a fucking date!"

"Not so good, huh?" said Yunis sipping her beer, smiling.

Clara shook her head in exasperation. She wanted to slap her sister. From far away, there was the sound of shattering glass, as if a heavy crystal vase had been dropped on the floor.

"Oh, shit," said Yunis.

Clara left the sunroom and walked through the dining room, turning off the stereo on her way to the stairs. At the top of the stairs, two young men in baseball caps and football jerseys were bent over, laughing uncontrollably. Right behind them, in the bathroom, a stepladder straddled the shards that remained of a light fixture.

"What happened?" asked Clara.

The two young men straightened up and tried to control their laughter, but the giggles escaped from their mouths. They were responsible for the joint she'd smelled downstairs, she was sure.

"Why is my light fixture broken?" she asked, hoping a more specific question would produce an answer.

"The bulb burned out," said the first, who wore a Miami

Dolphins jersey. This was all he could manage before breaking up again.

"We were trying to put in a new one," said the second, who wore the silver and black of the Oakland Raiders. "But we didn't screw it in right."

"I guess we screwed up!" said the first.

Clara looked at them for a long moment, at the completeness of their amusement. When was the last time she had laughed like that—high or not? She couldn't remember. "Out of my house!" she finally said.

This got them to stop laughing. "This is *your* house?" the second asked.

"Yes. *My* house. I pay the mortgage here. The party's over." Just as she said this, the music came back on, even louder than before.

"Damn," said the second. "I can't believe that. I thought this was Yunis's place. I thought she bought it with the inheritance money she got." They walked down the stairs, leaving behind the mess on the bathroom floor.

Clara watched them go and thought it best to check the three upstairs bedrooms before following them. With some relief, she discovered that the master was empty and, apparently, untouched. The guest room—now Deysei's—was likewise unoccupied and undisturbed. But opening the door to Guillermo's Pixar-themed room, she heard voices. The room was darkened, with the curtains drawn. Under the Buzz Lightyear quilt there was a mound that could only be a body—or two. Clara turned on the lights and immediately saw two pairs of shoes on the floor, a pair of Nikes and pair of red strappy fuck-me heels.

"Come on out," she said. "I know you're under there." This was a game she played with Guillermo sometimes in the morning and she used the same tone now.

The quilt was thrown back, revealing an old friend of Yunis's from Inwood named Aurora and a guy Clara didn't know. The guy's bare, muscular brown arm, emerged like a rifle from under the quilt. *Who the hell are all these people?* she asked herself. Hadn't she come to New Jersey to escape them? Aurora was sitting up now, buttoning herself back into presentability, her unhooked bra strap hanging out the armhole of her sleeveless blouse. The guy was reaching under the covers, obviously pulling his pants back up. He was sucking his teeth and sighing as he did so. Guillermo's Lightning McQueen lamp had been knocked over during their tryst and lay on its side. Some of the books in the bedside stand had also been bumped to the floor.

"Christ, Aurora!" said Clara. "In my son's bed?"

"Sorry," she said in the Dominican-inflected way—*So*-ree— getting out from under the quilt and stepping into her heels. She smoothed her blouse and her skirt.

"You too," Clara said to guy. "Out of the bed now."

"In a minute. I've got a boner over here."

"I don't care. Out!"

"I thought you said we wouldn't be disturbed," the guy said to Aurora.

"Shut up and let's go," she replied.

"Stupid fucking bitch."

"Take it outside," said Clara. "Both of you."

When they had gone, she stripped the bed—no condoms, no stains, thank goodness—and put the sheets in the hamper in the bathroom, taking care not to stand on the shattered glass. With the toilet brush, she swept the shards onto a week-old sports page Thomas had left draped over one of the towel rails. She carried the paper downstairs and wrapped it up in another sheet of newsprint before stuffing it into the garbage can, which was overflowing with chicken bones and plastic bottles. The party was not breaking up. There were people in every room, drinking and talking. The reggaeton had been replaced with merengue and a few people were dancing in the living room. It was like trying to kill a Hydra. She went into the sunroom looking for Yunis, but it was empty save for the teenager at the computer, blasting away at the alien spaceships.

"Where's my sister?" she asked him.

"I dunno," he replied without looking up from the game. "Some girl came in looking for her. I think they went downstairs."

"Christ," said Clara. She walked back through the dining room, past the dancing couples, this time unplugging the stereo midsong. "This party is *over*!" she yelled in the direction of the living room. Standing in the kitchen at the top of the basement stairs, Clara heard a scream from below, a wordless cry, as if the house itself were wailing. It was her sister's voice. By the time Clara got to the bottom of the stairs, she could hear her niece: "No, Mami. No!" Clara dashed past the washing machine and dryer and entered the den in time to see something she did not completely comprehend at first, but something she would never be able to forget. Deysei and Guillermo were still sitting on the couch. Guillermo was trying to get off the couch, as if a giant spider was approaching him. Deysei, unable to move like Guillermo, was holding up her hands to fend off her mother's foot, which, encased in its white wedge-heeled shoe, was descending toward her. "No Mami!" she called again. Clara was too far away to do anything. She saw Yunis's foot go into her daughter's midsection like a pizza maker's fist going into a ball of dough. Deysei screamed.

Yunis lifted her foot to stomp Deysei again, but by this time, Clara was moving. She raced across the room and jumped on her sister's back. They rolled to the floor, Clara's head colliding with the base of the couch.

Yunis was standing up. "I'm going to kill her. I'm going to *kill* you. Fucking my boyfriend."

"Stop it! Stop it!" shouted Clara, clutching at her sister.

"She's been fucking Raúl!"

"I know," said Clara. She could hear Deysei crying now and, on top of it, Guillermo shrieking.

"You *know* and you didn't tell me?"

The ruckus had brought people down from the party, a half-dozen of them, coming into the room, Manny in front.

"Somebody call the police," shouted Yunis. "They've got to arrest him. He's a goddamn rapist. I'll tell them where he lives."

"Calm down," said Clara.

"I'm *not* calming down. I ain't never going to calm down from this!"

Deysei was still on the couch, curled tightly, holding herself and moaning.

"We've got to get her to a hospital," said Clara to Yunis.

"Yeah, so they can take that fucking thing out of her," said Yunis.

THE HOSPITAL. AGAIN.

Hospitals were second only to airports in Clara's list of least-liked places. Just like airports, hospitals were venues for arrivals and departures, for beginnings and ends. A day that contained a visit to both could not be a good one.

The emergency room nurse sent them up to the triage section of the labor and delivery ward. There, Deysei was taken in as if she were going to give birth, the nurse asking lots of questions. Clara explained that her niece had been kicked in the stomach during a fight at a party. The nurse was unfazed, as if she heard this story every day. Very quickly, they had her undressed and into a smock, a fetal hearbeat monitor strapped to her stomach. The heartbeat was there, *beep-beep-beeping* away with comforting regularity. A doctor came in and performed an exam and then an ultrasound. The fetus was clearly visible on the screen, the spine like a row of little teeth, its still-forming limbs moving in that silent darkness.

"You are leaking amniotic fluid. Your bag of waters has been ruptured. There is no way for us to save this pregnancy," the doctor said.

Deysei began to weep. She'd been holding it in the whole time—in the car, in the emergency room, and through the examination. Now she let her tears out. Seeing it, Clara began to cry, too.

"It's OK?" asked Guillermo. Clara had brought him along. Manny was supposed to be taking Yunis back to Inwood. Back to his place or somewhere else. She didn't care.

"No, Gilly, it's not OK."

"Was the baby was hurt?" asked Guillermo.

"Yes," said Clara.

And then Guillermo began to weep, too.

Thomas

The second interview—a day-long series of introductions, meet-ings, and Q&As—had gone smoothly. It had been hospi-table, collegial, with no third-degree, no surprise quizzes to test his knowledge of Anglo-American cataloging rules or the Dub-lin Core. The company, Susquehanna Serials, was headquartered in a glass building off the Dulles toll road in northern Virginia. About midway through the afternoon, as a personnel officer was going through various benefits packages, Thomas realized that the job was his. They would not be putting themselves through all of this—the expense of getting him down here, the hours of meetings, the discussion of salary—if they had not already decided that they liked him. Unless he spat on someone or made an off-color joke before leaving, he could expect a call in the next week telling him that he'd been hired. The recognition filled him with happiness and relief. It was not the perfect job, but it was a job and that would do for now. He was going to be a salesman. That's not what the position was called, but that is what it was. He would be pitching Susquehanna's databases to corporations, universities, and libraries in the New York area and providing follow-up support for exist-ing customers. A certain amount of his salary would be based on commission; there was also the possibility of performance-related bonuses. The fact that he had worked with similar kinds of clients at BiblioFile—and the fact that one of Susquehanna's VPs was a former BiblioFile exec—seemed to please everyone. "We'll be in touch soon," the human resources manager said as they parted. "Real soon."

A cab took him to the nearest Metro stop, where he got on a train to Bethesda. The job would require regular trips back to the D.C. area, which was not a bad thing—he'd be able to see his mother more often than he did now. As he rode in the back of the cab, he tried not to get too far ahead of himself. Employment would be a good thing, definitely. It would erase one set of concerns, but there was still all kinds of other shit going on—with Melissa, with Deysei, with Clara's fertility problems.

He got out of the cab and, before going into the Metro, he called his wife.

"Hi? Thomas?"

"Yes. What's up?" He could hear something frying in the background. The radio. Guillermo saying something. The evening routine under way.

"Hold on, baby, I'm talking to Daddy," Clara said to Guillermo. And then to him: "So, are you done? How did it go?"

"Really well, actually. I don't want to jinx it, but—"

"Don't jinx it!" said Clara. "That's so great. When will they let you know?"

"Soon. Maybe next week."

"It was a long wait, Thomas, but totally worth it. OK, I don't want to count our eggs—"

"You mean our chickens."

"Yes. So, are you going to take your mom out to celebrate?"

"I think I might," he said. His mother was going to pick him up from the Bethesda station.

"Do you know what train you're going to be taking home tomorrow?"

"Not yet. I'll look at the timetable in the morning. Something in the afternoon, so I can spend a little time with my mom. So, how's everything there?"

"A little crazy, actually," said Clara without hesitation.

"Really? Like what?"

"Well, you remember how I said my sister might be coming back from D.R.?"

"Yeah . . ."

"She's flying in tomorrow."

"*Tomorrow*? What the hell happened?"

"She and my mother had a big fight and she stormed out of there this morning. She's staying with Plinio now. Tomorrow was the earliest flight she could get." There was a long pause. "She's going to have to stay with us for a little while, Thomas."

"Why? Doesn't she have an apartment?" he said. "Why can't she and Deysei move back there?" *That would solve a couple of problems,* he thought but didn't say.

"She sublet that apartment, remember?" said Clara. "The woman in there now is refusing to leave. I can't say I blame her."

"Your sister is homeless?" he said. "What about Raúl? Can't she move back in with him?"

Here Clara paused. "No. God knows where Raúl's living now."

"I don't get it. Why the hell is she coming back here so soon? Why's she giving up so quickly?"

"I don't know for sure, but I'd bet that she and the new boyfriend already burned through their little honeymoon period."

"A boyfriend? *That's* why she moved?"

"Like I said, I don't know for sure, but based on her history, I wouldn't be too surprised. That's just how it goes with her."

"Shit. And what about that inheritance? Didn't her grandfather leave her money or something?"

"There's a big legal battle over the estate. She might not see it for years. He had like ten kids with three different women and they all want their cut before Yunis gets hers. Anyway, it's not even that much, just a few thousand dollars."

"So, she's homeless, heartbroken, and penniless, and now she's coming to live with us?"

"Yes."

He collected his thoughts for a moment. "Speaking of boyfriends, did you talk to that Tito guy yet?"

Another pause. "No, not yet. Like I said, it's been a little crazy. I'll talk to him tomorrow."

"Don't humor him, Clara. Don't get sentimental. Tell him how it is."

"I will," she said.

"I'll call you tomorrow when I know what train I'm on. Hug Gilly for me."

The conversation wiped out all the good feelings he'd had after the interview. He boarded the train and stewed. This was one of those times when it seemed that every cliché about Latino immigrants was spot on, when every fear he'd had back when he'd first started dating Clara seemed to have been realized. He rued, if only for the duration of the journey to Bethesda, the fact that his marriage had brought him into such regular contact with these crazy Dominicans. Was that racist? Was that bigoted? He didn't know. He didn't care. All he knew was that this wasn't right. All he knew was that this kind of shit did not go on in his own extended family. All he knew was that he was now going to have not only his moody, pregnant teenage niece living under his roof but also his uncouth, loud-mouthed, and unstable sister-in-law. And all this would be happening while he and Clara were about to start IVF, which he'd gathered from the brochures the doctor had given them was a hormonal and emotional minefield. At this point he felt himself wishing he'd married into a nice, repressed family of New England WASPs; he found himself thinking that he should just ditch all of this and run off with Melissa. But he had not heard from Melissa in a couple of weeks—not since his visit with the flowers. She was waiting him out, letting him make a decision. Right now it seemed like an easy decision to make.

HIS MOTHER MET him in downtown Bethesda and led him to a new restaurant. Thomas no longer tried to keep up with his hometown, with its unrestrained development and prosperity. It was like a childhood friend who'd married into money and suddenly started wearing designer clothes and driving a Bentley. You were still cordial with them, but whatever connection had been there was long gone. Every time he returned, the town where he'd grown up was less familiar to him. The one benefit of it was that his mother's house was now worth twenty times what she and Thomas's father had paid for it in the late sixties. His mother's financial security was not something Thomas worried about.

She looked well, his mother. Her dark brown hair had grown back nicely and a healthy color had returned to her skin. She was dressing with care once again. Gone were the sweats and the T-shirts of her chemo days. Here she was in a nice pair of gray slacks and navy blue shell, a silver necklace, and matching earrings. She still wore the lymphedema sleeve on her arm, but she was, overall, looking better than she had in a long time. It had been two years, he realized, with some amazement.

At dinner, she told him she was planning a trip, her first since the diagnosis: a cruise around the South Pacific. She showed Thomas the cruise brochure—Fiji, Tahiti, Bora Bora. The Gauguin experience. "Erin Siegert is going with me. You remember her? We went to Scandinavia together a few years ago to see the fjords." (In the wake of her divorce from his father, Thomas's mother had established a substitute family, a network of women who lived nearby and looked after one another. Many of these women were either divorced or widowed. None had children living at home and most, like his mother, were retired from full-time employment in the federal government.) Thomas had to acknowledge

that the divorce had definitely been a good thing for his mother—
and for his father, who had remarried his much younger mistress
and retired to Albuquerque, where he could indulge in his stargaz-
ing undistracted by family responsibilities. From the rare e-mails
his father sent, Thomas gathered that he had become a nocturnal,
nonsocial animal. Still, looking at his own life through the lens
of his parents', he was spooked by the thought of an existence like
theirs, an existence apart from Clara and Guillermo. He did not
want to find himself twenty-five years down the road plotting
some bachelor vacation, some golf outing with a divorced pal,
waiting for news of a heart condition or an enlarged prostate to
come back from his primary care physician before confirming his
itinerary.

"Looks like a lot of fun," he said, handing the brochure back to
her.

"I tell you, I'm so ready. I want to go *now*," said his mother.

"I bet," he said. "You deserve it, Mom."

He told her about the interview and parceled out a few stories
about Guillermo. He'd even remembered to bring some recent photographs of his son. There was a good one, a family portrait taken
in one of Millwood's numerous parks. It looked like a piece of clip
art for a progressive, postracial America. Thomas found himself
on the verge of tears as he showed it to his mother, a tidal surge of
panic blocking his throat. It was the same way he felt when he said
goodbye to his son each day at the bus stop, when he was gripped
with the possibility that he might never see his son again.

"Oh, that's a good one!" his mother said. "Can I keep it?"

THOMAS SLEPT LATE the next day and took his mother
out for lunch at a restaurant near Union Station. On Amtrak, heading back to New York, his cell phone rang. He expected it to be
Clara—he hadn't been able to reach her that morning before leaving
his mother's house—but the ID on his phone told him otherwise.

EPSTEIN HISTORY ARCHIVE, said the display, the name Thomas had come up with just in case Clara ever went snooping.

"Hi, Tom," said Melissa, as if nothing had changed between them, as if there had been no ultimatum delivered, as if they had been talking every day the last two weeks.

"How did the interview go?"

"Pretty good," he said. "I don't want to jinx it."

"Are you in New Jersey?" she said.

"On my way back from D.C."

"Well, I'm in the city. Could I meet you in Penn Station? I've got a little surprise."

Thomas had planned to get off in Newark and take a cab home, but he'd also been unable to reach Clara to give her an ETA. She was probably at the airport picking up her sister, he realized. Yunis—another reason not to rush back to Millwood.

"OK," he said.

"I'll meet you at the Eighth Avenue exit. Look for my car."

He spent the remainder of the journey wondering what the surprise might be. The ultimatum, he now saw, had signaled a shift in Melissa. No longer was she the addled widow in mourning. No longer was she the lonely but privileged housewife. No longer did she seem weak and helpless. Since the ultimatum, Thomas had seen something else in Melissa—a tough-minded and ruthless competitiveness. He recalled a spring afternoon after he'd been laid off. Melissa, upon learning that he'd played tennis in his youth, had taken him to her indoor court in Montclair. They'd knocked the ball back and forth amiably enough until Thomas, with a couple of lucky shots, threatened to break her serve. At deuce, she'd clammed up and whizzed two aces past him, exclaiming, "Ha!" as he lurched after the ad point. The next game, she was back to her easygoing self, making him chase balls all over the court. That was the face Melissa was wearing these days, the focused and determined look of the competitor in midgame flow. Thomas had the sense that, one way or another, all of this was going to be settled before the afternoon was out. The realization filled him with a kind of plummeting fear.

AS PROMISED, SHE was waiting for him in her white Lexus on the curb near the intersection of Eighth Avenue and Thirty-third Street.

He got in. No kiss. But otherwise, it was a pleasant experience: the subtly air-conditioned interior, Schubert's Trout Quintet on the stereo, and Melissa herself, looking delectable in dark blue jeans and a crushed satin blouse that she seemed to have chosen because it perfectly matched the pewter gray upholstery of the car. "Hi," he said, tentatively.

"Hello, Tom," she said, with an unreadable little smile as she pulled into traffic.

"Where are we going?" he asked, and ventured a joke: "To make out in the Temple of Dendur?"

This got a laugh from her, which raised his spirits.

"No. But what a great idea." She turned right on Thirty-fourth and then right again on Seventh, heading downtown. "I thought maybe a change of venue would be good for us."

THEY MADE THEIR halting way downtown and Thomas tried to predict where they might be going. He realized that he was trying to predict this in the smallest and largest senses. Where *were* they going?

They drove without a word. Melissa didn't mention her ultimatum, didn't mentioned the pregnancy that wasn't, didn't mention the several times in the last month that she'd turned him away at her door, but it was all there, interwoven with the bars of the Schubert. In the Village, Melissa crossed to Hudson Street and found parking. They got out and walked. The building she led him to was on Greenwich Street, a modestly sized modern high-rise with an undulating facade designed by a brand-name architect. In Midtown or on Wall Street, it would have been unremarkable, but here, amid the brownstones and brick row houses, it seemed unreal, like something that had been added to the streetscape in Photoshop.

The doorman greeted Melissa by name, and she and Thomas went through the sparsely decorated but striking lobby. For a moment, Thomas thought they were entering a boutique hotel—someplace without a sign, known only to the initiated—but there was no check-in desk, no bellhop station, no concierge. He was suddenly nervous, as if this were another job interview.

"Very nice," he said, realizing, too late, how inane a comment it was.

Melissa still said nothing. The elevator took them up to the seventh floor and deposited them in a hallway with only three doors. Producing a set of keys, Melissa opened the farthest door and went in without waiting for him.

Beyond the door was a room filled with sunset light. Thomas had the sense of walking into an art installation on the subject of tranquillity, of celestial repose. The apartment was unfurnished, or rather it was furnished with hopes and possibilities, with potential. To one side there was an open-plan kitchen with an array of stainless-steel appliances. In the other direction, more doors—bedrooms, he supposed. He remembered a Frank O'Hara poem about "a pleasant stranger whose apartment is in the Heaven on Earth Bldg." This is was what he'd imagined the Heaven on Earth Building to look like when he first read the poem in college.

Melissa was traversing the broad expanse of shiny blond flooring to open a sliding glass door that led out to a terrace. When the door slid open, a warm breeze came rushing in and flowed around him. Thomas followed her out to the terrace. The river was on the left, and beyond it, New Jersey, the sun a slowly dropping wrecking ball of lava light. Straight ahead, they had a view over the neighboring brick row houses and brownstones to the ascending skyline of

Midtown—Penn Plaza, the Empire State Building, and Rockefeller Center. Lights were coming on in the city. Next to seeing Manhattan covered in newly fallen snow, he could not imagine it looking more magical, more inviting.

"When are you moving in?" he asked.

"Friday," she said. "The question is, when are *you* moving in?"

So this was it. No more stalling. No more thinking about it. No more hoping she would back down from her ultimatum. What she was showing him was the New York life he'd wanted when he first arrived in the city, the life many people imagined they would live once they made it in New York. It was the loss of exactly this kind of existence that he'd briefly mourned when he and Clara had moved to the suburbs, when they'd bought the Odyssey and begun commuting. Melissa knew. She and Thomas had talked about the draws of the city, the privilege of being able to walk out your front door to restaurants, theater, movies. How simple it would be to step right in, to shed his life in Millwood and reside here. No more crazy Domincans mooching off him, turning up pregnant in his house.

But he found himself doubting those dreams, those idle fantasies. Much of their appeal was that they were just that: idle. The likelihood of a job offer in the next week allowed him to see things more clearly now. What Melissa was offering seemed suddenly fraudulent, requiring, as it did, the betrayal of his wife and child. Melissa herself, meanwhile, seemed to require nothing more of him than his presence. She seemed to be saying to him: *You'll do. You'll save me from being alone. You'll save me the trouble of having to meet another man.* He found himself thinking the worst of her—that her choice of husband had been no more than a way of maintaining the privileged ease of her life. What a luxury to be able to make decisions that way! It was what she was asking him to do now. *I was married, but this great opportunity came along.* He was seized by the vertiginous possibility that he was about to fuck everything up and the converse realization that he could still salvage something—maybe everything.

"Six months ago, in the Botanical Garden, you said that there would be no complications," Thomas said.

"And I meant it. At the time. But it was naive of me—and naive of you to believe me."

"Why can't we just keep it the way it was? With you living in the city, it might actually be easier. Especially if I went back to work."

"I told you, Tom. When I thought I was pregnant, I realized that wasn't going to be enough. That feeling hasn't changed."

"This is what *you* want," he said. "This is not my life. I've had no say in choosing this apartment."

"It was my money."

"You mean Stephen's."

"Not anymore. It's mine now and I'm willing to share it with you."

"I don't know. I think maybe it's best for you to begin again."

"Don't tell me what's best for me. This is your last chance, Tom. If your answer is no, you will never hear from me again. It will be as if I had died."

The finality of those words—intended to be threatening—was liberating. Isn't that what he wanted? Wasn't that a good outcome for him? For her to disappear.

"I'm sorry," he said. "I can't."

Her mouth flattened into a scowl. "Are you sure? Are you really certain that's what you want?"

"Yes," he said, consciously appreciating her beautiful face, the seductive length of her neck, those blue eyes, in these final moments before she was no longer his mistress, no longer a part of his life.

"You're fooling yourself, Tom. Nothing would have happened between us if things were all right in your marriage."

"That's still my answer." His voice quavered as he spoke.

"Then you're going to have to find your own way back to New Jersey. Get out of my apartment."

"Melissa—"

"Goodbye, Tom. You're going to regret this."

He stepped back from the terrace ledge, retreated into the apartment, and crossed the shiny wood floor to the entrance. There he paused and took a last look at her, Melissa, silhouetted in the glass, leaning on the railing, and looking out over the city, as if already searching for someone else.

WITHOUT REALLY KNOWING what he was doing, Thomas headed over to the subway station on Varick Street. He felt like he'd just survived a mugging, or that someone had pulled him out of the way of an oncoming bus. He was keyed up, jittery, unable to focus on anything. He boarded the train and stood in front of the in-car map of the subway system. Looking at the map, he realized that he could go anywhere—not just in the city, but *anywhere*. The subway connected to the airports, to the Port of New York. He was free, but deep down, he knew the freedom was fleeting. The hiatus he'd taken from work and family life the last six months was coming to an end. It was a Sunday-night freedom, an end-of-summer freedom: precious, limited, and waning. Turning away from the map, he got off at Penn Station.

It was Saturday evening, but unlike a few hours earlier, the station was as crowded as if it were a weekday rush hour. This usually meant only one thing: delays. Sure enough, before he could even check the departure board, the announcement came over the PA: A train had broken down in the Hudson River tunnel. Delays of up to one hour. He went to the bar and ordered a beer. He tried calling the house to let Clara know that he was on his way home. He got their machine.

He was glad to have a little time to recover from the confrontation with Melissa. He felt enormous relief. He'd gotten away with it: He'd had his extracurricular activity and now he could get back to his family. Melissa would not have any trouble finding another companion, someone willing to be kept. He took a sip of his beer and eyed the score of the game. The Yankees were losing. Yes, everything was going to be fine.

IT WAS AFTER nine when he finally opened the side door and stepped into the kitchen of his home. It felt like he'd been away a long time.

His sister-in-law was in the kitchen, pouring tonic water into a tumbler. A bottle of vodka was on the table.

"*Heeeere's* Tommy!" she said, doing her best Ed McMahon. "What's cracking, my brother? Where you been? We was starting to get worried aboutchoo."

"There were delays," he said. "A train broke down in the tunnel." He'd forgotten that Yunis was coming back, forgotten about all of that.

"*Right.* Come on, man. You can't fool me. You was stalling. I know it." She lifted her glass and said, "*Salud,*" before knocking half the drink back.

Yunis looked browner than she had the day she left for Santo Domingo. Tanned and drunk, he thought, setting down his bag.

"How was your trip back?" he asked.

"The trip was fine," she said. "It was the shit that went down after I got here that was the problem." She glanced to her right, into the living room. Thomas followed her gaze and saw a large dark red stain on their couch—one of the new pieces of furniture they'd bought since moving to New Jersey. The shade of the floor lamp next to the couch was dented and torn.

"What the hell happened?" he asked.

"I'm gonna let my sister tell you," she said.

"Where is Clara?" Thomas asked.

"She's at the hospital with Deysei."

"The hospital?" said Thomas. "What happened? The baby?"

"Like I said, I'm going to let my sister tell you all about it." Yunis looked at him—a challenging look. A look that said: *That's right, bro, you missed some shit.*

"What about Guillermo?"

"With his mami." She took another drink from her glass. "All right, Tommy. I'm going downstairs to watch my shows. You wait up for your wife—I know she wants to talk to you." She walked past him to the stairwell. "Peace, my brother."

The kitchen, he noticed now that Yunis had gone, looked like it often did at the end of a party. Dirty dishes were arrayed on every surface and bore crumpled napkins, chicken bones, and congealed pools of gravy. On the stove, there was a pot of rice and a frying pan with an inch of oil in which two slivers of *plátano* were petrified. Dirty glasses abounded. The paper towel roll was empty, the tracks of adhesive on the cardboard tube like a nonwinning result in a slot machine. In a roasting pan, half-hidden by tinfoil, was the carcass of a bird, the rib cage plucked almost clean. Thomas smelled adobo and garlic and vinegar. This is what the kitchen in Yunis's apartment used to be like when he went there. It had taken only a day for her to make their house into hers.

He climbed the stairs, slowly and quietly. He felt weary. He showered and got into bed, intending to read, but he fell asleep, and the next thing he knew, Clara was in the room with him. Without forewarning, her arrival felt like a dream.

She was wearing a white terry cloth bathrobe over her favorite sleeping outfit— pink pajama bottoms and a black tank top. She'd come home, showered, and changed without waking him. What time was it? He looked at the clock: 1:23. Clara saw that he was awake. She sat on the edge of the bed and pulled a piece of folded letter-sized paper out of the side table. She held it up to him. "Who is this?" she asked.

He took the page from her and looked at the slightly out-of-focus image of the front of Melissa's house. It took him a moment to realize that he was in the picture, holding a bunch of flowers, talking to Melissa. Fuck.

"That's me," he said.

"I know that's you. Who is *she*?"

"What's going on? Why were you at the hospital? Is everything OK?"

"Who *is* she?"

"Come on, Clara."

"Answer my question."

"Did you have me followed?" he asked.

"No, I didn't have you followed."

"How did you get this photograph, then?"

"Never mind how I got the photograph. Tell me who she is."

"Her name is Melissa Epstein—I mean Melissa Logan."

"You don't even know her name?"

"Logan is her maiden name."

"So she's cheating on her husband, too?"

"No, he died."

"Wait, so *this* was the 'job' you were doing over in Newstead?"

"It was a real job," he said.

"I don't believe it. What a fool I am. And aren't those the same flowers you gave me a couple of weeks ago?" Clara asked.

"Yes."

"So you gave me flowers that this bitch didn't want?"

"It's not like that."

"Thomas. How could you do that to me?"

"I'm sorry," he muttered.

"How long have you been fucking her?"

"I'm not fuck—it's over. It's over now."

"How long did this go on?"

"Almost six months."

"*Six* months?"

"It started right after I was laid off. Right after the miscarriage."

"I can't believe it. You've ruined everything," she said. "You've ruined it all. We were just about to get out of this shit and you've fucked it up."

"It doesn't have to be over, Clara. Everything doesn't have to be ruined."

"How could you have been sleeping with her for *six* months? What am I supposed to think? The next time something bad happens to us, you're going to go fucking some rich housewife again? I can't even believe you when you say it's over. How do I know you weren't with her the last few days? How do I know you were really on an interview, with your mother?"

"I was down in D.C.," he said, indignantly.

"You've got no right to take that tone, Thomas. You have no idea what has been going on here." At this point, she paused and looked at him. "You're not the only one who has been tempted. You're not the only one who has had opportunity."

"What do you mean?"

"You think I haven't had my chances to screw around? You think Tito wouldn't have me back?"

"Tito?" said Thomas. "What's this with Tito all of a sudden? The guy you loved so much you aborted his baby?"

"I don't know," said Clara. She looked utterly confused and utterly despondent. "Sometimes I think I should have kept that baby."

"If you had kept it, we would never have met. You said that yourself."

"Well, maybe my life would have been better. Different, but better."

"Guillermo would never have been born. How is that a better life?"

"I would have had another child. Maybe two."

"We still can," said Thomas. "We can still do it. I'm ready."

"How am I supposed to believe that after what you just told me. I don't know what to think of you anymore, Thomas."

"Clara, please."

"Look what I went and picked up," she said. She held up a white paper bag with a blue stork on the outside. She dumped the contents onto the bed. Vials of medicine, syringes, needles, cotton swabs. "I was ready to start. I've been waiting so long for this."

"Come on, Clara," he said, and reached for the gap in her robe, hoping to pull her toward him in an embrace. And she did come closer to him, but not to kiss him—to strike him across the face with her open hand.

"Get the fuck out of here," she said.

"Clara—"

"No! I said get out!"

Tito

The path into the forested section of the park was illuminated by old-fashioned lampposts that were meant to look like Victorian gas lamps but actually contained modern halogen bulbs. About one in three had been vandalized, their glass faces shattered with rocks, creating areas of darkness on the path. As he stumbled along the walkway of hexagonal cobblestones, taking sips from his bottle, Tito was not seeing the park as it was—darkened, cooling, ominously tranquil. Instead, what he saw was the park as it existed in his imagination—a place of wonders, the park where he and Clara had spent their Friday afternoons more than fifteen years before. The sacred locations, like the stations of the cross, were arrayed on the map in his brain, and he intended to visit them all on his way to his destination. Just up here, where the path wound out of view of the ball fields and apartment buildings, was where he had first taken her hand. That was on their third date, the week after he had kissed her the first time. A little farther along, on a bench near an outcrop of stone, was where he had undone a single button of her blouse and reached in, his hand slipping under the cup of her bra, her nipple squeezed between his thumb and the knuckle of his forefinger. His hand had stayed there for a good fifteen minutes while they'd kissed, getting sweaty, his shoulder cramping from the weird angle in which he'd had to position his arm to reach in through the narrow opening. Then they heard a man walking his dog approaching along the path. Trying to withdraw his hand from Clara's breast, Tito found that it had become stuck. She had to dip into the opening, peel his palm away, and button herself up just before the dog walker came around the outcrop to find them both laughing. *Kids.*

Farther along, the path passed under the mouth of the Indian cave. As they worked their way deeper into the forest and deeper into each other's clothes, they were heading for that cave, where Tito hoped they would be able to have a little privacy, where they would not have to worry about people walking their dogs. Still, there were risks. The cave was reputedly the haunt of savage bums and violent drug users. It was also where several of his classmates claimed to have lost their virginity. As he and Clara approached the cave, they saw someone standing by the mouth: a teenager neither of them recognized, his head swiveling, on the lookout.

"Wait," said Clara, grabbing him by the elbow and pulling him back under the cover of the trees. They stepped off the path and watched the sentry as he looked nervously about, now and then glancing over his shoulder back into the cave.

"What do you think is going on?" she asked.

"Maybe they're in there smoking crack," said Tito.

"Or planning a robbery."

Neither, it turned out. After a few minutes, another teenage boy emerged from within the cave, holding the hand of an even younger girl. From this distance, she looked thirteen or fourteen, though she was dressed like someone older, in a short skirt and thin-strapped top.

"Oh, God," said Clara. "They were taking turns with her."

Tito understood that his hopes for the afternoon had been spoiled. They would not be going into that cave now. Not today. "Let's go over to the benches," he said. "The ones with the view."

"Yeah," said Clara. "I don't want to go in *there*."

They backtracked and took a different fork of the path to a little promontory with two benches and a waist-high railing overlooking the Hudson Bridge, the Metro North railroad tracks, the Palisades of New Jersey, the Spuyten Duyvil Creek, and the inlet to the Inwood lagoon. They sat on one of the benches, a warm breeze rising up off the water and blowing in their faces.

"I've never been here before," said Clara. "This is better than that cave."

He was glad he'd suggested it. He kissed her. "What do you like about it?" he asked.

"I don't feel like I'm in New York anymore. I could be anywhere. Europe. Africa." She looked out over the river. "Where would you go if you could go anywhere right now?"

"Nowhere," he said. "I'd stay right here, because that's where you are."

She smiled at him and took his hand. "That's sweet, Tito."

"I mean it," he said. "Where would you go, if you could go anywhere right now?"

"Back to my grandparents' *ranchito* in D.R.," she said. "Back home."

THE SHORE OF Inwood lagoon was, supposedly, where the Dutch had purchased Manhattan from the Indians. In the lamp-lit late-summer night, as Tito wandered through the trees, he imagined a little band of these Dutchmen in their billowy pantaloons and iron helmets sweating as they took their first walk around Inwood, surveying the wilderness they had just acquired for a few trinkets, wary of the wilderness and the savages they'd just done business with. They felt tired, exasperated, but also a little giddy, elbowing each other and pointing, expansive with new acquisitions and a sense of missions being fulfilled. Tito had seen the same expressions, the same gestures, on the faces of Dominicans coming through the international arrivals gate at Newark or JFK when he'd waited for his parents to return from their annual vacations home—trepidation and possibilities, the end of a long journey and the start of another.

Possibilities. He'd come in here to complete the tour of this sacred walkway and then throw himself off the Hudson Bridge or jump from one of the cliffs over the river. That had been his plan, but now, in the park, he had the sense that he'd walked right out of the world, the sense that he existed in some kind of purgatory unconnected to time and place, that his meeting with Clara might not have happened yet and that he could still do something to stop her, that, if he went back far enough, he might be able to prevent her from leaving. There was no telling where this path might lead him—to the jungles of Peru, to Shangri-la, or even to the *ranchito* in the Dominican Republic that Clara had wanted to get back to.

He kept going along the route that he and Clara had walked that afternoon when he had wanted to take her to the cave, eager to see what might happen. He had never had a chance to show off all the stuff he'd learned about Inwood. They were always too busy kissing and feeling each other up. There wasn't time to talk history. He took a sip from the bottle. If he turned left here, he would descend out of the trees and emerge onto the grassy bank that led to the Payson Street entrance opposite Clara's old house. The house had changed over the years since Clara's father's murder. It was owned by a family of Jamaicans now. They had gotten to work right away, fixing the place up. It was unrecognizable, restored, a house anyone would want to live in. The restoration had been a sad thing for him to watch—the slow eradication of one of the landmarks on the map in his brain.

But Tito did not go that way. He continued on, going west and north, toward the river, into the deepest part of the park, where the trees were the thickest and the sounds from the city all but lost, except for the wash of traffic on the Hudson Parkway, a white noise that seemed to further remove the park from reality. He walked on, a sense of urgency gathering around him.

Behind him there was a noise, a metallic, mechanical grinding. It was approaching quickly, like a swarm of steel-winged hornets. Through the trees, he saw a single beam of a light. Then, more lights—not hornets, but lighting bugs. Around the bend they came, a succession of riders on mountain bikes, the cleated tires thrumming the path, the lubricated shriek of their cranks rising to a crescendo. Before he could fully register their speed, they were upon him. "On your left!" the first of them shouted as Tito jumped to the edge of the path. They went by him too quickly to count—four or five or six, looking insectlike in their tight black pants and their lurid, clingy tops, the vented helmets glistening exoskeletally in the lamplight. "Whoo-eee!" said the last as they went around the corner and were lost once again in the trees, buzzing toward some bikers' hive deep in the forest.

Tito's heart was pounding so hard that his neck and biceps quivered. He felt feverish, overstimulated. He took a drink. Holding up the bottle, he saw that he'd downed more than half of it.

"Breathe," he said aloud. "Just breathe."

Once, in his early days with Cruz Brothers, when he was still on the trucks, still lifting heavy things all day long, he had come close to hyperventilating. He and another grunt, a fat, sweaty Puerto Rican kid named Cleber (pronounced *clever*, to everyone's undying amusement), were taking an antique dresser up the stairwell of an elevatorless prewar building on St. Nicholas. The apartment was on the sixth floor and they'd already made countless trips, everything carried up by hand. Idiotic with exhaustion, endorphins, and falling blood sugar, Tito had started laughing between the third and fourth floors of their climb. He was leading, which was harder on the back but also safer should one of them lose their grip or their footing—an occurrence that was increasingly likely as the day wore on and fatigue came into play. He'd lost count, even then in his early years with Cruz Brothers, of the number of broken fingers, sprained ankles, dislocated shoulders, black eyes, fat lips, and unexpected dental dislodgements he'd witnessed. He had a sense that something bad was going to happen on this ascent of the stairwell. The dresser, even without its drawers, was *heavy*. About halfway up the fourth flight, he and Cleber against all common sense had started shouting out comparisons, trying to one-up each other.

"This thing's heavier than a fucking piano."

"Heavier than Ozzie Cruz after a night at the all-you-can-eat buffet."

"Heavier than Ozzie Cruz's wife after a night at the all-you-can-eat buffet."

"Heavier than Ozzie Cruz's *mami* after a night at the all-you-can-eat buffet."

"Heavier than my *cojones*."

"Heavier than a goddamn *matrimonio obligao*," said Cleber. Heavier than an arranged marriage. It was something Tito's father often said when hauling garbage out to the curb and, in that moment, it seemed like the funniest thing he had ever heard.

"Stop laughing!" said Cleber. "You gonna drop this motherfucker on me."

That only made Tito laugh even harder.

"I'm serious. Cut that shit out."

"*Matrimonio,*" rasped Tito between guffaws. "*Obligao!*" Cleber was right. He was laughing so hard, he couldn't hold the damn thing. It was impossible to lift heavy objects when you were laughing. Guys on the trucks were forever trying to get each other to drop stuff by cracking jokes. If Tito let go now, the dresser would rumble and bounce down the stairs, squishing Cleber like a water balloon under a brick.

"I'm putting this shit down," said Cleber, lowering the legs of his end onto the steps. There were tiny metal wheels on the feet of the dresser. Still laughing, Tito squatted to bring his end down, but he couldn't hold it and let his side of the dresser drop the last three inches or so, chipping out a piece of the stone on the lip of the step. Relief released a new burst of hilarity from him. Now that his well-being was no longer endangered, Cleber was laughing, too.

"You shouldn't have started that shit," said Cleber, finally winding down. "Damn you for starting that shit when we're carrying something like this."

Tito had laughed so hard that he was coughing. He felt unable to breathe; his cough was turning into a choke.

"You all right, man?" said Cleber.

Tito was still coughing. He was not in control of his own body. It was an amusement park ride.

"You're turning red, Tito. Stop that," said Cleber.

But he couldn't stop. His cough was as uncontrollable as his laugh had been. He waved his hands, signaling distress, signaling that he was drowning. Cleber girded his jeans around his thick waist and squeezed past the dresser, climbing the stairs to reach Tito and slap him on the back. That didn't help. Finally, in desperation, he slapped Tito across the face, knocking him against the dresser. There was a silent, suspenseful moment in which Tito stopped coughing and the dresser, its tiny metal wheels set in motion, became unmoored from the step. They both grasped at the shiny, lacquered wood on the dresser's top, but it was too late. Down it went, teetering and bouncing noisily on its minuscule wheels like a rampaging, drunken rhinoceros, smashing against the wall of the third-floor landing, the wood splintering and buckling on impact.

There was another long moment of silence—one beat, two beats— as Tito and Cleber looked at the wreckage of the antique dresser and then at each other.

"Damn!" they said simultaneously, and began to laugh all over again.

TITO FELT THE same loss of control now. He could not inhale properly. He could not get air into his lungs. There was no

Cleber here to whack him on the back, to slap him across the face. There was no one here to tell him to take it easy, that everything would be all right. Because everything wasn't going to be all right. Either he was going to kill himself or he was going to walk back out of this park into a life he didn't want, into a permanent hangover, into an existence without Clara. He tried to calm himself, tried to slow his breaths, to deepen them, but no, he was going to die right here, he was going to suffocate himself and fall dead on the cobblestones. This is not what he'd had in mind at all. He had to do something. Dropping the bottle of whiskey, he ran down the path, running as fast as he could, trying to outrun his panic. He thought he heard someone shouting, then thought it was the wind in his ears, then realized that it was his own voice, his own freaked-out shriek wailing into the dark. He caught his toe on a stone and fell forward, belly flopping on the path, his chest and his chin striking the ground.

That did it—knocked the panic right out of him. He could breathe again. Lying there, feeling the epicenters of pain in his knees, in his torso, in his arms, on his chin, he admired the process. *How could we take this so much for granted?* he thought. *Breathing. All day, all night. We just assume it will keep happening.* He rolled over, lying on his back, breathing, looking up into the branches over the path. He rubbed his chin and looked at his fingers—blood. The branches beyond his bloodied hand were winding around each other, circling and spinning. Fuck. He was piss drunk. Slowly, he stood up, steadying himself against the slender trunk of a tree. He was now so far into the park that it would be faster to get out again by going forward, ending up at the soccer fields on the river by the foot of Dyckman Street.

He staggered on. He could hear the water now, the gentle wash of the river against the rocks below, the wash of traffic on the parkway and the bridge. Here was Spuyten Duyvil and the mouth of the lagoon. Another fact he had learned while researching the history of Inwood for his Fridays with Clara was that the course of the Harlem River had been altered a century or more before, turning part of Manhattan into part of the Bronx—only it was still considered part of Manhattan. He'd often thought that that was where he should live, in that weird part of the Bronx that was not part of the Bronx, on that part of Manhattan that was separated from the rest of Manhattan. The citizens of that little neighborhood had protested being relegated to the Bronx. They wanted to continue to believe in the dream that they were part of Manhattan. Here he was, still thinking of living—of where he should live. That meant something. He descended a fork of the path that went down to the outcrop of rock overlooking the lagoon. There, below him, on the left, was the Hudson Bridge. He could see the traffic coming and going. Across the river were the apartment buildings of the Bronx. He'd moved furniture in and out of most of them. To his right, the darkness of Inwood Hill Park, the ball fields and playgrounds with the backdrop of the neighborhood. He could see his father's building, and he imagined that one of the lights he could see was the once empty apartment where he and Clara had made a home for an afternoon. Here's where he could do it—within sight of all that, within sight of his entire life. The railing was low enough that all he had to do was lean forward a little too far and he'd topple off the edge and into a short fall that would end either on the rocks at the base of this little cliff or in the waters of the Spuyten Duyvil. Since he could not swim, they amounted to the same thing. He wanted a drink. He wished he still had his bottle. He leaned against the railing with his hands and hypnotically followed the progress of a car's headlights across the bridge and then another car's back in his direction. Like the ball in the game of Pong. *Blip.* Manhattan. *Blip.* The Bronx. *Blip.* Manhattan. *Blip*—

"I hear you was looking for me," said a voice behind him.

Tito turned and there was Raúl standing on the edge of the trees, holding the bottle of whiskey he had dropped in his panic.

At first he was more astonished by the bottle's survival on the path than he was by Raúl's unexpected appearance. Unsure whether to believe his eyes and well aware that he might be hallucinating, Tito said, "What?"

"I hear you was looking for me." Raúl took a step along the little path that connected the overlook to the main cobbled walkway. Tito heard the crumple of dirt, twigs, and leaves beneath his boot. Not a hallucination. Could his imagination be that vivid? Or was it just the alcohol? "This is some good shit," Raúl said, drinking from the bottle as if it were a can of cola.

"It's strong," said Tito, still worried that he was actually talking to himself.

"Mmm," said Raúl, wiping his mouth on the back of his hand. Raúl was dressed in his regulation homeboy outfit: a pair of baggy jeans, a muscle shirt, unlaced Timberlands, and a black Yankees cap worn askew. But something was off about him. It was like he was sleepwalking, like he was part of a dream.

"I hear you was looking for me," said Raúl. "Here I am. What you want?"

"It's OK," said Tito. "I got what I needed." Not sleepwalking, he corrected himself. Not dreaming. *High.* He had a hand on the railing, the drop into the river at his back.

"Yeah, I hear you took that bracelet from my girl."

"*Your* girl?"

"Deysei. She's my girl. That's my baby she's carrying."

"I didn't know she was—" and then he stopped himself, putting it all together, the throwing up, the stomach pain. Of course. But *Raúl?* Really? He must be dreaming this. There was no way.

"You got that right," said Raúl. "I fucked her good. Her mami wasn't giving me none, so I fucked her baby. She didn't want to at first, but I talked her into it. Girls who ain't got no father, they the easy ones. All you got to do is say a few nice things. They looking for a man to love them. And you know what?"

"What?" said Tito.

"She was a better fuck than her mami, too, under all them clothes. You ever fuck some sixteen-year-old pussy?"

"No," said Tito.

"You gotta try that shit. Young pussy is sweet pussy. I'm telling you. *Sweet.*"

"She's keeping the baby?" Tito asked.

Raúl snorted. "Ain't my problem."

Tito didn't say anything. Now that he'd decided that Raúl was probably real, he was trying to gauge if he could run past him and make it back onto the path. But things were unsteady. Things were still spinning a little. He couldn't quite focus. Could he outrun Raúl? Raúl was faster than he was, Tito guessed, but Raúl was also high. Could you run fast when you were high? Was it like trying to lift heavy things when you were laughing? Tito didn't know. He'd never tried it. Raúl was wearing boots, Tito thought. Unlaced boots that would slow him down. But then he glanced down at his own hard-soled funeral shoes. A wash.

"I hear you was looking for me," said Raúl, taking another drink and coming closer on the path. If Tito was going to make a move, now was the time. The closer Raúl got, the harder it would be to get past him. But Raúl kept coming in his stomping monster steps. The chance was lost. "I hear you was looking for me," he said again.

"Not anymore," said Tito. It was how you got rid of a salesman. Keep refusing. It was how people got rid of him, how Clara had gotten rid of him. Don't waver. Don't give in. Keep saying no. It was how you got out of a dream. You opened your eyes. Raúl was just a couple of feet away now, at the gap between the two benches. Tito could smell him, the whiskey, the body odor, and something scorched, like the smoke from an extinguished match. Raúl sat down on one of the benches, his legs turned to the side, blocking the narrow space.

"What, you telling me you don't want the money I took, too?" Raúl looked up at him.

"No," said Tito. "The client didn't ask for the money back."

Raúl held up the whiskey bottle to see how much was left and laughed. "'The client.' Shit. Listen to you. Talking like the Man. That was always your problem, Tito. You always do what people tell you. You want to be a good boy, don't you? But you know what? You leave money like that lying around when you got strangers in your house, you deserve to have it stolen. I *needed* that money. I had to find myself a place to live."

"Yeah," said Tito, stinging from what Raúl had said. "I heard your girlfriend left you."

Raúl rose suddenly and Tito braced for an assault. But Raúl was just standing up to vent. "She didn't *leave* me," he said, spitting. "She left the fucking country, didn't she? Can you believe that shit? Going back to that hellhole when everyone over there trying to get here." He looked at Tito for confirmation. "I said, can you believe that shit?"

"No," said Tito.

"Bitches, man. You got to be careful around the bitches."

"Yes, you do," said Tito, trying to play along.

"Damn straight. We got to drink to that," said Raúl, handing the bottle across. Tito took that bottle and swallowed a slug, figuring the alcohol would kill whatever germs Raúl had left on the mouth of the bottle. He was worrying about germs. Yes, he wanted to live.

"I hear you had your own problem with the bitches," said Raúl, looking at him with a kind of complicity. The anger of the previous moment seemed to have disappeared.

"What do you mean?" said Tito. He felt himself blushing and was glad that it was too dark for Raúl to see.

"Deysei told me you're sweet on her *tía.*"

Tito said nothing.

"Deysei told me you're in *love* with Clara." Raúl laughed. "I give you props, man. She's fine. Deysei said you fucked Clara back in the day, so I give you props. But things is different now. You got to understand. She's out of your reach, my man. Don't you know that? She's married to a white dude. She got the house in the burbs. Dream on, my man."

Tito said nothing. His eyes were tingling. He could smash the bottle across Raúl's face right now and get away. He held it, pondering.

"Gimme that," said Raúl, reaching for the bottle. "It's not like I don't know what I'm talking about," he said. "I know all about bitches think they better than you."

Tito said nothing.

"Like that one we moved. The teacher. Who the fuck she think she is with all that *art* in her house."

Tito knew that Raúl was waiting for him to make some sound of agreement, to continue the complicity, but he was silent. He was thinking again of trying to get past him, of trying to leap over one of the benches.

"Yunis, she was getting like that—she wouldn't suck my dick. Just 'cause she got some inheritance money coming her way, she thinks she don't have to put out for me. She thinks I'm going to support her ass without letting me fuck her. She's lucky I didn't do nothing, not like the other one. That one, she really thought she was all *that*. I mean, she had it coming. You know what she said to me?"

"Who?"

"That white chick. The one I moved over to Vermilyea."

"Vermilyea?"

"That's right."

"Rebecca?" said Tito, taking a wild guess, but suddenly knowing he was right, suddenly putting it all together.

"Becca," said Raúl. "That's right. How come you knew that?"

"What did she say?" said Tito trying to get him back on track. "What did she say that got you mad?"

"Man, you knew that? Becca. How did you know that?"

"What did she say to you?" asked Tito. "What did Becca say to you?"

"You know what she said? She said she don't date black guys. Can you believe that shit? How ignorant is that? Calling me black."

Tito said nothing. He didn't know what to say. He was trembling.

Raúl stood and stretched, holding the bottle high in the air. "I thought maybe that was why you were trying to find me. I thought maybe you'd figured it out. And I guess you did. That's why I thought I better come and talk to you. You know, I waited for her just up over there, had a little smoke and waited for her. I would have given her some. You know what's sweeter than young pussy? Young *white* pussy. Don't you think? You ever had some of that white pussy?"

"No," said Tito.

"She started fighting with me. Wouldn't put out. I had to fight back. She had it coming to her. That's what I say. She had it coming to her. Just like you got it coming to you."

Raúl's forearm slammed into Tito's chest, knocking him back over the railing. It was like something he'd done on the playground as a child with Clara, whirling around a metal pole, his feet over his head, momentarily free of gravity before landing safely, only this time there was nothing for him to land on, just open space and the water. It happened so fast that he was falling before he knew he'd been hit, dropping down into the darkness, the shock of Raúl's blow radiating through his chest. Plummeting toward the water below, he looked back up at the outcrop and did not see Raúl standing there. All he saw was the railing receding into the sky. His last thought before he hit the water was to wonder if he'd imagined the whole thing, to wonder if he would see Clara again—in this life or the next.

Epilogue

Clara

Each morning after breakfast, Clara drove the rented Nissan from the hotel in Santo Domingo out to La Isabela. Her mami didn't understand why her daughter and grandson were not staying in her newly constructed dream house, and Clara was tired of making excuses—that there was no air-conditioning, that Guillermo would be eaten alive by the mosquitoes, that she was concerned about the cleanliness of the water. Her real reason was much simpler: She wanted there to be a part of each day when she did not have to listen to her mother ask her about when she was going to take Thomas back. "Men can't help themselves," she'd say. "You're not going to make another baby? Maybe he cheated because you weren't putting out enough." Her mother had been asking her these questions for almost three months, by phone and now in person. For the sake of her sanity, Clara needed to be able to leave her mother's house every night.

Each morning, she drove through the capital, following the directions written by her Tío Plinio. Each morning, she followed the same directions, and each morning, she wound up taking a slightly different route through Santo Domingo to get to the highway that led to La Isabela. Some mornings they passed the gates of the presidential palace and some mornings they didn't; some mornings they passed the baseball stadium and some mornings they didn't.

Clara had never been familiar with the capital and even now she did not feel at ease in its noisy, shambolic streets. Its chief association for her was with the abduction, and in order to stifle those unbidden memories, she deliberately drove away from the pedestrian shopping district where her father had purchased her new-world wardrobe, where he had set about making her the person she was today.

But she didn't dwell on those things. She had more recent problems to contend with. During the drives out to her mother's, she felt herself to be in recovery from the events of the late summer and early autumn: her husband's affair, the loss of Deysei's baby, the discovery of Tito's body, and the funeral. It was more than two months since she had learned about Tito's death while watching a local newscast the day after Deysei's release from the hospital. Hearing his name on the reporter's lips, she felt like the victim of a practical joke. It was not clear, the reporter said, whether the death was a murder or suicide, but Clara knew that it was the latter and that she was the cause.

Thomas had called her the next afternoon at work to offer his condolences and, no doubt, to use the situation to get back in her good graces.

"I'm here for you, Clara. Whatever you need," he'd said.

"I really do need you now, Thomas," she said.

"I'll be right there," he said, and she imagined him standing up and walking toward the door of whatever friend's apartment he was staying in during this doghouse period.

"No," said Clara. "No, no. Stay there. Don't you understand? Now, when I really need you, I can't trust you. Now, when I really need you, you're not here. I've got to figure all this out on my own."

"You can't blame yourself," he said.

"You don't even know what you're saying. You have absolutely no idea what you're talking about."

"Tell me about him," said Thomas. "Tell me anything you want. I had no idea he was that important to you."

"It's too late, Thomas. Way too late for that."

"Clara. It was just one mistake. I made *one* mistake."

"How many times did you sleep with her? Did you sleep with her only once?"

"No."

"Then you made more than just one mistake, Thomas."

His tone finally changed. "Do you think you are ever going to be able to forgive me, Clara?"

"Right now, I'm not in a position to forgive you anything. I've got to forgive myself for a few things first. That's why I could really use my husband at my side."

"I'm sorry," he said. "It was over before you even learned about it—the day I came back from D.C."

"So you *were* with her!"

"In New York, not in Washington. I broke it off with her as soon as I got back."

"Good for you," she said sarcastically, not believing him for a moment. How did she know he wasn't actually in that woman's house right now?

"Tell me what to do, Clara. What should I do? Is our marriage over? Should I give up on us? Do I need to find somewhere else to live?"

"I can only answer your last question," she said. "You need to find somewhere else to live."

That was how she'd left it before her trip to the Dominican Republic, and during her time away from New Jersey she had not been able to convince herself—nor had she allowed herself to be convinced by her mother—that she should take him back. As far as she could see, there were two reasons to reconcile: her desire to have a second child and her need for help in raising the first. Shining Star had her husband's sperm stored in one of their freezers, which took care of the first reason. She wasn't sure yet what to do about Guillermo. Certainly she would not prevent him from seeing his father, but beyond that, she was unwilling to forgive Thomas. She was done being nice.

THE DAYS AT La Isabela were long. It was only her second trip back since she had graduated from college and her first since Guillermo was a baby. It was overdue. If she had waited much longer, her family would have written her off as a *gringa,* an Americanita: too good to remember where she had come from. She and Guillermo had flown in on New Year's Eve, and today, Three Kings' Day, was the last of their visit.

Her mother's house was the center of the action, and within the house, the kitchen was the hub. It was just as she had imagined it on that afternoon when she'd spoken to her mother—when she'd learned that Yunis was coming back to New York. On a given day there might be half a dozen aunts and female cousins in there, laughing and talking. They came in—rubbing their eyes and stretching—to drink coffee and eat breakfast and talk and capture Gilly, who spent his time playing hide-and-seek and tag and watching Spanish-dubbed Disney movies on the DVD player in the living room, the language barrier no barrier for him. Periodically, he would come bombing back into the kitchen to drink a glass of juice or snatch a handful of potato chips. On this final morning, after the kisses and hugs of welcome, he was led into the living room, where there was still straw on the floor (left there the night before for the Kings' camels) and a clutch of small, wrapped packages. Gilly leapt upon them with delight, liberating them from their papers. They were cheap, well-intentioned gifts from her family: a paddle-and-ball game with an elastic that broke on its third use, a Hot Wheels knockoff, and a T-shirt that said SANTO DOMINGO. The paltriness of the gifts did not diminish his exultation as he touted every one around the room. Within five minutes, he'd run off with his cousins to play in the fields.

Deysei came into the kitchen from her bedroom. Every time

Clara saw her during the visit she had the same thought: It was all for the best. Deysei was tanned and slimmed down. In the tropical heat, she had dispatched her cornrows, overalls, and hoodies for cropped hair ironed flat once a week by her *abuela,* knee-length skirts and shorts and tank tops. Once the doctors had determined that the fetus would not survive, the birth had been induced and the baby delivered. Clara had spent the next few days trying to broker some kind of detente between her sister and niece, but every interaction ended up with shouting and tears. Finally, Yunis had been convinced to move back to Inwood, essentially to sublet her own sublet. Clara, without her husband at hand to help her manage a rambunctious kindergartner and a despondent high-school junior while also tending to her own problems, decided that drastic action was needed. She bought a ticket for Deysei to go to the Dominican Republic and live with her *abuela*. She simply resigned herself to the fact that she would always end up paying the tab on her family's screwups and brought out her credit card.

What a crazy time it had been, she thought now, as she sat across the kitchen table from her niece. She could hardly believe she had come through it. In some ways, it had made her realize that the difficulties of the preceding year—Thomas losing his job and her own lost pregnancy—had been, relatively speaking, not so bad. Things could *always* get worse. She'd known that once but had forgotten it.

Deysei had settled down and enrolled in a bilingual private school in Santo Domingo. One of her uncles ferried her to and fro every day on his commute into the capital. The school was strict. There was a dress code, a hair code, and a ban on iPods, video games, and cell phones. Deysei had resisted at first, but with surprising alacrity, she had entered the life of the school and surrendered her old habits. The benefits were evident. Her Spanish was much improved, she no longer slouched, her grades were good, and she had stopped talking about Raúl. During the week she was in La Isabela, Clara helped Deysei fill out her college applications, proofread her admissions essays, and went over the packages of information about scholarships and financial aid. There was a good chance of her getting most of her tuition waived at one of the SUNY schools—Purchase or Stony Brook.

The other person who had settled down since Deysei's arrival was Clara's mother. Given a charge to manage, to fret over, to feed, she had risen to the occasion, providing stability and encouragement to her granddaughter. Somehow the extra generation that separated them allowed Clara's mother to parent fairly and Deysei to accord the proper respect to her grandmother. Perhaps it was also the more traditional society of the Dominican Republic asserting itself. During the week of their visit, Clara's mother was in full matriarch mode, orchestrating the preparation of food, catching Clara up on the familial gossip, giving her unsolicited advice on child rearing and sexual practices. Retirement had made her less severe if no less obstinate in the way she controlled things. Her mother had been planning to honor their visit by slaughtering and roasting a pig, but there had been no water for two days and so they had not been able to clean the animal. Like the presidential turkey, it had been given a holiday reprieve and was that morning cavorting in the mud in the pen behind her uncle's house. An array of other sundries were being prepared—less imposing in their presentation than a pig on a spit, but no less delicious. Her mother had brought in bottles of wine—an exorbitant gesture in the land of beer and rum. It was a gesture Clara would pay for indirectly with the check she would give her mother before leaving that afternoon.

Clara took her place in the kitchen assembly line, slicing yucca, rolling dough, chopping garlic, laughing, and telling stories. As much as she had longed for her life in the suburbs, as much as she loved the tranquility of it, she had to admit that it lacked this communal vivaciousness. But, after a certain age, wasn't everything in life a trade-off? She had made her choices and it was too late to change her mind.

IN THE AFTERNOON, her hands smelling of garlic and her clothes damp with steam from the rice pot, Clara walked up the drive to the town's main road. How different it was. When she was a girl, a motorized vehicle traveling along this road was an event. You came out of your house to see it—or you locked your door and hid in your house, depending on what kind of vehicle you thought it was. Now the traffic was incessant. In among the jalopies and pickups, the new SUVs with their veneer of criminality, and the overcrowded minibuses, there were the flatulent mopeds, often carrying as many as three people on their sagging seats, backfiring as they navigated the craters in the semipaved road. There was no visible reduction in traffic or noise because of the holiday. The tin-shack emporiums along this byway could not afford to close; many could not afford to lose a day's pay.

Earlier in the week when Clara was on an errand to get some cooking oil for her mother, a distant cousin, Angel, had approached her and asked her for money. No preambles. No small talk. Just: "*Hola, Clara. ¿Tienes dinero?*" Just like that. She had offered the coins in her pocket—six pesos and change—but he'd snorted at her, saying he needed a hundred. She said she didn't have a hundred. For a moment, she thought there would be a scene. Angel had looked around and must have decided that there were too many people nearby. He nodded at her and melted back into the street.

After that, she started varying the time of her daily trip into the town to buy the little treats and necessities that were expected of her—batteries, soap, cosmetics, and bottles of beer and rum. Sometimes she would bring one of her uncles with her, but to-day, her last in the country, she wanted to go alone. She made her rounds with no sign of Angel. On the way back, she stopped and bought apples. The individually wrapped red fruits were a seasonal treat—the Three Kings equivalent of an Easter egg, a memory from her childhood. She bought a dozen each day and distributed them among her cousins. They were Empire apples, available in any supermarket in America, but the context made them a delicacy and she relished eating them every afternoon. Apples never tasted so good. They tasted like gold.

The apples helped everyone fend off hunger until the late afternoon, when food began to emerge from the kitchen. The uncles, who were drinking beneath the mango tree in the driveway, got out the folding tables and more chairs and paper plates and glasses. The music was turned up. It was hot, but bearable, and it did not look like it was going to rain. More rum was poured. Sodas for the kids. And then the food. First, there were *pastelitos*. Deysei carried a platter of them around the compound, into bedrooms and living rooms, through backyards, summoning everyone, letting them know that the feast was about to begin. Clara watched the members of her extended family assemble under the mango tree with their half-eaten *pastelitos* in their hands, the crescents of dough and meat like invitations. After that, a sequence of dishes: *chicharrones, ropa vieja, tostones, yucca, bacalao, moro.*

While they were eating, Clara's cell phone rang. It was Yunis.

"Yo!" she said. "Y'all having a fine time there without me?"

"I'm eating a *pastelito* right now."

"I don't need to hear about that. You know what I'm eating?"

"No."

"Lo mein leftover from yesterday. And you know what else?"

"What?"

"It's fucking snowing outside."

"Well, it's only about eighty here," said Clara. "A little chilly, actually. I might need to put on a sweater."

"Shut up."

"So, how's the J-O-B going?" Clara asked. Yunis, unable to find an ex-con to support her, and no longer having a dependent child to use as leverage with the welfare office, had finally resorted to steady employment as a receptionist for a doctor on the Upper West Side.

"It's all right. I got to tell you, Sis, this working for a living sucks. Dealing with people all day sucks. When I get home all I want to do is go to sleep."

"That means you're a grown-up now."

"Shit. Who needs that? How's my girl?"

"She's good. You should see her. She's lost some weight." The earliest indications of forgiveness had started to surface between Yunis and Deysei. There were speaking. A month ago that had seemed impossible.

"OK. Pass the phone around so I can holla at everyone and then I got some big *bochinche* for you."

Her phone made the rounds of the gathering, and even Deysei spoke civil good wishes into it before it came back to Clara. She stood and walked away from the feast, as if she were heading back into the kitchen to get some food, but she turned at the last moment and headed between her mother's house and Tío Plinio's, walking toward the pen where the pigs were kept.

"Tell me," she said to Yunis.

"You ain't never going to guess who was just here."

"Who?"

"The police."

"The police?"

"Yeah. They came here yesterday, looking for Raúl. They said they wanted to talk to him about that girl that got killed in the park. The jogger."

"What?"

"That's right. The Cruzes moved her right before she got killed and Raúl worked on that move. He never told me that. Police just heard about this. They said he's a person of interest or some shit."

"Oh, my God. They think he killed her?"

"They didn't say that. Alls they said was they wanted to talk to him."

"Do you think he could have done that?"

"Before he fucked my daughter I would have said no. But now? Anything's possible. You live with someone for two years and you think you know them. You don't know anything."

"What did you do?"

"Are you tripping, Sis? I told them I'd do anything I could to help them. I had a pretty good idea where Raúl might be hiding out and I called him up and acted like I wanted to make nice with him. Told him to come over today for a booty call. But he never made it up here to the apartment. The police were waiting downstairs and they arrested his ass right in front of the building."

"Holy shit, Yunis. Are you worried?"

"About what?"

"That he might come after you for setting him up."

"He's going to be in *jail,* Sis. Whatever he did, it's a second of-fense. He's going to be in there a *long* time. I ain't worried about nothing. But don't tell Deysei, you hear me?"

"You're going to tell her?"

"Not yet—but soon. There won't be anything she can say to me then."

"She's not talking about him so much these days."

"That's good. I should have kicked him out a long time ago."

"So, you got a new boyfriend, Yunis?"

"Well . . ."

"What? There's a new man in the Yuniverse?"

"One of the patients at the office. Nice middle-aged white guy. Electrician. Anyway, he's been giving me the signals."

"Has he done time?"

"*No.*"

"Yunis!"

"What? You the only one who can go with a white guy?"

WHEN THE FOOD had been eaten and the rum had been drunk, when darkness had fallen and the mosquitos had chased everyone indoors, Clara and Guillermo said their goodbyes, a half hour of hugs and tears and kisses and wishes for a safe journey and promises to come back soon. They got into the rental and drove back toward Santo Domingo, waving their hands out the windows and beeping the horn. Raúl was going to jail. The thought of it calmed her. Once they were on the road, Clara began eagerly anticipating the moment when she would open the door to their hotel room and feel the air-conditioning chill the sweat on her face and arms. Dwelling on this and not paying full attention to what she was doing, she missed her exit. She got off the highway and attempted to backtrack from the next exit but ended up on another major route out of the city. "Shit!" she said, and got off the second highway to try and turn around again. She pulled into a parking lot in front of a little restaurant to make the U-turn. It was barely more than a shack with a hand-painted sign. She recognized it right away. "Oh my God," she said, and stopped the car.

"OUR FATHER'S BEEN murdered."

The voice on the other end of the line was her half-brother's. She had not spoken to him in years.

"Sorry?" she said. The call was so unexpected that she had the sensation that God was talking to her. She stood in the kitchen of her Morningside Heights one-bedroom, listening. She was partially undressed. She and her new boyfriend, Thomas, had been making out on the couch in her living room. He was in there now, watching the movie they'd rented as a pretense for getting busy with each other.

"He was killed last night, Clara, shot four times during a holdup of the store." This was Efran talking, she reminded herself. Not God.

It was too much for her to process. She focused on something smaller, something more manageable.

"How did you find me?" Clara asked.

"My friend's father works for the DMV. He looked you up." There was silence for a moment. "Clara, Papi's dead."

She said nothing.

Efran told her that there was going to be a wake in Inwood the next day and then they were going to fly the body back to the Dominican Republic to be buried in Dolores's home town, Higüey. The news of her father's murder filled her with guilt and remorse, triggered these emotions with such force that she felt compelled to take actions that would have seemed insane a day earlier. The following afternoon, she dressed in mourning black and went to the funeral home on Dyckman, just a few blocks from the store. There were a dozen people in the room with the closed coffin, and a murmur went through them when she entered. She looked at no one, walked straight to the casket, and kneeled, but she was not thinking about her father, not directly. She was thinking that she wasn't going to let Dolores prevent her from from paying the proper respect. She mimed a prayer and then let her hand rest on the flat surface of the coffin. When she stood up, Dolores was right behind her, looking haggard and deranged. Words of kindness from her stepmother in that moment might have gone a long way to healing the old wounds, but it was as if no time had passed, as if Clara was still a child newly abducted from the Dominican Republic.

"Now you come. Your father dies heartbroken because he has not seen his daughter in years and now she dares show her face!" This was said loud enough for everyone in the room to hear. Without a word, Clara walked out of the funeral home and got on a train downtown.

Two days later, she was on the same flight as Dolores, Efran, and her father's body. It had cost her a fortune, but the encounter with her stepmother in the funeral home was a challenge she would not turn away from. On the plane, Dolores and Efran sat up front and Clara sat in back. The whole flight down, it seemed that there was someone standing over her waiting to use the toilet. She had not slept much since learning that her father had been killed. She'd fallen victim to a panicked second-guessing of everything in her life. Again and again, she wondered how things would have been different if she had gotten back in touch with her father. She could not help but think that if they had found a way to settle their differences, he might somehow still be alive. At the same time, she raged against those guilty feelings. It was only by escaping from him and Dolores that she had been able to make any kind of life for herself at all. Still, the fact remained that her father was dead and she had done nothing to prevent his murder.

The plane landed in the early afternoon. Clara was met at the airport by her *tía* Augustina, her mother's youngest sister, who was less than a decade older than she was. Augustina had once been married, though it turned out that the union was bogus—that her "husband" was still married to his first wife. She had a grown child by that man, worked in an office in the capital, and owned her own car. She was about as close to an independent woman as Clara knew among her family. She and Clara waited in Augustina's car near the cargo area. From a distance, they watched as Dolores harangued and badgered the customs officials. "Can't you see I'm in mourning? I want to bury my husband." It took three hours for the body to be released, and as soon as the casket came through the door and the documents were signed (and, no doubt, a bribe paid, Clara thought), two relatives of Dolores's appeared, one in a station wagon and the other in a Jeep. They loaded the casket into the station wagon and then everyone else got in the Jeep.

It was a five-hour drive to Higüey. Augustina encouraged Clara to sleep while she drove, but she could not sleep. She was afraid they were going to lose sight of the station wagon in the traffic and never find their way to the funeral. The house was in the middle of farmland, off a small road. Cattle grazed in the fields. As Clara and Augustina pulled up, Dolores's people were unloading the casket from the back of the station wagon and taking it into the house. A small crowd had gathered to greet them and neither Augustina nor Clara knew any of those people. Clara had never met her father's relatives—he was the only one of his family who'd emigrated. She did not even know if the people they were looking at were related to her. She waited until everyone had gone inside and then she knocked on the door. Dolores opened it. "This is not your father's house," she said. "This is *my* family's house. You can stay out there, but I will not let you inside my house, you shameless daughter."

Clara went back to the car, where Augustina was flipping through an American magazine Clara had brought her, the radio on. Night was falling. It was six hours each way to La Isabela and the funeral was going to be held the next morning. Augustina offered to drive her home and back if Clara would pay for the gas.

"I want to stay," said Clara.

"I know he was your father, but what did he ever do for you that you want to put yourself through this?" Augustina asked.

Clara did not want to explain. "You can leave me here," she said. "Go spend the night at a hotel in Higüey. I'll pay for it."

"No," said Augustina. "I'll stay. We'll sleep in the car."

"I'm going to sleep over there," said Clara, pointing at the porch of Dolores's house.

"OK, *loca*. Go make yourself uncomfortable." Augustina looked back at the pages of her magazine.

There was an old, wobbly chair on the porch on which Clara sat while her aunt slept in the car. Though none of them knew her, the people who came to the house to pay their respects that night all said hello as they went in. On the way out they didn't give her a second glance. As Clara sat there on the rickety chair, she could hear the sounds of eating and talking through the window. Eventually, all the mourners left and the lights in the house were turned off and Clara was still sitting on that chair in a kind of stupefied daze when the front door opened again. She expected it would be Dolores telling her to go away and she was ready to fight with her stepmother, but it wasn't Dolores. It was Efran. He had a cup of water, a piece of *salchichón*, and a heel of bread. "Here," he said, and he stood there while she ate the food and drank the water so that he could take the cup back and wash it before his mother realized what he had done. It happened so quickly that Clara didn't even think to give some to Augustina, who had fallen asleep in the car. Before he left, Efran said, "I'm sorry for the way they treated you. I was young. I didn't know it was wrong." Clara thanked him for that and for calling with the news about their father's death. She told him it was OK, that everything was OK between them as far as she was concerned. He nodded and went back into the house.

Days later, when she thought back on the night on the porch, she couldn't remember sleeping, but she did remember falling off the chair several times during the night, falling onto the cement floor of the porch, a rude awakening from unhappy dreams. Which was worse? The bad dreams or the world into which she emerged? After the third fall, Augustina appeared and tried to convince her to come into the car with her and sleep, but she didn't want to; she felt it was important to stay there on the porch. She was proving something to herself, proving that she wasn't the terrible daughter Dolores claimed. In her delirious state, she followed the same thoughts around and around her head. Clara kept wondering why her father had left the Dominican Republic in the first place, why he'd moved to New York with her mother. He had always said what everyone always said—that he had come for a better life and to make a better life for his children, but she, in that delirious state, didn't see how a life in which you were gunned down managing a shitty hardware store in Washington Heights was better than a life in which you got to stay alive into old age in Santo Domingo. She wasn't sure the first part of it worked out for him. She wasn't sure he had had a better life in New York than he would have if he had stayed. What she was sure of was that *she* was better off because he had brought her to New York. She had gone to college and found a good job, and no matter what had happened between her and her father, it was hard for Clara to deny the idea that he died in order to give her this life. *He died so that I wouldn't grow up in one of these shacks, illiterate and a mother before I turned twenty,* she thought as she drifted in and out of sleep on the wobbly chair. *He died, but in order for me to have this life, I had to leave him behind, just like I had to leave Tito behind, just like my father had to leave Santo Domingo.* Was she talking in her sleep? Could they hear her in the house? Her mind raced on. That was a huge part of it—leaving things behind, shedding the old life and the people in that life. She could not deny the truth of this and it was the first time she'd ever figured that out, and it finally made sense to her that her first reaction when she heard her father had been killed was to blame herself. And maybe Dolores was right. Maybe she didn't deserve to go into the house and mourn for her father beside his casket, like a good daughter. Maybe that was true for every child of immigrants—they always betrayed their parents. She didn't know. All she knew for sure was that she could not have done things differently.

At dawn, Augustina came out of the car and saw that Clara was crying, that she was nearly hysterical. "*Tranquila,*" she said, and dug in her pocket for a bottle of pills. "Take this," she said, and popped one onto Clara's palm. "Come back to the car." The pill made her woozy and she fell asleep, deep into sleep, not the fugue state she had been in most of the night.

When Clara woke up, people had started arriving for the funeral. The casket was brought out and loaded into the station wagon and everyone followed the station wagon on foot. The sun was climbing higher in the sky and the day was getting hotter. It was a mile or more to the graveyard, and Augustina held Clara's hand as they walked behind the rest of the funeral party.

The grave diggers were still working on the grave when the funeral party arrived. They stood uncomfortably in the heat in their mourning clothes for another half hour while the diggers finished. Clara and Augustina stood apart from the rest, among the headstones and mausoleums, watching the grave diggers work. It was getting hotter and Clara was dizzy, hungry, dehydrated. She thought she was going to faint. And then, she got her period. Right there in the graveyard, she felt the blood seeping into her panties two weeks ahead of schedule. There was nothing she could do. The funeral was starting. The blood continued its slow descent between her legs, and she couldn't concentrate on what was being said. The ceremony was short, and soon the casket was lowered into the ground and everyone tossed in their handfuls of dirt and started walking back to Dolores's house. Clara looked at her aunt. "I can't walk," she said, sitting on a gravestone. "I got my period."

"Stay here," said Augustina. "I'll get the car." And then Clara watched her as she walked away down the dirt road back to Dolores's house. The grave diggers had left, too. Clara was alone with her father for the first time since his death. She looked down into the hole, just trying to stay awake. She didn't feel any kind of epiphany. She didn't feel like her father was near at all, but that's the way she'd felt for years, she realized—that he wasn't nearby, even when she lived under his roof. She remembered a day at the beach a long time ago, before her parents had separated, her first memory. Her Tío Modesto tossed her off the end of a jetty thinking she knew how to swim. She went in, eyes open, and came up to the surface, thrashing around, trying to climb out of it, her mouth filling with salt. She thought she was going to drown. Then Clara saw her father jump off the end of the jetty. He was there, beside her in the water, taking hold of her, pulling her back to the beach. She was a doll in his arms, pressed tight against him as he pulled them through the water. It was the only time she could remember feeling that way about him—safe and grateful. After a while, Augustina's car came along the road, and Clara picked up a handful of dirt and tossed it into the grave and said, *"Gracias, Papi. Gracias por todo."*

She slept in the car while Augustina drove them over the mountains and back toward La Isabela. When Clara woke they were just outside the capital and she was starving and realized that Augustina was probably starving, too. They stopped at a restaurant—the same restaurant that Clara was now parked in front of, with Guillermo, sleeping, in the back of the car. She and Augustina went in and ordered steak, and it was the most delicious food she had ever eaten. In each bite, she felt she could taste everything in the meat, from the grass the cow had eaten, to the iron in its blood, to the steel of the butcher's knife, to the woodsap in the coals that had cooked it on the grill, to the oregano the chef had used in his marinade. It was almost worth it—going through all she'd gone through in the previous twenty-four hours—just to be able to taste food like that.

Now she got out of the car and pulled Guillermo out of his booster seat, carrying him toward the restaurant. They went in and sat down at a table, the boy asleep, his head on her shoulder. The place was empty and unchanged—a bare floor, wooden furniture, a *bachata* playing from unseen speakers. The proprietor came out from the kitchen. Clara asked if he was open. He said he was. Not waiting for the menu, she ordered two grilled steaks with *plátanos* and salad. Then she sat and waited for the food to come, thinking about her father, and Thomas, and Tito—the men who had been the cause of so much heartbreak in her life. Guillermo stirred, his head turning on her shoulder, and then fell back to sleep. She knew what she was going to do. When the food came, she was going to place money on the table and walk out of here; she was going to leave those steaks for her father and Tito, sacrifices to the dead. That was her plan, but when the food came, she found that she was still hungry. She woke her son and together they ate, cleaning their plates.

ACKNOWLEDGMENTS

I would like to express my gratitude to the following people:

To my wife, Zoraida, and her family—Grecia Solano, Jansel
Botex, Eva Matos, Wilma Botex, Taina Hiraldo, Alexander
Matos, and Phil Turneur—for sharing their lives and stories
with me.

To my family—Grace, Michael, Cassandra, Joshua, Jason,
Marcus, and Thomas Michaud—for years of love and
encouragement.

To my friend Atar Hadari.

To my agent, Eric Simonoff.

To my editor, Jane Rosenman, and to Elisabeth Scharlatt,
Brunson Hoole, Courtney Denney, and the rest of the team
at Algonquin.

To my current and former colleagues at the *New Yorker,* espe-
cially Erin Overbey, Pamela McCarthy, David Remnick,
Kilian Schalk, Deborah Treisman, Cressida Leyshon, Carin
Besser, Field Maloney, Willing Davidson, Blake Eskin, Amy
Davidson, Rollo Romig, Macy Halford, Richard Brody,
Ben Greenman, David Grann, David Denby, Shawn
Waldron, Yvette Siegert, and Ligaya Mishan.

To my teachers and the early readers of this book: Gene Wolfe,
David Craig, Anne Spillard, Gordon Lish, Marian McCraith,
Shelley Krause, and Monique Callender.

Thank you one and all.